MISSING IN ACTION

The Walker was leaning at the counter, writing—drawing, was more like it—a series of tiny geometrical configurations on a lined page of a tall book.

Jack smiling, turning the tall book around so that Peter could take a look at a page full of tiny figurations. Peter thinking, You know what it looks like? The page? Like a high school sophomore's nightmare of a geometry final exam.

"They're back," said the Walker.

"Who?"

Jack pointed to a line of tetrahedrons and rhombuses.

"Squintik," he said. "And Jere Lee."

"Is *that* what that says?"

Jack smiling wider, nodding.

"Yeah?" Peter joining in, nodding and smiling. Then, abruptly, frowning. "What about Herb Dierickx?" He indicated the open book with his jaw. "He get back, too?"

"No."

Other Books by Tom De Haven

FUNNY PAPERS
SUNBURN LAKE
FREAKS' AMOUR
JERSEY LUCK
JOE GOSH
U.S.S.A.
CHRONICLES OF THE KING'S TRAMP, BOOK I:
WALKER OF WORLDS

CHRONICLES
OF THE
KING'S TRAMP
BOOK II

THE END-OF-EVERYTHING MAN
TOM DE HAVEN

SPECTRA ™

BANTAM BOOKS
NEW YORK • LONDON • TORONTO • SYDNEY • AUCKLAND

All of the characters in this book are fictitious,
and any resemblance to actual persons, living or
dead, is purely coincidental.

Special thanks to Lou Aronica,
Betsy Mitchell, Alan Lynch, and David Keller.

*This edition contains the complete text
of the original hardcover edition.*
NOT ONE WORD HAS BEEN OMITTED.

THE END-OF-EVERYTHING MAN
A Bantam Spectra Book / published in association with Doubleday

PRINTING HISTORY
*Doubleday edition published July 1991
Bantam edition / June 1992*

*SPECTRA and the portrayal of a boxed "s" are
trademarks of Bantam Books, a division of
Bantam Doubleday Dell Publishing Group, Inc.*

ISBN 0-553-29658-2

Published simultaneously in the United States and Canada.

*Bantam Books are published by Bantam Books, a division of Bantam Doubleday
Dell Publishing Group, Inc. Its trademark, consisting of the words "Bantam Books"
and the portrayal of a rooster, is Registered in U.S. Patent and Trademark Office
and in other countries. Marca Registrada. Bantam Books, 666 Fifth Avenue, New
York, New York 10103.*

PRINTED IN THE UNITED STATES OF AMERICA

OPM   0 9 8 7 6 5 4 3 2 1

For Mandy (who'll read it)
and Harry (who won't)

Thanks to Rick Raymo
for crisis intervention

"I travel not to go anywhere, but to move. The Great Affair is to move."

—ROBERT LOUIS STEVENSON

Part One

LONG NIGHT IN A SMALL CASTLE

PETER

IN THE GREEN ROOM (WHOSE walls are canary yellow), a makeup lady wearing a cop-show fedora with lilacs in the hatband keeps flitting around my chair, smearing my face with thick beige goop. Over there? In the corner? Past the trestle table with its plate of powdered donuts, sleeve of hot cups, and Braun coffee maker? Is a television monitor, and hey! there's Phil on the screen, Phil Donahue, folks, with his thick silver hair (still married to Marlo Thomas?) and his schoolgirl complexion, those sort-of-dated aviator glasses, and his navy-blue suit; man, he's looking *so* ⟋ . . . sincere, hopping up and down the red-carpeted steps with his big foam-topped microphone, working the studio audience.

I dunno, I'm thinking, maybe . . . maybe I shoulda done "Nightline" instead? Maybe this isn't quite *serious* enough? I mean, I'm not some . . . flake. I'm the most famous guy in the world. *Gonna* be.

The makeup lady steps back, squeezing her chin in a bony hand, crinkling her eyes. She's about forty, I figure, dressed in a gray blouse and stylishly wrinkled peach-colored slacks. "Okay," she says. "You're finished, Mr. Musik. Don't touch under your eye, though. Where you have that shiner? Don't touch it, you'll smear."

Shiner? What shiner? Which eye?

"All set, Mr. Musik?" A sudden growling voice, behind me.

It's—hey no, this can't be! It's my old editor from the *National Enquirer,* Alan Burns. Burnsie. What the hell is Burnsie doing *here?* Working for Donahue? Burnsie saying, "Just don't forget: look at Phil, or at the audience, but not at the cameras. Okay?"

"Burnsie? Since when're you—?"

But wait a second. Wait a second. It's not Burnsie, whatever gave me *that* idea? It's just some guy, a staff guy, might even be the director, who knows? Small and jowly, in a dark-blue suit and a maroon tie, smelling of talc, like he just stepped from the shower. Taking me by the elbow, asking do I have to use the john? Last chance. I tell him no, no thanks, then follow him out of the yellow green room, the guy saying, "And watch your language, we're live."

And now here's Phil Donahue saying welcome— "Welcome, Pete!"—above tepid studio applause. One second I'm walking down a hall under fluorescent tubes, the next I'm sagged in a padded swivel chair on the set, hot television lights baking my face. I don't get it, I don't—

Should I call him Phil?

Or Mr. Donahue?

Don't call him anything. Just, just . . .

And now Phil Donahue is holding up an oversized file card, he's reading from it out loud, that edge of incredulity in his voice that he reserves for self-declared messiahs and sexual quacks; he's saying, ". . . Peter Musik claims to have visited another world that he calls Lostwithal." Phil sticks the card back into his suitcoat pocket, then jiggles his glasses. "Is *that* what you claim?"

I go, "*Los*-twithal. You don't pronounce it 'lost.' It's *Los*-twithal. And *I* didn't call it that. That's what it's called."

"Oh come *on,* Peter. And how'd you get there— through a wardrobe? Down a rabbit hole?"

What's he want, a punch in the nose?

I say, "No." I say, "My friend Jack had a ring. He

just"—and with my left hand I describe a downward arc —"sliced through."

"Sliced through *what?*" says Phil, rolling his eyes and wrinkling his forehead.

"Through . . . nothing. Through the *air.*"

And now I'm thinking that maybe I should just stand up and walk away. Already this is going badly. Whose idea *was* this, coming here? Doing this show? Hell with it.

"Whoa," says Phil Donahue, as I start to get out of my chair. "Don't be huffy, *convince* us." He turns to a huge doughy-skinned woman (a necklace of red wooden beads, a charm bracelet, a hearing aid) seated on the aisle and dips his microphone toward her. "What do you think, dear? Are *you* willing to be convinced?"

"Phil, I *know* there's another world beyond this one. And it's a much *better* world, too. But you have to *die* first to get there."

This provokes loud, supportive applause.

You believe this?

"Convince us," says Phil Donahue. "Convince us!"

Applause, applause.

"All right," I tell him, "I will. If you'll let me speak."

Phil: "You're a journalist."

Me: "Yes."

"For the *National Enquirer.*"

"Once upon a time. Yeah. What of it?"

"Peter, don't get so belligerent. We're just trying to establish your credentials."

"You're *trying* to make me look like a jerk. Is what you're *trying* to do."

He think I'm stupid or something?

And now some lady—God bless her!—seated deep in the audience jumps up and says, "Let the man talk, Phil! You invited him here, let him talk!"

Phil Donahue looks startled, looks stunned. What, he hasn't been letting me talk? How could anyone accuse him of that? He's the fairest of the fair, he's not—he's not *Geraldo,* for God's sake!

To me: "All right," he says. "Suppose you tell us how you got there. I understand there was something about

. . . amnesia? You had amnesia? Could you enlighten us?"

To demonstrate that he's all ears, Phil sits down on one of the carpeted steps, resting the microphone across his knees.

So I begin. It all started, I say, when I happened to meet this chemist at a . . . at a . . .

(should I say it?)

. . . at a bar . . .

(are they gonna think I'm a *drunk* now?)

. . . in a marina, down in Florida. Interesting conversation. "Which," I say, "eventually brought me north to see a man named Eugene Boman, of Boman Pharmaceuticals."

"Excuse me," says Phil, heaving himself back to his feet. "You say Eugene Boman. Now, is this the same Eugene Boman—the billionaire?—who disappeared last Christmas time?"

What, there might be *two* Eugene Bomans?

But I go, "Same guy," then plow ahead: "And what I was investigating—what I'd heard about in Florida—were these things called Idiot Drugs. That's the *generic* name for experimental drugs, pharmaceutical drugs, that end up having side effects nobody foresaw. Like, say, an arthritis drug that ends up giving the patient—oh I don't know, kidney failure. For example. Drugs that never get past the laboratory. Or *should* never."

I stop there, and smile. Friggen proud of myself. Hot damn, the Musik Man's taking charge!

And Phil Donahue, for a change, seems genuinely interested, no longer condescending. "And what did Mr. Boman tell you?"

"Well, I don't want to go into all the particulars. I'll save those for my, um, book. I intend—"

"He admitted to you then that these so-called Idiot Drugs had gotten into wide circulation, is *that* it? Into our neighborhood pharmacies? Is *that* the scandal you uncovered?" Phil jabs his finger at me, and shakes it. He's outraged! He's appalled! Yet *another* fast one perpetrated on the American public! He spins around toward the audience. "What's going *on* here?" he asks rhetorically. Then, veering back to me: "Well?"

"Nothing like that," I say.

"Nothing like *what?*"

"Look, I really don't think I should go *into* all this now. Let me just say that for a variety of reasons Gene Boman let a very close relative have . . . access to a number of these Idiot Drugs. And when I found out about that, and when they *realized* I knew, they . . . injected me with something called Blue Mark."

"Sounds like a laundry detergent!" says Phil Donahue, and the audience roars.

This guy is really exasperating. I mean—really! But I don't lose my cool. Just say, "Well, it wasn't. It totally wiped out my memory."

Phil claps his hands together. "At last! We're getting to the amnesia! Maybe by next week we'll get to Lostwithal! But first we're gonna break here. Be right back."

Abruptly, some of the set lights go off.

"Listen, you're doing great." From Phil, hunkered beside me now, whispering. "This Boman connection, though—do you have proof?"

"Well, you don't think I'd—"

"Just between us. Who was this 'relative' of Gene Boman's?"

"His father-in-law. Major Richard Forell."

But then I'm thinking: Why'd I tell him *that?* I should be saving all this *good* stuff for my book. My book. Gonna be a bestseller. Gonna make me rich. Gonna—

Phil Donahue springs up the moment the overhead lights flash. "We're back. With Peter Musik, scandal-sheet journalist, alleged sojourner in another world . . . and recent amnesiac. May I assume, Pete, that you've regained your memory? All of it?"

"Yeah. Thanks to my friend Jack."

"Jack. Let's *talk* about him." Phil glances once more at the file card. "This is the so-called 'King's Tramp.' The Walker of Worlds. *That* Jack."

"Yeah."

"And how'd you two meet?"

"Well. After I got amnesia, I was . . . I found myself living on the street. Where I met this guy. A bum. Who said he was from another world. Another universe. I reacted to him . . . at first . . . same as you're all reacting to me. I thought he was, um . . . I didn't *believe* him. But he convinced me."

"Like you're gonna convince us."

"Well, Jack had some means of persuasion that I don't. Unfortunately."

"Such as?"

"Such as a wasp that's really a witch."

"A wasp," says Phil Donahue. Punctuating that with a guttural "uh-huh," meaning: loony tune alert!

A collective murmur of amusement, and disdain, rolls down from the audience, making me squirm. Pissing me off.

"She can turn herself into a wasp, but she's actually—"

"A witch," says Phil, widening his blue eyes.

"A woman."

"Named what? Tinker Bell?"

Laughter. Applause.

"Named Lita."

"Okay," says Phil. "For the moment let's just assume that your friend Jack had a pet wasp. Witch. Named Lita. Everybody got that straight? All right. So what'd she do, Pete? Sting you?"

"In this band shell, yeah, in a park, and—"

"She *stung* you?"

"Which put me under the Walker's control. He was, like . . . *in my head.* In charge. And from there on, I kind of . . . helped him out. See, there was this *other* guy from Lostwithal who was looking to find Jack. To kill him."

From someone far back in the audience, a college boy: "Sounds like *The Terminator!*"

His friend: "Sounds like *Starman!*"

"We have skeptics," says Phil. "Refute them?"

And I go, "Life imitates adventure movies—what can

I tell you?" Showing a little quick wit, yeah? I smile, keep smiling, then peer toward the "skeptics," and see . . . I'm not sure what. A shape, a silhouette. A bulk.

With yellow eyes.

Way up there, in back.

And now Phil is saying, ". . . want to hear what happened with you and this Jack and Jack's wasp and Jack's ring, and so forth!"

I lean forward again, squinting, but that shape, that bulk . . . is gone.

Phil Donahue is glancing at the file card again. "Says here that some *other* people accompanied you and your friend Jack to *Los*-twithal. Am I pronouncing it correctly?"

"Lostwithal, right. Yeah, there was . . . there were a few other people went with us. You see, Jack has this *talent* to make coincidences happen. Accidents, he calls them. Accidents that, like, bring a whole bunch of different people together to, um, *accomplish something*. So what happened was, we all just kind of met up at this hospital and then we all . . . went over. Together."

"To Lostwithal," says Phil.

"To Lostwithal, yeah. There was Gene Boman's girl-friend, a college girl named Money Campbell. And Boman's chauffeur, a guy named Herb. And there was a woman . . ."

Phil's eyes cut to the file card. "You're referring to the bag lady?"

"Hey, she's not a bag lady! She was just living on the street, but she wasn't. . . . Her name is Jere Lee."

I realize suddenly that the audience is murmuring, that it sounds like an office Christmas party, there's even the occasional outburst of laughter, the laughter sounding mean and dismissive. Someone up there, some jerk, hoots and calls, "What'd he say—*Sara* Lee?"

"Her name," I go, "is *Jere* Lee."

"Jerry Lee *Lewis?*" From the smart aleck.

"J-e-r-e. Jere Lee *Vance*."

Phil Donahue is staring at me, his expression dogged and inflexible, like a prosecuting attorney's.

I go, "You must've read about it, for crying out loud. We all disappeared from a hospital room. It *must've* been in all the papers. Jack killed the Finder . . . the guy who'd been sent to kill *him*. Then we all went to Lostwithal. Together."

"Peter . . ."

"So that Jack could tell the King—"

"The *King*?"

"Agel. So that Jack could tell King Agel about what the Mage of Four, Mage of Luck was trying to *do*. That he was trying to conjure up this . . . monster. Called the Epicene."

"Peter. Where have you *really* been? Isn't it true that you've been a patient in Greystone Psychiatric Hospital?"

Jumping to my feet, I go, "The Epicene! It's made of mud and grass and stone and it's *growing!* And when it's fully grown—"

"Peter. Please. Sit down."

All of a sudden I feel . . . stupid, and slump back into my chair and look slowly from Phil Donahue to the audience, and everyone's expression—Christ, everyone's! —is identical, is pitying.

Murmurs and snickering, and Phil is clearing his throat.

"Let's see—let's see if anyone has any questions for Mr. Peter Musik," he says, climbing the steps, going into the audience. "Yes. You have a question?"

A heavyset woman in a floral-pattern tent dress, standing, leaning toward the microphone as she keeps her eyes straight ahead, locked on me (the lunatic). Speaking with a Texas or an Oklahoma twang, saying, "Yes, *I'd* like to ask Mr. Musik about Gene Boman. I was reading about him in *People* magazine and he doesn't seem to *act* like a billionaire. He's not at *all* like Donald Trump or . . ."

And I go, "You're absolutely right. Gene Boman is, well, he's kind of a *flake*. Easily manipulated."

The woman nods—just as she thought! *Just* as she thought! "Could you also tell us what's *happened* to him? I read that he might be living in a little town in Virginia. That he didn't *want* to be rich anymore and that he—"

"No," I tell her, "he's in Lostwithal, too."

Phil Donahue can't help it, he laughs out loud. "Who isn't? What about Judge Crater? He there, too? And Jimmy Hoffa?"

"You're not listening to me. You're not listening! I *told* you. When you get involved with Jack and Jack's enemies, these . . . accidents happen. I don't know *how* Boman got there, but . . ." I give another shrug. "These accidents happen."

"I'll say!" says Phil. "Do we have another question? Yes. You have a question?"

"I sure do," says a young brunette woman, very slender, very pretty, dressed in a white blouse and a plum-colored tight skirt. "I've been a big fan of Anne McCaffrey's Pern series. I just *love* them, and I wanted to ask Mr. Musik if he's going to have any dragons in *his* novel when it comes out."

What? *What?* I go, "I'm not writing a *novel!*" I go, "This all happened!" I go, "It's *still* happening! It's not over yet!"

"If that's the case," says Phil Donahue, "then, Peter, what are you doing *here?* Why aren't you back there, helping out your friends?"

And I—I can't answer him.

And the studio lights—all of them—cut suddenly off.

And the monitors.

And the Exit signs.

And I'm in darkness.

In silence.

I move to stand up—"Hello? Hey!"—and can't.

My legs are too heavy, my arms too numb.

Darkness. *Black* ness.

Except for two small points of light. Up there.

Yellow.

Two points . . . ovals . . . *lozenges* . . . of yellow.

Eyes.

That begin to move.

And with their forward movement, comes sound.

A slapping, sucking, *oozing* sound.
If mud—
If mud . . .
If mud could walk. . . .

CHAPTER 1

DIDGE

RAIN DRUMMED ON THE roof of the coach, and on the team of six green horses, running three abreast. Forks—and flashes—of lightning. Peals of thunder. A shrieking wind, and the coach tipped, then slammed back down, chassis bouncing, sidelights hissing, driver grunting, high wheels churning mud that splattered the door.

Inside: a Mage of Court, opposite a slender young woman named Didge. Her knees (she was wearing coarse gray trousers) brushing his (beneath a brown cassock). Didge saying, "The Isle of Mites? Perhaps? I *know* we've met somewhere."

Patiently, the mage smiled, then winced at yet another volley of thunder, lifted massive woolly eyebrows, resumed smiling. "I've had no . . . occasion," he said, "to visit the Isle of Mites."

"Oh!" And Didge laughed. "I wasn't suggesting that you were there for—oh!" She blushed, in the dark. "I just meant . . . I thought that perhaps you were there *officially*."

"No."

"Then I've seen you somewhere *else*, Master Amabeel."

He shrugged, turned sideways, and looked out the window, at the downpour and the darkness. Along his jawline, vaguely reflected in the glass: a faded tattoo, of a salamander.

The mage could scarcely keep his eyes open. He was exhausted and still vexed, still depressed that he'd been roused and summoned on such a night; that his dreams— of symmetrical shapes and fluctuating, fiery numbers— had been so violently interrupted. Scattered. Lost . . .

MAKE HASTE, the beetle-fly had said, MAKE HASTE!

Amabeel had tossed off the bedclothes, and thrown on his vestments, his scapulars, and bustled from his chambers (then, with an oath, he'd bustled right back: the fly having pointed out to him that he'd forgotten his tongs and his gunnybag). Then: moving quickly along the castle's maze of galleries, the floors strewn with rushes and herbs, his sandals slapping noisily, descending stairs, more stairs.

To Rampike's apartments.

Amabeel pensive and serious, trying not to yawn, saying, Yes, Prime Minister. Of course, Prime Minister. At once, Prime Minister.

Then: rapidly descending still *more* stairs, stepping outside into the cold rain, hurrying across the bailey to the stables, where he'd finally climbed into this coach and discovered this . . . Doveflesh. This . . . Didge.

Who said now, "You're probably wondering what *I* was doing on the Isle of Mites. I don't want you thinking—"

"No, of *course* not."

"For secondwork," she said, "I was a Walker. I used to ramble for an art-prince named . . ."

But she didn't finish. Instead: "I'm sorry."

The mage lifted his eyes.

"You don't want to hear all this. Please excuse me. I'm just . . . nervous."

"You mustn't be," said Amabeel, reaching out to touch her lightly on the wrist. Her left wrist. "There should be no danger. Now."

"Oh, I'm not worried about *that*. It's just . . . truth is, Good Mage, I don't know why *I* was chosen for this. I'm sure it must be according to the Order of Things, but. . . . You don't think it's a mistake, do you? I arrived in Beybix only yesterday. To visit my brother." And to escape, for a time, the tedium of her life.

Amabeel's lips skinned back over sharp white teeth. "I'm sure there's been no mistake," he said, looking directly into her eyes. Searching them. "How long have you been Talented?"

"As a Dispeller? Since the last rains, that's *all*. So you see. And I haven't *done* anything with my Talent. To speak of. I live out on the Minor Coast. In Drawl."

The mage nodded.

"You know Drawl?"

"I've been there, yes."

"Really? When? Do you know Landholder Jix? He's my . . ." But her voice trailed off, she became self-conscious, and then, barely audible, she whispered, ". . . uncle."

Again, the mage nodded. (Though of course he didn't know Didge's uncle, he was just . . . nodding. Sourly.)

Didge turned her head away, avoiding his bright blue eyes, wondering if she ever *had* met him before. Likely not. (Oh face it, Didge-girl, you never laid eyes on this old man before in your life. You're just . . . chattering.)

Oh Schoolteacher, she thought, what am I doing *here*?

What am I *doing*?

Thinking, A Dispeller? *Me*?

Wrong. All wrong.

Didge could see that now; *now* she could.

But nine seasons ago, it had seemed a fine and sensible choice.

No, that's not true. She was deceiving herself (again); she'd never *really* wanted to become an ordinary, inconsequential spellbreaker; that was just a . . . compromise.

An admission of mediocrity.

Worse: of failure.

For a time, Didge had thought she would pursue the Walker's calling—*that*, she'd reckoned, would be her thirdwork, her *life's* work. She would become fourth degree, then fifth (why not? she would "wear out the leather," in tramp argot), rambling throughout Lostwithal and elsewhere (oh *please*, elsewhere!) in service to His Majesty-Most-Still.

But those plans had become impossible.

After what had happened (Self-deceiver! What she had *caused* to happen) one High Summer day, twenty seasons past, in the northern city of Sett. . . .

(But don't think about *that*.)

(Don't think about . . . *him*.)

(What's past is past. Is past.)

So.

So, she'd decided, if she could not continue to live as a Walker, she would become a—*what?*

Didge had had no aptitude for conjuring (she couldn't keep numbers straight in her head, much less remember two thousand Perfect Shapes) and no aptitude —none!—for the farming life (even Uncle Jix said that), but she *was* educated (somewhat) and charmed (partly), so . . .

Didge, a Dispeller.

Clarifyer of muddied wells, unsticker of tongues, healer of boils. Undoer of mischief, of magic.

Earning a scanty, and sometimes precarious, living with just a dash of salt, a few bland words, a drop or two of blood.

Didge, a Dispeller.

She pulled her cloak around her, nestled her cheek to her shoulder, slumped against the dithering coach wall, and finally closed her eyes.

Even so, lightning penetrated, erratic and flickering. The old mage—Amabeel? Was studying Didge again:

her frizzy head of orange hair, her small, thin face and high, scalloped cheekbones, her pale-gray complexion. Her dark-gray lips.

Her wet, glistening lashes.

This stranger, this woman, this Doveflesh, this . . . Didge.

CHAPTER 2

AFTERMATH
OF A LEFT HOOK

PETER MUSIK KEPT POKING AT his swollen right eye, saying, "Why'd you *do* that, man? Jack! I'm talkin' here."

The Walker gave a half-shrug, then took another bite from—from whatever the hell it was that he was eating, some kind of meat roll; looked like a fat link of Italian sausage left too long (say, five, six hours) on a barbecue grill. Disgusting thing. Peter didn't want to think about what it *really* looked like. He watched Jack chew, and kept tapping his shiner. Thinking, Hey Jack, you hit me. You friggen *hit* me!

Saying, "You friggen *hit* me!"

They were sitting—Jack on a stool, Peter on the cot —in a dark, tiny room that smelled rank, like sewer gas or rotten eggs, and made Peter think of a jail cell, a *dungeon* cell: stone floor, open latrine, chittering mice (Peter couldn't see them, exactly, but he preferred to *believe* they were mice, not . . . the *other* possibility), and a small, round-headed window with rain leaking through the shutters. Creepy. Well, jeez, the whole place was creepy. This . . . Manse Seloc.

"You finished your snack? Good. So why'd you hit me?"

"Because I was afraid you were going to *kill* that man."

"What's it to you? That 'man' is the sonofabitch filled me so full of—"

"Drugs, yes." Jack's eyes shifted. Away from Peter. "But somehow he's ended up here. Hasn't he? Which, to my way of thinking, makes him part of the Order of Things." Jack stood up suddenly, then glanced through the open doorway and into the corridor, where a soldier in a bright-red tunic passed by carrying a resin torch. "Besides"—Jack was grinning now—"he's just a little fat guy."

"You didn't have to hit me so hard."

"You were *strangling* him. Come on."

Peter shrugged. Okay. *Okay.* So he'd lost his head, a little bit. Who wouldn't have, under the circumstances?

Think about it. Here's Peter, right? Peter and Money and Herb Dierickx and Jere Lee Vance and Jack and Jack's frail old magician buddy, that guy Squintik; here they all are, slipping out of that hospital room through a Cut into Lostwithal (no, darlin', no dragons), then fighting their way to the King's castle.

(Would've been nice if Jack were more of a Schwarzenegger; *Schwarzenegger?* Christ, if Jack looked like anybody from the movies, it was Willem Dafoe, a scruffy Willem Dafoe.)

Yeah . . . so finally they get to Beybix, to the royal castle (well, not *all* of them: Herb was lost along the way, the bats got *him*), where Jack tells the King about the Epicine. About how the Mage of Four, Mage of Luck made this *mud baby* that's gonna grow into a monster—

(Peter thinking, This is the part gave Phil Donahue such a canary)

—that'll destroy everything in existence, and now here's Peter riding with soldiers to Manse Seloc . . .

(this creepy place, this kind of small castle)

. . . and *now* here's Peter watching the soldiers try to break down a door to get at . . . well, at the *villain*, right? That Mage of Four guy, that nutcase . . .

. . . and *now* here's Peter seeing the door suddenly explode, and when the smoke clears, here's Peter ogling a big hole in the castle where there used to be a turret room.

Yes, and *now* here's Peter looking down a corridor in this creepy old castle, this Manse Seloc, and seeing—

Eugene Boman, the bald fat billionaire, Mr. Idiot Drugs himself.

Gene Boman?

Who'd turned Peter into a bum on the street, a bum without a memory.

At first, Peter thought he must be hallucinating—like maybe the strain of the whole adventure was starting to wear on him, or maybe . . . maybe he just hadn't had enough food to eat in the last couple of days, but . . . no.

It *was* Gene Boman. Here. In Manse Seloc.

Like: Delivered (somehow!) on a silver platter.

Who *wouldn't* have gone for the bastard's throat?

Under the circumstances. . . .

"I wasn't gonna *kill* him," said Peter. "I was just . . . hey, come on, Jack. Revenge is sweet. You didn't have to sucker-punch me."

"Your opinion."

"Yeah. Yeah. It is."

"You feeling all right now?"

"Well . . . considering." He rubbed his jaw, touched his shiner.

"Then come on," Jack said, and stepped out into the corridor.

Peter promptly followed; what, he was gonna stay behind with all those . . . mice?

Peter saying, "Hey, Jack, wait up."

Saying, "I never knew you dreamed when you got knocked out. Did you? After you hit me? I had this *weird* one. I was, like, on television, and—"

Then saying, "Jack? So where's the sonofabitch Boman *now?*"

SITTING IN FRONT OF HIS BIG
Zenith console TV, that's where, and wishing like crazy that he had some program listings, so he could know what shows were coming on.

What night *is* this, anyhow? If it's Tuesday, "Bonanza" 'll be on, followed by "The Bold Ones." But maybe it's Thursday. If it's Thursday—great! Start with "The Waltons" on CBS, then switch to NBC for "Ironside."

Gene Boman almost rings for one of the house servants, almost goes over to the wall, there, and presses a bell-button and has one of the servants come upstairs to his bedroom, so he can ask, "Would you find me the *TV Guide?*" But he really doesn't want to bother anybody; even though his mom says that's what servants are *for,* to serve, still Gene Boman always feels awkward, asking them to do stuff for him.

He doesn't like to impose.

Which, of course, inevitably gets him into big trouble with his father. His father staring at Gene with that flat, exasperated look, saying, "You have to start showing a little more temperament, Eugene. And a lot more character." Gene promising that he'll try, but . . . it's so *hard.* And he doesn't think he'll *ever* be able to scare people the way that his father does. On any number of occasions he's watched Eugene Boman, Senior, intimidate this, that, and the other company executive; Gene's even watched him intimidate a bunch of United States *senators,* the time his father testified in front of a pornography commission, blaming dirty movies and dirty books for everything that was wrong with this great country of ours—absenteeism, inefficiency, drug addiction, street crime, loud music, divorce rates, earrings on men—the whole magillah.

Gene Boman admires his father, but doubts that he'll ever learn to be *like* him. And that makes him miserable, fills him with despair. Sometimes—*often,* as a matter of fact—he wishes he'd never been born so rich. Rich at all.

Be nice just to be a normal kid. Well, in some ways he *is* normal. What he likes most in the world? Is watching TV. (That's normal—right?)

Television is better than real life, Gene's been thinking more and more lately.

At the age of twelve, he's just about convinced of it.

Best thing in the world? To sit here on the bedroom carpet, with your back to the wall, and watch shows like—

Like: "The Sonny and Cher Comedy Hour."

Sonny and Cher? Then it's Friday! Gene thinks. So what's on later?

"Room 222" and "The Odd Couple."

Followed at ten by "Banyon."

Friday. This is great! This is fabulous! It's his favorite TV night.

Leaning forward now, watching Cher kid around with Sonny, Gene Boman starts thinking, Boy, wouldn't he just love to touch *her!*

And then he blushes, feeling . . . bad. It's shameful and stuff, all these thoughts he keeps having about Cher, about Mary Tyler Moore, about that wife on "Bob Newhart"—Suzanne Pleshette; geez, even about Sandy Duncan. Gene even has this secret lust thing for little Sandy Duncan. Skinny Sandy Duncan. His father would beat him to a pulp, if he could read his mind, but—

When two servants step into his bedroom, he cringes like a felon caught in a searchlight.

They really should've *knocked,* but Gene'll let it pass, this time.

And now he's blushing, trying to smile, saying, "Could you fellas bring me up a Coke? Please? And some Doritos? But only if you're going back downstairs. Don't make a special trip on *my* account."

And then, just to be safe, he reaches out and switches to another channel, to "The Brady Bunch." Safer to watch "The Brady Bunch." In case, you know, his father ever asks these two servants what he was watching on television Friday night. . . .

°   °   °

"DORITOS?"   SAID   JACK,   A
Walker.

"And a Coke," said Peter Musik.

They stood just inside the storeroom door, in dimness, in dampness, and stared with shuddery fascination at the bald fat man sitting cross-legged on the beaten earth floor, a dreamy look on his face, gazing at the open end of an empty bushel basket that was tipped on its side.

Jack saying, "You think he wants regular or diet?"

CHAPTER 3

THE END-OF-EVERYTHING MAN

WELL, THERE IT IS, SHE thought. Manse Seloc. And, shaking her head, Didge remembered: she'd been here before.

It must've been, what, more than a hundred seasons ago—on a daytrip with her father, and her mother, and her mother's husband, and her father's brother Jix (her own brother hadn't yet been born; she herself was no more than eight or nine: her hair was straight then, it was yellow, golden yellow, and she wore it proudly in a long gleaming horsetail), and, and . . .

Didge remembering: as a treat, Uncle Jix had brought them all to the capital, to Beybix (he'd had some business there, perhaps a tax to pay), and one afternoon near the end of their visit (after they'd seen Agel's castle and filed through the Schoolteacher's Museum and prowled the market squares and wandered through the labyrinthine Public Garden of Our History) they'd rented

(Uncle *Jix* had rented) a horse and small wagon, and they'd gone out of the city and into the pitch-pine barrens, following the old Sand Road, for a picnic.

And in the late afternoon Didge had wandered off alone, not far, not lost, just . . . alone, following a switchback trail (and there was fetterbush . . . and turkeybread . . . and a sweet bay magnolia: Didge proud that she could identify every shrub, every tree, and flowering plant; she was a smart little girl, was Didge, *everybody* said so), and finally she'd come to a bluff, looked down, and *seen* it: the small black castle. At once, she'd known what it was.

Manse Seloc.

(Where lived the End-of-Everything Man.)

(Don't be foolish, children, he's just a mage, like a thousand others.)

And Didge had stood there, transfixed and trembling, on that bright, hot Low Summer afternoon, till her uncle (with his bald sunburned pate) had come along and found her. And then *he'd* stood transfixed (and maybe trembling, too, Didge couldn't really tell).

At last, she'd said (murmured), "The End-of-Everything Man."

And Uncle Jix had said, "Time to go home, child."

"Time to go home," he'd said.

Not: don't be foolish.

That was years and years ago. Fifteen or sixteen.

More than a hundred seasons.

A bright, hot day, in Low Summer.

And now, on a cold, dark night of torrential rains in Late Blaze, Didge sat with her nose pressed to the coach window, transfixed once again by the ancient (and greasy) black walls and towers of Manse Seloc, where torchlight jiggled in several slitted windows. Her head began to buzz. And—small hands clenched, both hearts pounding —she trembled.

The End-of-Everything Man.

She flinched when the mage's hand dropped upon her knee, and tightened there.

"Master . . . ?"

"Come along, woman, don't *worry* so."

Cloth cap plastered to his skull, the coachman pulled open the door and held out a hand to assist Didge to the ground, where she promptly sank into mud past her ankles.

When Amabeel had joined her, they slogged across the courtyard, their heads bent against sleet and rain, the surly wind blowing their hair pell-mell, his cassock whipping around his knees, her cloak snapping behind her. Didge felt a rush of excitement (and of dread, and of misgiving).

What am I expected to *do?*

The mage rapped upon the great iron door. Almost immediately it swung back with a grating sound, and there stood a tall—some six-and-a-half-feet-tall—grim-faced soldier in the gaudy red tunic and white crossbelt of a King's Guardsman. A captain of the Guard. (On the dorsum of his nose was a spider tattoo, emblem of valor.) After he'd rattled off the fitting, and tiresome, words of welcome, according to the Order of Things, he made a slow, grave bow, to Amabeel.

But then he merely glanced (with perplexity? or was that just her imagination?) at Didge.

Who moved impulsively forward and dropped a curtsy, which she ought *not* to have done, but . . . well, she was flustered.

The Guard captain led them through an arched passage (chimneyed lamps burning in wall brackets) and into a cavernous, beam-ceilinged octagonal hall. There, a score (at least) of other soldiers stood warming themselves by the hearth's log fire, or were squatted at gambling, or sat morosely on the bottom steps of a broad winding staircase.

A number of the men's tunics were torn and scorched black.

There were six long windows hung with blood-red draperies, but no furniture.

And the floor (Didge recoiled with a sinking, then a spinning, sensation)—the stone floor was strewn with animal bones, and with chips and flinders of bone, and with bone powder that wet boots had tramped into gummy white paste.

"Come along," said Amabeel, vehemently, "we've services to perform."

She drew a deep breath, to still her trembling. Then, half-running, she crossed the hall, passing the mage (which, again, she ought not to have done), and started up the stairs behind the Guardsman. Whose sword hilt clinked softly as it bounced in its scabbard.

Suddenly Didge's hands felt very cold. Something was wrong. She glanced upward, and then saw him—a man. In shadow at the top of the stairs. Leaning against the balustrade. Arms folded. Clearly waiting.

The—

—End-of-Everything Man?

CHAPTER 4

FLESH ON FIRE (I)

BROTHER, WHAT PETER Musik wouldn't give right this second for a piece of paper and something to write with. It was driving him nuts, all these weird people traipsing around, and him not able to make notes. Just his luck, to pop into some alternate universe without so much as a Bic pen in his pocket!

He wouldn't have trouble remembering the first-graf stuff, so to speak—all the major *incidents;* it was the picayune things, the telling *details,* the choice bits of business he was afraid he'd forget if he didn't write them down now.

For example: this small, cute woman with the orange hair and pale-gray skin? Peter would *try* to remember that she had a slight limp on her right leg and a jeweled brooch, shape of a cat, pinned to her cloak, but he'd *definitely* remember how she reacted seeing Jack at the top of the stairs. She was shocked. So badly it seemed possible that her legs might buckle.

He'd remember, too, that Jack, seeing *her*, seemed taken equally by surprise—and that he'd reached out and grabbed her, drawing her up the last two steps, into the gallery, and that he'd called her Didge.

Peter the pro, the working journalist, stood five feet away, taking everything in: seeing Jack smile, Didge frown, start to cry. Peter watching, nodding, not knowing what the hell was *up*, but certain it was juicy, and then—

Then a very tall, white-haired geezer, a magician-type in a soggy brown cassock, came hobbling off the staircase, puffing and blowing, and suddenly Peter Musik (Your Correspondent in Lostwithal) was faced with a serious dilemma.

Should he stick around, see what happened between Jack and this Didge person—

(whose toenails were filed to points)

—or should he follow the old magician?

(who had a scuffed leather bag slung over his shoulder, and carried a pair of tongs)

Peter thinking, What would Jimmy Breslin do?

He glanced at Jack (still talking low, speaking Losplit, saying to the woman, ". . . your brother?"), then made a hasty decision, hoping it was the right one: he moved briskly along the gallery, trailing after the geezer.

JACK SAID, "BLADEN? IS AT THE castle?"

Didge said yes, hadn't she just *told* him that? Bladen was at the royal castle. Doing his firstwork. Didge sounding cross, adding, "You want to talk about my brother, fine, we'll talk about him later. Right now I'm supposed to perform a service. You want to show me what it is?"

Jack didn't move. He just stood there with his back pressed to a bulky stone pillar, his eyes fastened on Didge.

He'd never expected to see her again.

No, change that: a fifth-degree Walker didn't think in terms of "expect" or "not expect."

He'd never *wanted* to see her again.

   And what was most unsettling about this? Wasn't so
much *seeing* Didge here as being startled by her sudden
appearance.

   A Walker wasn't supposed to *be* startled. By anything.

   Jack saying finally, "I'll take you down to the cellar,"
then led the way, his mind drifting back, much against his
will, to that *other* time she'd surprised him; remembering
a humid, High Summer day when he'd woken in his bed,
in his cottage in Sett, and there she was, spooned against
him, naked and beautiful; the morning she'd ruined her
life, and very nearly had ruined his. . . .

                                WIND-DRIVEN RAIN BLOWING IN,
slanted, through a big hole in the turret's stone wall, pouring down through gaps in the conical roof, bouncing
on and puddling what remained of the floor—further
drenching Master Amabeel as he crawled about on hands
and knees, examining rubble.

   Occasionally, he'd use the tongs to pick something
up—a splinter, a singed clod of plaster, a chunk of iron, a
chip of glass—and drop it into his gunnybag.

   Peter Musik stood in the doorway, one hand braced
on the sooty jamb, watching, seeing the Court Mage un-
snap a little pouch-pocket in his cassock, and take out a
small white tablet—it resembled, no kidding, a piece of
Chiclet gum—and then stick it on his thumb, the tip of
his left thumb.

   This called for a closer look.

   Taking it slow, moving carefully—there were places,
rifts, in the so-called floor where you could look straight
down to a gallery twenty feet below—Peter stepped into
the turret room and crouched.

   The better to see Amabeel press the tablet to a
splotch of mud that clung to a rocker on what looked
like—

   —a baby's cradle?

   Peter took another step, easing forward slowly, saying to himself, Yeah, an old-fashioned wooden cradle.

There was a blinding flash—of blue—and Peter stumbled backwards (thinking, I'm gonna fall!) and the blue light, dense and glossy, began to pulse, strobing like crazy all around Master Amabeel, whose body shook and twitched, and whose face burst suddenly into flames.

THE PRISONER IS BURNING!

What am *I* supposed to do about it?

Put out the fire, that's what.

Perform your service.

Dispell.

When her hands started to shake, Didge made fists.

The burning prisoner, a powerfully built man with dark red hair and bushy eyebrows, hung shackled to a greasy wall in the cellar, thousands of bright, tiny, hissing flames rippling upon—but not consuming—his naked body.

Abruptly, they all died, blew out, leaving his flesh dazzlingly red.

His chest rose and fell.

And the flames blossomed again.

He never made a sound.

But Didge groaned, recognizing the spell, and knowing how difficult it could be to break, that a pythoness had cast it, and—

And if Jack, a Walker hadn't been standing right there, she would've thrown up her hands, pleaded inexperience, turned around and fled. Faced the consequences later.

Consequences. What was the worst thing they could do to her? Take away her documents? Stain her Heart of Talent? Say, Didge of Drawl, you're unfit to be a Dispeller—now go home?

Would that be so awful? It would be a relief!

Except that . . . discharged from her thirdwork, she'd have no other life-choice but to find a host, someone to support her, and that might get a little unpleasant. Lead to all sorts of complications. Like what happened to her mother—abstinently married to one man and producing children, as though they were fruit pies, for another.

Yes, well, the whole thing was moot, because she wasn't *going* to throw up her hands, plead inexperience, and run.

Not with Jack standing there, she wasn't.

She might *fail,* that was a real possibility, but she wouldn't fail without first giving it a try.

Not that she had to *prove* anything to Jack—to the Void with him!—it was simply that . . .

He was looking at her.

And she knew exactly what he was thinking. She did! She *knew!* He was thinking, Didge isn't worthy of a Talent, it's wasted on her.

Isn't *that* what he was thinking?

"You can go now."

Jack said, "Go? What're you talking about?"

"And take this man with you." Gesturing at the big red-faced soldier, a posted guard. "I prefer," she said, "to be left alone."

"Didge. We have no idea who this prisoner is, he could—"

She flared and drew back her shoulders. "Don't interfere! I've been formally summoned." (Formally summoned, indeed: by a Castle Dog that had scratched at the door of the visitors' hostel. MAKE HASTE! MAKE HASTE . . .)

Jack looked at her for what seemed to Didge a long time, his eyes piercing blue, then he nodded at the soldier, and they both went out.

The flames had died again on the prisoner. Whose eyes stood open, were glazed, and seemed sightless. And whose lefthand fingernails curled like talons.

Didge's gaze moved from the prisoner to the door. Then to a trestle table, to a water pail in a far corner, to a slug line that glistened across the stone floor. Stalling. That's what she was doing, she was stalling. Just *do* it, she told herself. Do it now.

You don't need . . . anything.

But she did. Oh, but 'Teacher, she did!

She couldn't *do* this without—

Reinforcement.

Turning her back to the prisoner, Didge shoved up a sleeve, exposed a wristlet of braided rag. Loosened one of the braids, spread it, and pinched out a winged beetle nestled in a twist of cloth.

Pinched it out, finickally, then squeezed it till it popped, and licked the ooze.

Half a minute later, when she turned again to face the burning man, her lips had gone flaccid, but her eyes were keen and bright.

Crooking two fingers, she worked them down beneath her collar, fished out a string pouch from around her neck.

Salt.

Removing the brooch from her cloak, she pricked her thumb with its post.

Blood.

Her mind was sluggish now, a faraway planet. She was moving erratically, unsteady on her feet, but . . .

But given just a few moments longer, she felt certain she could . . . that she would . . . that she'd even *want* to recall the Twenty-first Injunction, the Coda, the Relent, and the Low Paradox.

Words.

Just give her a few moments. A few moments, Schoolteacher.

First comes pleasure, *then* comes service.

To Didge, a Dispeller that seemed only fair.

CHAPTER 5

PLAYING
WITH UNCLE MILTY

THE BURNING PRISONER IN
the cellar at Manse Seloc wasn't a Lostwithalian. He was,
like Peter Musik, a visitor from Kemolo. His name was
Frank Luks (rhymed with "kooks"), and Frank Luks could
deal with pain. He had it down to a science. Or something.

Thanks to Uncle Milty's game room.

Frank Luks had never told *any*body about Uncle
Milty. A guy like Frank, who made his living, most of the
time, as a mercenary, just didn't go around telling the
sorts of people that *he* knew about some albino midget in
a pineapple shirt who lived in a wood-paneled room deep
in his brain. They'd think he was crazy, they'd peg him as
unreliable, the word would spread, and that'd be the end
of Frank Luks's career.

So he'd always kept Uncle Milty his own little secret.
Too bad. Because how he'd met Uncle Milty, how

he'd *invented* him and the game room, made kind of an interesting story.

It goes back to when Frank was nineteen, to his Ranger days in 'Nam, and to a Saigon brothel called The Tight Spot, where there was always reading material lying around on tables—not that you ever got too much opportunity to read. There'd be plenty of raggedy-looking American magazines—*True* and *Time* and *Sports Illustrated*—and usually a lot of paperbacks, too. Frank had found *Rosemary's Baby* in that whorehouse and swiped it; another time he'd found *The Godfather* and become so engrossed in it that he hadn't even bothered getting laid. And then one day, in the fall of '72, he'd come upon a copy of something called *The Mind Shop Method*, by T. Nelson Poole.

When Frank spotted it, he figured it for a science-fiction novel. But it wasn't. It was kind of a weird self-help book. A *very* weird self-help book. He skimmed it, and it seemed fairly interesting, and had nice short chapters, and so later, on his way out, he grabbed it from the table and stuck it in his pocket.

Over the next few weeks, he'd read the book, twice. What it was about—the gist of it—was this: you could increase your productivity and accomplish all sorts of creative problem-solving just by building an imaginary workshop deep inside your brain.

The book told you how to do it, step by step.

See, first you'd go into this trance. It was like self-hypnosis. *That* was cool. Then you made believe that you were walking down a staircase through your brain (you had to visualize the stairs, the tread pads, the bannister, any hand smudges on the wall, everything), and at the foot of the stairs you'd find a room, your workshop, and in this workshop there'd be—

Well, whatever you wanted there to be.

Tables, chairs, a couch, bookcases, whatever. A stereo. A typewriter. A wet bar.

You'd also find an assistant (it could be a guy, or it could be a woman, it could even be a *naked* woman, it was entirely up to you) just waiting to help you figure out some really clever ways to deal with life's big problems.

Sure, it sounded flaky as hell, but it also sounded kind of neat, too.

Frank Luks decided to give it a try.

Only it didn't pan out.

He could get into his trance all right, no problem, but whenever he tried to visualize that staircase through his brain? Nothing happened. And if he couldn't even get to the stupid staircase, how was he supposed to reach the goddamn workshop?

So he threw away the book, and forgot all about the Mind Shop Method.

For about three months.

Till he was gut-shot in the filthy jungle and thought he was dying.

That January—this would be January of '73—he'd been sent into the boonies with three other Rangers, to stalk gooks and rattle them. The Rangers would snipe and vanish, snipe and vanish—sometimes they'd even crawl into a VC camp at night, do a little spooky-dooky number, like pin a Nixon/Agnew campaign button on the commanding officer's blouse, then slip away. Head games. Except for the brutal heat, the rain, and the bugs, it was a lot of fun.

But then they'd walked into that ambush.

The other Rangers bought the ranch in about four seconds, but Frank Luks managed to scramble the hell out of there. How he did it, he never knew. Afterwards, he was unable to recall anything about his flight except the blood. And the pain.

He'd never forget the pain.

He could deal with the fact that he was dying: he was a professional soldier, a Ranger, a cowboy—you took it as a given that you'd probably get killed.

But the *pain!* Jesus. He didn't know how to deal with it.

He was a bloody mess, flies in his wounds, and the pain just kept getting worse and worse, and he wanted to pass out and he couldn't, wanted to die and he didn't, then finally—and this was truly weird—of all the stuff in his life that he could've remembered at that point, what popped into his head was that little paperback book, that buck-twenty-five Bantam paperback, the one about mind control and the imaginary workshop.

So he gave it another try.

But still he couldn't visualize the staircase through his brain.

Okay, thought Frank, if I can't make a staircase, know what I'll do? Take the elevator.

And bing, just like that, he was descending.

He could *see* the damn elevator, he could see it! The gray walls, the top exit and ventilator grille, the handrail, the directory, the floor-selector buttons. What an imagination! He pressed B, figuring it meant "basement."

And kept descending, and wondered what his workshop ought to look like. The only real workshop that Frank Luks could remember seeing in any detail had belonged to his dad, and that hadn't been much of a workshop, just a one-car garage with some elementary tools on pegboard, a greasy bench, a vise, a jigsaw, and a bunch of stapled-up *Playboy* centerfolds. Frank started thinking, Well, maybe he'd recreate his dad's garage, but, like, make a few improvements. Add a well-stocked refrigerator, a gun rack, better lighting.

When the cage doors slid open, though, and Frank stepped off the elevator, he was surprised to find himself standing not in a one-car garage but in a cozy little knotty-pine rec room with pink-and-black-speckled asphalt tile on the floor. There was some hard plastic furniture, all blue, a card table with a burbling electric percolator on top, and several pogo-stick lamps that dated from the first years of the Atomic Age.

The walls were lined with chip-core shelving units filled with boxed board games. Frank—who'd always loved board games as a kid—recognized Clue and Monopoly, Stratego and Scrabble, the old standbys, the classics.

Wait a minute, he thought as the elevator closed behind him, aren't I supposed to be in charge here?

What kind of dumb workshop is *this?*

Way down deep in his brain, Frank Luks scratched his head.

He was baffled (a rec room?) and disappointed (where was the assistant? where was the assistant he'd decided in the elevator should look a lot like Michelle Phillips, from The Mamas and the Papas?), but he wasn't *mad* or anything. How *could* he be? His pain had stopped. Entirely.

Frank sat down in one of the butterfly chairs, thinking that maybe he'd died. Which was such a goofy idea—heaven (even hell) as a rec room, a *game room?*—that he had to laugh. Then he got up, looked around for a cup, found a heavy white diner mug (there were exactly two in the room, on a shelf), and poured himself coffee. Good thing he always drank it black because there was no milk or sugar. When he sat down again, he kicked off his shoes, a pair of Thom McAn Romas with the nice cushioned insides, the kind he'd always worn before he got drafted. He was wearing white socks. Jeans. And a black t-shirt with a stencil of Jim Morrison's face on the front.

Totally relaxed, he closed his eyes, stretched out his legs. He felt lazy, invulnerable, and secure.

" 'Ey, Frank," said a voice next to him.

When Frank opened his eyes again, a man was standing directly in front of him: a stunted, pink-eyed, white-bread man with thin hair the anemic color of drawn butter.

What happened to Michelle Phillips?

The little man—the albino!—was wearing a short-sleeved Hawaiian-vacation shirt (palm trees, pineapples, hotels, and volcanoes), beige chino pants, a brown skinny belt, and tan Earth Shoes.

Back in the real world, if Frank Luks had seen a guy that looked and dressed like this, he would've felt compelled to bait him, would've said, That's some shirt you got there, uncle. (Where Frank had grown up, it was common usage to substitute the word "uncle" for "asshole.") You know what you ought to do with that shirt, uncle? Wash it and burn it. That's what Frank would've said if he'd met this character in the real world. That shirt you're wearing? Wash it and burn it.

But down here, deep in his brain, in the game room, Frank just smiled thinly and said to the guy, "My problem is, I figure I'm bleeding to death—you got any great ideas what to do?"

The albino assistant cocked his head and shrugged. "Are you in any rush to get back up top?" When he spoke —and Frank thought this was pretty strange—he spoke with a slight Hispanic accent. *Mucho* strange, since Frank Luks, as a matter of course, despised all Hispanics— Cubans, Puerto Ricans, Mexicans, any of those types. Shit, you wouldn't think he'd invent an *Hispanic* assistant, now would you?

Yeah, but *had* he invented this guy?

He decided not to worry about that right now.

Company was company.

"Am I in a rush?" said Frank. "No, I'm not in a rush. What's back there? I got a hole in my stomach, back there. Up top. Whatever you wanna call it."

"So let's just hang out," said the assistant. "Feel like a board game? You like Clue?"

Frank thought for a moment, then said Clue was okay, but it wasn't one of his all-time favorites. But, yeah, he'd play, he said. Then he said, "What's your name, uncle?"

He'd expected the albino to say something like, Well, that's entirely up to you, Frank. But he didn't. He said, "Milton Bradley," and reached down Clue from one of the shelves.

"What'd you say?"

"Milton Bradley. You asked my name, it's Milton Bradley."

Frank said, *"The* Milton Bradley?"

The albino made a face and said, "How could I be *the* Milton Bradley, Frank?"

Was this weird, or what? An albino Hispanic named Milton Bradley, same as the game company?

Frank was thinking that maybe he hadn't read *The Mind Shop Method* as carefully as he'd thought.

"You remember the rules?" said Milton Bradley, opening the game board on the table.

"Whyn't you run them by me, quick," said Frank. "Refresh my memory."

So Milton did, then they started to play, the pair of them tossing dice and moving their tokens (Frank's was black, Milton's white) through the country manor, the scene of the crime. After a few minutes, Frank started to call Milton Bradley "Uncle Milty." It made him feel at least a *little* bit in control of the situation. The albino scowled the first time, but otherwise didn't seem to care.

Up the elevator, meanwhile, a chopper was landing . . . medics were scrambling out . . . and Frank Luks —the Corporeal Frank, the bloody one in camouflage garb—was being hustled onto a field stretcher.

Down in the rec room, the Essential Frank was taking a wild guess, saying that he thought it was Colonel Mustard in the library with a lead pipe. Then, as Uncle Milty watched him with just a hint of petulance on his mouth, Frank checked the envelope, smiled, and said, "I win."

In the almost twenty years since then, he and Uncle Milty had played a lot of board games together. Dozens.

The time Frank had had his spleen ruptured in a traffic accident just outside Toledo? In '74? He'd taken the elevator to the game room and played Risk with Uncle Milty. Conquered the world while the Highway Patrol cut him out of his Mustang with an acetylene torch.

And that time in Detroit? Doing repo work, dragging a box spring out of a public-housing slum, and that lunatic woman, mother of nine, had jammed a chef's knife between his shoulder blades? Frank had sat down with Uncle Milty for a good long game of Stratego—Frank naturally blowing the albino clear off the playing board. The battlefield.

Then, in San Salvador? Summer of '83? Just about a month after he'd arrived, his first time out as a mercenary, when he'd taken two machine gun bullets through a leg? He'd beaten Uncle Milty at Aggravation, bankrupted him at Monopoly.

In Nicaragua? When his plane had been shot down, and he'd spent three days in a mangled wreck, with a concussion and a broken shoulder? He'd played Master Detective, Sorry, Pokeeno, Yahtzee, Hangman, and Classic Concentration. And won every game.

Down in the rec room, Frank Luks was unbeatable.

These last two days, while his body hung shackled and burning in Manse Seloc, he had bested Uncle Milty at Chinese checkers, Rags to Riches, Quicksand, Payday, Pictionary, Trivial Pursuit, and Whodunit.

Now they were playing Wheel of Fortune, and Frank was squinting at the puzzle board, where an H, two Ps, two Ss, two Ns, and a G were exposed. He rubbed his chin. He'd already spun the wheel and the arrow was pointing to $600.

He said, "Are there any Bs?"

Uncle Milty picked up the booklet, flipped to the B-page, ran his little pink eyes down to number 35 (they were playing Puzzle Card 35) and said, "No, no Bs."

Frank was startled. No Bs?

He watched Uncle Milty lean over the wheel, ready to spin it.

"Wait a second," said Frank, and stood up.

"What's the matter?"

"I'm getting tired of this."

Frank jabbed the elevator button. Immediately the doors slid open. "I'll be back, all right? Don't look at the answer."

"I never cheat, Frank."

Which was true; as far as Frank knew, the creepy little guy never did.

Frank stepped into the cage and pressed P; he didn't know exactly what the P stood for—maybe "Penthouse"? —but whenever he pressed that particular button, he was conveyed promptly up through his brain and let out behind his eyes. (Nothing at all happened when he pressed any of the number buttons.) Slumping against the handrail, Frank listened to the cables zing. He was going crazy with boredom. He'd often been bored in the past, but this time it was specially bad.

In the past, whenever he'd been hurt, gone into his trance, and taken the elevator? There were just two possibilities. Either he'd croak, and that would be the end of the game room and Uncle Milty, or else he'd recover, and take the elevator back up to his real life.

But *this* time . . .

Jesus Christ, *this* time it was different.

The doors opened, and Frank Luks stepped into his eyeballs, seeing the same skinny woman that he'd seen earlier, the one with pale-gray skin and hair the color of orangeade. Dressed in corduory pants and a cloak that was sopping wet.

Then he wasn't watching her any longer; he was suffering.

His shackled body in flames.

The flames not burning his flesh.

Just torturing him.

Always before, either you'd die or you'd recover.

But this.

Christ, *this* could go on friggen *forever!*

Frank caught the elevator back down.

" 'Ey, Frank," said Uncle Milty. He was pouring himself a cup of coffee from the bottomless percolator. In nineteen years, they'd never refilled the basket, or put in more water, and yet the coffee was always fresh, always great, always strong the way that Frank liked it. "Ready to play? It's still my turn." Uncle Milty sat down at the table.

Frank just stood there glaring.

Was that the only thing this stupid ugly albino ever thought about—playing board games? Christ. *Jesus.*

"Frank? What's the matter?"

What's the matter? This stupid ugly albino *spic* had the gall to ask him what was the *matter?* All of a sudden, Frank Luks snapped and grabbed Uncle Milty by the front of his retarded shirt, lifted him off the floor and flung him halfway across the game room, where he slammed against one of the shelving units. It lurched forward, and a dozen board games toppled down. A cascade of tokens, luck cards, play money.

"Don't blame me, Frank," said Uncle Milty, his voice

eerily mild. There was the faintest trace of a smile on his lips. "I didn't get you into this mess. You wanna blame somebody? Try that crazy Major you been working for."

Frank spread his fingers and pushed both hands through his hair, repeatedly. "You're supposed to *help* me, uncle. That's the whole idea, isn't it? But all you wanna do is play *games*. It's crazy."

Uncle Milty calmly picked himself up off the floor, sat down again at the card table.

Silence fell between them.

Frank began to pace. At last he said, "I could be hanging up there burning and not-burning for *years.*"

"I suppose that's possible," agreed Uncle Milty. "But like I said, it's not my fault. You're the one went to work for Major What's-his-face. That man's a lunatic, Frank. He got tossed outta the Marines, didn't he? It's a wonder he didn't end up in some federal penitentiary."

"How come you know so much about him?"

"I don't know so much, Frank. All I know's what *you* know. We just see things different. I say the man's a nut. I say the man's an animal. And I say *you* were an idiot for taking his offer. Now. You ready to play? It's my turn."

"You're calling me an idiot?" Frank raised a threatening hand. "You wanna die, uncle?"

"Grow up, Frank. You gonna *kill* me? And just how you figure on doing that?"

Frank looked blankly at the albino. "It was good money."

"Terrific." Uncle Milty shrugged. "How you gonna spend it here?" He glanced to the elevator. "You never use your head, Frank. When you found out what that crazy guy wanted, know what you shoulda done? Said thanks, pal, but no thanks. Really, Frank, nobody'd ever mistake you for a great human being, but even *I* was surprised you'd sink so low."

"What?"

"Stealing those people off the street—"

"They were only *bums!*"

"—so they could end up being guinea pigs. Low, Frank, very low."

Frank Luks couldn't believe he was hearing all this. Nineteen years they'd known each other, and the little prick had scarcely said anything more than "Good game" or "What do you want to play?" and now, now he was calling Frank names, *judging* him?

"Watch your mouth, uncle."

But the albino wasn't intimidated. He leaned back in his chair. "And to volunteer *yourself* as a guinea pig. Frank, you've surprised me over the years, but I gotta tell you, *that* just about bowled me over."

"Oh, it did?"

"Yeah," said Uncle Milty, "it did. I never thought *you'd* take one of those idiotic drugs."

"*Idiot* Drugs. And there was a good reason."

"Sure, sure, sure."

"You don't understand anything, uncle. That drug was special. It got me *here.*"

"Big deal."

"Christopher Columbus. Neil Armstrong. Frank Luks. If it had worked out—"

"If, if, if. *If* you'd come here and then gone *back,* sure. You'd be rich, you'd be famous. But 'ey, Frank? It don't seem too likely you *are* going back. Ever. Does it?"

"I'll get out of this. Always have before."

"You always have. I'll give you that."

"The Major and Gene Boman were coming through after me. They'll find me."

"Maybe. But what if *they* got snatched by that little witch, same as you—uh? What if they did?"

"I think I heard enough of this crap."

Uncle Milty spread his hands.

Again, silence fell.

And again, Frank was the one to break it. "I have to do something. I can't just hang around here, I have to *do* something!"

"Exactly!" Uncle Milty pointed at the puzzle board. "It's my turn." He spun the game wheel. The arrow stopped at FREE TURN. "I'd like to buy a vowel."

Impassively, Frank studied the gray doors of the elevator.

"I'd like to buy a U, please," said Uncle Milty.

With an exclamation of disgust, Frank Luks crossed the game room, thumbed the elevator button. When the cage opened, he stepped inside. "How the *hell* did I ever end up with you?"

"Ditto," said Uncle Milty.

"What?"

"I said ditto. Ditto, Frank. How'd I end up with *you?*"

Frank couldn't be bothered worrying about the implications of *that* statement, not *now* at least. So—in a voice that was thin and cold and contemptuous—he just said, "If I die, uncle, you die with me."

It seemed to him the albino waved a hand dismissively, but he couldn't be sure, since the doors closed before Uncle Milty could complete his gesture.

The elevator ascended.

CHAPTER 6

FLESH ON FIRE (II)

NOW DIDGE CAME TO THE part she hated, that she'd always hated, where she had to rub her face till it stung with mineral salt, then roll her eyes, and get down on the ground and wriggle. All that stuff was so . . . *primitive*. Made her feel like a savage. It was stupid, a complete waste of time. Waste of motion. Her considered opinion.

Back at the Craft, she'd got into a lot of trouble for expressing those views to her Third Masters; they'd called her self-conscious and vain, accused her of being squeamish and lazy, a troublemaker. But they didn't understand: she was just practical. Modern. Look, everybody *knew* it wasn't salt that reversed a spell of magic, and it wasn't a lot of jigging around, either. Why pretend? Words did the trick—actually, their *vibrations* did. The rhythmic and modulated *sounds*. It didn't even matter what the words *meant*. It was all in the vibrations.

The rest of it was a lot of antique nonsense. Superstition.

But for saying that, for saying what everyone already knew, Didge had nearly been expelled from the Craft, nearly Stained, on two separate occasions. Once she'd even had her bags packed.

Finally, she'd learned to keep her big mouth shut.

That didn't mean, though, that she'd ever *accepted* all the rigmarole.

But she *had* taken an oath, and so . . .

She knelt down, stretched out full length on the cellar floor, and writhed.

As she began to utter the Relent, her mind was still hazy from the beetle 'sap, but her voice was clear and strong. She did, however, stumble over a word or two. But just a word or two.

When she was finished, Didge stood again, feeling slightly dizzy, and brushed off her cloak and trousers.

The prisoner was watching her.

Didge met his gaze, then looked away the moment his chest (but *only* his chest this time) darkened again with the red glow of fire.

His body strained against shackles, and his head jerked back. He grunted in pain.

It was the first sound of any kind that Didge had heard him make.

He grunted again as she raised cupped hands to her lips and began to articulate the Low Paradox, her thumbs moving deftly in and out of her mouth, pressing front teeth, side teeth, back teeth, manipulating her tongue.

A Paradox was to be uttered without hesitation (at the Craft she'd spent more than half a Wet Season just learning to breathe correctly), but now, midway through it, Didge drew a complete blank. Suddenly she couldn't remember what to say next, and in a panic she murmured three or four words from a stanza of the *Child's* Paradox. She broke off, in horror . . . shook her head to clear it . . . then went on, stammering, and finished.

She was afraid to look at the prisoner.

She was certain she'd botched it. The entire service. If the prisoner were still in flames, what then?
Then what?

The sweat stood out in beads on her forehead.

Slowly, she raised her eyes.

His body glowed. He moistened his lips. Then clicked his teeth together. Didge could sense him bracing for more fire.

She held her breath.

But nothing happened.

Nothing!

She rubbed a hand across salty lips and sagged with relief.

The prisoner cleared his throat. Seemed about to speak, but then didn't.

His eyes followed Didge, though, as she moved confidently across the room, unlocked the door, and pulled it open.

"I'm finished, Walker," she said. "It's done."

IT HAD BEEN MORE THAN twenty minutes since Peter Musik had seen Master Amabeel go up in flames. And still he couldn't stop trembling. Thinking, Jeez, the guy's *head!* The guy's whole *body!*

He stood in the gallery now, opposite the turret room. Propped against a low balustrade. His mouth sandpaper-dry.

The Guard captain in the blood-red tunic was staring at him with his lips pressed tight together.

Peter straightened, rolled his shoulders, assumed— or at least *tried* to assume—a professional, inquisitorial demeanor. Brows knitted, head cocked, a hand on his hip. Then: "What happened in there?"

Which only made the Guard captain laugh.

Ever since Peter Musik was a kid, that had been the one sure thing to set him off, make him crazy, start him swinging. Being laughed at. He took a step toward the Guardsman, then stopped. His heart pounding. "What's so funny?"

"You're speaking the liquid language."

"The *what?*"

"You can always tell somebody who's learned Losplit from a cup of cold water."

Saying "learned" with a sarcastic, insolent edge.

Peter had learned—acquired the facility to speak—Losplit from quite a *few* cups of cold water, as a matter of fact: cold, cloudy water drawn from a well at a place Jack called The Preserve.

"What if I did? So what? You understand me. Now do you think you could answer my question? *What happened in there?* The old man was on *fire.*" Yes, and then he wasn't. Just as suddenly as the flames had started, they'd ceased, and the mage, without so much as a blister, had calmly resumed canvassing the room. He was still at it now. "What's he looking for?" said Peter. "What's he doing? What'd I see?"

What, what, what, what, what.

Narrowing his eyes shrewdly, the Guard captain crossed the gallery. Then pressed his left palm flat against Peter's chest. The right side.

"You have only one heart," he said. There was a pause. A long one. "You are . . . too-human?"

Peter nearly made a wisecrack, but wasn't sure it would translate well into Losplit—into *liquid* Losplit, at that—so he just nodded. Feeling a slight glow, a tiny buzz, like a TV personality who's been recognized.

Immediately, the Guard captain drew his sword.

JACK WAS THINKING HE SHOULD
maybe tell Didge she'd done a good job. That might smooth things over. But on second thought? It was a bad idea. She'd take it the wrong way, figure he was just patronizing her. So he said nothing. Merely reached out and touched the prisoner's chest.

The right side.

Didge behind Jack now, saying, "What?"

"He's a Kemolon."

"He *is?* But how—"

"Did he get here?" said Jack. "No idea. Maybe he'll tell us." Then to the prisoner: "Care to?"

The prisoner blinked.

Didge saying, "If he's from Kemolo, he doesn't understand—"

Jack saying, "I think he does," then pointing at a pail of cloudy water. "You do, don't you? Who was it gave you a drink, the little witch? Sister Card?"

Still, the prisoner refused to speak.

So Jack switched to English: "I can help you. But first you have to talk to us. All right? Just tell us your name, how you got here. Don't be an asshole."

The corners of the prisoner's mouth tightly crimped.

"What, you don't like being called an asshole?"

"I'm not talking to anybody," said the prisoner, "so long as I'm hanging here. You let me down, then we'll see."

"First your name."

Jack had reverted to Losplit.

"No, first the iron comes off." Now the prisoner was speaking Losplit, too—the liquid dialect—though Jack figured the guy probably didn't even realize it. "First the iron."

"Oh, let him down," said Didge. "If the Mage of Four hung him up, then he *has* to be all right."

Jack, over his shoulder: "Oh? Really?"

Her eyes flashed, and her face turned two shades grayer.

Jack, to the soldier: "We'll leave him there, for now."

"No—wait!" The prisoner. In English. "My name's Frank Luks."

"All right," said Jack—in Losplit—then he turned again to the fat soldier. "You have a key?"

"Key? What key?"

"To unlock the manacles."

"What do you think," said the soldier, "I live here?"

"Hurry it up and get me down," said Frank Luks. In English. And: "Come on, come on, come *on!*" In Losplit.

FOR A MOMENT, A VERY BAD MO-
ment, Peter Musik had been sure the Guard captain was

going to run him through, slice 'im up, but instead of that what he'd done was turn his sword around, in a kind of ceremonial way, kind of *offering* it, then make Peter look closely at the hilt; see that, see what it said, there?

MADE IN GREAT BRITAIN.

The Guard captain had then laughed explosively, and introduced himself. His name, he said, was Ukrops, a Red Guardsman. And *then* he'd clapped Peter on the back, as if they were buddies. Two old pals. With so much in common!

Ukrops saying then, "Are you from London of England Great Britain?"

Peter thinking, *What?* Saying, "Um . . . no. Fort Lauderdale."

"Lauderdale." Ukrops struggled over the pronunciation. "That is . . . of England Great Britain?"

"The United States."

"The United States. No, I was never there." Ukrops shook his head, with, it seemed, profound regret. "But I *was* in England Great Britain. *London* of England Great Britain!"

"You *were?*"

"As a Walker, oh yes. I rambled through London. I loved the trains below! And the paper cones with fried potatoes. You know England Great Britain?"

"I've been there."

"Well!" Ukrops was beaming with pleasure, and Peter found his smile contagious. "A Kemolon! I like Kemolons! At least the ones I met in London of England Great Britain." He sheathed his sword. "But what are you doing *here,* Kemolon?"

"It's a long story," said Peter. "But I came as a Witness. Know what I mean?"

Ukrops nodding, his smile slipping just a little. Then he sighed, squared his big shoulders, and once more reached out to touch Peter gently on the right side of his chest. "It's so peculiar . . . just one heart."

"I guess," said Peter. "But somehow we muddle through. We Kemolons. Listen, Ukrops. About that magician in there." Peter gesturing with his thumb.

"The Mage Amabeel."

"Right. Mage Amabeel. What's he doing?"

"Seeking Iteration."

"And that means . . . ?"

Ukrops tilted his head, thinking. "Iteration means . . . it means . . ." He smiled apologetically. "I can't explain to you what it means."

"How about just the general idea."

Ukrops thought some more. Suddenly his face brightened. "You know Sherlock Holmes," he said, "from London?"

"Yeah . . . ?"

"Mage Amabeel is Sherlock Holmes . . . from Beybix."

Peter thinking, Man, it just keeps getting stranger. Don't it?

ACCORDING TO THE ORDER OF things, the fat soldier Sollox had just twelve days left till he was required to choose his thirdwork.

Before tonight, he'd intended to stay on in the military, though in another rank and capacity, of course.

Why not? It was a good life. There were no wars to fight—how could there be? There were no nations. Lostwithal was everywhere. It *was* the world. And there'd been no civil insurrections for a thousand years, maybe longer—Sollox had always been a poor student of history.

Soldiering was the safest profession that Sollox, a peaceful man, a phlegmatic man, could imagine, which is why, nineteen seasons ago, he'd selected it for his secondwork and had enlisted. He'd done his share of traveling since then. He'd even helped to build a few good bridges. Now, that was *satisfying*. And he was well-fed. And he enjoyed wearing a bright uniform. Ladies loved uniforms. And the pay was very good; the pay was excellent. What more could he want?

But now? Tonight? He was reconsidering his future. Because here he was in this dismal black castle way out in the pine barrens, the middle of nowhere, and he was scared to death.

Because suddenly it seemed the old stories were true. . . .

In Lostwithal, for thousands of years (maybe longer) there had been stories told about the Epicene. Children's stories. Campfire stories. Barracks stories. Stories good for a listen, a nod, a pleasant shudder. But stories. Just *stories*. Imaginary.

Nobody had *believed* them; nobody (well . . . except for a few crackbrained cultists, and who paid attention to *them?*) truly had believed in the Epicene, or in the Moment of Bulcease, or in a fourth human world. Not *anymore*. Not seriously, not for a thousand years (maybe longer).

But now? Tonight?

It seemed the stories were true.

That the Epicene was real. That it lived.

That it had been conjured to life by the most crackbrained cultist of them all.

The Dark Aristocrat.

The End-of-Everything Man.

The Mage of Four, Mage of Luck.

Which is why a full battalion of field militia had been rushed here tonight to the Manse Seloc.

To destroy the Epicene in its infancy. In its cradle.

Before it could grow strong and long and tear its way into the Moment of Bulcease, to release the Last Humans, whose hearts (according to the oldest and scariest stories) were made of mud.

Soldier Sollox was thinking that perhaps he might become . . . a fisherman.

Spend his days bobbling in a boat on Black Lake, and never worry again about the Epicene, or the Last Humans.

Unless.

Unless the old stories were really true. Really *really* true.

In *all* their details.

In which case, why bother even to *think* about his thirdwork?

Since, in a matter of weeks, even days, maybe *hours*, he'd be dead. Along with everyone else.

Every human being in Feerce and Kemolo and Iss. . . .

Down in the dungeon at Manse Seloc, the fat soldier Sollox gave a low groan. Then he pulled open a drawer in a greasy wooden chest.

Moist black dirt in the drawer bottom.

And several thick-bodied slugs.

And a heavy iron key.

Which he picked up and handed to Jack, a Walker.

Then, with an air of heavy gloom, Soldier Sollox sat down on a stool, braced his elbows on his knees, leaned forward, and squeezed his face between his hands.

IN HIS CAREER (OF SORTS) AS A journalist, Peter Musik had specialized in writing about obsessive types—though not too many people noticed this, or appreciated it. Peter was at his best when his subjects were . . . colorful, let's say. Monomaniacs with quirky personalities.

In the early eighties, he'd written an original paperback book about the Hunt brothers of Texas—those guys who'd tried to corner the world silver market. What had attracted Peter to the Hunts wasn't so much their financial finagling as their ingrained strangeness. Filthy rich, yet they drove around Dallas in wheezy old cars, bought their brown suits off the rack. Oddballs.

Peter loved obsessive oddballs.

Which is why he'd once done an article for *Parade* about the world's second-most tattooed man (who just so happened also to be an Episcopal priest), and a feature for *Philadelphia Magazine* about the heart surgeon whose life goal was to get into the Guinness book for composing the longest detective novel ever written, and a series of columns for *Playgirl* about female daredevils.

In fact, what had enticed Peter to start investigating

Eugene Boman last year wasn't his criminal activities, it was the guy's hobby of collecting TV memorabilia. The cheesier the better. Here was this billionaire pharmaceuticals baron, and his biggest thrill in life was paying thousands of dollars for a "Brady Bunch" pencil sharpener or an "I Dream of Jeannie" lunchbox.

For some reason, and he had no idea what that reason might be, Peter Musik was drawn to kooks.

And right now, in the Manse Seloc, he was absolutely enthralled by this Ukrops character.

Talk about obsessives. Know what he had stashed away inside his tunic? A dog-eared copy of *London A to Z*. A guide book! Yes, and a silver medallion commemorating the marriage of Prince Charles and Lady Diana. Ukrops, it seemed, had been in London (of England Great Britain) at the time of the royal wedding. Doing what, Peter couldn't imagine, but he'd been there all right, part of the cheering crowd! This human from another universe caught up in all that furor. An anglophile, for crying out loud!

Ukrops was asking Peter now how they were, Charles and Diana—did they have any children?

Peter saying, "Yeah. Two, I think."

"Males?"

"I'm not sure."

Ukrops frowned and shook his head. "Is Charles the King yet?"

"Not yet."

"Is—?"

"Ukrops, excuse me—do you know where we're going?"

"Of course. Just come along."

Ukrops, carrying a resin torch, turned a corner; Peter hurried to catch up. They were down in the bowels of the manse, negotiating a dark, musty, narrow corridor, heading—Peter hoped—for the dungeon where (according to the Guardsman) Jack, a Walker had taken the young woman with the pale-gray skin. Didge.

"How old is the oldest now?" said Ukrops.

"What?"

"The oldest child of Charles and Diana. How old—"

From somewhere just ahead, and reverberating down the corridor, came a shrill wail of pain. And outrage.

And despair.

THREE MINUTES AGO:

When Frank Luks had stepped away from the wall, both his legs had buckled. He'd staggered, he'd reeled, struggling to keep his feet, then crumpled up and pitched forward.

The guy with the long hair and the raggedy loose clothes—the *bum*—grabbed him just before he hit the floor, then eased him onto a bench.

But if that bum thought that Frank Luks was going to say thanks or act grateful, he could just forget about it.

Shoot, this could be a trick—you know? Maybe that tall creep with the snails—or whatever the hell they were, the *slugs*—on his face, maybe he was standing right outside the door. Bet he was. Right out there. Eavesdropping. Oldest trick in the book. Send in somebody who *says* he's on your side, down go your defenses, next thing that happens you're blabbing out your guts, digging your grave.

Well, Frank Luks didn't trust this bum, and he didn't trust the gray girl, either. Frank thinking, On *my* side, yeah sure. To hell with them. Hell with them both. And to hell with that little round dork in his stupid March of the Wooden Soldiers costume, sitting over there on a stool.

Frank wasn't grateful, and he wasn't talking.

His legs, though, were quivering like crazy, and his wrists and ankles were bloody, chafed raw.

Other than that, he was all right.

Not a burn on him.

Frank thinking, What was it, hypnosis?

He couldn't *really* have been on fire. Right?

Hypnosis.

What were these friggen people, bunch of hypnotists?

He pressed down hard on his thighs, digging in with

his fingertips, kneading the sore muscles, trying to stop their quivering.

Two minutes ago:

The bum, the guy who'd talked to him in English— who'd called him an *asshole!*—dragged over a bench and sat down.

"So." Talking English again, and talking it like somebody from Brooklyn. Sounding clipped and nasally. Saying then, "Did you come here with Eugene Boman?"

Which wasn't what Frank Luks had expected to hear; it surprised him, gave him a real jolt.

But he'd recovered immediately. And said nothing.

Damn, though, he was thinking. Is Eugene *here?* Is the *Major?*

When Frank Luks—using the talons that used to be his fingernails—had torn his way into this . . . place, this other world, other dimension, other *something,* Major Forell had promised to follow in a few hours; he'd be coming, he said, don't worry. Hey, Frank? Don't worry.

He'd be coming, he said, and bringing along his son-in-law.

That dweeb who'd supplied them with the weird pharmaceuticals. The Idiot Drugs. That had grown Frank's talons . . .

The bum with the ratty hair and the dirty clothes, the black shoes and the flat metal bracelet on his wrist had leaned in closer then, saying, "Did Eugene Boman *bring* you here?"

Frank blinked, pressed his lips into a straight line.

". . . or did you just come by yourself?"

Then: the bum snatching at Frank's left hand, squeezing it tight, holding it up, the two of them, together, staring at his talons, long and gray and thick and curving, with tips and edges like sharpened knives.

The bum had craned an eyebrow. . . .

One minute ago:

Frank thinking he might try to get out that door. *The* door. The only one. God only knew what was outside, but —if he *could* make a break, break into a run, all he needed was maybe twenty seconds, if that much, to *really* escape.

All he had to do was fix an image in his mind (picture the barn at Mancelot Farms, where he and the Major had played around all those months with the Idiot Drugs), and then . . .

Use the talons to slice a way *back*.

To the world. The *real* world. Of gas pumps and toll booths, Cheerios, and Sly Stallone movies. Anchor Steam Beer. Nintendo. Real *life*. The *world*.

Twenty seconds was all he needed.

He'd have to get past the bum, though . . . and that soldier. But *he* wouldn't be a problem. Look at the guy, just sitting over there on his fat butt, looking gloomy as hell. Man, he probably wouldn't even *notice* Frank sprinting for the door.

And the girl was no big deal, either.

What could she do, trip him?

No, the only problem was the bum.

Who continued to stare at Frank with that wise-guy half-smile. Waiting for him to start talking.

Hey, bum, guess what? You're gonna have a mighty long wait.

Frank clenched his toes . . . and the muscles in his calves . . . and thighs. Drew in his stomach. Steadied his nerves.

He raised his eyes and smiled at the bum.

"All right. You want me to tell you 'bout Eugene Boman? Okay . . ."

As Frank had figured he would, the bum leaned back, a little. Relaxed, a bit. Assuming Frank was ready to cooperate.

That's when Frank lunged, pushing off with the balls of his feet, shoving hard with both hands.

And the bum—what an amateur!—toppled over backwards in an awkward, flailing spill.

Frank had leaped halfway across the room before the lard-ass soldier displayed any sign of life.

And the idiot—the stupid *uncle!*—didn't even look at

Frank; no, he just turned and glanced frenziedly *behind* him, at the grayskinned girl.

Who'd shouted.

Frank was already pulling open the door—even heavier than he'd expected—by the time the soldier realized what the hell was going on and lurched to his feet, one hand reaching across his big soft belly to grab his sword.

This was a piece of cake. Wasn't it? Piece of *cake*.

Motor running. Adrenalin pumping. It was great. Back in action. Frank doing what he was meant to do.

Now he was out in the passageway, looking left, then right. One sputtering Frankenstein-movie torch in a wall fixture, a pile of bones *(bones?)*, and a puddle of greasy water. But that was all. That was *it*. Nothing else.

And nobody.

Which meant that Frank Luks was home free.

Almost.

He ran—to his left, though direction didn't matter. He wouldn't be running long. All he needed was a few more seconds.

A . . . few . . . more . . . seconds.

But then every pore in his body erupted with flames.

THE STUFF THAT POPS INTO YOUR head when you think you're going to die. In Peter Musik's experience, it had been so utterly banal, so downright *stupid* that whenever he'd remember it later, he'd feel ashamed of himself. Embarrassed.

For instance, as a twenty-year-old in college? He'd been flying from Boston to New York one Thanksgiving to visit a girlfriend when the shuttle's engines abruptly quit. Know what had gone through his mind in the ten, fifteen seconds before they'd kicked in again? A lyric from an old Shangri-Las' song: *Betty, is that Jimmy's ring you're wearing?* Now, what in hell did *that* mean?

Nothing. But it's what he'd thought about when he'd thought he was going to die.

Betty, is that Jimmy's ring you're wearing?

Another time, years later, he was in Peru, riding up a steep mountain in a rinky-dink railroad train; suddenly, something had . . . slipped, and the train had plunged back down the track, picking up speed, wobbling like crazy. Know what had passed Peter's mind then? *I think I can, I think I can, I think I can.* From that children's book, *The Little Engine That Could.*

That was as philosophical, as existential as he got.

And only last summer, when Major Richard Forell had stuck a gun in Peter's face, and Peter knew for *sure* that he was going to die—know what he'd thought then?

That it was a real shame he'd never gone to bed with Money Campbell, the dizzy college girl with the big breasts who'd helped him get the goods on Eugene Boman.

Sometimes Peter wondered if it was just him, or if everyone else in the world also faced death with such dimwit stuff flickering in their heads.

He hoped it wasn't just him, but . . .

How many *other* people were likely to think of James Arness, the star of "Gunsmoke," when a naked guy whose body was enveloped in writhing orange flames appeared from nowhere and charged at them down a narrow passageway, screaming and acting homicidal?

James Arness, James Arness . . .

Peter was suddenly paralyzed, thinking about James Arness.

If anything equally as dumb had popped into Ukrops's mind (a fond memory, perhaps, of Lady Di in her wedding dress), it certainly didn't hinder *him* from taking prompt action. He pulled his shining Brit sword from its scabbard, wrapped both fists around the grip, and raised it. Then he planted himself, Peter thinking, like a major-league batter, and waited for the screaming man— the burning man—to come within striking distance.

Peter thinking, James *Arness?*

Thinking, Oh, man, know how come? That old black-and-white horror movie—*The Thing?* It was Arness played the alien from another planet. And there was that scene: Arness covered in flames. Running like hell through that Quonset hut at the North Pole.

Peter thinking, James Arness, right.

Then thinking, Holy good God—it's Frank Luks! The Major's flunky.

Thinking, What the *hell* is Frank Luks doing here? On *fire?*

—As Ukrops swung.

A fine hot jet of blood splattered Peter Musik's face.

"FRANK? SIT DOWN, WHY DON'T you? Frank?"

Uncle Milty got up from his chair at the game table as soon as the elevator opened.

"Come on over here and sit down. Frank?"

But Frank Luks didn't move from the cage. Just stood inside with a glazed expression.

"Frank? You in pain?"

"No, I'm . . ." He cleared his throat, and swallowed.

The whitebread midget walked over to the elevator, extended his little hand.

Frank looked at it for half a minute, then heaved a sigh, and let Uncle Milty lead him back to the table.

"Sit down, Frank."

Frank nodded, did as he was told. Uncle Milty poured him a cup of coffee.

"Something's . . . different," said Frank.

"You feel like finishing the game? Let's finish it."

"What's . . . different?"

"I think it's still my turn, Frank. I bought a vowel, remember? I bought a U." Uncle Milty picked up and consulted the answer booklet. "No Us. Frank? It's your turn."

"My turn?"

"You wanna try to solve the puzzle, maybe?"

Uncle Milty turned the puzzle board, so that Frank could see which letters were exposed. An H, two Ps, two Ss, two Ns, and a G.

Frank opened his mouth, closed it.

"Give it a shot, Frank. Let's finish this game."

"Something's . . . different."

"Just sound it out."

As Frank turned his head slowly and looked at the puzzle board, Uncle Milty stood up from the table.

On the wall shelves, all the other game boxes were fading . . .

Were gone.

And the shelving units: fading.

Gone.

The linoleum floor glowed brightly . . .

Was gone.

Frank said, "Huh . . . pah. Sss—sings?"

Uncle Milty, hovering in the air, in space white as milk.

On the table, the coffee pot winked out of existence.

Frank said, "Hope? Sings? Hope *sings?*"

The elevator door faded, vanished.

"Springs! Hope springs! *Hope springs eternal!*"

He reached out, flicking down several plastic toggles with his index finger, and uncovered all the hidden letters.

HOPE SPRINGS ETERNAL.

Then the table vanished, and all that remained then was the puzzle board, the spinning wheel, Frank's coffee mug, Frank's chair, and Frank. Floating in white.

Frank's legs dangling.

Uncle Milty drifted near.

"You're dying, Frank."

Frank nodded.

"And I can't help you. I never could."

Again Frank nodded. Then looked up at the albino. There were tears in his eyes, on his face. "Milty?"

"Yes, Frank?"

"Are *you* dying, too?"

Before he vanished, Uncle Milty smiled fondly, and said, "Good game, Frank. Good game."

What passed through Frank Luks's mind as he faced, and then experienced, his own death was a crisp image of a pretty blonde woman in a slinky black gown, happily waving good-bye.

CHAPTER 7

FURTHER INVESTIGATION

MAGE AMABEEL HAD completed his detective work in the turret room and was now anxious to get started on the trip back to the royal city. His discoveries had filled both his hearts with dread, and a cloud of anxiety had swept through his spirit. He needed rest. He wanted to leave this wicked place, this place of chaos, immediately. But where was the Dispeller? He couldn't just leave her there, much as he might like to. She'd come with him, she ought to return with him. In life, circles should be complete. It was the Order of Things.

Clamping both hands around the stone balustrade, he leaned forward and peered down into the great hall, searching for Didge among the milling soldiers. He didn't find her.

With an irritable sigh, the mage turned and stared up the long gallery, to where he'd last seen the Doveflesh, in hissing conversation with a King's Tramp. His left hand went to the pouchlike pocket in the front of his cassock. He took out a small white tablet, and walked pensively to the head of the staircase.

The Dispeller, he recalled, had been standing right . . . there.

Slowly, Amabeel genuflected. His back was needled with pain, from all of his crouching down and crawling about during the past hour. He narrowed his eyes, extended his hand, and pressed the white tablet to the floor. He kept pressing upon it till the first digit of his index finger began to pulse with a pale-blue light. When light turned to flame, a spray of extravagant numbers blew through his mind. He added them up and uttered the sum beneath his breath.

There was a loud snapping sound, then a second one, directly in front of him.

The light winked out around his fingertip, and the flame died, but the snapping sounds continued, intermittently, becoming louder as they moved farther and farther away, down the staircase.

In such sounds, for Mage Amabeel, were echoes, were visions. Was Iteration.

He grunted now, seeing—in a flicker, till the next *snap*, when he saw them both again, again in a flicker— the King's Tramp and the Doveflesh moving away, farther and farther, down the staircase.

Amabeel descended, his expression one of thoughtful melancholy, and was thus led across the great hall and through a passageway and down more stairs, and down still more, into the damp cellars of the Manse Seloc.

Snap
—then
Snap
—then:

The King's Tramp and a Red Guardsman knelt beside a dead body that lay sprawled and still bleeding in the passageway. They were talking to each other in low, controlled voices. Behind them stood a portly soldier and the gaunt young stranger whom Amabeel had seen earlier, who'd been so impudently curious about the mage's investigation of the shattered turret room.

The Dispeller emerged from a doorway, trembling, sucking her lips in between her teeth, and shaking her head in violent denial.

Amabeel watched the King's Tramp rise to his feet slowly, carefully, as if holding himself, and his temper, in check. When he approached the Dispeller, she flinched.

"I performed my service! I performed it well! To the Void with you, Jack, a Walker—I performed my service well!"

Her hands, Amabeel noticed, were bunched tight.

The King's Tramp raised his left wrist to his mouth, and bit it.

When he spat, his saliva was mixed with blood.

Then he turned his back on the Dispeller and strode up the passageway, stepping over the dead man and continuing swiftly on, heading toward Mage Amabeel, his face stony, his coloring dark, almost purple, with rage. Amabeel pressed himself against the wall. The tramp went by without taking notice of his presence—which, according to the Order of Things, he ought not to have done.

"Excuse me," said the young stranger a moment later. He, too, squeezed past Amabeel and went tearing after the Walker. Amabeel's eyes widened. Not only was the stranger speaking the liquid dialect, but the mage could detect the beating of only one heart in his breast! "Jack! Wait for me!"

Then Didge, a Dispeller whirled around and fell to the floor with a shriek.

The Red Guardsman began to clean his sword's blade with a scrap of cloth.

Amabeel sighed, unbuttoning the pouchlike pocket at the front of his cassock. This had been a long night, a too-long, long night. And it wasn't over yet.

That corpse. . . .

CHAPTER 8

DOT DOT DOT

GENE BOMAN WAS WATCHING a private-eye series called "Banyon," tonight's episode guest-starring Stefanie Powers, when Peter Musik and Jack, a Walker burst into his bedroom—actually a small pantry—and grabbed him under the armpits and dragged him out.

"Hold on, fellas, it's not my bedtime! Fellas?"

He became indignant then and began to struggle, threatening to have them both fired—he'd see to it they never worked in household service *ever again*—and Jack told Peter that on second thought maybe the guy *did* deserve to be strangled, and Peter said, "You see? What'd I tell you?" Then he hooked an arm around Boman's neck and gleefully applied pressure till the billionaire's tongue quit wiggling, and his eyes rolled up in his head, his face turned blue, and he passed out.

They lugged him down a series of crinkum-crankum passageways, finally ending up, much to Peter's relief, at the entrance foyer. There, they let go of Gene Boman, and once he'd spilled to the floor, they stepped over him and went outside to look for their saddle horses.

Even though, every ten or fifteen seconds, branch lightning continued to flash in the dark sky, the storm had ended. The ground, however, was sloughy, a mass of gurgling mud, and the humidity was brutal. Delightful place, this Lostwithal, thought Peter Musik, and slogged after Jack.

The horses—as enormous as Budweiser Clydesdales, and as green as 7-Up bottles—stood just where they'd left them, at the north wall of the manse. A short distance away, several young grooms kept watch on the soldiers' mounts. One of them was playing what sounded like a flute or recorder.

Peter, unlooping reins from an iron ring: "Jack? That guy on fire? I knew him."

"Frank Luks."

"One of the Major's crew. But I don't *get* it."

Jack grunted and started leading his horse around to the front of Manse Seloc.

Peter saying, "First Boman shows up here. Then Frank Luks. What's going on, Jacky?" (First time he'd ever called him *that:* Jacky. *Jacky?* Christ, he must really be exhausted.) "You have something to do with it?"

"Did you see his left hand?"

"Whose? Frank's? No, what about it?" Peter thinking, what, he'd missed some important detail? Him, Peter Musik, the *journalist?* Damn.

"Claws," said Jack.

"Claws? Like animal claws?"

"We'd always thought it required a Schoolteacher's Ring to pass from Moment to Moment."

"Yeah?"

Jack, looking at Peter, giving a half-shrug: "But the points on those rings? Who knows what they're made of, really."

Peter saying, "Claws?"

"Maybe."

"But how did Frank Luks get—?"

"It's what I'd been hoping *he'd* tell me." Jack's expression hardened, and Peter suddenly remembered the way that the Walker had bitten himself, back there in the cellar, bitten himself then spat, spat at the feet of the grayskinned woman. Peter thinking: An insult, right? Definitely a serious insult. What'd she do to make him rebuke her like that, spit his own blood?

Peter saying then, "That woman . . ."

"A fool."

They'd walked their horses to the front of the manse, tied them to a post, and were swashing through mud, their feet stumbling. Going back inside to collect Gene Boman.

"A fool?" Peter saying, "A *fool?*"

Dot dot dot. The old reportorial dot dot dot: meaning, *you* complete the sentence. Elaborate. A *fool* . . . ?

Jack halted, his right hand on the door latch. "She was sent here to perform a service. To cancel a spell of magic."

"What, on Frank? Somebody put a magic spell on Frank Luks?" Peter thinking, A *spell?* Thinking, Whoa. Thinking, Just like in Disney. "The Mage of Four put a spell on *Frank?*"

"I suspect it was Sister Card."

—Whom Peter Musik had killed last night in the Public Garden of Our History. With an automatic pistol. He'd killed a *witch* in a world of *magic,* using a United States Army-issued Colt .45. Wait'll he got hold of some paper and a pen! Notes now, a book later. Guaranteed bestseller! That'd make Carlos Castaneda's Don Juan stuff read like *Scuffy the Tugboat.*

"But you were telling me," said Peter, "about this grayskinned woman."

Dot dot dot.

Jack, rubbing a hand up and down the back of his neck: "She failed. She was sent to perform a service, and she failed through foolishness." There was that look again, of pure disgust. "And now Frank Luks is dead."

He dropped his hand, leaned a shoulder against the door, pushed it open.

In the entrance foyer, Gene Boman sat tailor-squatted on the floor. He suddenly guffawed—something funny happening on "Banyon."

Peter saying, "Hey Jack. We know each other. Since when're *you* such a hardcase? *She failed through foolishness.* That's not like you, man. Doesn't sound like you at all."

"Know me? You don't *know* me, Peter." And his eyes snapped, narrowed. "Never assume you do."

"Wait a second, I'm—"

With a sigh, Gene Boman reached out a hand and gave it a half-turn. Going through the channels. Nothing on any of the networks now, except news. Stupid news. Richard Nixon, George McGovern, President Thieu. *Boring!* He turned to a local station, maybe there'd be a good rerun. Paydirt! "I Dream of Jeannie," starring the fabulous Barbara Eden. Jeannie saying to the astronaut played by Larry Hagman, "Oh *please,* Master."

Peter saying to Jack, a Walker, "I didn't mean to offend you."

For half a minute they stared at each other over the top of Gene Boman's bald head.

At last, the Walker lifted a shoulder, and his smile briefly reappeared. "I'm sorry." Sounding as though he meant it.

"No, hey. Look, it *was* kind of presumptuous. You tell me she failed through foolishness—okay! She's a fool. That's it, lady screwed up and you're angry. I understand. She's—she's a fool."

Dot dot dot.

Come on, Jack: dot dot *dot*.

And finally Jack said, "She is also . . . my mate."

—As Gene Boman burst out into peals of falsetto laughter, 'cause you know what that Jeannie just did? Turned Larry Hagman into a spider!

CHAPTER 9

CODA

ER TEMPLES THROB AND
she feels sick to her stomach: Didge in an alley tapping
at a whitewashed door, as the first gray of dawn streaks
the sky over Beybix. The door opens, but just a crack, an
inch, scarcely wide enough for the old woman inside
to peer out. Crossly, she looks at Didge, but then, ah!
she recognizes her—the young Dispeller who was
summoned last evening by a Castle Dog. It's not often
that someone with royal business stays here, in *these* hum-
ble lodgings.

"Come in, child, come in! Let me fix you a cup of
tea," says the old woman as Didge, making feeble gasps,
slumps into the hostel. Smell of charred firewood. Soiled
plaster walls, a wide-plank floor, a small table with a clay
basin on top. Water in the basin. Beside it, and mounted
on a black wooden base, a rusty iron ball the size of a shot
put. "Arrive yourself, my dear, and have some tea."

Didge completely immerses three fingers in the stale

water, then describes a wet triangle with them on the iron ball, and so arrives, according to the Order of Things.

The old woman nods with satisfaction—some visitors scarcely moisten their fingertips, so rude! She turns and limps back toward the kitchen, calling over her shoulder, "Your clothes are still damp—we'll make a nice fire in the stove. We'll toast you, eh? We'll have tea. We'll talk. My dreams were trifling—just more old men talking nonsense. The silly things that men say to women in dreams!" The long train of her gray robe is snarled with hair and dust balls, flecked with splinters. "I'm *glad* that you woke me!"

Practically blind with migraine, Didge puts the heel of a hand to her forehead and presses. When she speaks, her words all run together, under her breath: "Ineedto . . . Needtosleep."

The old woman is staring at her now with cautious sympathy. "Of course. Can you find your own way up? Are you—?"

"I'mfine." Didge nodding, turning, lurching toward the stairs. Worn treads. Climbing slowly, stumbling once. Then: a landing, a short hall, a doorway. Ashen light through a grimy shoebox window. She hears two men talking in low affectionate voices, someone snoring, someone coughing, someone clearing her throat of phlegm. The dormitory air is thick and close. She touches a bedstead, momentarily bracing herself, silently counting. Eleven, twelve. Her bed is the fourteenth (the fourteenth?) on the left side.

Thirteen.

Fourteen.

Unfastening her cloak, dropping it.

Please let this one be mine. Please let it be empty.

Please, Schoolteacher.

She crawls onto the hard mattress, odor of straw and stale herbs, and her breath comes in short ragged gasps. When she closes her eyes, the blackness is awriggle with dazzling red wires.

It's not my fault!

Thinking, The way that Jack *looked* at me.

But it *was* my fault it was it *was* my fault. I failed.
Again.
As always.
She lifts her face, eyes wide and feverish, and breaks
out into dry sobbing. Failed. As always! Again! She flops
onto her back, stretches both arms above her head,
knuckles lightly rapping the wall. Draws one hand slowly
down over the opposite palm, fingers unknotting fabric,
loosening the wristlet.
My fault.
A failed service, spoiled service, *all* my fault.
His flames returned! Myfaultmy fault.
Ooze on her tongue.
As bitter as her life.
Didge smiling, as the red wires in her boiling mind
begin to pale, and to wink out of existence.
Didge falling.
Thinking, If I only I could—
like the wires
—cease.
And she's no longer falling; she's here, somewhere (a
'sap dream, of course), and she's moving, not floating,
walking, feeling her way through the dark. Now stopping.
At the head of a staircase, be careful, don't fall, just . . .
one step at a time, careful, careful, Didge going down,
counting eleven twelve . . . twelve thirteen fourteen,
fourteen steps, and
I'm at the bottom.
She moves forward, headache gone, no longer sick
and full of contrition.
Just . . . walking.
Toward a rectangle of weak light.
An open doorway.
She slackens her steps and halts at the threshold.
Seeing, beyond, a small room with a square deal table and several straight-backed chairs. A spotless wooden
floor. A shelf on the wall. And on the shelves, five decks of
pasteboard playing cards, a jar of black and yellow could-
stones, a doubling cube, dice in a glass, and a schema
board with its game tiles arranged in files, ready for play.

Didge thinking, A schema board! And thinking, I haven't played in fifty seasons.

I used to be good.

Used to beat my brother.

Even my uncle, sometimes.

And just *look* at those could-stones (as she steps into the room), they're beautiful.

With a pang, she remembers long rainy days, herself as a girl, juicy with life, eagerly clutching a coarse yellow stone in her left fist, crying, *Maybe I should, bet I can!* Then flinging it across the table, bursting apart the cluster of smooth blacks.

Playing Could . . .

Playing Schema.

Playing Mage's Memory, and Full Castle Empty, and Your Father's Old Blood, and Drown the White Dog, glancing repeatedly at the cards in her hand, her body trembling with the terrible need to *win!*

To win.

And she *did* win, she won often, when she was very young. . . .

Didge picking up and putting down the dice glass, admiring the finely incised pips and characters in the game tiles, then flinching when a high thin voice beside her says, "Hello, Didge—feel like a game?"

Didge seeing: A tiny, tiny man. Pink eyes and chalky white skin. Pale yellow hair. And pictures on his shirt. Color pictures. Of fruits and trees and mountains and . . . are those *buildings?*

"If you're not in a hurry," says the tiny man, "let's play a game. Want to? Sit down, Didge, sit down. *Sit.*"

Part Two

ADDICTIONS AND DEPARTURES

MONEY CAMPBELL

"**M**ISS CAMPBELL? DEAN Broumas will see you now." And I say, "Oh?" like I'm really surprised, like I haven't been sitting here in his outer office *waiting* for him to see me, sitting here, all sweaty, feeling gritty, with nothing to read but college alumni magazines and nothing to look at but that blue-haired-grandmother of a secretary and her big white IBM computer, and a wall full of old prints—dogs with dead game birds in their mouths, really gross pictures. "Oh? Thanks. Thank you." And I stand up, and I straighten my skirt, and I smile at the secretary, and I wonder if people her age with their bulges and their liver spots and their chicken-skin necks ever have sex. Ever get laid. Be weird if they did. Gross as those pictures. "Thank you."

And I walk across the blue carpet, and I knock at his door, solid as a yacht, and I go in.

Dean Broumas. You know who he looks like, a little bit? Like Jane Fonda's father, not when he was real old, not how he looked in *On Golden Pond,* but like how he looked in that movie I saw last year in my American Film course, it was black-and-white and about Wyatt Earp. *Henry* Fonda. Dean Broumas looks a little bit like Henry Fonda when he played Wyatt Earp, only Dean Broumas has these real long ears; bet you when he was a kid other kids called him Dumbo. I bet you. And he's sitting behind his big desk, it's a polished antique, could be chestnut, with lots of folders on top, but everything's in very neat piles, scarily neat piles, and he says, "Miss Campbell," and nods at a chair, and his ears are really something; I've seen pictures of Lyndon Johnson, and he has Lyndon Johnson ears on a Henry Fonda head, and I feel all queasy at the pit of my stomach, and I sit down.

And I go, "Sorry to bother you, Dean, but I wanted to come and explain to you what happened. I mean, why I missed all my final exams."

He smiles, but it's not a friendly smile; we've had our little run-ins before, and I guess he doesn't like me too much. There was that time I had to come see him 'cause I'd plagiarized a lot of junk for an English term paper about some guy, I forget who exactly, some poet. I had to beg and plead don't expel me. "You might've come before this, Miss Campbell," he says.

And I go, "But I only got *back* this morning."

"Oh? You went away, did you?" Boy, listen to him— that sarcasm? He sounds like my father. "On a little trip, were you?"

And I go, "Well, it was a trip, all right, Dean. But I didn't plan on taking it, believe me. I really meant to be here. I worked hard all last semester, you could ask my professors. This was an . . . unexpected trip."

"Was it a family emergency? Were you ill?"

"No. No, it was . . . Dean, would you do me a favor? Will you just listen to what I wanna tell you, and not say anything till I'm finished?"

"Miss Campbell, I'm afraid that I have to warn you. Unless you have a valid medical excuse, or had a death in your immediate family, there's not much chance that—"

But I cut him off right there, going, "This college gets a lot of money from Boman Pharmaceuticals, doesn't it? I mean, like, endowments and stuff?"

Lookit how he's looking at me *now*: surprised, interested, maybe just a tiny bit scared. What's Boman Pharmaceuticals got to do with anything? So I *tell* him, just give it to him straight.

"I've been Eugene Boman's mistress for more than a year."

"Miss Campbell!" He's shocked, he's angry, oh yeah, but he's turned on, too. Old Dean Broumas. Know how I know? His eyes are traveling all over me, now to my tits. Men. All a woman has to do is mention sex, and suddenly they're hot as dogs. It's true. I know what I'm talking about. And Dean Broumas, his face red, goes, "I don't care to hear anything further along these lines." Yeah, right, sure.

"Well, I'm sorry, Dean. But I'm gonna tell you anyway."

And I do, saying how Gene Boman propositioned me when I was working part-time at his stupid company, just up the road from the college, me working there to pay my tuition.

Dean Broumas saying, "Really, Miss Campbell, what's all this have to do with the fact that you missed the last two weeks of classes and didn't show up for any of your examinations?"

And I go, "I'm *getting* to that," and then I tell him about how I met this kinda sleazy, but kinda cute reporter named Peter Musik, who was trying to find out how come Gene Boman had given his creepy father-in-law a bunch of really dangerous drugs, and—

"Miss Campbell, enough." Dean Broumas looks at his watch, mutters something about having to be at a meeting of department chairmen in five minutes, and I go, "Wait, wait! All I want to tell you is this: the reason I missed so many classes? And all my exams? Is because of Gene Boman, when you get right down to it. And since Gene Boman gives the college, like, millions of bucks every year, I think, I think, I really think you should let me come back to school. 'Cause it's really not my fault."

Dean Broumas leans forward in his chair, he doesn't look convinced. Or sympathetic, either.

"Miss Campbell. One question. Where have you been?"

"Well, it's kind of complicated—"

"Where have you been? That's all I want to know."

"Lostwithal."

He blinks.

And I go, "It's, um, another planet. I think. I don't really know *what* it is. Or where it is. It's kind of like the Middle Ages there, but not really. Know what I'm saying? It's weird."

"Miss Campbell. Are you under the influence of drugs?"

"Ah jeez. No! Listen, please? It's all Gene Boman's fault. If he hadn't done a head job on Peter Musik? Peter would never have met and got mixed up with this guy named Jack. Who *looks* like an ordinary street bum, the kind of guy that talks to himself and makes you nervous? But he's *really* this person from another planet. And then I went looking for Peter, and so *I* got mixed up with Jack, too, and then a whole bunch of us ended up traveling to this place called Lostwithal. And *that's* why I missed all those classes. *That's* how come I missed my final exams. Honest, Dean. I wouldn't lie to you. You think I just cut for a lark? I almost got killed! First by a bunch of giant bats, and then by a witch! A witch, I'm telling you! You think I'm just an airhead with big boobs? I've been trying to save the *universe*, Dean. I'm not kidding! There's a monster! It's called the Epicene. Don't ask me how to spell it, but it's called the Epicene, and it's made out of mud, and if it doesn't get killed soon it's gonna wipe us all out. *That's* how come I missed my exams, I been trying to make sure this monster doesn't wipe us all out."

Dean Broumas jabs a button on his telephone, says, "Mrs. Ostriker? Please call the campus police." Then he hangs up, then he stands up, then he says, "Miss Campbell, I'm going to ask you to submit to a drug test. Will you submit voluntarily?"

"Go to hell."

"Then, Miss Campbell, please leave now."

And I get up, sure I get up, sure I'll leave, what do I care about stupid college? I hate college, I never wanted

to come in the first place, college sucks! I got more important things to do. Like, like—

Like *what?*

And I plop back down in the chair, feeling dizzy all of
a sudden, and drained out and crampy, like I'm getting
my period, and I got this killer headache, and there's a
roar in my ears, and Dean Broumas flickers in and out of
focus, shadows and bright light flashing across his face like
Henry Fonda's, and I'm afraid I'll be sick, don't wanna
throw up, and now it's quiet, like four in the morning, and
when I look it's dark, dark as a coal mine, and I'm scared,
I'm a little girl and I'm scared, and something touches my
throat, it's wet and it's sticky and it's pebbly and it's cold,
it's mud.

A muddy hand is squeezing my throat—

CHAPTER 1

PORTRAIT

Hunched forward, hug-
ging herself tight, Money Campbell sat trembling near the
window in a chair she'd dragged across the little bedroom.
Man. Christ. Holy God. I thought I was dead.

But it was only a dream, it wasn't real, except for the
part about getting her period. That was real, all right, and
wasn't it just wonderful. Swell. Just great.

What do you do in stupid Lostwithal when you get
your dumb period?

It wasn't too bad yet, but some months—by the second day?—it was like the Colorado River, almost. Money
thinking, *Then* what am I supposed to do? Are there any
drug stores here?

She leaned forward and whispered fiercely, "Hey,
Lita? You awake?"

No reply.

Jack, a Walker's girlfriend—or whatever the heck she
was—snuffled once, and turned over on her side, cot
squeaking. Definitely not awake.

Well, it wasn't an emergency yet. Money could wait. She could wait till morning to ask Lita, female to female, about what you did at this time of month in a place that was kind of like the Middle Ages but wasn't really. Maybe they used magic? Maybe you just spoke a few magic words and the cramps went away and the flow dried up? That'd be cool. That'd be really cool. Better than Midol, cheaper than Tampax. Money wouldn't mind *that* at all.

But wait a second. Hold on. Maybe women didn't *get* periods in this goofy place. Nah—they were humans too, right? 'Least that's what they kept saying. And they sure looked human, everybody she'd seen so far. Weird, definitely a little weird, some of them with gray skin . . . but *human*.

Maybe that Lita can turn herself into a wasp, Money thought, but when she's regular? She's got all the human parts. And she's cute, too. Short. But cute. Everything nice and compact. Money envied Lita for being so clean-limbed and compact—delicate.

Money wasn't too sure, though, what Lita felt about her. Last night? As they were getting ready for bed? Lita took one look at Money stripped to her underwear and said, "Are you a wet nurse?" Not being nasty or anything, not sounding jealous, just looking at Money's big chest and going, "Are you a wet nurse?"

Which made Money Campbell feel like an absolute *cow*. Freaken Holstein.

Are you a wet nurse?

And Money had quirked her mouth to one side and said, "I guess so, yeah. But to big babies only."

Lita hadn't caught the irony, though. She'd just seemed perplexed, then nodded, then told Money to go ahead and take the bed, she'd sleep on a cot.

But as soon as they'd settled down? *Ka-boom!* It had thundered and lightninged and rained like hell. Money hadn't been able to fall sleep. No way. Not with that *noise*, not during *that* storm. And so, for hours she lay on her back in the hot muggy dark, hands clasped behind her head, elbows sticking out, eyes wide open. Thinking about Peter Musik—that prick! Galloping off with Jack, a

Walker to the Manse Seloc. Leaving her behind with Lita, Lita taking her to this little poky apartment down a smelly cobblestoned alley. Don't you just love it? You gals stay where it's safe, us guys'll go off with the big strong soldiers. What bullshit. But typical. Money thinking, This may not be earth but if you're talking 'bout humans? You're talking 'bout the same old sexist crapola! Isn't that true? Isn't that so true? Boy.

Finally, as the rain slackened and the wind became less shrill, she'd dropped off to sleep.

Only to dream that dream.

Man. Christ. Holy God.

She got up now from the chair, figuring there wasn't any point in trying to fall back asleep. She wet her face with tepid water from a cracked pitcher (Money thinking, Like you see them do in old cowboy movies). Then, even though they were filthy and full of tears, a little blood-stained, she put on the baggy brown shirt and drawstring pants she'd worn yesterday. (They were the only clothes she had, and she couldn't very well borrow any of Lita's, could she?) Finally she pushed open the window and stuck her head outside, hoping for a breath of cool air.

No such luck. It was as muggy outside as it was in; *muggier*.

She could hear water dripping intermittently from eaves and spouts up and down the deserted alley.

Moonlight wriggled and split, and split again, in a multitude of rain puddles. She could see her reflection in one: her bright yellow hair. Cobblestones gleamed.

Money pulled her head back into the bedroom, rubbed a hand across her neck, then walked directly into the front room.

"Lita?"

She'd decided she needed some company. Hell with being considerate.

"Lita?" And no more whispers, either, she wanted the witch to wake up *now*, and talk to her. Calling, "Lita? Lita?" as she stood over the cot. "Wake up—please?"

Money reached out and touched Lita's shoulder, intending to give it a gentle nudge. Instead, she snatched back her hand, instantly, with a small yelp of surprise. Christ, it was like an electric shock!

Now her fingertips tingled. Felt all pins-and-needles.

Humans? Money thinking, Humans?

So they say.

Tottering a little, she turned toward the door.

Considered. Did she want to go outside for a couple of minutes, get some air, or did she want to see if there was any chicken left. It was good chicken—she'd had some last night, with a glass of sweet wine—but hey, it was almost morning now. She was hungry, but not for cold chicken. English muffin'd be nice. Even a Pop Tart.

With a cup of strong coffee.

They *got* coffee here?

What if they *don't?*

Money thinking, Don't torture yourself.

Thinking, I wanna go home.

She opened the door and stepped out into the alley.

Boy, what she wouldn't give for a jolt of caffeine. A cup of coffee—or a Coke. Even a Coke, a bottle of Coke. Even a *warm* bottle of Coke. Forget the bottle, just a *swallow*.

She leaned against the damp wall, wanting Coke, wanting coffee, wanting company, wanting a bath, wanting to go home.

And wanting to see Peter again.

Wanting that badly.

Aw, come on, Pete, come back. This isn't fair.

She pushed away from the wall, looked up the alley. Maybe he was coming . . . now.

Right . . . this . . . second.

But he wasn't.

All that Money saw were puddles and more puddles, all of them riffled now by a gritty breeze. A small bird on a windowsill, and a wooden barrel with a mangled-looking wheel leaned up against it. Everything dismal.

She gave an irritable shrug and turned to go back inside the bungalow when, from the corner of an eye, she noticed—well, she wasn't sure what it was exactly. A splotch of color. Bright yellow. On the wall of a two-story clapboard building twenty or so yards away, just before the alley turned.

A splotch of golden yellow.

It wasn't curiosity so much that eventually made her walk down there for a closer look; it was boredom.

A way to kill ten or fifteen seconds.

Ten or fifteen seconds to walk there, two seconds to check it out, another ten, fifteen seconds to walk back.

As she walked, the big spot on the wall seemed to glisten. *Did* glisten. Was lustrous. And now, now there were other colors, too, below the yellow, and framed by it. Money thinking, suddenly knowing, It's paint.

Coming nearer, thinking, Hey neat, it's a picture.

A wall painting.

A portrait.

Then the colors resolved. Yellow became hair, ivory became flesh. Crimson became lips, tan became nipples.

Lamp black became leather, became a dog collar, and silver became its leash.

Money gaped, then went cold, then felt dizzy, emitting a feeble, interrogative moan—a sleeper's moan.

Something clattered slightly behind her, but she couldn't turn. Couldn't turn.

She could only stare at the wet painting on the wall—

Me!

—till her eyes rolled in her head.

He caught her as she fell.

His fingers were long, very long, and tapered, and they were slick with bright pigments.

CHAPTER 2

AT BEYBIX

THE GROUND MISTS WERE
gone, burned away. Both moons had set, and the sun was
climbing. Pine needles dripped steadily. Birds shrieked,
heat bugs ticked and rattled. And the air, as usual, was
thick with gnats.

Peter Musik kept squeezing his eyes shut, then snapping them open, fighting the urge to doze. He wanted to
fall asleep—God knew he did, more than anything—but
he sure as hell didn't want to fall asleep on a horse, end
up on the ground with a broken collarbone. Broken *neck*.
Peter stifling a yawn, now asking Jack for the tenth time in
the last half-hour, sounding (he knew) like a whiny kid in
the back of his parents' car, "We almost there?"

And the Walker pointed ahead—through those
trees? that glimpse of white? The city of Beybix.

They were almost there.

Eugene Boman gave a loud snuffle and made a sticky
mouth-noise. He was riding with Jack, who'd had to give

up the comfort of a saddle to make room for him. Every
so often during the trip from Manse Seloc, he'd picked up
his lolling head and voiced some complaint—I'm getting a
hernia! Or, Doesn't anybody have citronella oil, the flies
are eating me alive! And once, about five miles back, he'd
mumbled for a while about hoping they'd get to where
they were going soon because daylight was coming and he
wanted to watch Saturday-morning cartoons. Think we'll
be there by ten? For "The Scooby-Doo/Dynomutt
Hour"?

The guy was off his rocker. Nuts. No doubt about it.
Which put Peter Musik into a funk of frustration. Ever
since he'd snatched his memory back, his identity? All
he'd been waiting for, all he'd wanted to do, was to nail
Gene Boman, and nail him good. See the bastard crawl.
Ruin him. He wanted to flip on the TV news, sit back with
a cold beer and watch old Gene, on videotape, being
whisked into booking court by plainclothes detectives. See
him shield his face from flash cameras, flinch at microphones. Handcuffs glinting. Sweet revenge.

But now? Man, now it seemed that Eugene Boman
was *already* ruined, and crawling, and nailed, and there
were no microphones here, no cameras, no courts, no
"News at Eleven," no beer (for all that Peter knew), but
the most frustrating thing of all? Peter was feeling almost—

(Thinking, No! No way! Never!)

—sorry for the big fat slob.

He widened his eyes and rubbed his cheek, grum-
bled under his breath and gave his horse a perfunctory
nudge with the heels of his heavy-soled boots.

Then, at last, they were there.

Gene Boman frowned at the ancient city wall, the
battlements, the pointed arches, the iron gates, and said,
"We home, Dad?"

"Almost." Jack, a Walker, patted him lightly, kindly,
on the shoulder before dismounting. Then, looping his
reins around a hitching post outside the gatehouse, he
told Peter, "Stay here."

Which was okay with Peter Musik, no problem, he'd

gladly wait outside. But now that he had an opportunity to get down off the goddamn green Clydesdale for a few minutes and stretch his legs, he sure as hell meant to take it. His thighs ached dully, and so did his lower back. He'd never been much of a rider. Or keen on riding. He used to have a girlfriend, her idea of fun was driving to a stable on Saturday, saddling up, going off into the woods for an hour's gallop. Lord love a duck. A person could get his head lopped off from low-hanging branches.

The things that Peter Musik had done for love. Or sex. Whatever.

Now, in morning's lemony light, he stretched his arms above his head, did some deep knee-bends, and started touching his toes—to the accompaniment of creaks, crackles, and loud pops.

Living on a city street for three months, he hadn't kept too physically fit. Not that he'd *ever* been very big on working out. He'd always walked a lot, and swum twenty, twenty-five laps maybe twice, three times a month, but that had been the extent of it. That, plus the fact that he'd usually skipped lunch, had kept his weight about 170, 175. Till his days as an amnesiac bum, that is. Between Labor Day and yesterday, September to December (it was December back on earth; what month it was here, Peter couldn't say), he'd dropped a lot of weight. A lot. He hadn't been on a scale recently, but he guessed that he was, oh, somewhere around 150 now. And on a five-eleven frame, that was skinny. Skin and bone. The Idiot Drug Diet.

All things considered, though, Peter figured he was in decent shape. For a thirty-one-year-old guy who'd been through all the shit that *he'd* been through.

Oh man, though, the way his body was creaking now? The way he was huffing and puffing after only ten toe-touches? You'd think he was *fifty*-one. You'd think he was—

Several men, all of them identically dressed in nubby oatmeal-colored blouses and dark-brown trousers were staring at Peter; one of them—the one with a cage of birds and butterflies hoisted on a shoulder—was laughing outright, as if he'd never seen anything more ridiculous. What *was* this person doing, bending down and straightening up, bending down and straightening up, bending down and—

Peter stopped, nodded, and all the men nodded back. Quite amiably. Then, still nodding, and watching Peter sidelong, they walked off together, following the curvature of the wall. One of them limped, two carried (Peter guessed they were) rakes (though the tines were crossed into Xs), and two others carried spading forks. The butterflies in the cage were black. Jet black. The butterflies in the cage were jet black. The birds in the cage were red.

The birds in the cage were red and resembled cardinals.

The birds in the cage were red and resembled cardinals, except their beaks were thick and hooked and yellow-and-black, like a macaw's, and—

Damn! Damn, how much longer did Peter have to wait before he got hold of a lousy pencil and a piece of paper? Crying out loud, what *was* this place, anyhow—the Albania of alternate worlds? It was driving him batty trying to keep all this good stuff in his head and not lose anything.

He watched the men disappear around the wall—

(black butterflies, red birds, red birds, black butterflies)

—then glanced behind him, and: oh *shit!*

Eugene Boman was gone.

Where? Where the hell could the bastard have gone *to?* The gates were closed, so he couldn't have just walked into the city. Back up the sand road? No. No, it was a good quarter-mile till the empty road bent away into the pine forest; there was no way Gene could've gotten that far in, what, two minutes? At most.

Oh Jesus. You believe this?

Peter made a fist and slammed it down on the hitching post. Then, with a kick at the ground that scattered gravel, he walked to the gatehouse, yanked open the door, and went inside.

The place reminded Peter (when he'd first seen it last evening, and again right now) of the rangers' station at a state forest—where you get assigned a campsite? Yeah, weirdly enough, that's exactly what the place reminded him of. Rustic. There was an unpainted plank floor, several topographical maps on the wall, a wood-burning stove, and a long counter made of pine. The guy standing behind the counter even *looked* like a forest ranger: tall and fit, and ruddy, and short-haired. The only thing missing? Something with Smokey Bear's picture on it.

"Jack?"

The Walker was leaning at the counter, writing—drawing, was more like it—a series of tiny geometrical configurations on a lined page of a tall book.

Peter's eyes zeroed in, covetously, on the pen in his fingers.

"Jack? We got a problem."

The guy behind the counter who looked like a forest ranger (only, he was wearing a dark-yellow tunic and had three intersecting small circles—sort of like the Rheingold beer logo—tattooed on a cheek) leaned down, folding his elbows on the counter, and studied Peter with openmouthed surprise.

(Peter thinking, Yeah, yeah, I speak the liquid dialect . . .)

"Jack? He's gone! I don't know how he did it, but he got down off your horse and—"

The Walker interrupted, to point into a corner of the room.

Where Gene Boman sat perched on a stool, staring raptly at a square wall map (watching Scooby- and Scrappy-Doo mix it up with a bunch of ghosts in a dark and creepy haunted house). (When a commercial for Peter Paul Almond Joys came on) he groaned suddenly, and put a hand to his stomach. He looked around (to see if there were any snacks on top of his bureau), and when he saw Peter (Peter?) he cocked his head and blinked.

(Gene thinking, Peter? Peter Musik?)

(Thinking, Oh my God.)

(Remembering.)

(Denying what he remembered.)

(Turning back to the wall, letting focus seep out of his eyes, everything turning furry, then refocusing, sharp: seeing Scooby and Shaggy and Daphne and Velma and Fred scramble up a staircase whose treads and risers suddenly collapsed into a sliding pond . . .)

When Gene Boman leaned forward, the tip of his nose practically touching the map, Peter shrugged (what're we gonna do about this guy? he's a basket case!) and went over and joined Jack, a Walker at the counter.

Jack smiling, turning the tall book around so that Peter could take a look at a page full of tiny figurations. Peter thinking, You know what it looks like? The page? Like a high school sophomore's nightmare of a geometry final exam.

"They're back," said the Walker.

"Who?"

Jack pointed to a line of tetrahedrons and rhombuses.

"Squintik," he said. "And Jere Lee."

"Is *that* what that says?"

Jack smiling wider, nodding.

"Yeah?" Peter joining in, nodding and smiling. Then, abruptly, frowning. "What about Herb Dierickx?" He indicated the open book with his jaw. "He get back, too?"

"No."

Peter considered a moment, then pressed his lips together, shrugged, and turned from the counter.

Jack's hand shot out, grabbed Peter by the elbow.

"I thought you'd be glad that Herb Dierickx didn't return."

"That what you thought?"

"Peter . . ."

"All right. So maybe I blamed him, a little. For what happened to me. Maybe I did—for a while. But . . ."

Jack was staring hard into Peter's eyes.

"But I'm not glad he's dead! What do you think I *am*, Jack? Huh? Christ, you and Money, the two of you. Think I'm such a bastard. You say I don't know *you?* Jack? You don't know *me*, either. Jesus H. *Christ*."

He'd stiffened, and his face had turned scarlet. Now he made a short, down-chop motion with his left hand, crossed the room, grabbed Gene Boman roughly by the shirt collar, and dragged him away. The door banged shut a moment later.

Jack, a Walker smiled grimly, then nodded to the gateman, and followed them outside.

CHAPTER 3

THE SPELLMAN OF SOOLKY

IN THE TINY VILLAGE OF Soolky, on the northern shore of Black Lake, a leather tanner had summoned the new Spellman, a nervous young man called Pindrix.

"I want you to make my wife agreeable again," said the tanner, not looking at Pindrix but continuing to measure a variety of salts into a tanning bath of sumac, oak bark, and hemlock. He was a tall, burly man of advanced age and was dressed in a brown leather apron.

"Agreeable?" said Pindrix. The door stood open, and through it he could see the tanner's wife as she crossed the dooryard, moving from the woodpile to the ice house with an air of fatigue. She looked only slightly less old than her husband. Her gray hair was braided and her spine bowed. "You mean in temperament?" asked the Spellman.

"I mean in a *wifely* way."

"Oh," said Pindrix.

"Well—do it!"

"I . . . excuse me, but I am a servant of the village," said Pindrix. His throat felt constricted. His voice quavered. "I am not at liberty to do favors for citizens."

"Don't insult me! I'm not asking a favor, I intend to pay you."

The Spellman squirmed uncomfortably, removing his gaze from the tanner's lined and homely face and glancing toward the open doorway again, again seeing the old woman as she carried a block of ice between heavy tongs into the cottage. There was a gray ewe cropping grass in the yard. A dog slept in shade beneath a fig tree. The tree was heavy with fruit, the fruit clustered with yellow jackets. Clouds of midges whirled in the bright morning sunshine.

The tannery was hot and humid and fetid.

"I suppose I could give you a powder," said Pindrix, "to put in her tea."

"I don't want a powder! I want you to cast a spell!"

"Impossible," said Pindrix. "There is no such spell."

That was a bald lie. There were a *variety* of such spells, only young Pindrix had not mastered any of them, as yet.

Grunting his disgust, the old man flung away the stave he'd been using to stir his tanning broth. "What good are you?"

What *good* am I? Poor Pindrix sorely wished he could answer that question, which happened to be the same one he asked himself nightly in his bed of straw, basil, daisies, and fennel, and daily as he wandered in gloom from planted field to planted field, mumbling his poorly memorized incantations, hoping that crows would oblige him and disperse, the soil heed him and bring forth wheat in abundance—please?

Oh, what a sorry Spellman he was! And everyone knew it. Not just this conjugally unhappy old tanner, but everyone in Soolky. Well, thought Pindrix, coming here wasn't *my* idea! If he had known he would end up posted to the insipid countryside, he would never have chosen Useful Magic as his thirdwork. Never!

Since boyhood, Pindrix had had ambitions to become a scholar. Though he'd been born and raised on the remote Isle of Meeres (celebrated for its cabinetmaking and fine colored inks), he felt that he belonged in the great city of Beybix. At court. Glimpsing His Majesty-Most-Still from time to time, and living among shrewd mages who passionately studied the Perfect Order of Things. Instead, here he was out in the boondocks being told to make an old peasant wife behave as a ripe and lusty young bride. Feh!

"Perhaps," he said now to the tanner, "perhaps you might . . . celebrate something tonight with—with strawberry wine, perhaps. Perhaps *then* she might—"

The tanner roared displeasure at all that perhapsing and reached for his stave.

Pindrix grabbed up his heavy satchel and bolted.

Fleeing across the dooryard, he nearly tripped on the skirts of his pale-green cassock.

The dog, roused from its sleep, commenced to bark.

Arms flailing, Pindrix plunged through midges and kept running till he was some distance down the road. Then he took to the cool woods, where he stumbled along for some time—glimpsing the lake, then losing sight of it —before stopping to rest on an oak tree blown down in last night's ferocious storm. He was sweating freely, and his nipples had leaked clear mucous that now darkened the front of his long garment.

When he'd again resumed breathing normally, Pindrix hauled his satchel onto his lap and undid several buckles. Reaching inside, he withdrew a folded slip of paper from between the pages of a small, thin book with a pale-red cover.

As he glanced over his day's itinerary, which had been given to him the previous evening by the village council, Pindrix felt his stomach queer. A rat banishment? A *rat banishment?* Ohhh 'Teacher. He shut his eyes, trying to recollect the words and sums and conformations of a rat banishment—did he have a mnemonic? Sometimes, for some services, he had mnemonics. But for rats, a rat spell . . . no.

With climbing panic, the young Spellman riffled through the red book. When he found the spell he was looking for—under "Vermin"—he read through it once, silently, then covered the page with his hand and spoke the words out loud, while silently adding numbers and imagining a miscellany of triangles.

Nearby, a creature—certainly not a rodent—yelped in anguish.

Oh 'Teacher, thought Pindrix, what have I done wrong *now?*

The yelp was followed by several slow groans that were carried on the stillness of the morning air.

Pindrix cautiously rose from the tree trunk.

Yet another groan . . .

It was a man, the Spellman discovered moments later. A heavy-set man sprawled at broken angles on a cove beach. Lake water lapped his feet and ankles. His clothes were torn, and there were dozens of raw puncture wounds in his throat and in his arms. He continued to groan, his breath short and raspy.

Pindrix stood paralyzed. Only his lips moved. He wasn't at all certain that he could remember what he'd been taught at the Craft about the curative arts.

But he couldn't just *leave*—he couldn't just ignore this poor man, this stranger, he had to do something. *Something.*

So he cast an elementary spell that raised the man from the beach and floated him slowly through the first-growth forest—and that's how the misbegotten Spellman of Soolky became involved with a half-dead too-human chauffeur from earth named Herbert Leslie Dierickx.

CHAPTER 4

DUBROVNIK

PASSING THROUGH THE WAK-
ing streets of Beybix, Lostwithal, Peter Musik was thinking of Dubrovnik, Yugoslavia.

As a senior in high school, way back in '77, he'd bad-
gered his parents, who could ill-afford the outlay of a
couple thousand bucks, to sign him up for a summer stu-
dent-exchange program: six weeks traveling by rail
through Europe with a group of thirty-five hormonally
antic American kids. It had been Peter's first trip on an
airplane, his first time out of the United States. What an
experience! Castles, museums, cathedrals, crypts,
campaniles, red-light districts. Baguettes and pâté, gelat-
tis, chianti, wheat beer. He'd seen the *Mona Lisa,* and ten
zillion Michelangelo sculptures, and the Sistine Chapel.
He'd strolled the grounds at Versailles, gone swimming in
the Rhine, hiked through the Black Forest, bussed
through the Alps, gotten sick-drunk in Munich. Yes, all
that, and he'd gotten laid, too—had his very first experi-

ence with a twenty-two-year-old group leader from the University of Miami and subsequent ones with prostitutes in Amsterdam, London, Florence, and Salzburg.

But of everything he'd seen and done that summer, what stayed sharpest in Peter's memory over the intervening years was one particular day, a drizzling August Thursday, in Dubrovnik, a week before the flight back home.

That morning he and another boy, a rich kid from New York City named Dean—who grew up, fast, to become a notable Republican, then one of the apostles of the "trickle-down" theory of economics, then a high honcho in the Budget Department during the Reagan years, and ultimately a jailbird—Peter and this kid, Dean Datlow, had, on their own, decided to explore Dubrovnik without guides, without chaperones, and without a street map. (Dean, who'd recently read a bit of Nietzsche, called it taking the leap of faith. Peter called it having a cool adventure.)

So just after dawn they'd slipped out of the youth hostel (built during the Renaissance, they'd been told, and they could believe it, too: it sure looked, and smelled, old). They'd crept down the staircase and across the stuffy, high-ceilinged lobby, unlatched the front door, then scrammed down the steps, run to the corner, turned it, and then . . .

For the first time that summer, Peter had truly felt the strangeness, the *otherness*, of another country, another culture. In the tour group, you were always protected, you made your own little moving American ministate, passing safely, and blandly, through foreign streets and vast train stations with the giddy, unserious air of amusement-park visitors.

But that morning in Dubrovnik? Was the real thing, and the real thing was mysterious, and scary, absolutely wonderful. Peter loved it that he couldn't communicate with anyone he passed, that he couldn't read signs. He noticed a different . . . tang to the air, and different sounds, and the odd arrangements of goods in the shop windows—the odd *assortments* of goods. He studied faces, and clothing, and was mesmerized. This was no amusement park—no Six Flags, no Disney World, no Busch Gardens—built for the pleasure of vacationing Americans with disposable incomes. This was a foreign country, man, a foreign city—real. And *different*. The people were different, and acted differently; even the things they did that were familiar to Peter—like buying vegetables, like looking at their wristwatches, like folding a newspaper—they did with a slightly (or significantly) different quality than people did them back home.

Peter had been intoxicated.

Same thing this morning in Beybix.

Same damn thing. He was intoxicated, he was delighted, and though he was buzzing with exhaustion, that thrill of otherness was as striking now as it had been that morning in Yugoslavia, thirteen years ago. . . .

They'd returned the horses to the castle (as though they were Hertz cars, Peter had quipped) and were crossing a huge open market square, Peter's head swiveling this way and that, his eyes narrowing to study a wooden cart heaped with mounds of plump and gleaming fish, a kind he'd positively never seen before. Their splatter-markings, in primary colors, were as distinctive as a drip-painting by Jackson Pollock. Peter turned his attention from the fish to the fishmonger, and to the small metal cup of curling gray vapors he kept passing back and forth in front of his open mouth as he gulped, deeply.

Weird.

Wonderful.

They kept walking.

Peter watching (now) two women set fire to heaps of green—shrimp? no, *beetles* . . . that filled a raked metal tray; the beetles crackled and turned black. One of the women beat the flames out with a scorched wooden paddle.

At various places around in the square, young boys and slightly older girls were dipping their hands into white sacks that were slung across their chests, grabbing handfuls of white ash, which they sprinkled onto paving stones.

An old man pulled several thick pins from the sides

of his wagon—he stepped back, the sides crashed down to reveal plank shelves crammed with leather boots and sandals, and various-shaped bottles of colored water. Colored water?

Peter Musik cocked his head and kept walking. Kept looking.

There was a line of young men, girl-children, and very old women outside a bakery—at least Peter assumed that's what it was, from the smell of warm bread wafting through the open doorway. There were, however, no breads, or cakes, displayed in the window; instead, there were several small piles of brightly painted stones surrounding a large copper sphere that was mounted on a black base. A tetrahedron.

Eugene Boman also must have sniffed the bakeshop aromas, because he pivoted abruptly, and would've joined the end of the line if Peter hadn't snatched him by a sleeve, given him a sharp, two-fingered poke in the lower back, and set him walking—sleepwalking—again in a straight line.

Peter turned his attention back to the marketplace, and watched a pretty woman string pennants above her wagon. Thin blue fog circled her throat and her wrists. Not jewelry, fog. Pale-blue . . . fog.

This was better than Dubrovnik, boy. Way better.

Out of habit, Peter started wishing again that he had some paper, some paper and a pen, and—and a camera. A camera'd be so great. But you know something? He wasn't wishing *all that hard.* He was feeling, well, he wasn't quite sure what, exactly, but the sensation that was stealing over him, gradually, was reminiscent of the sensation that he'd had—and vividly could still recall having had—back in August of 1977 as he'd wandered the Stradnum, the main street of Dubrovnik, and the winding maze of old side streets, and the public gardens, and the sea fortifications on the Adriatic.

As he'd been then, he was again now: charmed, and glad to be so baffled.

Content to be startled by what he saw.

Content. And not particularly curious. Scarcely curious at all.

Content merely to see.

Questioning things, making sense of them, *reporting* them—all that stuff could wait, till later.

Later, Peter said to himself now, instead of asking the Walker, Why're they doing that, who's she, who's he, what're those things, what's going on over there? What's that foggy stuff?

Later. Later.

Peter stopped dead in the middle of the market square, startled. He put a hand to the top of his head and scratched mildly. Whoa. Jeez. He hoped he wasn't going screwy. As screwy, in his own way, as Gene Boman.

Later? Peter Musik, obnoxious and tenacious media pro, saying *later?*

Really weird.

Hey, it was probably just flat-out total exhaustion—some brain chemical or something kicking in after days and days without any good Zs. It was probably that, sure; some chemical making Peter feel this way, this strange and flaky way, making him feel like he was eighteen again, and in love with his own senses.

But so what if it was? So what?

It felt good. Yeah?

And *he* felt good.

He was on his way to see Money Campbell again, and when he saw her? First thing he'd do? Kiss her like in the movies—like he was Dennis Quaid and she was Ellen Barkin, like in *The Big Easy*, yeah, really do it, serious kissing, maybe he'd even stick his tongue into her mouth. Knock her off her feet.

He whirled on his heels and went jogging after his companions.

As he ran, he ran through a spume of fine white ash flung by a small boy whose right earlobe was tattooed with a tiny black ant.

The stuff had a familiar and kind of pleasing odor—Peter thinking, Quaker Oats before you add the hot water. He smiled, amused by his own schizzy flip-flopping

(I'm gonna be an observer/I'm just gonna *live),* and then he flinched, was jolted to a halt.

By an exclamation of surprise, followed by a high-pitched cry of alarm, from Gene Boman.

And by the sight of Jack, a Walker's head being surrounded by—now seemingly *hooded* by—a droning, clicking black swarm of yellow-faced bees.

CHAPTER 5

HER FATHER'S PULPS

AT THE SAME TIME THAT
Peter Musik found himself recollecting his salad days in
Dubrovnik, Jere Lee Vance—as she crumbled lumps of
black confectioner's sugar over a slice of buttered corn
bread in an apartment not far from the big market square
—was thinking about her dad's collection of science fiction pulp magazines.

God, whatever happened to them? Hundreds of big,
chunky, ragged-edged dime and quarter magazines filling
up, almost bursting through, a couple dozen soap and
soup cartons. When she was young, in the early 1950s,
Jere Lee had discovered those pulps down in the cellar,
stuck away where the coal bin used to be. Most of them
were cover-dated 1936, '37, '38, '39.

Girls, she'd known, weren't supposed to like science
fiction, but Jere Lee had. She was never a great *fan*, but
she liked the stories well enough. She could still remember the names of a few of her favorite writers. Raymond

Z. Gallun. Frank Belknap Long. Manly Wellman. L. Sprang? Stang? *Sprague* de Camp.

What she'd liked most, though, were the covers. The magazine covers.

Every one of them seemed to feature a pretty girl (wearing a two-piece bathing suit) squirming in the clutches of a tentacled alien with sea-creature eyes. As young as she'd been, she'd nevertheless realized that the illustrations had more to do with what grownups did together behind locked bedroom doors at night than with personal injury and violent death. Those aliens didn't mean to rip the arms off those pretty blondes and brunettes, they meant to, well, *marry* them. And to Jere Lee, at the ages of nine, ten, eleven, twelve, that had been a tantalizing notion, indeed.

Later, as an adult (working woman, newlywed, young mother, battered wife, negligent parent, sloppy drunk) she never read any science fiction magazines, though she occasionally would buy a supermarket tabloid if there happened to be a scream headline about an ordinary housewife from Arkansas or Oklahoma who'd been abducted by a visitor from outer space. It was always such a load of bull, but even so, somewhere, in some deep fissure in Jere Lee's brain, the story would give her a satisfying thrill. A cheap satisfying thrill. The same sort she'd known as a girl.

Jere Lee figured she was slightly perverse, a little bit kinky, but what the heck: her fantasies were harmless.

It wasn't like she'd been stuck on the notion of jumping into bed with somebody else's husband, or a motorcycle guy, or a delivery boy, or the census man. Her fantasies were utterly impossible. Sex with an alien from another planet? Yeah, right. Tomorrow.

Right, she thought, tomorrow, and smiled thinly as she chewed her sugar bread in a high-ceilinged apartment that belonged to an enormously tall, exceedingly thin . . . alien from another planet.

Two days ago, she'd been at the end of her rope—penniless, homeless, wandering the streets, buffeted by December winds, afraid of catching pnuemonia, of starving, of being arrested, mugged, murdered. Estranged from her grown children, disengaged from . . . practically everything. A forty-five-year-old woman who felt seventy in her bones, a bag lady with no inclination to fantasize about anything. A city ghost. A statistic.

And now look where she was.

Here. She was here, and feeling alert and energetic again—alive. Even better, totally *interested* in being alive. So interested that she was thinking about those old pulp magazines again, feeling that old warm tingle, smiling. Even blushing.

Jere Lee, wiping black sugar from her lips, taking a swallow of hot tea, and thinking, Here's what you get for holding on. The corniest of corny platitudes. And it happens to be true. Hold on. Your life can change.

My life has changed.

I've changed.

Because here I am, and there he is, and—

I'm happy.

Yeah? Jere Lee thinking, Yeah? And you also sound like Little Orphan Annie. Cinderella. You big banana. Banana brain.

And she said to herself (as Peter was saying to *him*self around the same time): So what?

Carrying her tea cup, and a second cup, and walking gingerly, careful not to spill any, she crossed the big white-walled room. Jere Lee guessed it was the living room, but how could she be certain? Maybe it was the dining room. The study? Whatever. There were several tall windows that let in sunlight, which lay in broad bands across an area rug patterned with red, orange, and gold ideographs and geometric shapes. The wooden—possibly mahogany—furniture was heavy, squarish, and undecorated. None of the chairs, set between the tall windows and arranged around a long refectory table, were upholstered. They looked, and Jere Lee could vouch that they were, brutally uncomfortable, as much fun to sit on as a church pew. No pictures on the plaster walls. A stone fireplace. And a granite plinth supporting a sphere of solid blue ice that was, apparently, exempt from natural law, as

Jere Lee understood natural law: though the temperature in the room must've been eighty degrees, the ice showed no sign of melting. There wasn't so much as a drop of water on the stone base.

Using an elbow, since both hands were occupied, she tapped on a door that stood eight feet high, was oak, and had a glass knob shaped and faceted like a cartoon diamond. She tapped again.

"No need for that. Enter, woman."

It was something of a shock, still, for Jere Lee to hear that high-pitched whistling language—Losplit—and an almost guilty pleasure to realize she could understand it perfectly; that, in fact, she could speak it herself, and speak it without the slightest forethought.

Thanks to the cloudy water she'd drunk so much of yesterday on the road to Beybix.

Master Squintik, the Cold Mage, was sitting up in his bed.

"I made some tea," she said. "At least I *think* it's tea. If I turn into a statue or something, be sure to turn me back, okay?"

He smiled, then moistened his lips before he spoke. "You're quite right, it's tea. Thank you," he said, as he reached for the cup and took it. His fingers were the longest and thinnest that she'd ever seen on anyone. Long and thin, but not brittle-looking. Quite the opposite.

Jere Lee sat beside the bed on a hard chair, the only kind there was.

"That's some stove you got in the kitchen."

Squintik opened his eyes a little wider.

"I say, that's some stove. Is it always hot?"

"Yes."

"But where's . . . what *burns?* There's no coal, there's no wood. And God knows there's no gas or electric." (She said "electric" in English.)

"No," said Squintik, smiling again, but offering her no explanation. Then he lifted the cup of scalding tea to his mouth and sipped, the steam drifting lazily up his long, pallid face, curling around his sharp beak of a nose, and in the hollows of his cheeks, and leaving tiny droplets of moisture in both places.

Jere Lee watched him for a minute, then emptied her cup, set it down on the bedside table, and stood up. Her buttocks could take just so much punishment. After the soldiers had brought them both here earlier this morning—here, being a stone building on Dwindling Street—she'd tried to fall asleep in one of the highbacked chairs in the other room. Forget it. Over the past half-year, she'd slept in tunnels and doorways, on benches and the hard cold ground. She was no finick, but jeez, this place was murder—there was simply no way she could get comfortable on anything in the apartment.

Of course, she hadn't yet tried the bed.

She said now, "How are you feeling?" And it was a funny thing: she badly wanted to address him by name, but wasn't sure how to. People like Jack, a Walker—and like the soldiers who'd come and fetched them from the pine forest—kept calling Squintik "master" or "good mage," sounding very formal. For a while, Jere Lee had done likewise, most of the time. And whenever she did call him just Squintik, she invariably got the feeling that he'd stiffened a little bit, that she'd been presumptuous and disrespectful, that she'd broken protocol.

Hell, though, she had feelings for this man, very strong feelings—and you didn't go around calling somebody you had those kind of feelings for master.

Unless you were kinky in a way that Jere Lee had no interest in being.

So she'd stopped calling him anything.

"How are you feeling?" she said. "Stronger?"

He looked up, slowly examined her face, then nodded several times, earnestly. "Much."

"You had me scared last night. I didn't think you were going to—I was afraid that you might . . . Well, anyway. I'm glad you're feeling better. And thanks again."

He craned an eyebrow. (Jere Lee thinking, Odd, how so many of their gestures mean the same things as ours. Then thinking, *Theirs.* Thinking, *Ours.* Then thinking, *Very* odd.)

"I mean . . . thanks for saving our skins." She moved her narrow shoulders. "Those bats. The way you . . . froze them."

His smile became rueful, and he nodded again, but just barely. Then he looked from Jere Lee's face to the bedroom door.

"I mean, we all could've ended up like . . . like poor Herb. Being carried away." She frowned, bit her bottom lip, felt awkward. Noticing that Squintik had finished his tea, she removed the cup from his hands (they were so cold to the touch) and set it down on the table.

(cold to the touch)

Jere Lee suddenly remembered this: When her ex-husband used to smoke marijuana? Right away, his body temperature would drop, and then he'd always want to make love (so to speak), but his hands would be like ice cubes, that's what she'd tell him, Your hands are like ice cubes, don't touch me. Don't touch me, your hands are like ice cubes, your hands are

(cold to the touch)

Squintik was staring at her with puzzled eyes.

"What's wrong?"

"Nothing."

"Tell me. Please."

She looked at Squintik, and her face flushed.

(cold to the touch)

"Nothing's the matter, really."

"If you're worried about your friends—the young woman and the young man—please don't be. They're quite well."

"How would *you* know? You've been out like a light for the last—"

The mage cocked his head sidewise, and if she weren't mistaken (if this gesture and expression held the same significance as it did at "home") he seemed a bit . . . smug. "Trust me, Jere Lee, they're quite well. You'll be seeing them again shortly. And then, with our undying gratitude, we'll send you all back to your own world, to your own lives, and— Jere Lee?"

Her face had suddenly turned a bright blotchy red.

And then (Jere Lee thinking, Thank God!) someone was knocking at the outer door.

"That," said Squintik, "will be the Walker."

And so it was.

The Walker: standing in the gloomy hallway with dozens of bees snarled in his dark bushy hair, crawling on his cheeks and his temples and the backs of his hands, clinging to folds in his raggedy white shirt.

With a weary nod at Jere Lee, he stepped across the threshold, dipped two fingers into a bowl of cloudy water, sketched a mark on a bronze sphere, then strode across the living room or dining room, or study, whatever room it was, and went directly into the bedchamber.

Jere Lee glanced at the wet mark that Jack had made. It was an isosceles triangle. She moved her head slowly from side to side, shrugged one shoulder, and closed the door.

CHAPTER 6

A MOMENT OF
FELICITY

WITH AS RESPECTFUL A VO-
cabulary as his tired brain could muster, Jack was saying
he'd appreciate it greatly if Master Squintik could just
. . . send the bees away? They'd discharged their duty,
delivered their message, conveyed the mage's summons,
but now they were starting to irritate Jack. A couple of the
miserable things had even stung him. He was sitting
slumped forward in a chair beside Squintik's bed, his
hands folded in his lap. His skin looked putty-colored, he
kept blinking, and now he pressed his lips together against
a yawn.

Squintik looked at the Walker, then made a bow
from his waist. The bees removed themselves from Jack's
hair and face and clothing, then moved in a swarm to the
window and collected on the bubbled glass. Jere Lee was
watching from across the room, staring so intently that
her eyes bulged.

"I'll get it," she said, and pushed open the window, and the bees flew off.

Jack dug his fingers into his scalp and scratched. Then: "Your friend Amabeel was at Manse Seloc," he said to the mage.

"Of course. Who else would Rampike send?"

"Who else. Do you want to know who else? I'll tell you—"

"Didge," said Squintik, "yes. I know about Didge."

Raising his head, Jack looked sullenly at the mage. "Why would the Prime Minister send such an incompetent?"

"Don't ask that kind of question, Jack. Be assured, though, it was according to the Order of Things."

The Walker made a low, miserable groan of disgust. Which annoyed the Cold Mage: his brows knit sharply, and his nostrils flared.

"You're tired," he said.

"Tired? I'm exhausted."

"My apologies. But there are things I need to know."

"What things? Already you seem to know—"

"*Some* things. I know only some things. Amabeel was in contact with me."

Jere Lee blurted, "Who's Amabeel? And when did he—?" She broke off when Squintik turned his head and shot her a reproachful look. "I'm sorry," she said. "Excuse me," she said. For *living*, she thought.

"Tell me about your reception at the castle."

"We nearly didn't make it inside," said Jack. "Sister Card was waiting at the garden. If it hadn't been for our two Witnesses, she would've killed Lita and me."

Jere Lee opened her mouth to speak again, thought better of it, and merely smiled. The Witnesses. Peter, of course. And Money Campbell. That's who he meant. Money Campbell and Peter Musik. Who else?

"And what happened to the pythoness?" said Squintik.

"She's in the Void."

"Continue."

"Agel received his Tramp most graciously."

"Jack, please. You're tired, I'm tired. Kindly dispense with the standard language. You told him of your Ramble . . ."

"And he immediately called for Rampike. There were no questions."

"None? At all?"

"No."

Squintik lay back against his pillow, studied the ceiling for a moment. "Good," he said. "Continue."

"His Majesty informed the Prime Minister that he was convinced that Perfect Order had been violated."

"Violated. Is the word he used?"

"Yes."

"Not disturbed."

"Violated. He said violated."

"Excellent. Continue."

Jack rubbed a hand over his face. "Then"—he squeezed his puffy eyes shut, opened them—"His Majesty said that the Epicene—"

Squintik sat up again, abruptly. "He called it by that name?"

"Yes. He said the Epicene was to be destroyed—"

"Burned?"

"Destroyed. It was to be destroyed, he said, and the Mage of Four, Mage of Luck, he said, should be seized and brought to Beybix. And then Rampike ordered out the Red Guards, and then Agel's light faded, and we were all dismissed from court."

"Jack, tell me. The gallery—"

"Was filled, good mage. Yours must've been the only empty seat."

That information brought a triumphant smile, and spots of color, to Squintik's chalk-white face. "Continue."

"Then one of the Witnesses and I accompanied the soldiers to Manse Seloc."

"Why?"

Jack blinked, looked down at his hands. Looked up. "Why?"

"Yes, why? Your service was done."

"Peter . . . the Witness called Peter wished to see it through to the end. I thought I owed him that much."

"But not you?"

"Good mage?"

"It couldn't be that you, also, wished to 'see it through to the end'?"

Jack sighed, and slumped; he moved his hands listlessly. "Perhaps."

"But you're a Walker, and not just any Walker, a King's Tramp. What you're suggesting to me is that—"

"Is that I wished to see the Dark Aristocrat punished. You're quite correct." He cleared his throat. "I did."

Squintik was grinning. "Unprofessional."

"Agreed."

"Continue. No. Wait." He turned his head to Jere Lee.

She'd been standing against the wall; now she lurched forward, eagerly. "Yes?"

"There's a cabinet in the other room. Inside, you'll find a tall green bottle. Would you mind getting it? And you'll find glasses in there, as well."

"How many should I bring?"

The mage smiled. "Three. Bring three."

"Right back," she said, and went out, wondering if Squintik really wanted the bottle, or whether he just wanted to be rid of her for a moment, to tell, or ask, Jack something in private.

She found the cabinet, a teak cellarette, and the glasses, little tulip glasses, and the bottle. The bottle resembled a champagne magnum and was stoppered with a black cork. It was surprisingly heavy.

When she returned, the Walker was standing at the open window, peering into the street. He glanced around at Jere Lee, then looked at Squintik. "It had already exploded by the time we arrived," he said. "Do you think he would've destroyed himself and . . . and the monster, rather than be taken?"

"No," said Squintik.

"Nor do I. It's possible they weren't even in that room."

"They were there," said Squintik.

"And?"

"We'll learn soon enough what happened to them." The mage beckoned Jere Lee to his bedside, took the bottle, twisted the cork free. A gray wisp escaped. He nodded for Jere Lee to set the glasses down on the table. She did, and he carefully filled them. The liquid was clear as gin, and odorless. He pushed one of the glasses toward her.

Jere Lee said, "Should I be drinking this on an empty stomach? Should I be drinking this, period?"

It was a joke, yet it wasn't.

She'd sworn to herself years ago that she'd never touch alcohol ever again. Not after all the damage it had caused in her life, all the grief.

But she didn't want to make a big thing of it now, a big production, and anyway, it probably wasn't even alcoholic, it was probably—

Probably what?

She picked up her glass, watched Squintik pass Jack his. Jack accepted it with a vague, distracted expression.

"A moment of felicity," said Squintik with a nod to each of them. "Which we all have earned." Then he sipped at the liquid. Jack did likewise, and with a shrug, so did Jere Lee.

A dizziness came over her, swept through her. Then —suddenly, vividly, definitely—she was twelve years old again, was strong and fresh and graceful, wearing a pale-pink t-shirt with a red heart appliqué, and blue shorts and clean white sneakers, was sitting on brown grass and crispy leaves in the county park near the house where she'd grown up, was staring at bunched-up fair-weather clouds that scudded across a bright autumn sky; was happy, was blissful.

She shuddered, turned deathly pale, and dropped the glass.

Which broke.

CHAPTER 7

SPLINTERS, GRANITE, MUD

BY THE TIME MASTER AMA-
beel arrived, some ten or fifteen minutes later, Jere Lee
had recovered her composure, though she continued to
feel like an absolute nincompoop. Dropping her glass like
that—come on! How corny.

Feeling like a real nit, she'd apologized to Squintik,
stooped and collected up all the chips and chunks of broken glass, then had withdrawn, hastily, to the outer room,
leaving the Walker and the Cold Mage to carry on their
discussion in private. She sat down on one of those horribly uncomfortable chairs, and tried to reconstruct in her
mind the so-called "moment of felicity."

Impossible.

Oh, she could remember it all right, remember it
happening, she just couldn't *feel* it any longer. And my
God, it had felt so *good,* to be twelve again. Christ, it was
the *realest* hallucination she'd ever had. And you could

ask anyone who'd known her back in the "old days"—
she'd had more than her fair share of *those*.

Moment of felicity? *Felicity?*

Jere Lee thinking, Felicity.

That's when Amabeel—though to Jere Lee, a white-
haired stranger in a shiny brown cassock—startled her,
violently, and she'd jumped to her feet. He'd entered the
apartment without knocking. His face looked drawn. His
eyes were tense and strained and pouched.

He stared at her staring at him, then shook his head
several times, and gravely lifted an index finger. "One?"
he said. His voice harsh, rumbling.

"Excuse me?"

"I say, one? Heart?"

She pointed to herself, smiled uncertainly. "Are you
asking if I only have one heart? That what you're saying?
Yes," she said. "I do. Have only one heart."

"Everywhere I go!" exclaimed Amabeel.

Again Jere Lee smiled, but this time as if humoring a
crackpot. Then (What am I, the butler?) she asked, "May
I tell Master Squintik that you're here?" Already, she was
inching back toward the bedroom, cautiously. "Your
name, please?"

She didn't get to announce him, though. Behind her,
the door opened, and Squintik, dressed now in a black
cassock, stepped out. He moved past Jere Lee and walked
directly to Amabeel. The two mages embraced, broke the
clinch, and then pressed the pads of their left thumbs
together.

Each thumb turned blue, each thumbnail frosted.

When Jere Lee's eyes widened, Jack leaned forward,
and whispered, "Don't worry, they'll melt."

The two mages were seating themselves at the refectory table.

"I'm not worried," she said. Then asked, "What *was*
that stuff we drank?"

"Jack," called Squintik, "come and sit."

And Jack did, with a long, uneasy sigh.

Leaning against the door jamb, Jere Lee folded her
arms. She kept peeking back into the bedroom, at that

green bottle on the table. An idea began to surface in her mind: What would happen if she had another drink? Just . . . one more. *Another* moment of felicity. Another drink, and maybe—maybe she'd see her mom and dad again, be *with* them again, wouldn't that be nice? Or see her daughters. *Be* with her daughters. There'd been lots of small moments she'd enjoy reliving with Karen and Anne Marie. Her tongue suddenly felt thick, and her mouth dry. Her throat tickled.

God, she hadn't felt this thirsty in a long time.

Years.

All at once, she straightened up, alarmed.

Years is right. Not since, since . . .

She pulled the bedroom door shut, walked over to the refectory table and, though uninvited, sat down.

Squintik, to Amabeel: "This is Jere Lee, a kindly woman from Kemolo. I am in her debt."

Jere Lee thinking, Kindly woman. Great. Me and Mother Teresa.

Amabeel nodded, perfunctorily, and returned his full attention to Squintik. "The dead man in the cellar at Manse Seloc," he said, "was also a Kemolon."

"Yes."

Amabeel snapped open the pouch attached to the front of his cassock. Dipping a hand, he took out five small gray . . . somethings. Jere Lee craned to see, but couldn't tell what they were. They resembled little bones, sort of. Or shark teeth, or—

"I removed these from the fingers of the dead Kemolon's left hand," said Amabeel, and Jere Lee felt nauseous, paled noticeably.

Fingernails.

When Amabeel tossed them all onto the table, they softly clicked.

Squintik studied them for several seconds, then raised his eyes.

"I cannot prove it, good mage," said Amabeel, "but I feel it likely that . . . these are how he stepped from his Moment to ours."

Squintik picked up one of the fingernails, examined

it. Holding it between thumb and first finger, he gestured with it, striking downward (Jere Lee thinking, Like somebody trying to scratch a window glass with a diamond ring).

A tiny, inch-long tear appeared in the air.

It quivered, almost obscenely, then vanished.

Squintik dropped the fingernail back onto the table. Turned and looked at the Walker. "Jack?"

"The Kemolon's name was Frank Luks."

"Continue."

Jack frowned, moistened his lips. "There is another too-human here named Eugene Boman who may be able to tell us how this Frank Luks came to have such claws." But then he added hastily, "Or he may not."

Amabeel opened his mouth to speak. Shrugged instead. Slumped back in his chair. Scratched at the tattoo —the salamander—on his jawline. "Shall we turn now to more pressing matters?" He looked at Squintik, at Jack, then back at Squintik. "The Epicene is not dead."

"No," said Squintik. "But where is it? I fear the Dark Mage has taken the monster and fled to Feerce, or even to Kemolo."

"He has not. I can tell you this much: They are still in Lostwithal." Once more Amabeel opened his pouch and dipped a hand, but this time he removed a few small chunks of granite, some splinters of charred wood, several friable clots of dry mud. "From the turret room at Manse Seloc," he explained.

Using only his index fingers, he arranged the objects in a circle directly in front of him on the table. Then, from the pouch again, he took out a small white tablet. He placed that in the middle of the circle. Finally, he glanced up at Squintik, who nodded.

"Proceed," said the Cold Mage.

Amabeel bore down upon the tablet with his index fingertip as if (thought Jere Lee) he were pressing an intercom button.

There was a faint click.

Followed by another click, slightly louder.

Granite, splinters, and mud seemed to twitch. *Did* twitch.

Jere Lee glanced from Jack's face to Squintik's to Amabeel's (their eyes were narrowed, their lips tight, their nostrils flared), and when she looked back to the miscellany of objects on the table, her jaw dropped and she prickled with gooseflesh.

CHAPTER 8

AT LITA'S

LITA THE WITCH (SEATED IN a fan-back chair, wearing a long, glossy blue robe of close weave and looking imperturbable) kept telling Peter Musik the same thing, over and over: that the girl was *gone.* Money Campbell was gone.

And Peter kept saying, But where? Where'd she *go?* Saying, Gone, gone *where?* What do you *mean,* gone? as he rubbed an open hand across his bristly face, or shook his fist, or squeezed and kneaded the back of his neck, absurdly prowled the little apartment, moving from one room to the next, idiotically opening cupboards, a wardrobe, getting down on his knees and peering under the cot, the bed, behind a chest of drawers. What do you mean she's gone? Gone? *Gone where?*

"Sit down," the witch finally said, to break the loop.

"How can I sit down? My friend's gone. She was supposed to be here, and she's gone."

Lita took a deep breath, held it, exhaled, and the exhalation was faintly colored pink.

Abruptly, Peter quit his roaming, winced with a sudden headache, pressed splayed fingers to his temples, looked around for somewhere to sit, spotted a small sofa, and sat.

"You just did something to me," he said. "What'd you do?" He slapped his thighs petulantly.

Lita smiled at this. But there wasn't much humor in her smile, and it lasted only a moment.

"I don't know where Monica is," said the witch. "She was here when I went to bed, she was gone when you woke me with your pounding at the door."

"But—"

"Where is the Walker?"

"How should I know? He just . . . left."

The witch leaned forward.

"We were coming across the big plaza—the market. And all of a sudden, these . . . bees started buzzing around his head."

"Bees?"

"Bees. Not wasps. Nothing like you, sweetheart, when you get fancy. Ordinary fat bees. Messengers, is what I figure."

When she craned an eyebrow, Peter shrugged. "I'm starting to get savvy to your funny ways." He quirked his mouth, shrugged again. "So anyhow, Jack says he has to go someplace, and he points me in this direction. Tells me yours is the white door. The white door, he says, and the last I see him he's headed off in the opposite direction. All these bees buzzing around his head. So I don't think we have to worry about Jack, do you? All we have to worry about is Money. *Where the hell is she?*"

And Gene Boman, who was standing with his face three inches from a blank wall, said, "Would you people mind keeping it down? I can't hear my program!"

CHAPTER 9

THE VICTIM

YOU ASSHOLE. YOU JERK.
Complete jerk stupid asshole jerk. Berating herself like
crazy, Money Campbell was able to keep her terror in
check.

Some of it.

You are the biggest, stupidest jerk that ever lived,
you stupid—jerk!

And know what else? You know what else? You're a
born victim. That's right, asshole. A victim. It's the only
job you've ever been any good at.

Money thinking back to when she was, like, fourteen,
fifteen? And already had the figure of a backup singer for
the Rolling Stones? She'd thought she was so cool, so
sophisticated. Why? Just 'cause I had big boobs, that's
how come. Yeah, and a great ass, and a pretty face. *So*
cool, scorning every boy-jerk in her high school, sneaking
out nights with college guys, grown men, married men
with Saabs and Triumphs. But what'd that get her?

Some nice clothes and two secret, all-expenses-paid trips to an abortion clinic in Cincinnati.

Jerk. Nitwit. Victim.

And later on? Still so full of herself, still convinced she was a real piece of work, a pistol, a smart cookie, totally in control of every situation, she'd listened one summer day to Eugene Boman stammer to her about his quote powerful attraction unquote, then she'd giggled inside—so amused, *so-o-o* scornful, and with a shrug agreed to become his girlfriend. Quote, unquote.

Big jerk idiot.

That had turned out just great, hadn't it? Oh yeah. Wonderful. She'd expected a lark, a hoot, and ended up in a nightmare. And when she'd tried to get out of it? When she'd tried to help Peter Musik after his brains had got scrambled? Some whacked-out bounty hunter from another universe mistook her for a witch and nearly killed her.

Money thinking, See? See what I'm saying?

No matter what I do, no matter whether I think about it or I don't, it always ends up the same damn way. Same stupid way.

'Cause I'm a jerk. An asshole. An idiot.

A victim.

She was sitting (cowering is more like it) in the dark hold of some kind of boat (hearing water slosh and burst into spray, hearing sails snap, breathing in mildew); her clothes were damp, she had a scratchy throat. And killer cramps.

But no recollection how she'd gotten here, or any idea how much time had passed since she'd seen that wall painting—

(that painting: a naked woman on a leash. A dog leash! And the woman was Money. At least, the face was hers, undeniably, and the body, but the details were . . . wrong: her nipples weren't dark tan, they were pale pink, and she had a wide, ragged scar just above her pelvic bone—from an old bicycle injury—*not* a tattoo of a goddamn *beetle*, for Christ's sake)

—had turned to run, but instead (damn damn *damn* —you girly idiot) fainted dead away.

All she could remember of the incident was that somebody had caught her by the arm, and around her waist.

Somebody who'd reeked of—

(like the art department, back at Old Tappan College, where right now, *right now,* she was supposed to be taking first-semester final exams)

—oil paint. Oil paints.

When she'd returned to consciousness (an hour ago? *half* an hour ago?) she was lying here, lying on her side, alone.

Across the hold (the wide floor planks were filthy black and gummous; the overhead timbers were green with mold) were four narrow steps leading to an open hatch through which Money could see a rectangular piece of sky and fast-moving white clouds and, occasionally, a white gull.

The floor pitched suddenly, sickeningly, and Money flung out a hand to brace herself.

Then the floor pitched in the opposite direction, and she struck her head, glancingly, against the wall.

And now she heard voices, above.

Then something (somebody) blocked the sky, and a shadow fell across the stairs, and the floor.

She drew herself back into the corner, arms locked around her legs.

The man who came down was no more than three feet tall, had dry, wizened, pebble-textured skin, and walked crookedly (she could see that one hip was wildly out of alignment). He was dressed in a gray blouse, a cape, and tight-fitting trousers that limned his immature genitals.

His thick hair, his fingernails, his toenails (he was barefoot), and his lips were an identical bright yellow.

Dye, nail polish, and lipstick, Money presumed, till he limped nearer and she saw that the "whites" of his eyes were the exact same yellow. (Education at work: From a studio art course she'd taken her freshman year at college, Money remembered, *cadmium* yellow.)

The whites of his goddamn eyes were cadmium yellow!

So was his tongue, when he opened his mouth to speak.

His teeth, however, were cobalt blue.

Don't be a jerk, she thought, don't scream.

And she didn't.

No, what she did, she put back her head and howled.

CHAPTER 10

WAVE FRONTS

ABOUT A YEAR AGO, WHEN she still had a job, and an apartment, when she was still . . . respectable, Jere Lee Vance went to the movies one Saturday with a woman her age named Helen Shepherd. Helen wasn't a good friend, not a friend at all, really—just an acquaintance; both she and Jere Lee worked in the same midtown office building, but for different companies. They used to eat lunch together.

That Saturday had been the first time they'd seen each other socially. Helen had selected the movie, an obscure and depressing thing from France about several poor families living in a slum; Jere Lee had expected nudity, but there was none. Just a lot of yelling and misery, with quivering subtitles.

Anyway. The movie theatre was a tiny "art house" way downtown, where Jere Lee rarely ventured. When the picture let out, it was only four in the afternoon, so Helen suggested they go to a few nearby art galleries be-

fore having a bite to eat. Jere Lee had never been much
interested in art, but what the hell, let's go.

It was a disaster.

Helen, who'd been to college (but never graduated)
and was once married to an accountant who prepared
income taxes for several "prominent" artists, was very en-
thusiastic about nearly every picture she came upon. Jere
Lee, on the other hand, was flabbergasted by how ugly,
how willfully ugly, everything was. Why was there so
much violence in the paintings, such pain? No matter
what gallery they walked into, it was always the same
damn thing: screaming men, burning women, numb
faces, headless torsos. She may not've been well-edu-
cated, but she was no philistine, and whenever she'd
heard about censorship, she'd always bristled, but why—
why was contemporary art so ugly?

It was disgusting, she felt, and said as much to
Helen.

Who recoiled as though slapped in the face by a lunatic.

Embarrassed, Jere Lee didn't say another word.

Till quite a bit later, when they were back on the
street again and strolling past yet another gallery, which
Helen seemed pointedly disinterested in. The gallery was
called The Wave Front, and what caught Jere Lee's attention was a tiny cat—not a kitten, an adult cat that just
happened to be very tiny, almost miniscule—seated on a
white pedestal. Its head moved as Jere Lee went past. A
cat in an art gallery? In a grocery store, maybe, but an art
gallery? And it was such a tiny thing, it was—

Lord, it wasn't real, it was—

She laughed, tugged at Helen's arm, said, "Look! It's
one of those things, what do you call those things, like in
science fiction?"

Helen pressed her lips together in utter disdain. "Lasers."

"Yes, but that's not—"

"Holograms," said Helen.

"Right!" Jere Lee had turned back and was studying

the cat in the window. Thinking, Look at that! It's, like, three-dimensional!

She was charmed.

Helen was not. "I don't consider that stuff art," she said.

"Why not?"

"It's a silly little cat. Where's the art there? It's just technology, that's all it is."

Jere Lee blushed (again), then (to her great surprise) felt herself grow warm with anger. God, she was so sick and tired of people who thought they knew everything — all her life she'd been browbeaten by "experts." Her parents, her relatives, her husband, her bosses. Why would you want to be friendly with *those* people, Jere Lee? It's October, Jere Lee, you can't wear white pants in October! Nobody paints their kitchen lilac, Jere Lee, nobody! I'm paying you to *type* my letters, Mrs. Vance, not rewrite them. Blah blah blah. Everybody was an expert. Except her. Well, dammit, she was tired of experts.

Jere Lee Vance said to Helen Shepherd, "I think it's good, I like it."

"Well, of course, you're entitled to your own opinion."

"I guess I am."

"You want to go in?"

"I might, yes."

"Well," said Helen, "then go ahead."

"You're not coming?"

"I don't want to waste my time."

Jere Lee smiled slowly, looked from Helen's face to the small light-cat in the gallery window, and said, "No, of course not. But don't worry. I'm sure that someday, somewhere, somebody'll make a scary ugly hologram."

The reason she was reminded of that misbegotten Saturday outing and of that silly, silly quarrel was because—

Someday (now), somewhere (in Master Squintik's apartment), somebody (the mage Amabeel) was making a truly scary and *very* ugly hologram.

Well, not a hologram, exactly.

But a reasonable facsimile thereof.

Using magic, instead of lasers.

Within the circle of mud and splinters and stone: a round 3-D room. Dollhouse scale. Curving stone walls, and several slit windows. A table, some chairs, a glass-fronted chest. A wooden baby cradle, and a cot.

And two men, both looking anxiously at a door, that shook.

One of the men was dressed similarly to Squintik and Amabeel, but his face (Jere Lee recoiled: she'd never, *ever* liked horror movies) was covered with tiny white wriggling . . . things. Slugs.

The other man (Jere Lee remembering Sunday mornings, nine o'clock mass, Drake's brown-crumb coffee cakes, the color comics) was dressed like Jungle Jim. Like Jungle Jim, in the old funny papers.

Black gunbelt, big holster, trousers jammed into high shiny boots.

And his face was familiar. Somehow.

From . . . television?

Jere Lee thinking, Television. I saw that guy on television.

He's—

But she couldn't remember, couldn't . . . place him.

It would come to her, though, later; she was sure of it.

Don't wrack your brains now, just . . . watch.

Watch Jungle Jim draw his sidearm, point it at the door.

And: the Monster Movie Man hasten to the glass cabinet, pull open the doors, reach in and take down a paper cone.

Hear Amabeel say, "You see? His dust. Not the rings."

And hear Squintik grunt.

Now: Watch the Movie Monster Man shake black dust from the cone, and watch the dust, suspended in air, begin to swirl.

Jere Lee thought it looked like one of those satellite weather pictures: a tropical storm.

Now upgraded to a hurricane.

She glanced away from the . . . hologram, to Jack, whose lips were drawn back from his teeth, whose teeth were clenched.

And then:

The Movie Monster Man bent over the cot and lifted into his arms—

Jere Lee, under her breath: "Oh my God . . ."

—a long-limbed wriggling child of mud.

Then: Blue light sizzled, and when Jere Lee could see again, she saw only those chips of scorched wood, those few snicks of granite, those several tiny crumbs of . . .

Mud.

Amabeel glanced from Squintik to Jack, then reached out with both arms and gathered back his miscellany, put everything away in his cassock pouch.

"You see why I tell you they've not gone far," said Amabeel. "He has rings to all the Moments, yet chose to escape through a tunnel of dust."

"Why?" It was Jack.

"I merely reconstruct the actual," Amabeel replied. "I am not versed in motives."

"Perhaps," said Jack, "the Epicene must reach maturity *here*. In Lostwithal. Does that—?"

"No. It is not necessary," Squintik said, and (if Jere Lee wasn't mistaken) his remark seemed to puzzle the Walker and amuse Master Amabeel. Wait a second, maybe not amuse: What it *really* looked like (the narrowing of his eyes, the tightening of his thin lips, the slight tilt of his head) was that Amabeel had had something confirmed which previously he'd just suspected.

He said, "According to the Order of Things, I should now petition for an audience with His Majesty, but I wonder . . ."

Squintik, crisply: "What?"

"Agel will listen to me, will believe me, of course. Will thank me. Then seek counsel from Rampike, and

Rampike will consult with his ministers, and his ministers
will duly summon the mages of court, and then we mages
will argue precedent. We always do."

Squintik leaned back in his chair, made a brief, circling, impatient motion with his left hand.

"And finally," said Amabeel, "it will all return to
Agel's full attention. *Then* what will occur? Finders will be
engaged. Yes? Finders." He lowered his voice, and
colored it with contempt. "According to the Order of
Things."

"I mark your tone. What are you saying?"

Amabeel hesitated, picking at the snap on his pouch.
He lifted his chin, thrust it out. With a tentative smile
(Jere Lee thinking, He's nervous), he said to the Cold
Mage, "Perhaps we might speak . . . alone?"

"I don't—"

"It would be best."

Squintik considered. "As you wish." He turned to the
Walker and Jere Lee. "I apologize," he said, "but my col-
league . . ."

Jere Lee followed Jack into the bedchamber.

As she was pulling the door shut behind her, she saw:
Amabeel pointing a finger stiffly, almost accusingly, at
Squintik, Squintik pressing, and turning, a fist against his
forehead.

(Now *there* was a gesture she was unfamiliar with.
Unfortunately.)

Jack had crossed the bedroom to the window; he sat
down on the deep sill, rubbing his eyes.

"What's going on?" she asked (talking to the Walker,
but staring again at the green bottle on the round-topped
table).

"I'm not sure."

She didn't know whether or not to believe him. Decided she would, merely because . . . she wished to.

"That little scene we just saw, on the table. Was that
—that was the Mage of Four, wasn't it? The Mage of
Luck?"

Jack nodded. "Last night."

"And the other man?"

"I'm not sure."

Jere Lee grinned: Well, if he wasn't, she was. She'd remembered. She'd known that she would, and she had, and now said, "His name is Forell. He's from . . . where *we're* from. Peter and Monica and me."

Jack raised his head. "Yes. It's what I thought."

"I used to see him almost every day, on television. Years ago."

She'd said "television" in English, which meant there was no such word in Losplit, so she figured she ought to ask Jack if he knew what television was.

He made a face.

She said, "Well, I wasn't sure . . ."

"What was he doing on television?"

"Testifying. What he was really doing, I guess, was trying to get himself out of trouble. He was somebody in the Army . . . or the Marines, something like that. A lieutenant, or a colonel. A *major!* Major Forell. I forget the details, but I think—I think he may've tried to start a little war—at least that's what most of the senators were saying. He'd tried to start a little war in Central America, all on his own. He always struck me as . . . there was something about his eyes. And the way that he smiled. He scared me, but a lot of people liked him. I even saw his picture on a t-shirt once." She was running on, she realized, blabbing. So she pressed her lips together and moved one shoulder in a half-shrug. "I can't imagine how he got *here*, or why . . ."

Jack got up from the window sill. "Your friend Peter knew him."

"*Peter* did?" It was still difficult for Jere Lee to call him Peter; when she'd known him, as a bum on the street, he was Geebo. Called Geebo. That was his name. Geebo. "How did . . . Peter know a guy like that?"

Jack wasn't willing to answer that one. He stood still for a minute, a faraway look in his eyes. Then he walked to the table, picked up the green bottle, pulled the cork.

"Need a little more felicity, do you?" she asked.

He smiled without warmth and poured some liquid into one of the glasses. (And didn't ask if she'd care to join him.) He held up the glass to the sunlight. (And *still* didn't ask if she cared to join him.)

She realized that she wanted to be asked. Badly wanted to be asked.

So she might have the satisfaction—the pleasure—of hearing herself say, "No. No, thank you."

"Felicity," said Jack, as if to himself. But then he frowned, and sighed, and put the glass back down on the table without drinking.

There was something deeply sad, and touching, and mysterious about that little act of self-denial, and she felt sorry for him all of a sudden, and liked him, very much. And was unaccountably afraid.

(He *deliberately* didn't invite me to join him in a drink. He *knows*. Somehow, he knows.)

They exchanged smiles across the room.

Which disappeared from their faces almost immediately, when Master Squintik flung open the bedroom door, and angrily ordered them both to leave his apartment, at once. At once! *At once!*

CHAPTER 11

PEASANTS

SHE WAS SHORT, WITH A squat, almost heavy build. She looked—at least Herb Dierickx thought she looked—like a forest woman in a Grimm's fairy tale; a peasant wife, the mother of doomed children, certainly not . . . certainly not a wicked witch. She was dressed in a plain skirt, blouse, and apron. Her black hair, shot with iron gray, was braided. There were sandals on her feet, red insect bites on her calves, shins, and ankles—and now she crisscrossed both hands through a cloud of steam rising from a black cauldron over the fireplace. Herb could smell meat rendering, and it turned his stomach.

Gradually, the steam cloud took on a soft pink coloring, then roiled, and became red droplets that rained back into the pot.

A peasant wife, the mother of doomed children—a witch, perhaps, but not a *wicked* witch. Herb felt sure of that, though he couldn't have said why.

He was lying on a bed of straw and hay, covered by

only a coarse linen sheet. For some time he'd been secretly watching the woman (who had large but well-mod-
eled features, a full bosom, a slight limp), shutting his
eyes whenever she'd turn her face toward him, and keeping them shut whenever she'd come over and check on
him. She gave off a brisk, clean odor, vaguely spearmint.
Once, she'd moistened his lips with a grass swab, then
daubed it gently to one of the many infected cuts on his
cheeks. Cuts and punctures and bites. She'd applied lo-
tions.

Good Christ, Herb felt sick! And sore, miserably sore
all over, but there were a couple of places—in his lower
right shin, and deep in his groin—where the pain was so
constant, and so wretched, that it scared him almost to
death. Was he mutilated? Going to be crippled? Were
bones broken? Shattered? Oh God, sweet Jesus, what if
I'm crippled? What am I gonna *do* if I'm crippled and not
dreaming?

He moved his mouth and said, "Margie . . . ?" His
wife's name.

The woman turned, too suddenly for Herb to shut
his eyes and pretend he was still unconscious. She wiped
her hands on her apron and hurried across the floor.
She'd been blocking the little hut's only window, and now,
as she moved away from it, Herb glimpsed milky blue sky.
And saw, too, a mound of smoldering cordwood outside,
the smoke pale and diffused. Then he saw the woman's
sunburned face close to his, and her eyes were green.

At one corner of her mouth, what he'd taken for a
tiny mole turned out, upon closer inspection, to be a black
tattoo.

Of a spider.

She leaned nearer, her red round face looming, and
smiled. Carefully, she reached up and felt his burning
forehead with the fingers of her left hand. They felt cool
and dry, but rough, and good. Then she said something,
and her voice was high, weirdly high, a whistling sound,
though punctuated often with gutteral clicks and with an
occasional almost telegraphic ticking of her teeth.

Losplit.

Which Herb understood, perfectly. Him, a 56-year-old guy with a tenth-grade education who'd never spoken anything besides Eastern-Seaboard city English in all his life.

She was asking him if he felt better, was there something she could get him? Bring him? Then asking how he'd ended up all broken and bleeding and floating in Black Lake. Asking, Were those bite marks, *teeth* marks?

Asking, "Who *are* you?"

Herb played dumb. When in doubt, gape. He shook his head slightly, and gave a small shrug.

And the woman, who was squatting beside him, rocked back on her dirty heels and narrowed her eyes.

She stood up, still looking at him—shrewdly now, doubtfully—and took a step backwards.

He wanted to say don't go, but decided to think things out some more before tipping his hand, so he said nothing, and she went, slipping sidewise through the doorway, and stealing away without closing the door behind her. A moment later Herb saw her flash by the window, then she was gone, and he was by himself, and terrified.

What if she brought somebody back, an *unfriendly* somebody? Oh God. How'd I get into this? I'm just a guy who drives a rich man's car. And here I am where there *are* no cars—no stoves, no toasters, and where peasants do magic.

He forced himself to sit up, moving slowly, and bracing an arm against the hut's cool stone wall.

I'm just a guy drives a rich man's car. Did. Used to. Before I came here.

And last night—or the night before, or last week—a bunch of bats the size of bald eagles plucked me into the sky, carried me off, then dropped me.

Oh, Margie, Margie . . .

Slowly, he turned back the sheet and looked down at himself. There were clots and lines of dried yellow mud applied to a dozen cuts, the skin on his legs was purple where it wasn't the color of oatmeal, and there was a linen bandage on his left shin. His penis and testicles seemed all right, though. (Thank God!)

He moved to stand up, felt dizzy—but followed through. In a minute, he was on his feet, his knees quivering. He looked around for his clothes, and spotted them, bloodstained and torn badly and hanging on a wall peg: a pair of coarse trousers and a loose, tent-sleeved blouse.

He didn't know if he could make it across the floor unassisted, but he gave it his best shot. . . .

ACCOMPANIED BY A LEAN AND gangly young man whose head was shaved and polished to a high Yul Brynner gleam, the woman returned half an hour (or so) later.

Herb had seated himself at the only table, and there he'd stayed, thinking, fretting, awaiting his doom. There'd been no point in trying to wander away; it was a cinch he couldn't make it far in his condition, and besides, where the hell would he go? He couldn't imagine how anybody could be a greater stranger. He was on another planet. In another dimension. Reality. Universe. Name your poison. He wasn't on earth.

The young man was wearing a cassock. The magician Squintik, who was partly responsible for Herb's being there in the first place, had dressed similarly—only Squintik's cassock was black and the young man's was green, forest green (and overlarge, too long). So was this guy also a magician? (A postman? An executioner?)

He let them stare at him, the bald young guy and the stocky woman straight out of the Brothers Grimm.

Their move.

At last, the woman said something in a low whistle (". . . go on, go *on!*") to her companion. He grudgingly nodded, and stepped forward, tripping on the hem of his cassock, stumbling, blushing brightly. (Jesus. Herb thinking, Jesus Christ, who *is* this guy? A comic-strip character?)

As he sat on a chair across the table from Herb, he slid his hand down the neck of his cassock, and squeezed his right breast. When he withdrew the hand, the flat tips of his long fingers were tacky with a kind of white paste. Like Elmer's.

Tentatively, he extended the hand, then gestured with it, as if coaxing Herb to do something, or at least display some recognition.

Herb shook his head. Sorry. No comprenday.

The young man glanced back around at the woman, then shot to his feet, and stood very stiffly, as though annoyed. (Herb was loath to read these people's body language the same way he'd read people's back home.) Stepping around the table, he roughly grabbed Herb by the shoulder, leaned forward and rubbed the paste across Herb's lips.

Herb resisted simultaneous impulses to spit in disgust and shove the bastard's hand away. The paste tasted almost—mentholated.

His lips went numb, and he felt abruptly dizzy.

Things turned purple.

WHEN HE CAME TO AGAIN, HE was back on the straw bed, and the young man was pressing his ear to Herb's chest, on the right side.

Their eyes met.

The young man's narrowed—in delight, it seemed to Herb, but again, he didn't want to go jumping to any conclusions.

Then Herb was aware of several other people standing around the room, but keeping a safe distance from the bed; they all looked elderly, except for a blonde-haired man whose features struck Herb as Nordic. Craggy. He looked, Herb thought, almost like Rutger Hauer. That actor who was in *Blade Runner,* and that crummy remake of *Wanted: Dead or Alive.*

(Hey, Marge, that scary android in *Blade Runner,* the one with the white hair, the ringleader—that's Rutger Hauer.)

It was this man, this Rutger Hauer look-alike, who produced a small flagon from a pocket sewn into his cloak.

The guy dressed like a magician (only in green), took the flagon, carefully removed the stopper, and pressed the bottle to Herb's mouth.

It could be anything, Herb thought.

They could be killing me.

For some reason, though, he wasn't upset. He felt . . . calm. What happens, happens, he thought. And drank.

It was water. Not particularly cool, but sweet.

They were giving him more of that funny water he'd had yesterday, the stuff that he and Jere Lee Vance called Berlitz Water, as a joke.

Hey: One sip and you speak Losplit.

Herb thinking, Now what? *Now* what do I do?

The young magician pulled away the flagon, said, "You have only one heart."

Herb pretended to not understand.

The old people in the hut turned each to the other, with looks of surprise.

Yes, of surprise. Herb would've bet money on that interpretation.

"He understands us!" said the Rutger Hauer guy. "He's faking, don't trust him." Then he took back his flagon and said, "He's a Kemolon. You've all heard the parables. Watch he doesn't steal from you!" And with that, he turned and left the hut.

Herb thought, What a jerk!

Then he sat up, indignant, and said, "Don't listen to him. The man's a bigot."

CHAPTER 12

MORNING AIR

"**A**NOTHER?"

"No, thank you, Captain. I think—with your permission, of course—I should return to barracks now."

"Another," insisted Ukrops. "Just one more," and Sollox, who was seated across the small table, smiled weakly.

"Thank you, Captain, you're very generous."

Exceedingly generous. For the better part of an hour, Ukrops had been buying vapors for the pair of them. The first several bowls had been mild, the mildest of morning stimulants, but then, quite abruptly, he'd summoned the waiter and called for quickeners—first salts, then sugars, then flakes. For the last twenty minutes now, they'd been inhaling the sorts of warmed air you bought and breathed at the end of a long night, in a dark, noisy tavern. Intoxicants. Sollox had been letting most of these vapors escape, averting his face whenever he sprang his bowl's lid, and keeping his mouth tightly shut; he was hoping that Ukrops hadn't noticed. Normally, he had no aversion to inhaling vapors so early in the day; he just didn't want to get silly or stupid or, worse, confidential with an officer. No, indeed.

Nonetheless, he'd still inhaled enough that his head was spinning, and his pupils were dilated. And his lungs felt on fire.

At a gesture from Ukrops, the old waiter came trotting over with two more white ceramic bowls, set them down, and made another helical mark with his gold crayon on the tablecloth. He hesitated a moment, then bit his lip, and glanced around to see if anyone else was in need of service.

There were twelve tables set outside the tavern in brilliant morning sunshine; of those, only a few were occupied, and those by farmers who'd slipped away from their nearby market stalls for a benign jolt or two. Even at this time of day, and in good weather, most patrons preferred to inhale their stimulants indoors, where the air was thicker and food was served. You couldn't get so much as a sausage outside. Public Ordinance. The Order of Things.

"I used to be a Walker, you know," Ukrops was saying now as he lifted his face from his bowl.

"Yes, sir, you've told me."

Only about fifty times, thought Sollox.

"Fourth-degree. Everyone expected me to stay on, make it my thirdwork. Become fifth-degree, a King's Tramp. I expected it myself."

"What changed your mind?" said Sollox. "If you don't mind my asking." (It was the vapors talking: With a clear mind, Sollox *never* asked questions. Another part of his strategy for survival.)

"What changed my mind? Baron Dag. Of course."

Sollox said, "Oh?"

"You recall Mad Dag?"

"Of course. Well . . . I've heard his name."

"I pursued that Whisper myself, you know."

"Whisper, sir? I'm afraid that I don't—"

"As a Walker. As the *Prime Minister's* Walker, I pursued that Whisper. 'Ukrops,' says the PM, 'hear this Whisper and Ramble.' The Whisper, of course, was that old Dag meant to raise an army of grayskins against King Agel."

"An *army?*" said Sollox. Stunned.

"A Doveflesh army. And it was true, he did. Though I wore out much shoe leather before I was able to confirm it. When I returned to Beybix, I was convinced there'd be civil war within a season. Well!"

Sollox looked perplexed, cocked his head. "Sir?"

"I simply mean—if that was to be, I certainly had no wish to stay a Walker. If war came—the first war in fifty thousand seasons, or a hundred thousand, who even *remembers* how many?—I wanted to be *in* it. Part *of* it. A Walker, it's true, is freer than all other men, but, still, a Walker is . . . passive."

Slowly, Sollox moved his head up and down.

Thinking, Passive and *poor*. Free and *penniless*.

Which is why *he'd* never considered the occupation.

Ukrops hunched over his bowl and breathed up the last few curling vapors. Then he slumped and smiled sadly.

Being politic, Sollox tried matching the smile.

"Of course, after I'd gone to my Craft and resigned, then came back here and joined the Red Guards . . ."

"Yes?"

"Mad Dag's own mother—his own mother!—poisoned him. Which meant no grayskin army! No civil war! And no . . . King's Tramp named Ukrops."

Ukrops looked wistful.

So did Sollox. He hoped.

"I miss the life," said Ukrops.

Sollox knew what was coming. Though he'd been Ukrops's aide for barely a month, he knew *exactly* what was coming now.

London of England Great Britain. Again.

Ukrops reached inside his doublet and pulled out a small book with a shiny soft cover. He opened the book, unfolded a map, then leaned across toward Sollox and peered solemnly into his face.

Sollox, to himself: Of all the places that I rambled as a Walker . . .

"Of all the places," said Ukrops, "that I rambled as a Walker—"

Then he stopped.

Stopped so abruptly that Sollox flinched, and paled, terrified that he'd let some of his boredom register on his face.

But Ukrops wasn't even looking at him now; eyes suddenly wide and merry, he was gazing into the market square, then grinning as he rose to his feet, bellowing, "Peter Musik! Peter Musik! Peter Musik of Fort Lauderdale United States of America—hello! Come join us!"

Sollox didn't bother turning around to look. No, he just gave a long, quavering sigh, then leaned forward, and stuck his face into his ceramic bowl.

CHAPTER 13

WOMAN WALKING ON A HILL

JERE LEE VANCE COMING
slowly down the high granite stoop, pausing, frowning,
half-turning, looking back up at the front door, then flinging off the Walker's hand: Don't rush me!

And saying, "What'd *we* do?"

"I doubt that we did anything. If you mean something *wrong*."

"But so why'd he throw us out? I don't get it. He just
—what's the matter?"

"Come, I'll take you to Monica now. And Peter."

"I'm not leaving."

"What?"

"You heard me. I'm not going. Not yet I'm not."
Reaching the narrow pavement. Shaking her head. Hands
on her hips. "I thought we were . . . friends."

Jack saying, "We are."

"Not you! Not *you* and me. Me and . . . him." Gesturing back at the graystone building, raising her eyes to the window (shut now) on the third floor. Then looking to Jack. "You understand?"

He started to shake his head no, then stopped. His eyes widened, slightly.

"So you go ahead," she said. "I'll stay here."

"For what purpose?"

She didn't reply, just sat down on the stoop, folded her arms across her knees, rested her cheek upon a wrist.

Jack asking again, "For what purpose?"

"You're supposed to be human—*you* figure it out."

"Don't be foolish."

"Sorry. I can't help it. That's just the way I am." She removed a hand from her leg, and with her fingers made a brisk sweeping gesture. "Run along. But I'm staying here. Come back for me later, if you like."

"I don't think you know what you're doing."

"Oh, I'm sure I don't. Go on. Go *on.*"

"You are telling me that you have . . . affection for Master Squintik?"

Mutely, she stared out toward the cobblestone street; color was rising in her face.

"Jere Lee Vance, I'm telling you now. Come with me. We are in Lostwithal, you don't understand—"

"No."

"—anything. You came here as a Witness, you performed your service."

"Oh God, you people. Don't you ever relax? Don't you ever talk normal? Don't you ever feel—anything? 'Witness.' 'Purpose.' 'Perfect Order.' You know what you all sound like? Bunch of nuns teaching catechism. Listen." She got up from the steps, put her face close to Jack's, her eyes big, her forehead stretched tight. "Just listen, okay? I know about your monster, and all that stuff. I do. I *understand.* It's a big deal." She smiled. "But forget about that for just one second. Can you? And look at me. Will you? Just look at me?"

Jack crooked an eyebrow. "I can't help but look."

"So look, then. What do you see?" She touched her yellow hair. "Straw, right?" And touched a cheek. "Lines, yeah?" Then touched her forehead. "*Lots* of lines. Pretty drab lady, aren't I? All in all?"

Jack didn't speak. Didn't blink. Just stared.

"But let me tell you something. Underneath all this . . . drab? Guess what? I'm alive. I heard all about your monster, and how maybe it's the end of the world, the end of everything, but . . . I'm alive."

She smiled radiantly, and the lines on her face vanished for a moment, and her blue eyes glistened.

"Two days ago I was dead. Good as. End of the line. Nowhere to go. No friends. Nothing. Nothing and nobody. And for some . . . reason, I walked into a bus station and there was this funny-looking bald guy bleeding on the floor. And I helped him, and now . . . I'm alive again. I still look the same, but I'm not the same. You understand? *Do* you? *Can* you? Maybe it's wrong and maybe I'm an idiot for being happy when everybody else is so worried about . . . Epicenes and blah-blah-blah, but I *am* happy. And *he's* the reason."

Again, she looked up at the closed window.

"So make fun of me, Jack, and hate me if you like, but just . . . go. Leave."

Still, Jack's eyes didn't blink. His face was immobile.

"I took care of your Master Squintik when he was bleeding in that stupid bus terminal, and I went to him at the hospital when he needed me, and I stayed with him in the forest last night after he destroyed those bats and nearly killed himself doing it. I stayed with him in the pouring rain. And I put him to bed when the soldiers brought us here. And this morning? I made him tea."

She turned away, blinked, sleeved her eyes, looked back at the Walker.

"And now I'm supposed to just go away? No. I won't. I'll wait here, if you don't mind, and then—then I'll go back up and . . . I'll talk to him. See what's the matter. See if I can *help*. All right? Okay?"

Jack, a Walker took a step backwards. Then, with quiet intensity, he said, "There's a Schoolteacher's parable about Kemolons. Very well-known. A young Kemolon woman is walking on a hill, she is walking to her lover's house. She looks to the west and sees a bolt of lightning set fire to a field of wheat. It's her mother's field. The woman stares at the flames for a moment, then continues on her way. She comes to her lover's house, but says nothing of the burning field, and they fall into each other's arms. The wind shifts, and the house catches fire"—he paused, and glared—"and the two lovers burn to death."

With that, he abruptly turned and crossed the street. "Oh brother," said Jere Lee, "they *are* nuns!"

ZICKAFOOZ

FROM THE VAPOR TAVERN, IT was a twenty-minute walk—down winding secondary streets lined with tawny brick tenements, through a series of thronged market squares (the booths in this one displaying sides of red meat hung from great hooks, in this one lumber and charcoal and wool, in this one barrels of spice), then around an open stockyard, and into a broad cobbled avenue fronting the great black lake and its seething, hectic quayside (a multiplicity of clipper masts and tangled rigging, lofts and warehouses, carts laden with baled freight, mobs of jostling and bellowing mariners, most of them grayskinned), then under a viaduct, past an archaic-looking gristmill—to the small weather-beaten house where Ukrops said they would find his older brother, Zickafooz.

But, as the Red Guardsman headed for a gate in the low crumbling wall that surrounded the house, Peter Musik (who'd had to prod Gene Boman the entire trek,

Boman's endless inclination being simply to plop down for a fixed stare into space) called suddenly, "Wait a second, wait a second. Would you just . . . wait? I don't know if this is really necessary. I appreciate your offer, but—"

"You want to find the female, don't you? You *told* me you need to find this female."

"I do," said Peter, "but . . . well, maybe she's not lost. Maybe it's no big deal. I'm just overreacting. Maybe."

Ukrops was staring at him, puzzled. "It is nothing extraordinary to engage a Finder. Citizens do it every day. For big losses *and* little." He smiled. "Come." He continued briskly on.

Peter caught him by a sleeve. "I've had some run-ins with a Finder," he said. "He had these little monsters that followed him around. Things that looked like—weasels?"

Soldier Sollox flinched, and paled.

"Where was this?" Ukrops asked.

"Back ho—in Kemolo," said Peter. "The Finder was called Eudrax, and the guy he was supposed to find was Jack, a Walker. He killed a lot of people before he did."

"Ninth-degree," said Ukrops blandly.

"What?"

"This Eudrax was surely ninth-degree—an assassin. My brother Zickafooz? Is hardly the same . . . kettle of fish."

He said "kettle of fish" in English, pronouncing everything perfectly, and with a genial smile.

"No?"

"No."

"Not ninth-degree?"

The corners of Ukrops's mouth turned up in a thin-lipped, smile. "Second."

"And no little furry monsters? You promise?"

"Just a small dog, Peter. Come along." He turned and strode ahead.

*   *   *

A SQUARE ROOM, SHUTTERED windows. Low rafters dotted with living flies and the smeared remains of dead ones. The walls sticky with beeswax, dark with smoke. Several flickering lamps that yielded hazy light, plenty of gruesome shadows. A pallet and soiled bedclothes. Earthenware bowls, plates, and cups soaking in a tub of scummy water. And a big storage trunk with its lid standing open—a jumble of . . . *stuff* inside: sheets of fine marbled paper, a coil of rope, a surcoat of purple velvet, several pornographic candles, an ivory bust of Sad King Agel, a jeweled dagger, a cannister of hard candies, a leather apron, a gold clasp, a demijohn of cheap ruby-red liquor, an embroidered belt decorated with thick, milled-edged silver coins.

In the center of the room, a rickety table. Where Theek, a Tattooist (without tattoos; a slight, almost-old woman in a blue homespun gown; her gray hair, below a small white cap, was coarse and cropped short) sat hunched, staring with a crabbed, verging-on-venomous expression at a little man with a short pointed beard who sluggishly paced the floor. She wanted to jump up and grab him by his shirtfront, shake him. Tell him, Make up your mind! What little mind you have? Make it up! Decide! She'd been sitting there for an hour. She had places to go, other clients to see. Decide, Zickafooz, decide.

Slight as a boy, and balding, his forehead sprayed with freckles the size of lichen, his throat pebbled with a rose-colored rash, his left arm withered, his left hand limp, Zickafooz, a Finder paused in mid-stride, then cocked his head as if entertaining an attractive thought. Had he made his decision? *Had* he? No—because now he moistened his lips (again!) and merely raised his right shoulder in nonplussed irresolution. "I *thought* I knew what image I craved. But . . ." Another careless half-shrug, as he cast a fond glance at the young silky white spaniel dog that followed him eagerly back and forth across the room. "Be patient, woman, I'll—"

"I've *been* patient! How long do you expect me to remain here?"

"Landholder Sisk paid you, did he not?"

"To perform a service, not to spend my day sitting here with the likes of you!" Theek's face screwed into a grimace. Finders! Were all such . . . they were all so— loathsome. And it wasn't just their waxy complexions, or their spots, or their bad odor (like wetted ashes), or even their withered arms, no, it was, it was . . .

Around them, a decent person couldn't help but think of darker things: illness, disappointed love, the death of your parents, your own inevitable end.

The nature of their Talent (and the guarantee of their tenacity, their Usefulness) was to want and want and want, but their greed was so—lugubrious. Oppressive. Infinite. They came from their Craft addicted to bounty. Extravagant bounty or worthless bounty, it made no difference to a Finder. So long as it was promised, and bestowed. Theek wouldn't deny—no good citizen of Lostwithal would deny—that Finders had their place in the Order of Things, that they were a necessary element in Perfect Order, but they were just so . . . detestable. Insipid. Yet frightening. Very. Even the lowest-degree Finders—like this insect here, this Zickafooz—could set your teeth on edge, make your skin crawl. Plunge you into paralyzing depression. "Perhaps . . ." she said.

The Finder looked sharply at her.

"Perhaps I might come back another time, when you've decided."

"No! Today I collect my bounty, today! As promised. I spent half a season in the Western Hills looking for the Landholder's daughter. Half a season—and found her. And brought her back to him. I earned my bounty. I deserve it. I asked for a tattoo, on this day—and I shall have one, on this day."

His face was dead white, haggard, but his small green eyes flashed bright, dispatched anger. And though his lips scarcely moved, his high, piping voice quavered with petulance and—Theek felt—an implied threat. She nodded, spread her hands.

"Whenever you are ready, then," she said at last, and lowered her head, clasped small hands in her lap, slumped. She could taste, all of a sudden, sweet phlegm in her throat. Her lungs seemed to burn. She shivered at the thought of herself wasting away from a cancer. Such a bad death . . .

UKROPS KNOCKED, BUT DIDN'T wait for an answer—he just turned the knob and pushed the door open. He glanced back at his three companions, standing together below a gnarled willow tree, then jerked his head once, and stepped inside.

His forehead ribbed with worry lines, Soldier Sollox followed without enthusiasm.

Peter hesitated, still not convinced this was a great idea. Since he'd come so far, though, he might as well . . . see it through. Might as well. He shrugged, snagged Gene Boman (who was now humming the theme song from Hanna-Barbera's "Wheelie and the Chopper Bunch") by a belt loop, and dragged him through the low door and into the little one-room house.

First impression: how friggen dark the place was. And hot. Suffocating. And that pungent smell? Peter couldn't place it at first, then could: a fire scene, the morning after. Hosed ashes. (Hosed *ashes?*)

There was a squawk of surprise, a burst of laughter. Eyesight adjusting to the gloom, Peter (with a small gasp of surprise) saw:

A woman seated very stiffly at a table—and Ukrops embracing a thin, small, deathly pale man who was dressed in a caftan.

Peter (back in the news business again) thinking, *Dark-green* caftan.

And pink spots on his neck. Like measles.

Thinking, His left arm all shrunken. Palsied.

And the woman. Looks angry.

Meanwhile, Gene Boman took it upon himself to get down on the floor, stretch out on his stomach, cross his ankles, plant his elbows, prop his chin on folded hands, and squint hard at the dented-in side of a large storage box.

(Time for "The Superman/Aquaman Hour"! All *right!*)

A white dog (with flopping ears and one milky blue eye, Peter noted) padded over, sniffed Boman briefly, and then stretched out next to him.

Sollox, eyes on Boman and the dog, heaved a sigh.

The awful little man was clearly delighted to see Ukrops, and reluctant to break their fraternal clinch. He did, though, finally, and then, with a merry cackle, pulled the Guardsman to the open trunk. Stooping, he gestured at it. "I've been so busy," he said. "So busy! You see?" With his right hand, he rummaged through the miscellaneous contents and plucked out a pair of dusty leather pants. "See this, brother? A treasure, eh? For a lost husband! And I scarcely had to look!" He laughed, tossed away the pants, grabbed out a candle. "And this? Merely to find a thieving dairyman!" Flinging down the candle, snatching up the sumptuous belt of silver coins. "Nice? Yes? Very nice, yes? Yes?"

Ukrops nodded. "Oh yes," he said. "It's all . . . wonderful."

"So busy, so busy," said Zickafooz, standing back up. "No emptiness, no pain. So busy!"

He flung himself impulsively at his brother again, again embraced him.

Theek, raising her eyebrows fractionally, cleared her throat. "You are not the only busy one, my friend." Then, to Ukrops: "Good and wholesome breath to you, Captain."

"And to you, Mistress Theek." He bowed from the waist.

Zickafooz twitched in surprise. "You are—acquainted with this woman?" He didn't seem at all pleased.

"Well acquainted," replied Ukrops, touching a finger to the tip of his nose and tapping the little spider tattoo.

The Finder narrowed his eyes a moment in thought, then widened them (they seemed wet all of a sudden) and smiled. "She is here to bring me bounty." He leaned forward, his lips almost touching Ukrops's ear. "So busy!

More bounty than any other Finder in Beybix—I swear! No pains, no emptiness—I sleep well!"

With a small, sad smile, Ukrops reached out and squeezed his brother's shoulder, then gave him an affectionate pat. "I'm happy for you."

"Yes?"

"Yes."

"No pains, never. Not like before. I sleep through the night."

"I'm very happy."

"I sleep through the night, every night. I do. I could tell you my dreams! I've written them down! Well—not me, I've hired a scribe. I have a dream book, I keep a dream book, you could see it, you could read it. I'm just like everyone else now. I'm doing very well. I . . . dream." Zickafooz had worked himself into such a lather that some color had even come to his cheeks. But now, abruptly, he slumped, as if spent.

Theek rose from her chair. "Captain Ukrops," she said through clenched teeth, "I would be much obliged if you might speak to your brother—now? I need to perform my service here and be off. Already I've—"

Ukrops lifted up a finger to his lips, and silenced her.

Then: "Zick?" he said lightly. "Listen. Listen to me. Yes?"

"Of course. Always. Yes." Blinking, nodding—listening.

"I've come to you in need of your service."

Zickafooz's eyes widened in shock. "Mine? You come to offer me a bounty, brother?"

"My companion does," replied the Red Guardsman with a flick of his head to Peter.

"I've been so . . . busy."

"Yes, and I'm delighted. But are you busy today?"

"I . . . today I have to accept a bounty."

"Afterwards, though."

"Afterwards," said Zickafooz. "I would be free, yes. Yes." His antic enthusiasm of a moment before was damped now, altogether. He was staring at Peter Musik with cold calculation. "Depending, of course. So far I've heard no talk of bounty. No one has offered me bounty. You come in here speaking to me of a service—but no bounty has been offered."

When Peter opened his mouth to speak, Ukrops stepped in front of him. "We mean no insult, Finder of Bottles Hill."

Zickafooz looked at Ukrops as though he'd never laid eyes on him before, and with deep suspicion. An acid look.

"To come under my roof seeking my service—and then offer me no bounty? *Is* to insult!" He put his head in his hands and shook it in gaudy, theatrical frustration.

"We thought we might tell you first what service it is we propose, so that you might set the bounty most . . . appropriate."

Zickafooz nodded. And folded his arms. "Very well."

"We seek a young woman."

"A wife?"

Ukrops glanced at Peter, who shook his head.

"No," said the Red Guardsman.

"A lover?"

Instinctively, Peter said, "Yes," and the Finder arched an eyebrow.

"She is gone of her own free will?"

"We don't know," said Ukrops.

"How long?"

"A few hours."

The Finder shook his head and gestured dismissively. "A few hours only, and you come to me? Find her yourselves."

"She is a Kemolon," said Ukrops.

That bit of information had a startling effect upon Zickafooz: he recoiled for a moment, his eyes snapping, his mouth dropping open. "You are—you wish for me to find a too-human? Here, in the City of Beybix?"

"Unless such a service requires someone of . . . higher degree?"

"No! I could do it! You imply that I couldn't?"

"I merely wonder—"

"Insult!"

"I beg your indulgence."

The Finder had started pacing again, stroking his little beard, moistening his lips. His eyes were keen and bright. "A too-human! Their body waters are different, you know."

"Yes," said Ukrops.

"Their *tides* are different. It is no simple find."

"No," said Ukrops. He looked to Peter and winked. "But I could do it!"

"That's why I suggested we come here."

"Their tides, you know. Different, very different . . ." Zickafooz came to a sudden halt, scowled. Then he threw back his head and laughed. "Imagine, a too-human! Good, good! I could write it up—have it written up! Second-degree! Feh! I'd be third—overnight!"

"At least," said Ukrops.

"I'll do it," the Finder declared.

"Excellent! Might we hope, then, that you'll get started . . . soon?"

"Soon, soon, yes. But—there is the business of my bounty to be discussed.

Ukrops gestured magnanimously. "Of course."

Zickafooz crossed the floor, passing Ukrops, and peered intently into Peter Musik's face. Peter squelched an impulse to backstep, then felt himself go weak and wobbly, suddenly filled with grief. It was terrifying, inexplicable, and immobilizing: he stood perfectly still and let the Finder's eyes study him from head to foot.

When Zickafooz turned away, Peter slumped with relief.

Gene Boman was still flat on his stomach staring raptly at the big storage trunk. (What with Aquaman tying a mutant squid's tentacles into complicated knots) he didn't notice either the small white dog gnawing the button on his shirt cuff, or the Finder now crouched beside him.

"This," said Zickafooz firmly, glancing up at Ukrops. "I covet this. And would have it upon completion of my service."

He was pointing to Boman's six-thousand-dollar Rolex wristwatch.

"Done deal," said Peter Musik, in English.

"Agreeable," said Ukrops.

The Finder gave a chortle and sprang to his feet. Then, business completed, his eyes lost all their flint. Looked, suddenly, almost . . . meek. He flung himself at his brother, embraced him once again, laid his head upon his shoulder. "So good to see you!"

Ukrops patted him lightly, indulgently, and with indisputable sadness. "And to see you. Shall we be off, then?"

This whole affair had finally become too much for Theek. With a loud groan, she thumped the table with an open hand. "*I* would be off, as well!"

Zickafooz smiled, gazed fondly, gratefully at Ukrops, then approached the table. "I've decided, woman," he said, and with great effort lifted his withered arm and pressed a pale crooked finger to the tip of his nose. "A spider, madam. For my bounty."

The tattooist looked flabbergasted, colored darkly. Looked at him reproachfully. "You must be—"

"A spider, madam. Identical to my brother's."

She waved a hand back and forth. "It is a mark of valor; you cannot just *ask* for a spider. A sparrow, a cat— all right. A wolf. But a spider? No, not a spider. You must *earn* a spider."

"I've earned—"

"A bounty. Merely a bounty."

"But I insist."

"Then I refuse." She folded her arms. "The idea!" She snorted.

Ukrops stepped forward, placed a hand upon Zickafooz's shoulder. "The Finder of Bottles Hill is a most valorous man."

"Good captain!" said Theek, astonished. "Consider this testament."

"I do," said Ukrops. He gave the woman a very direct look—no nonsense. "He has suffered much, and manages again to dream. Would you see his dream book?"

"No, but I—"

"He has earned his bounty. I say it. I say it twice."

"Captain," Theek protested with half-closed eyes.

"The spider recognizes another—according to the Order of Things."

Theek pressed her thin lips together, sighed through her nose, finally nodded. Then she pushed her chair from the table. When she stood, the Finder slipped away from Ukrops's side and presented himself to her.

On tiptoes, Peter worked himself around the room, to have a good look at what was going on. He'd expected to see the woman produce a needle, a bottle of dye, the usual paraphernalia, but no—all she did was purse her mouth, as if to plant a kiss, and then lean toward the Finder, deep revulsion twisting her face. When her lips brushed his nose, Zickafooz flinched, gave a small yelp: like a faintheart getting a flu shot.

When Theek lifted her head—there it was, a tiny black spider stamped on the fleshy tip of the Finder's nose. "Bounty bestowed," she said stonily.

Without another word, she turned, brushed past Peter, past Sollox, and left the house, slamming the door behind her.

A moment of silence, then:

"I have no mirror," said Zickafooz.

"It is an admirable mark."

"Truly?"

"Truly," said Ukrops. "Now—the woman."

"The too-human."

"Yes."

"Different tides. Very difficult."

"But not *too* difficult—not for one as skilled and valorous as the Finder of Bottles Hill."

"No!" agreed Zickafooz quick as a flash. "Absolutely not!"

He seemed so . . . happy.

Peter Musik, on the other hand, tingled with melancholy and felt dangerously—ridiculously—close to tears

CHAPTER 15

JACK AND DIDGE

From Dwindling Street, the Walker cut across the Great Market Plaza and into the oldest part of the city, where nearly all the square-topped buildings, though made of stone and brick, seemed on the verge of collapse. Up and down the alleys, screaming children chased after balls and cats and one another, pointing tourists wandered between aisles of vendors, and old women sat in doorways—pins in their wrinkled mouths, sewing baskets on their laps. Here were noisy ale houses and cook shops and gambling arcades. A number of sad-looking men sold peanuts from wheelbarrows, and skewered sausages and grilled fish and candied sand flies from cramped little booths.

It was midday now—major bells marked it—and Beybix had come fully alive. Tired and despondent as he felt, still Jack took some pleasure in the bustle and confusion.

But then he saw Didge.

With a traveling sack slung over her shoulder and banging her ribs, she came out the door of a visitors' hostel and down the steps. Her face was puffy, her hair wildly unkempt, and the limp on her right leg more pronounced than ever before. She didn't notice Jack—or anyone else. Awkwardly, she moved up the street, turned a corner, disappeared. Jack suddenly remembered to breathe again. Then he made to follow her—but stopped. Throughout his body: a sudden, confusing pressure.

(You spat blood at her feet.)

(Blood.)

(Spat *blood.*)

(You are not on a Ramble, you are not obliged to be Curious.)

(Go to Lita. *Lita* is your life, not *her.*)

(Once, though.)

(Once . . .)

He sprinted ahead.

THE LITTLE RATTY-FACED MAN behind the board counter glanced up, then nodded a mild welcome. His eyes were quick, his eyelids flickery. His complexion was a livid mingling of saffron, purple, and green. Didge closed the shop door behind her. The bell tinkled again. She crossed the floor, dragging her sack by its thong, feeling awkward (as she always did, in these sorts of places). She looked up at the glass tanks upon shelves lining the walls. Beetles of various size and color bounced frantically against their sides.

The little man had already slid from his stool and picked up a wire scoop. He was closely following the movement of Didge's eyes.

"Bell blacks?" she finally asked.

"Best of the season! Nine for a dull cent, twelve for a bright penny."

"Could I—would it be possible . . . to have just three?"

"Nine for a dull cent, mistress, twelve for a bright penny. And you'll find no better price in the capital."

"All right."

"Which is it, then?"

"The nine."

He grunted, then hooked a grimy foot (he was wearing sandals) around a stepladder, and spun it to him. Climbing it, he carefully reached down one of the larger tanks. He set it on the counter, slid open its grooved lid. Didge held her breath, chewed her bottom lip, watched him scoop beetles. He counted out loud, she counted to herself. Then, while he tapped them all into a small jar (which he then fitted with a fluted paper cap), Didge untied her purse and fingered through it till she found a dark-brown copper coin with a triangular hole punched through its center. She laid the dull upon the counter.

Taking the jar: "Do you have a dreamerie here?"

"We do." Inclining his head.

She managed a smile, grabbed hold of her sack, and was starting toward the curtained doorway when the man cleared his throat. "I'll have to ask you for an eighth, mistress. Stay as long as you please, of course, but the stool will cost you an eighth. The floor is swept, though, I can tell you that. And the walls are waxed very nice, very nice. Cleanest walls in the capital. Lovely pictures. And the table is smooth. No splinters! No one has ever complained of splinters, not here. Not to my knowledge. Stay as long as you please. An eighth."

She produced it, and paid him, and went into the back room.

The dreamerie was scarcely more than a large closet, a cubicle. Drawn on three shiny walls: huge cartoons, in black crayon, of drug beetles. Thin candles, here and there, burned in small red cups, and in their quavering light Didge could make out three others in the room, two picket-thin women and a fat man, each of them squatted upon a stool fitted in between points of a star-shaped oaken table. Heads cradled in folded arms, breathing labored, congested. Smoke rose in a column from a heavy brass censer, and hung in layers over the table, and twined around the rafters.

Didge claimed an empty stool. Then, after lashing

her sack to her ankle, she took from the jar three bell blacks (long spindly legs, whiplash antennae, markings like fluid mercury) and crushed them against the tabletop with her left thumb.

She'd brought a tiny spoon to dig out 'sap . . .

JACK STOOD ACROSS THE ALLEY from the beetle shop. He'd watched Didge go inside, and for a moment had nearly charged in right behind her, to snatch her like a thief and drag her back out. But he'd stopped himself. In time, he'd stopped himself.

(Lita is your life, not her.)

(Not her.)

(Though once . . .)

He frowned and rubbed his chin in thoughtfulness. Once . . .

A thin young man with white teeth, a round green cap upon his head of straight dark hair, printer's ink still speckling his hands, grouting his fingernails. Blue eyes bright with anticipation of the Great Affair. Traveling the red-clay roads of Little Egg Peninsula, quite alone.

Till a crossroads, where they met.

The dark-haired boy-man and the lithe, grayskinned girl-woman. Both (they discovered, startled) with the same destination: Walkers' Craft, at Bleeding Heath. So: companions on the day's long journey—though hardly speaking, each too wrapped up in separate anxieties, speculations.

But that evening—that night, by a campfire, the talking began, and so the friendship.

Jackvasdik, a Printer's Devil? She laughed. Jackvasdik, Jack*vas*dik? No. Oh no, she said. Call yourself Jack.

And with a shrug, he decided, All right. Jack. Jack it is.

In time: Jack, a Walker.

Sounds good, she said.

And he agreed, watching the orange firelight dance across her face.

Didgeebus, a Gatherer?

Just, he said, be Didge.

New names (they said) for the new life to start.

And later (fire dead), when he slipped beneath her blanket, she let him stay; but when, timidly, he touched her breasts, she grabbed his hand and bit it. His thumb.

Said, One adventure at a time.

Said, Later.

Said, After the Craft.

And he lay all night spooned against her, lightly, sleeping some, waking often—to grit his teeth.

After the Craft.

After the Craft . . .

Now—long, long after the Craft, with all its liquors and lessons, trials, mazes, examinations, punishments— Jack, a Walker crossed the narrow cobbled Old Town street and stepped inside the beetle shop.

'SAPWALK.

Darkwalk.

Didge feeling trembly, bitter cold—then blazing hot.

Smelling . . . sweet bay magnolia. Stumbling from darkness to sunlight, to stand upon a bluff, looking down.

At a small black castle.

Where lives The End-of-Everything Man.

Behind her, a swishing noise. And she turns (it takes forever, and ever, and her poor head whirls), now seeing Uncle Jix (ephemeral, now corporeal) come puffingly through the fetterbush. Looking all over for you, child. And he takes her small damp hand in his big callused one, presses it kindly, then makes a sharp, keening sound. Intake of breath. Seeing for himself the black castle, below.

Where lives The End-of-Everything Man.

Time to go home, says Uncle Jix.

Time to go home.

Home.

And it's so dark again, so oily dark, and she's feeling her way . . . home, lurching, sluggish, following the sound of her mother's anxious voice—

Didgeebus!

Mother?

Mother at the cottage window, baggy brown dress, breasts leaking milk, belly swollen—big with another child: the sur-husband (who Didge likes for his deep, rumbling laughter, hates for the coiled hair in his ears) visited again last 'Teacher's Month, then stayed for nearly a week.

Didge, ripe girl of sixteen, standing in the open doorway, hot sun baking her shoulders. Mother, what do you want?

Mother pointing. Saying, That filthy man on the road.

Yes, Mother? What?

Why do you speak to him, child? I saw you.

Didge half-turning (it takes forever and ever, and her poor head whirls) to glance behind her—

At that filthy man standing in the road: small and brown-haired, big-nosed, homely, his old clothing infinitely mended. His shoes, though. His shoes! New leather, and thick soled—fine new shoes as black as Black Lake!

He's a Walker, Mother. He said so.

Send him away. Now quoting from the Book of True and Cruel: A Walker is a ghost of flesh and blood and vitals and bone. Send him away, child—I tell you.

But he's a King's Tramp, Mother—a King's Tramp!

Send him away, child. Tell him he'll not hear any Rumors at this place. Now go do as I say!

Good girl, obedient daughter. Doing as Mother says —but. But moving from the cottage across the grassy dooryard (the yard now in moving-cloud shadow, now in blue-black darkness) takes . . . forever and ever, and her poor head whirls.

Mother says to go away, I can't speak to you. She says you'll not hear any Rumors at this place.

But I already have, says the Walker in the road: small and brown-haired, big-nosed and homely.

What? What Rumor? Tell me!

Says the Walker, There is a girl—

Me?

Says the Walker, A Doveflesh girl—
Me!

Says the Walker, Who would be a ghost of flesh and blood and vitals and bone.

This Rumor, says Didge, is it true?

A Rumor is neither true nor cruel, says the Walker. Merely possible, always dangerous.

Neither true nor cruel.

Merely possible.

Always dangerous.

"ALWAYS DANGEROUS," MUM-
bled Didge, and ground her back teeth, and shivered feverishly, elbows nipping in tight against her ribs. Her face, turned to one side, slick with perspiration, was pressed down flat upon the dreamerie table.

Jack stood behind her, his mouth set grimly.

"An eighth—I must ask you for an eighth."

The ratty-faced little man stepped forward, then retreated, smiling slackly, apologetically. His arms hung limp.

"Leave."

"But you must pay. An eighth. Perfect Order insists upon the just transaction."

"Leave," said Jack, "or I'll kill you."

The man snapped his jaws shut, swallowed, and glared—but left.

And the Walker plucked up a stool and set it behind Didge's, and sat, then rested his forehead upon her warm, twitching shoulder.

Always dangerous.

What was she dreaming? Remembering?

A Rumor is neither true nor cruel. Merely possible, always dangerous.

A Rumor, thought Jack. . . .

One high-summer night, long ago, the boy-man that he was: wearing an inkstained apron, dropping letters and pieces of type into a composing stick, rubbing his eyes, yawning. His master ill at home with cat-scratch fever;

here, a job to be finished, promised for morning. The manuscript interminable, written on dirty scraps of paper in a small finicky hand, pages full of long numbers and dreary poetry—a forester's treatise on the motion and meaning of wood smoke.

The boy-man-that-was-Jack lifted his head, blinked, groaned, continued his tedious work; hours passing (his *life* passing) till: the scrape of shoes on plank, and with a bright pang of alarm, he turned round on his bench, and there she was, a tall woman with the road's yellow dust powdering her clothes. I beg a drink and something to eat, she said. Said the woman with the road's dust powdering her raggedy black clothes, who seemed half-dead with exhaustion, and whose shoes were as black as the waters of Black Lake.

A Walker!

The boy-man's two hearts lurched painfully in his chest.

A Walker! At this door! *This* door! *Now!*

Was he being called, at last?

Something to drink, something to eat, said the Walker. For which I cannot pay you.

The boy-man-that-was-Jack replying, Of course! Of course not! Then ladling salted milk into a cup, and fetching a rice cake. Which she accepted gratefully and sat, exhaling a long, trembling sigh, in the master printer's roomy chair. She stretched out her legs, studied her shoes. Then said, See these, Jackvasdik? I've nearly worn out the leather.

And he laughed, suddenly giddy, euphoric, and she narrowed her eyes, slowly looked him up and down.

Have you heard something I have not? That makes you laugh so?

No, it's . . . (And he laughed again, even louder.) It's merely . . . I haven't told you my name, but you know it!

The Walker continued to stare at him over the rim of her cup, a smile crinkling tired eyes.

The boy-man-that-was-Jack rocked back and forth on his heels then bent from the waist, impulsively, and put lips to the Walker's ear. For three seasons, he whispered, I've told every passing stranger of my desire to . . . serve. Has it been repeated, elsewhere—has it been heard?

She laughed, shot a finger at him. Why would anyone repeat the noise of a printer's boy? Do you suppose travelers remember *you* once they've traveled on?

With a look almost of pity, she handed him back the cup.

And he blurted, But am I called? You must tell me: Am I called?

To what?

The Walker's work.

Called? Is anyone? she said, amused. Or is that merely a Rumor?

She got slowly to her feet, thanked him again for his kindness, then moved toward the door, and the boy-man-that-was-Jack dashed the cup to the floor. It bounced, and the handle broke off.

But if you *feel* yourself called, said the Walker at the threshold, then walk, Jackvasdik. All instincts of the vocation are not instilled at the Craft. Some we are born with. As you must know.

Some we are born with, she said. *We. We* are born with.

He saw black threads swirl before his eyes. . . .

And he saw them again now, in the dreamerie.

Black threads in antic motion.

He blinked to dispel them, then reached his left hand toward Didge, and gently stroked her hair. The back of her neck was sweaty, seething with warmth. She twitched convulsively. He let his hand fall away. So wrong. It had all gone so wrong, for her. For her especially, but for him, too. Yes, for him, too.

Thinking, A Walker is a ghost of flesh and blood and vitals and bone. . . .

CHAPTER 16

THE MERRY SPACEMEN

D URING HIS SEVERAL LOST months living as Geebo the Blank, Peter Musik had met hundreds of characters like Zickafooz—alternately twitchy and calm, maudlin and callous, benevolent and malign. Former psychiatric patients, sometimes. Addicts, almost always. Watch out. Peter thinking now, Watch out. Don't turn your back on this guy. I don't care if we *are* in some other friggen universe. A junkie, babe, is still a junkie.

Bells were ringing throughout the city when Peter led the others into Lita's alley—at least he *hoped* it was Lita's alley. He could be mistaken, maybe it just *looked* like it—but no, this was the place: he remembered that rain barrel with the bent-out-of-shape wheel rim propped against it. And there was the witch's whitewashed door. "We're here," he told Ukrops, who nodded and then immediately turned to his creepy sibling.

Saying, "Should we do this formally?"

"I insist," replied Zickafooz in a voice saturated with arrogance.

Amused, the Red Guardsman drew himself up straight, cleared his throat, reached out with his right hand and lightly touched the Finder's shriveled left forearm. "I would," he said, "have your service begin now, at this beat of our hearts, and bid you return a lost woman to—" Ukrops frowned, then smiled slightly "—to Peter, a Witness."

Zickafooz looked suddenly crabby again.

"You didn't say anything about her being too-human!"

"Bid you return this lost *too-human*," said Ukrops.

"And the bounty, what about the generous and fit bounty!"

Ukrops shut one eye, and moistened his lips. (Struggling to keep his temper in check? Sure looked that way to Peter.) "For this completed service, your patron promises to bestow upon the most worthy Finder of Bottles Hill a bounty that is both generous and fitting, according to the Order of Things." Then to Peter, as he pointed at Gene Boman's wrist, "It's called a what? That thing."

Peter said, "Wristwatch." In English. Which surprised him, a little.

To Zickafooz, Ukrops said, "It will give your patron satisfaction and pleasure to reward you with that . . . clock you so desire."

The Finder's head snapped back. "It's a *clock*? I thought it was a bracelet! Well!" He laughed happily. "I covet it nonetheless!"

With that, his whole demeanor changed—again. His eyes lost their luster, his brow furrowed, his nostrils flared, and the ends of his mouth turned down. He gestured everyone away! away! with his one good hand, and with painful slowness raised the crooked one to his lips. With a growl, he bit it. Small teeth puncturing the skin, drawing blood. His eyes rolled up in his head, and he staggered.

Then, murmuring, he began to pace, up and down the alley. Walking ten paces, turning, walking back. Turning, walking the same ten paces . . .

His white spaniel dog, meanwhile, scurried along beside him.

And it was the dog, the silly little dog, that made Peter Musik suddenly think of something he hadn't thought of in twenty-five years: the Merry Spacemen.

He grinned, laughed to himself, thought, Jeez. The Merry Spacemen.

And their dog named Rocket.

Jesus.

When he was a kid in grammar school, Peter and a bunch of friends had called themselves (God knows why) the Merry Spacemen. It wasn't a gang; it was more like a club, but nothing official. Just a bunch of twelve-year-old Florida boys hanging out together, dreaming up stuff to do to pass the time before puberty set in. You wanna try chewing tobacco? Yeah, let's. What do you say we all go buy sailor hats? All right? Let's get drunk on your father's gin. Okay? Yeah, okay. What the hell.

There were only five Merry Spacemen. There was Peter and then there was a tall, handsome, wiseguy with amazingly white teeth named Jacky Loesser and this flaky fat boy named Richie Stafford and this really-timid-always-afraid-of-getting-into-trouble-sort-of-kid named John D. (for "douche") Edwards and then there was— Koz. Crazy Koz. Some days Koz'd be a goof, a real hoot, a clown, great to be around; he'd talk in funny voices, be full of great ideas about what to do (Let's go down the Army/Navy, steal us some bathing suits!); but other days, man, he'd come out of his house all surly and ready to fight, a real scary pain in the ass. Like his old man. Koz. Peter thinking, Crazy Koz.

And Koz had this mutt, this little fuzzy white ball of a mongrel street dog called Rocket. Jesus: the stupid dog was called Rocket.

Loesser, Stafford, Johnny Edwards, Crazy Koz, and brainy, cranky Petey Musik: the Merry Spacemen.

With Rocket, their Wonder Dog.

Circa 1972.

Peter thinking now, Jeez, I wonder what ever happened to those guys.

Standing in an alley in Beybix, Lostwithal, trying to remember what happened to his childhood pals.

It seemed to Peter that he'd heard something about Loesser becoming a priest, and Johnny Edwards a fireman . . . but maybe not, maybe it was Stafford became a fireman, Edwards that opened a shop selling scuba gear. And Crazy Koz? Vanished. He'd turned eighteen and gone away, and nobody had ever heard another thing about him. Or about Rocket, either.

The Merry Spacemen.

And now, as Zickafooz stopped his pacing and scowled, and his little white dog went yipping around his legs, and as Soldier Sollox leaned back against a building wall, looking worried, and Gene Boman squatted on the cobbles and stared blankly at the rain barrel, and as Ukrops regarded everyone with an expression of sly amusement, Peter said to himself, the Merry friggen Spacemen live again!

And laughed out loud.

The sound of his own laughter startled him, and he felt instantly . . . idiotic.

This is no joke. Peter saying to himself, Come on, already. You're getting goofy, Musik, you're turning stupid, you need to go to sleep.

The Merry Spacemen. Jesus. Christ.

Be *serious*. Money is missing. Money Campbell. *Money!* The girl you're—

Money is missing—all right?

Pay attention.

So he did, grimacing to get rid of his sappy, sentimental smile and focusing intently on the Finder, who was now striding back up the alley, now stopping, now turning toward a clapboard wall, now staring at a door in that wall.

Peter glanced at Ukrops. Who lifted an eyebrow, then inclined his head toward his brother. "Perhaps," he said, "the lady hasn't gone too far, after all." And walked up the alley. Eagerly, Peter moved to follow, but stopped dead in his tracks when someone called his name.

Lita: in her open doorway. An incredulous expression on her face.

Peter, with a shrug, and pointing with his thumb: "I hired a Finder. To find Money. She's not *back,* is she?"

Stepping barefooted into the alley, Lita moved her head from side to side, which Peter took to mean not only that Money wasn't back, but also (especially) that she thought Peter had lost all his marbles.

Peter saying then, "How about Jack?"

Lita looking past him, up the alley, saying, "He hasn't returned, either. How could you have *done* this?"

"Done what? Get a Finder? Look, it's all right—citizens do it every day." Then he laughed. And then he pressed the heel of his hand against his forehead, squeezed his eyes shut tight. "I don't know what I'm saying, I'm so tired." He opened his eyes, looked at Lita again, Lita standing maybe two feet in front of him, studying him with those almond-shaped eyes of hers, made her look almost Japanese. "He's low-degree, so don't worry," said Peter. "I have to find her, don't I? Money. I have to find her."

Lita touched his arm, and he could've kissed her.

Little sympathy: man, just what he needed right about then.

"Peter!" Ukrops shouting down the alley.

Then pointing, when Peter came at a run, appeared at his side. Ukrops pointing to the door his brother was still staring at.

"She in there?" said Peter. The Red Guardsman grunted (Peter thinking, That's a definite *no),* then breathed down through his nose, and finally, brusquely, reached out and—

tore the door off the building.

(Correction: the *sailcloth* off the building. Upon which someone had *painted* a door.)

A portrait was revealed.

Peter saying, "Oh Christ!"

Ukrops saying, "Is that her?"

Peter saying, "Ah Jesus!"

Sollox saying, "Look at the signature."

Peter saying, "Jesus *Christ!*"

Lita saying, "An art-prince."

Peter saying, "Goddamn!"

And then nobody said anything.

Till Gene Boman wandered over, took one look at the portrait on the building wall, flinched, shook his head, blinked, blinked again, opened his mouth and said, "Her nipples aren't *brown*, they're *pink!*"

Whereupon Peter Musik stepped forward and punched him right in the nose.

CHAPTER 17

BEHIND YOU,
THE WORLD ENDS

A GHOST, SAYS THE TATTER-
demalion Walking Master, as he leads Didge down a stony
path, around and in between prickly dark hedges twice as
tall as she. The Maze. The Master saying, A ghost of flesh
and blood . . . , and Didge listening, nodding, but also
glancing behind her, secretly, straining to see through a
twilight gloom. Only . . . he's not there. Jack. Jack's not
. . . there. And she hasn't seen him, nor even glimpsed
him, not once, since they arrived here together at the
Craft, but every day she keeps expecting (hoping) to meet
him, but she never does. And it's such a small place, the
old gabled Craft house on the heath . . . 'way back
there, where the Maze begins. Never sees him. Thinks of
him, though. She thinks of him constantly, and her poor
head whirls.

. . . vitals and bone, says the Walking Master, and
Didge hears the irritation in his gravelly voice, turns to

face him, and he's scowling. Behind you, he says crossly, there is nothing. Behind you, the world ends.

And Didge says, Yes. The world ends behind me.

Cheeks warm from the rebuke, she puts Jack from her mind (but can't, not really) and presses on alongside the Master. The sky above the Maze grows purple, turns dark, and now a low, a very low and droning sound—Walker's Noise, already familiar, wondrous, frightening—fills her ears, and she closes her eyes, concentrating hard, trying to Compass it, determine its source.

But stumbles.

And is rebuked again, for stumbling.

I beg your forgiveness, Master.

Sit. Sit, he tells her now, and suddenly here's a low round-topped table, a topiary, and a single chair, of black wrought iron. *Sit.* She does, and Walker's Noise grows louder, a sea roar, and in it she can . . . almost . . . distinguish individual voices, conversations, quarrels. Boasts. Promises. Was that laughter? And that? A howl of pain? And that? That whisper? A conspiracy to kill?

Look at me, says the Master, and she lifts her eyes, watches him as he turns, very slowly turns, his left hand, and then—

Snatches at the night air, clamping his fingers shut tight: a fist. Which he puts to his ear and then, less clenched, to Didge's.

I am your patron, he says.

She nods. (Her patron . . . and catechist.)

And you, he says, are my Walker.

Yes, says Didge. (His Walker . . . and catechumen.)

He withdraws the fist, shakes open his fingers.

You have heard?

Yes, says Didge. A Rumor, says Didge.

Says the Master, Is it true?

A Rumor is neither true nor cruel, says Didge. Merely possible, always dangerous.

Then I would not ask you, says the Master, to seek out its provenance, though I would know it.

To seek out its provenance, dear patron, I would gladly Ramble in your service.

And put yourself in danger?

A Walker, says Didge, is not afraid.

Says the Master, But all humans are afraid.

All humans, dear patron. But a Walker is—and Didge's throat constricts, but she forces herself to swallow, to go on—a Walker is a ghost of flesh and blood and vitals and bone.

The Master smiles thinly. Leans toward Didge. Then Ramble, he says. And return to me at Ramble's End.

He turns (now corporeal, now ephemeral), and disappears into the Maze, leaving Didge alone, quite alone, in the dark.

Thinking, I did well.

I did . . . well.

But now she presses all thoughts from her mind, ignores Walker's Noise that continues to buzz around her head like flies. Concentrating. On the test. The game. Her patron's Rumor.

Concentrating till there is silence.

And then a hum; quavering.

Compass it.

Follow it.

Ramble.

She rises from her chair (it takes forever and ever, and her poor head whirls).

The humming grows louder. Didge steps toward it, and it withdraws, becomes faint, teases her, slips away like the cunning north wind in a children's tale, slipping down that passage, and around that corner, where the tall shrubbery is shaped like a bell.

Smiling, Didge walks on. Following.

And once again she hears the humming.

She means to follow it, to follow that Rumor (a man . . . or perhaps a woman intends to plant a seed . . . or perhaps a jewel . . . in a garden of ashes) till she finds its source. Though she may walk all night through this Maze, Didge will know its source. The man or the woman. (Perhaps the child.) The seed or the jewel. (Or perhaps a corpse.) The garden of ashes.

Or perhaps—perhaps a teller of lies.

To ramble for the patron, to wear out the leather, to know, and to pass on her knowledge at Ramble's End is all that matters.

Nothing else.

Because a Walker *is* a ghost, a ghost of flesh and blood and—

She draws suddenly to a halt, frowns, cocks her head.

At a sound?

Or a thought?

A thought.

Jack.

No, says Didge, out loud, there in the Maze, alone.

Saying, No. Thinking, Jack.

Thinking, I heard him. Yes! I *know* that I heard him.

Behind me.

He is here in the Maze, behind me.

Didge thinking, But . . .

Behind me, there is nothing.

Behind me, the world ends.

And thinking, A Walker is a ghost.

Not a woman. A ghost.

She clenches her teeth, gives her head a violent shake, and continues on.

Past tall shrubbery shaped like a bell.

Jack.

It won't leave her mind.

Jack.

And now she's certain that he's here in the Maze, too. On a Ramble. Perhaps just beyond that hedge.

Behind her.

And if she might stop for just a moment, turn around, ignore the hum—

for *just* a moment

—she might see him.

There are things she's wanted to tell him.

Words she's wanted to *say* to him.

A touch she's wanted to give him.

And if he's just back there—

(and he is! she *knows* it)

—and if this is only a Craft game, a test

(and it is! she *knows* it)

—then. Then . . . ?

Didge thinking, No!

A Walker is a ghost of flesh and blood and vitals and bone.

Compass the Rumor, follow it, Ramble. Didge-girl. Telling herself, *Follow* it.

But turning round—

(so the world *doesn't* end behind me!)

—and striking off in a new direction, turning this corner, passing an alabaster fountain, pushing through *these* hedges, hearing nothing now except her own labored breathing.

Calling, Jack?

Jack? Are you . . . ?

Now stopping abruptly, hands cold, hearts pounding, mouth dry as sand.

Lost.

And nothing to lead her out.

No Rumor.

No Rumor, no Walker's Noise, and no Jack.

Just Didge, alone in the Maze, in the moonless dark.

In a panic, she runs, and trips, and picks herself up, and runs again, runs into brambles that tear at her clothing and face, pulls away, gasping, and runs, pebbles underfoot, then gnarled roots, then sand, then—

Nothing.

She flings up her arms, to catch something, anything, and grab hold. But there is—

Nothing.

She falls, twisting in space (forever and ever) and lands hard, bright splinters of pain exploding through a leg, her right leg. Dirt in her mouth. Blood in her mouth. And she's broken her leg. Her leg!

And she lays there, breathing hard, and she knows—

What will happen next.

Because this is a 'sapdream, a darkwalk, a memory, she knows what will happen next. She will lay in this pit, in the dark, in agonizing pain, and the night will pass slowly, and the sky will lighten, to gray, to pink, and then: she will hear footsteps.

And then: there will be a face looking down at her.

Not Jack's.

And not the Walking Master's.

A bland, kindly face, a face with light-green eyes and a ginger-colored beard.

The Sheriff-at-Craft.

And the Sheriff-at-Craft will say to Didge, You've been missed, and Didge will gaze up at him miserably and call for a rope, beg for his hand, but he will shake his head sadly and, instead of rope, instead of his hand—

He will merely smile.

And turn away, saying as he leaves, I'll tell them I've found you. They'll come eventually.

Eventually.

In two days they will come.

For two days, she will suffer.

A Walker is a ghost of flesh and blood and vitals and bone.

And Didge is down in the pit, and the sky is turning gray, turning pink, and she wants this 'sapdream to end, to end—

(I want everything to end)

(everything)

(the end of everything)

—and she hears the footsteps and knows who is coming, and she almost laughs (and her poor head whirls).

A face, looking down at her.

Not Jack's.

Not the Walking Master's.

And not the Sheriff-at-Craft's.

A small round face, a white face, a pink-eyed face.

Frowning.

I've been looking all over this crazy garden for you, says the tiny, tiny man with the pale yellow hair and the pictures on his shirt, color pictures, of fruits and trees and mountains and . . . are those buildings?

"Let's get out of here," he says. "Want to? Let's go someplace comfortable. Want to? Let's play a game," he

says. "Want to? Want to? Want to? Didge. You want to?
Want to . . . ?"

JACK GOT UP FROM HIS STOOL,
feeling shaky, perplexed. For nearly an hour he'd been
sitting there watching Didge twitch and shiver and scrabble the tabletop with her fingers; he'd been listening to
her moan and sob and click her teeth and cry out. But
now—now she was still. And quiet. Her breathing easy,
and measured. And when he touched her—there was no
seething heat.

She felt . . . cool.

Whatever torment she'd gone through had passed.

Suddenly. Quite suddenly.

He shook his head, glanced toward the dreamerie
door, looked back at Didge.

(Who'd been his life.)

(Once.)

Leaning down, he kissed her on the temple, lightly,
then straightened up and started to leave.

He stopped, though, when he heard her laugh: a
loud, clear, trilling laugh. Turning back to the table, he
watched her, still unconscious, extend a hand, her left,
and make a fist, and shake it, then fling it open.

As though—

As though she were playing a game of Could.

He grinned, and nearly went back to her side, tried
to wake her—but then he frowned and rushed out the
door and shut it, and the world ended behind him.

Because he was a Walker, and a Walker was a ghost
of flesh and blood and vitals and bone.

CHAPTER 18

THE FIRST ARGUMENT AGAINST GRIEF

NOW JUST WHAT IS *THIS* SUP-posed to prove? Jere Lee thought. Standing out here, fidgeting, twiddling your thumbs—proves what? Huh? What? Thinking, You crazy old broad. Almost forty-six, and what're you doing? Same thing you did as a moony fifteen-year-old. Remember Carl Timm? Sophomore year in high school? 1960? Beautiful Carl. Tousle-headed, snub-nosed, and what a gorgeous smile. Jere Lee remembering (as she plodded slowly up and down outside the frilly iron fence in front of Master Squintik's apartment building) all those October and November late afternoons when she'd dawdle on a certain street corner in the old hometown, just waiting for Carl Timm to come out of his house. Hoping. Praying. And whenever he did appear, Christ, she'd always feel such a terrible *vacancy* inside of herself, a cold vacuum, and she'd lose her breath, as though she'd just fallen on a rock, and her palms would grow sticky, and she'd flash her big smile of feigned surprise—but Carl? He'd just duck his head, every single time, and never glance her way, not once, not ever. But he saw her; oh, but he saw Jere Lee, all right. Saw the stringbean girl with the straw-colored straight hair and the bald eyes and the not-so-great complexion standing on his corner in a hand-me-down pea coat, looking stupid. Looking stupid, acting—foolish. And *very* fifteen. Well, she told herself now—her lips moving—you're acting fifteen again.

With a jerky motion, she stopped walking, then froze on the spot. "Big banana," she said out loud, and choked down a sob. "You big soft silly banana." Then she flinched, and spun half-around, surprised and embarrassed to see a young fat-faced boy with shiny cheeks watching her with open curiosity.

He was dressed in a baggy white shirt, the sleeves rolled back to his elbows, dark trousers, and rope-soled sandals. Slung across his chest was a bulging canvas sack —it reminded Jere Lee of the sort of bag newspaper delivery boys used to carry, maybe still did. One of his hands was dipped into the sack, the other was squeezing his jaw. His eyebrows lifted, and he made a slight bow.

"Mistress," he said, uncertainly.

"Oh—hello," she replied, a little manic. She bet she was blushing, and she hated herself for it.

The boy shot a quick glance at Squintik's building, then looked back to Jere Lee. "Are you lost?"

She put her hand up and rubbed it across her hair. She laughed. "Do I look it?" When he frowned, though, she added quickly, "No—no, I'm not lost, but thank you." Her eyes glazed. Go away, she thought. Leave me alone.

He nodded, then withdrew his hand from his sack and drizzled the sidewalk with a sugary white dust. He walked on, broadcasting it every which way.

"Excuse me!" Jere Lee had broken out of her trance and taken a few steps after him. When he halted, looked back at her, she asked, "Could you tell me—what you're doing?"

For a moment he seemed perturbed, almost insulted, but then, abruptly, his expression softened. He grinned. "Ah! You're from my Craft!" he said. "The Craft! Come to test me—to find me worthy or not!"

Jere Lee thinking, The *Craft?* But saying, "I'm just wondering what—"

He scooped out yet another handful of dust, held it in his palm, belled his cheeks with breath—and blew powerfully.

As the dust burst, swirled, began to settle, the fat-faced boy made another bow, this one splendidly formal —from the waist. "Dio," he said, "a Scatterer."

"Scatterer? Of what?"

He struck a pose—parade rest: legs spread wide apart, hands clasped behind him. "Of those that *were*—to remind us who *are* of our own too-brief time in the Order of Things." Then he cleared his throat, cocked his head. "Mistress, if you wish, I can recite to you the Nineteen Arguments Against Grief—shall I?"

Jere Lee was blinking, reeling a little. "Are you telling me that's—*remains?*"

"Mistress? Do you find me worthy?"

"Ashes? *People* ashes?" She was staring at the boy and her eyes had that glazed look again.

"The Nineteen Arguments Against Grief," intoned the boy. He squared his shoulders. "The First Argument: The Dead don't remember they lived. The Second Argument—"

But then he broke off—and flung up both hands to cover his head—when a sudden fusillade of hailstones came pelting down from the sky.

No, not from the sky.

Jere Lee (covering her head, too, and wincing) looked up and saw Master Squintik standing upon the roof parapet. He was dressed as she'd never seen him dressed before, in shiny black trousers and a loose white blouse. His arms were outstretched, his fingers were spread; his fingers were frozen—and the source of the hail.

It kept falling, in two discreet columns, and bouncing on the pavement.

Unlike Jere Lee, Dio didn't have the common sense to step out of the way: he merely stood there gawping, iceballs ricocheting off him. "It's a Cold Mage!" he cried.

"Yes," said Jere Lee, "I know. Thanks."

"I'd wager a coin it's Mage Plinthix!"

Jere Lee just nodded, then stepped backwards, off the pavement and into the cobbled street, to see from a better vantage.

She pressed her lips together, hugged herself tight, and stared, a little numb, unable to imagine what this meant, or what might happen next.

Hey, I'm just a rube from Kemolo.

A rube, all right: even after all she'd been through, and seen, in the last twenty-four hours, still she went dizzy and weak-kneed and pale when Master Squintik's long body suddenly burst into a billion splinters of ice, which spun around and spun around, then coalesced and became an enormous white owl, which took wing, swooping gracefully over Dwindling Street and then flying on, flying away.

Jere Lee's heart sank. She let out a loud groan, and started to run. She could still see it—him! If she could keep him in sight, she'd—

Follow.

"Mistress! Mistress!" The boy, Dio, running along beside her, snatching at her sleeve. "I haven't finished! Let me finish, please? The Second Argument Against Grief . . . the Second Argument—Mistress?"

"Oh shut up!" she said, and kept running.

As though her heart belonged to a girl of fifteen, and was young enough still to be broken.

CHAPTER 19

FOOL IN THE HOLD

H E SEEMED ALMOST . . .
sweet, the crooked runt with the yellow hair and the yellow eyes and the yellow tongue and the dark-blue teeth.

When Money had opened her mouth and howled? He'd jumped, then skittered back across the hold and stood at the foot of the stairs with a tentative, guilty, almost pleading expression—almost like: I'm-sorry-I-scared-you-it's-not-my-fault-please-so-don't-do-that-again-please?

Then he twisted his short cape around in front of him, turned it inside out (it was lined with red satin), stuck his hand into a slit pocket, and produced a perfect-looking little plum. Which he proffered to Money with an extended hand as he took a few mincing steps toward her.

She declined it, naturally: her mom and dad had read her enough fairy tales, and taken her to enough Disney features, that she wasn't about to fall now for the old poisoned fruit trick. Not Money Campbell. But jeez, how her mouth salivated! Nicest looking plum she'd seen in a long time. Maybe ever seen. No fooling. The supermarkets near the college, back home? You wouldn't *believe* how crummy their produce looked; it always seemed pawed! Spoilage spots galore—and so expensive!

This, on the other hand, was a great-looking plum. A *very* great-looking plum.

Nevertheless, she (no stupe: a victim, yes, but a stupe? never!) kept shaking her head in a vigorous negative.

The kind-of-sweet runt with the yellow eyes, etcetera, looked at the beautiful plum, shrugged sadly, and then stuck it back into his cape.

So far, he still hadn't spoken a word.

But then, neither had Money. Her lips scarcely apart, her breath sissed in and out. She sounded like a frying egg. (Or: your brain on drugs.)

The runt suddenly held up both index fingers. He revolved them, slowly, and then (as Money did a double take, scowling) he hooked the fingers around the ends of his mouth and stretched his lips into a high, goony smile, wrinkling his forehead repeatedly as he did so. Then he kicked up his heels and did a herky-jerky dance. Ended up with his legs being crossed and his big feet twisted together, and so down he crashed, hard. The floor shook.

Money stared for several long seconds, then—oh man, she couldn't help it—she giggled, then laughed hysterically.

Rolling onto his side, the runt propped his jaw in a hand, and looked at Money with open relief.

"Finally," he said.

She stopped laughing at once.

"No, no, please," he said, "continue! You're clearing my throat." He coughed.

Money saying, "What?"

He coughed again. "My throat." Touching it, squeezing it, right above his adam's apple. "Your laughter is clearing my throat. Go on!"

But, of course, she couldn't. You can't be *told* to laugh, so Money's laughter died as abruptly as it began.

He picked himself off the floor, dusted off the knees of his trousers, the elbows of his shirt, then made a sweeping, gallant bow to Money Campbell.

"Mother's Last," he said.

She stared at him.

He tapped himself on the sternum with two fingers.

She shook her head. "Excuse me?"

"My name," he said.

"Yes?"

"Is Mother's Last."

"It *is?*"

She giggled again (thinking, No, stop it!), and he beamed at her.

"A Fool."

"You," she said.

"Yes!"

"Are a fool . . . is that what you're saying?"

He nodded eagerly.

Money eyed him hard for several seconds. What she was thinking, This guy is . . . maybe a little retarded, maybe? Dangerous? *How* dangerous? She smiled slowly. Instinct and wiles recalled to life. "Okay," she said. "Fine. Now, Mr. . . . Mother, could you tell me what's going on?"

He rocked back and forth, then pointed at the overhead timbers. *"He* took you."

"Who?" Money thinking, *Took* me?

"Him. Up there." Still pointing. "Come. He wishes to see you now."

Money shook her head, no. *Oh* no. "Him. You still haven't said. *Who?"*

"The best."

"What?"

"No one better. Ever. In history. In history no one better, ever." The Fool snickered, winked, lowered his voice: "I *have* to say that. Or else he'll paint me changed. Again."

"What?"

"The best prince of art, the best, no one better. Not in history—never! Come see him." When he reached a hand toward Money, she recoiled. "Please? He'll be angry if you don't come. With me. Angry with me. Please? Come. Meet Presquit."

Money thinking, No way, José.

Then thinking, But what're you gonna do, girl, sit here the rest of your life?

Thinking, Be brave, you stupid coward.

She stepped away from the wall.

Mother's Last smiled gratefully. Then he started toward the stairs, but stopped, turned back, produced that beautiful plum again, again offered it to Money.

This time—why not?—she accepted it.

What a perfect-looking plum. No kidding. A beauty. Deep glossy purple—dewy, even. Sitting there in the palm of her hand.

As she was lifting it to her mouth, though, it quivered, and then, with a wet, ripping sound, bits of fruit pulp exploded, spraying wildly, spraying her, and a tiny, leering painted doll's head, chittering mechanical laughter, sprang out atop a thin, coiled, vibrating wire.

Money was surprised by her reaction. Very. Instead of going walleyed, hysterical? She merely raised an eyebrow, shook her head once, and then with a dry chuckle, calmly flipped the crazy plum over a shoulder. Thump. Jesus. What next, a hand-buzzer?

"So let's go," she told the Fool, who was grinning from ear to ear.

Happy happy happy.

WHEN SHE'D CLIMBED THROUGH the hatch to stand on deck, Money was astounded by the vastness of the lake. To her, it looked like the friggen ocean, a weirdly calm ocean that just so happened to be as black as motor oil. Birds shrieked overhead. Not a cloud. Sunlight hurt her eyes like pins. The air, though! Was so fresh, and so cool, that it made her head spin. She gulped it greedily, then slid, almost slipped, on the wet deck. The Fool caught her by an elbow, but she immediately shook him off.

"Let's get this over with, all right? Where is he, this Mr. Presquit?"

Mother's Last pointed directly ahead, then led the way, Money stepping gingerly, trying to squelch the queasiness (hell, the fear) that kept trying to push into her stomach and her heart, but also trying to check things out. Take inventory.

For good or bad, looks like she'd picked up a few traits hanging out with Peter ("Where's my Pulitzer?") Musik.

It kind of helped, even, to think of Peter now.

She could imagine him saying, Okay, tell me all about it. Where were you?

On this boat.

This boat. What *kind* of boat? Come on, Money, you gotta be specific. That's the name of the game.

That's the name of *your* game, babycakes.

(Babycakes? Nah, she'd never say that, not to Peter.)

That's the name of *your* game. Yeah, she might say that. That's the name of *your* game.

And Peter? He'd say—as he'd said often enough in the past, when he was always pumping her for more and more details about Gene Boman's office, his vacation house, the contents of his closets—he'd say, Just try? Okay? For me.

And Money would say, Well, it was like—a sailboat. Then she'd frown, and cancel that with a wave of her hand. I don't mean like a *little* sailboat, I mean—a boat with sails. Hey! All right! I got it, she'd say. You know down the Seaport Museum? 'Member that time you took me down to the Seaport Museum? And we saw that ship was supposed to be a model of Christopher Columbus's? 'Member? And I said, man, people actually crossed the *ocean* in that thing? Well. This boat where I was?

(Where I *am!* Oh God, oh God . . .)

This boat where I was? It was like that, almost. It was almost like the *Niña.* Sort of. Or the *Pinta.* Kind of. The *Niña* or the *Pinta.* One of those guys. Or the *Santa Maria.* Like, it was like this wooden ship from, like, 1492—okay?

That'd be all right to say, wouldn't it?

How's *that* for specific, Mr. Peter Musik?

She'd been gawking like a rapt tourist (no! a reporter!), craning to see the masting and rigging (strictly for Peter, 'cause he'd be proud of her), and now, paying no attention to her feet, she stumbled up the last few stairs leading to—

Money thinking, Oh jeez, is this the main deck? the foredeck? the poop deck? What do *I* know from decks? Sorry, Peter!

—a *higher* deck.

Again, Mother's Last snatched her by the arm, saved her from a nasty spill. Soon as she felt steady again, though, she shook him off again, roughly.

Lifting her eyes, she flinched: half-a-dozen bare-chested sailors stood directly in front of her, blocking her way, and staring. All of them were of jockey height, but as prodigiously muscled as old-time smithies, and they all wore fingerless gloves, dark-gray balloon trousers cinched tightly just above their calves with coarse twine, and soggy footwear that resembled (absurdly resembled, Money thought) ballet slippers.

Once she'd recovered from her surprise, she kept her face immobile. And folded her arms across her breasts. Bunch of sailors? One bosomy blonde? Hey, she'd read her fair share of historical romance novels back in high school. The beautiful wench en route to Jamaica sometime in the 1700s? Captured by snarling, lustful pirates. Bad news.

She glanced sidelong: no land in sight to swim to. So forget that. She wasn't jumping overboard. At least not *yet*.

When Money looked back at the sailors, they were all moving aside, opening a passage for her, and that's when she saw him: a thin, almost scarily thin, man wearing a tall black hat with a curved brim and dressed in a long, paint-splashed black gown. His eyes, deep set, were all pupil, it seemed to Money, from where she stood; his complexion was sallow, slightly pitted. A long bony nose, and a ferocious moustache. Also black.

It struck her suddenly: this was the first man she'd

seen in Lostwithal with any sort of facial hair. (Peter Musik's protégé strikes again!)

He beckoned her to step forward.

She didn't move.

He crooked an eyebrow.

She pursed her mouth.

That's when Mother's Last nudged her gently in the spine, and whispered, "Be careful."

"Be careful," he said, "and be gracious. If you value your face and your form."

CHAPTER 20

THE HANDS
OF OUR MOTHERS

"... THEN WOMEN ..."

Dark forest. Tamaracks with scaly bark, needles dripping water. Girl-children with almond eyes, holding hands, slowly circling, then circling back the opposite way, a pool of clear water. The water churning, a soft-gray mist rising, drifting.

The children, in thin, sweet voices: "First water, then mist, then women. First water, then mist, then women. First water, then mist ..."

Lita stood watching. She had no particular expression on her face, till the robed and hooded figure beside her, grinning coldly, whispered, "Then women. *Then* men. *Then* misery."

Whereupon Lita frowned.

"I know the full sequence, Mother," she said, her eyes still fastened upon the children. "Teach *them*."

"Perhaps . . . not." Her mother's grin was suddenly distressed. Then, just as suddenly, gone. With her head, she gestured toward the trees behind them and then walked in that direction, shoulders hunched, hands in the pockets of her coarse brown robe. Lita followed.

Tremulous mist scattered.

"Daughter, I give thanks that you came," the old woman said presently.

And Lita smiled. Saying, "It is a great pleasure to visit the woman who bore me, when she wills it." Thinking, And too painful not to.

A burning in the knees, in the finger joints, a migraine, and a choking panic: Mother calling.

Lita saying now, "Is there a service I might render you?" Formal, showing the proper respect. But nothing more. She looked at her mother, then past her, toward a stand of hemlocks, and the mist there lifted, to reveal: Lita's apartment at Beybix. The white walls, the military cot, a low chest of drawers.

The front door opening, the Walker (her life!) standing on the threshold, frowning.

When Lita saw Jack tip his head quizzically, then call her name (his voice didn't carry into the forest), a fond smile drifted across her face.

"Lita. Lita, pay attention, girl. To me."

"I always—"

"No, you do not always. You do not ever. But you must now."

Lita nodding, continuing to stare at the Walker: as he moistened his neck with water from the basin, then lay down on the cot. But then he sat up again, immediately, looking puzzled.

"I'm listening."

And her mother said, "We made the world, child." Then, a trifle louder: "And lost it."

Lita winced. Was *this* why she'd so abruptly summoned her to the Mist? To jabber platitudes? And nurse old grudges against the House of Agel? *Again?* Lita could scarcely conceal her irritation when she said, "This is so.

This is truth." The proper response. Followed by a sip of breath, followed (properly) by: "This is sorrow."

Her mother nodding, saying, "The world was lost to us, and we lived. The Preserve became a prison to us, and we thrived. But now, child, I think . . ." For just a moment the old woman shuddered. A look—a wet light, a glint—of sheer animal terror flashed through her dark eyes. ". . . it is the end of everything."

Lita said nothing. But her knees felt weak.

"Last night we dreamed of it, and this morning the children all wept."

She withdrew both hands from her robe, and slowly held them up to her daughter's face.

Shapeless stumps glistened.

First water, then mist, then women.

We made the world, and lost it.

And in the end, the hands of our mothers will turn to mud.

"It is the end of time, Lita. The time of Last Humans."

When she reached, Lita recoiled, would not be touched, and shook her head in vigorous denial.

"Stay with us. You are *of* us, a Woman of Mist. Stay. You left us for the Walker, and we forgave you, but now you must return. To go with us into the Void."

"No!"

"Lita. Child. Listen!"

But she clapped her hands to her ears, and moved backwards, away. Then turned, stumbling, and ran toward the hemlocks, blood roaring in her head. Breath scalding her lungs.

And then she was gone.

JACK CAME AWAKE SUDDENLY, lurching up, feeling a damp chill, seeing, across the room, a swirl of semilucent mist. Then seeing: Lita staring back at him, breathing rapidly, raggedly.

Jack smiled. "So how's your mother? Still wish I were dead?" When she made no comment, he frowned.

"Where's Peter? Where's the girl?" And when *still* Lita made no comment, he stood up, saying, "What's the matter? What's—"

With a howl of wild anguish and despair, Lita flung herself against him.

CODA

MEMORY IS DRAINING OUT of him, and it's becoming hard even to think. A few blurred images (castle room, cradle, funnel of dust) and high, meaningless numbers that vibrate in flickers through his mind, then burst like Catherine wheels: Major Richard Forell standing naked on a beach, legs spread apart, urinating. Now hunkering down, idly stirring the wetted sand with the barrel of an automatic pistol.

It's so very hard to think. . . .

Cupping his hands, he scrapes together some light-brown mud, scoops it up and then daubs it on his sunburned cheeks, smears it across his forehead, and into his hair. Scoops more, slathers that on his throat. Then his legs and thighs. Genitals. Then across his chest, packing it over his heart.

Trying to think.

He remembers a . . . promise?

(spurt of numbers, in yellow flame)

Of what? Promise of *what?*

Squatted down like an ape, he whirls quickly, so quickly that he almost loses his balance. Sees dunes, high striated dunes. And the vast black lake. And on the lake: a small barge with a rounded cabin, drifting toward shore.

He watches it come, hears it crunch upon the sand, beaching itself. And waits for someone to appear from the cabin, but no one does.

Richard Forell steadies himself. His breathing is shallow, the odor of ammonia is strong in his nostrils, and he's trying to think. Where am—

(torrent of numbers, in bright green flame)

—I?

Promise of—

(green flame blowing out, fresh pale numbers)

Promise of what?

His mouth drops open, and he hauls himself to his feet.

Slogs down the beach, blinking, letting some vague instinct

(or memory?)

guide him, lead him, and he climbs a transverse dune, with great difficulty, and tops it, and looking down sees a crude shelter made of driftwood and beach grass and mud. Hive-shaped. With a fist-sized hole poked through the top, three perpendicular slits cut into its side.

Richard Forell stands there trembling and feels suddenly faint, too much sun, too much . . .

(thought?)

He lifts a hand to his head, staggers forward. Knees buckle. And now he's falling, tumbling fast, sand in his mouth. In his eyes, stinging.

He rolls to a stop, and his neck throbs, his shoulders burn, and—

There's a skeletal man in a black cassock crouched beside the shelter, his fingers laced together and his palms turned up, and his lips are moving, and he bows his head and lifts it. Again. And again.

Thick-bodied gray slugs writhe upon his face.

Major Richard Forell now drags himself upright, then kneels, aiming his eyes at the shelter. From inside it comes a wheezing growl.

(It's so hard to think, but)

He stays kneeling there in the merciless sun, flies buzzing around his head, mud baking upon his body.

(but I think)

(burning numbers numbers burning fiery numbers think I remember)

(infinite numbers burning)

(a promise of numbers becoming suns you will)

And he shivers, and his eyes become fixed, become glassy.

You will be there, Richard Forell, at the end of everything.

Said the man in the black cassock.

Promised the Mage of Four, Mage of Luck.

Part Three

ISLE OF MITES

JERE LEE

THIS TOWN? IT'S LIKE THE town in that movie, that old movie they show on television every Christmas—with James Stewart? The one where he wants to kill himself? Jump in the river? But this angel, this sweet codger of a guardian angel played by Henry Travers? Takes Stewart all around, shows him what a sadder world it'd be if he'd never lived. God, can anybody watch that movie and not have a good cry? I never could. I sure never could, I can tell you that. I bet I seen that picture a dozen times—and when my girls were little? We always watched it together. Donna Reed was in it. Played the wife. And she was never prettier. And now she's dead. In real life Donna Reed is dead—and, ah Jesus, Jere Lee, you big banana, don't. Oh don't. Don't. . . .

Now you've done it. Everybody's looking. That tiny woman all bundled up in the shiny blue parka? Those kids, who *were* throwing snowballs. That big husky red-headed man coming out of a corner drugstore, even the couple in the gray Volvo station wagon stopped for a light. Everybody's looking at you, staring at you—

(you silly big banana!)

—standing here on Main Street, bawling your eyes out.

Because Donna Reed is dead?

Yes, why not?

And because this town reminds you of that old black-and-white Jimmy Stewart picture, and because that Jimmy Stewart picture reminds you of your girls when they were little, and because—

He sent you back. Wouldn't have you. Your bald and homely (sweet and sour) magician wouldn't have you, didn't want you. You would've followed wherever he was going, flown away with him, sailed off with him into the sunset, but—

He didn't want you.

Wouldn't have you.

Master Squintik wouldn't have you.

One moment you're sweating bullets in Lostwithal.

The next, you're shivering like crazy here in—

Maine. Bangor, Maine.

Thank you, Master Squintik.

I don't know how you did it—

(don't know how you do anything)

—but thanks, at least, for sending me here, and not back to where you found me.

Bangor, Maine: a place I've never been.

But a zip code I know by heart: 04401.

A zip code . . .

"Miss?"

A leather-gloved hand on my arm.

"Miss?"

A stocky man with dark-green eyes, snow twinkling in his brown curly hair, in his eyebrows, on the fur collar of his bomber jacket. "You going to be all right, miss?" His voice steady, friendly. But the way that he's looking at me! Trying not to be too obvious about it, but he can't help it, can he? Poor dear. Looking at me like I might go suddenly berserk right here on Main Street, scratch out his eyes, claw at his throat, this crazy woman in a summerweight caftan and leather sandals, thong sandals in the falling snow, this crazy bawling woman.

And when I clear my throat, he drops his hand, and steps back quickly to join several other coated and sensibly booted men and women who've come from—wherever, to see what's going on. I give everybody a comic sort of shrug. At least I *hope* it's comic. Please God, don't let it be pathetic.

And I tell them all, "I'm fine. Excuse me."

But that doesn't do the trick, not quite: they keep ogling me, and I catch the sidelong glances they're exchanging among themselves now. I sure do. And know all too well what *those* mean. Any minute now, somebody's gonna slip away and call a cop.

So before these good people of Bangor can have me arrested (or worse, put me in the clutches of a social worker), I say, "Can someone please direct me to Farragut Place?"

There's just the slightest relaxation among them all now, but still—there's still a whole lot of Yankee suspicion.

Till I say, "That's where my daughter lives. I'm here to visit my daughter. Anne Marie Windling? Do you know the Windlings?"

Jaws drop. It's almost funny. Jaw, jaw, jaw, jaw: dropping.

"I've come to visit for Christmas. It *is* Christmas today—isn't it? Isn't it?"

Of course it is.

I've known that all along.

Somehow . . .

And now I'm waving good-bye to the nice young man in the bomber jacket who was kind enough to walk me here to Farragut Place (a very short walk, an amazingly short walk, it scarcely took any time at all), and I open the front gate and go up the walk, admiring Annie's big house: it's a real solid Andy Hardy kind of house with a wraparound porch strung with colored lights, a lovely Christmas wreath on the door. I can see the decorated tree through the steamed-up window: popcorn and garland and glass balls and tinsel and pinecones dusted with glitter, and a silver angel perched on top.

It's so beautiful that I—

I can't just barge in like this. What was I thinking?

Squintik should've sent me back where he found me; that's where I belong: camped out in a bus terminal. I don't belong here, he should never've sent me here. I'll ruin everything, I'll ruin their day, their Christmas. And I start to back away, quietly as I can, and the little voice startles me, saying, "Hello" with a big question mark.

And my granddaughter, who doesn't know me from a bowl of soup, who's seven, almost eight, and hasn't seen me since she was two, is standing at the foot of the porch steps, dressed in a Red Riding Hood coat, quilted pants, and a pair of shiny white snowboots. Her head cocked to one side. Her blond bangs. Her blue eyes. And Beth looks *so* much like Annie, when Annie was her age, and I don't want to stare, I'll frighten her. So I turn my head slightly, and squeeze my eyes shut, and smile.

An enormous brown dog comes scrambling around the side of the house, barking and spraying up powdery snow, charging straight at me. Oh dear God, he's gonna bite me! But little Beth shouts, "Bear, no! It's my grandma!" Then shouting, "Maaaa! It's Grandma! Grandma's here!"

And now I'm sitting in an overstuffed chair in the parlor (it's just *exactly* like the chair my dad used to have, his favorite one, it's even upholstered with the same white-and-red fabric: isn't that . . . odd), and there's a fire in the fireplace, and a log falls apart with a soft thump and a bright shower of sparks, and the tree lights are twinkling, gift boxes all around and torn wrapping paper, and Bing Crosby is singing "God Rest Ye Merry, Gentlemen" on the stereo. I could shut my eyes, could doze, could probably sleep for a week, but that's silly, I just got here. I want to talk to Annie, haven't seen her in so long, it's been so long, we used to be so close, but . . .

Things happen.

The record ends, and now I can hear voices, Annie's voice, and Harold's, and I get up and go out into the hall, and now there's a good smell, a turkey roasting in the oven. "Annie?" But nobody answers me.

Some framed black-and-white photographs hanging on the walls, and as I go past, I glance at them: a wedding picture of Annie and Harold, and several pictures of Beth, typical little girl poses, Beth in a gardening hat, Beth in footed pajamas, Beth posed against a studio backdrop.

And coming nearer the kitchen, I hear my son-in-law's voice, Harold saying in a loud, anxious whisper, ". . . just show up! I mean, my God!" He sounds annoyed, and I know at once that he's talking about me. Of course. And now Annie's saying, "She seems so disoriented. The way she just stared at me when she was on the porch! It's . . . sad."

Harold saying, "I don't want to be unkind, I *know* it's Christmas, but—*what is she doing here?* And the way she's dressed! Where on earth did she get that outfit?"

Annie going, "Sssh," when I appear in the kitchen.

Harold putting on a phony smile, adjusting his glasses, asking me how I feel—he even pulls out a chair from the table for me to sit down. "You sure you're feeling okay?"

"I'm fine," I tell him, taking the seat. Look through the back window, and there's Beth in the yard playing with two of her little friends. A half-finished snowman out beside a utility shed. It's a great big yard, it's a beautiful yard, and I say so, but they're both staring at me, Annie and Harold, just staring at me. Annie wearing a holiday apron, a Christmas corsage, an oven mitt on her left hand. Harold holds a carving knife. A carving knife.

"Mother," he says, "we're . . . so happy to see you, of course, but—we don't understand."

"No," I say, "I'm sorry." And then smile and say, "Well, you want to know what's going on? All right, I'll tell you, but . . ." I break off to look at Annie. Reach a hand toward her, but she doesn't take it. Won't take it. What was I expecting? A Frank Capra movie, really? It's a wonderful life in real life? Expecting Annie to forget all the bad times, all those years of living with a drunk for a mother? Just put it all away, forget it, start all over? Welcome me with open arms? Oh Mother, I love you? Was I expecting that?

Dream on, Jere Lee.

So I drop my hand, smile, look out the window again

at Beth, and say, "I really don't know where to begin. Should I begin with my living on the street, or should I—"

Annie and Harold exchange glances, then Harold lays the knife down on the counter. "The street? What're you telling us?"

"That I lost my job, that I lost my apartment, and was ill for a while—and I had no cushion. You never suspected?" Maybe I shouldn't have said that, it sounds so accusatory. But I don't mean it to, really. Honest. "I thought you might've . . . when I got that post office box."

"No! We just thought . . ." Annie shakes her head; she looks white. Comes and slips into the chair opposite me at the table. "Are you *still* . . . ?"

"No! Oh no! Well, I'm not living anywhere right now. But I've just come back from . . ." I roll my lips together, shake my head. Never mind. I'd have to be crazy to tell them about Lostwithal. A magician named Squintik? Sure. Right. They'd have me committed before I got to the part about the giant bats.

From a drunk to a bag lady to a psychotic.

No, thank you.

And it grieves me, not being able to tell my older daughter, my first born, what's been going on. That Mom had a big adventure. That Mom fell in love with a bald magician.

But we're really not connected anymore.

She wouldn't listen; she'd freeze and she'd stare.

And Harold would be on the telephone calling a hospital.

So I just say, "No, oh no—I'm not living on the street anymore. I have a nice little apartment. On a very nice street. And I have a job. I'm doing—fine. Just fine!" I stand up and inhale, look at the oven, rub my hands together. "That smells so *good!*"

And Harold says, "Mother Vance, how *did* you get here?"

"On a bus, of course." Saying that as I take a quilted potholder from a hook above the counter. And now I'm checking all the pots on the stove, picking up lids, peeking underneath: green beans, mashed potatoes, yams. The oven bell dings, and Annie says, her voice so cold, so unfriendly, Annie saying, "Mother, I'm sorry, but you can't stay. You don't belong here; you just can't walk into my house and—you just can't!"

Of course I can't. Of course I can't. I know that. My life is . . . elsewhere. I don't belong here, I know that, I belong with *him,* insane as that sounds.

"You don't belong here," says Annie, but I pretend I don't hear her. I was always good at pretending. At pretending my marriage wasn't a stinker, at pretending I could stop after one more drink, at pretending my daughters would still love me no matter what I did. I was always good at pretending.

"Mother," says Annie, "you don't belong here."

And in a bright festive voice, I say, "Let's have a look at that turkey, it smells so *good,*" and I pull open the oven door, and slide out the rack, and then stare in horror at the small wooden cradle with its monstrous infant, an infant of mud that opens its eyes, and its eyes are bright yellow bright yellow bright—

CHAPTER 1

◆

ARDOR

HERB DIERICKX WAS SIT-
ting outside the charcoal-maker's cottage, enjoying the
pink sunset. And the smell of smoldering wood, too,
which made him hanker suddenly for a cigarette, even
though he'd quit last year, spooked into it by a phlegmy
cough that just wouldn't go away. He'd had an awful time,
giving up his beloved Parliaments—life had seemed so
utterly pointless without nicotine.

But he'd got over it, finally, thanks to a clinic and a
hypnotist, lollipops and orange juice, and his wife Marge.
Her, most of all. Margie saying when he'd lose his temper
for the fifth time in two hours, "Hey toots, you wanna
smoke? Go ahead. But you smoke, you die. You die, I'm a
widow. I'm a widow, what am I supposed to do, sleep in a
cold bed the rest of my life? You die on me, Herb Dierickx, I'm getting married again. Think about it." And he
had. Herb had thought about it a lot.

Sitting outside now, he inhaled deeply and then exhaled: wood smoke didn't count.

Hey, Marge? Breathing in wood smoke doesn't count.

He smiled to himself, rolled his shoulders, stretched out his legs. Then he poked a finger between his ribs, amazed by how good he felt, how *recuperated.* Whatever the hell it was that Mithik had put into all those poultices, all those cups of tea? It had done the job. And then some. Sure, Herb still felt a tiny bit sore, a little beat up, but all of his aches and pains? Felt . . . old; that was the only way he could describe it to himself. It was as if what had happened to him had happened weeks ago, not yesterday. Same with the cuts and punctures and bruises. They looked two-weeks healed. At least.

Maybe the folks around here dressed and lived like people in a Robin Hood movie, but they sure knew a few things worth knowing. We got Bactine, we got Tylenol, we think we're hot stuff. We think we're so great. Herb talking to himself.

It was growing dark now, and there were fewer and fewer curiosity-seekers from Soolky wandering out here, stopping on the road to gawk. In fact, now that he thought about it, he hadn't seen anybody poking around in maybe half an hour. Well, that was kind of a relief. He didn't much like being the center of attention. It made him feel awkward.

The one time in his life—before this?—when he'd been a bona fide celebrity he'd thought he'd go crazy. That had been, oh, fifteen years ago, when he was working construction. No—no, it was actually seventeen years ago. He'd been thirty-nine.

What happened, a big crane had toppled over, smashed right into Forty-fifth Street, pinned a young woman. Could've easily chopped her in half, but—a miracle—it hadn't: instead, it trapped her under debris and crushed both her legs, but left her conscious. Herb had reached her first, and stayed. Holding the woman's hand and talking to her, saying anything that popped into his head, so long as it was positive, to distract her from what was happening.

It took hours to get her free, but even before then,

Herb had become the big cheese. On the eleven o'clock news, in all the newspapers. Two days later, the mayor gave him a medal. For what? What for? Talking to some poor, frightened woman? Jesus. *That's* being a hero? For days this went on, days and days of local celebrity. It drove him nuts. People stopping him on the street, shaking his hand. Or pointing: There he is, that's that guy. He felt so stupid, so awkward—and every time he was interviewed? His scalp started itching so badly it was like the world's worst case of dandruff. You could take being famous. You want it? Take it. As far as Herb Dierickx was concerned, he preferred to live a wallpaper life.

But now he was locally famous again.

And just like before, for no good reason.

Famous for having one heart instead of two.

For being from there and not here.

All afternoon, when the villagers had kept traipsing out here to point? Herb had suffered that terminal dandruff sensation, all over again. And, of course, he hadn't *scratched*, that would've looked real bad. They only would've figured he had fleas, or something worse, this stubby guy from another universe. Thank God, they'd all gone home for the night, were having supper, putting the kids to bed, whatever.

Now, he could hear Mithik moving around inside the cottage, could hear plates clattering, and something cooking start to burble, and here it came again, that gang of indescribable feelings, and a bright dizziness—the realization of where he was (not that he had any idea where the hell he *really* was) mixed together with a sense of loss that made him nauseated.

Marge.

Jesus Christ, I may never see her—

But he stopped himself: no. Don't think about it. Just . . . don't.

Instead, he glanced toward the cottage window, glimpsed Mithik carrying bowls and plates, brushing moisture from a cheek with her sleeve (like Marge always did).

When she noticed him staring, she smiled. "Do you have an appetite?"

"Yes!"

"Good. Then come inside and eat."

"I'm on my way." He stood up from the log chair and started toward the door. But then he stopped, seeing somebody come hurrying up the road. Oh Christ—another celebrity seeker?

No: the skinny Spellman who'd rescued him from the lake, the tall, gawky young fellow.

Pindrix raised a hand, waving, then veered off the road and cut through the yard behind the mound of glowing charcoal, his skirts swirling around his ankles. He seemed excited, extremely pleased with himself. Didn't say hello, just, "I went down to the crossroads. Three travelers passed by—I told them all about you." From the way Pindrix was beaming at him, Herb got the strong impression he was supposed to be equally delighted by this particular piece of non-news. So, to not offend, he nodded eagerly.

"Oh, it's you, Spellman." Mithik, wiping her hands in her apron, standing in the cottage door.

"Mistress!" said the Spellman, then repeated what he'd just told Herb. She gave an indifferent shrug, which had a crushing effect upon Pindrix.

"He is trying to turn you into a Rumor," she said to Herb.

"Not trying, Mistress—have! Three travelers!"

Herb stood there baffled. Making me into a what? A rumor? Is that good?

Pindrix shaking his head, gesturing emphatically. "King Agel hears all Rumors that circulate throughout Lostwithal. He will shortly hear of Herb, a Dierickx, and send a Walker."

Herb brightened. "A Walker! Maybe he'll send the one I know." Then, his smile slipping a little, he asked, "Is that the only way you people pass information? It's a little . . . undependable, don't you think?"

Mithik smiled. "I'm afraid it's our way."

Herb saying, "You're kidding, right? What about

messengers, what about—?" Then he stopped, and
cocked his head. Jesus Christ, what'd he want to do, make
these people *feel* bad? Who was he to criticize the way
they did things? Him, a guest. His mother would be
ashamed of him, if she could hear him. She'd always told
him, "Everybody doesn't do the same things we do, Herbert. Remember that, and never criticize. It's not polite."

These Lostwithalians wanted to circulate rumors instead of send a message, like normal people? Hey. Fine.
Who was Herb Dierickx to criticize?

So to get off the topic of rumors, he said, "I'm hungry. Whatever you got cooking, it smells just great!"

The three of them went inside. Pindrix hadn't been
invited to supper, but he parked himself at the table anyway—not that Herb was going to think any the less of him
for imposing.

Imposing!

There he went again, passing judgment.

Everybody doesn't do the same things we do, Herbert.

Herb smiling as he took his seat, smiling at the
gummy-looking stew that Mithik ladled into his bowl,
smiling at Pindrix who kept squeezing his left breast and
then wiping his sticky fingers on the sleeve of his cassock.
Herb Dierickx smiling his head off, trying to be polite.

Trying like crazy not to pass judgment.

But thinking nevertheless, Rumor? I'm a rumor?
Like, War is imminent? Like, Paul is dead? Like, Elvis is
alive and living in Florida? *That* kind of rumor?

MITHIK SERVED AN AROMATIC
red wine with the meal, and Herb found himself drinking
plenty of it. The stuff generated a nice soft buzz, kind of
like the buzz he got from that cheap Yugoslav merlot
Margie had started picking up at the Safeway last year
instead of the Bolla they'd been drinking forever. By the
time he'd finished his fourth glass, he was sitting there
with a dreamy smile on his face, and every crude piece of
furniture in the poky little hut seemed as cozily charming

as anything by Ethan Allen, and Mithik struck him suddenly as being quite beautiful (in a large-bodied way). Even the high-strung, scowling Pindrix, whose Adam's apple kept bobbing, seemed the nicest guy he'd met in ages —well, of *course* he was nice, he'd saved Herb's life!

Herb slung his arm around Pindrix's shoulder and gave him a hug.

The Spellman looked appalled.

"It's great to be alive," said Herb. "Who cares a fig about some old mud monster!" He reached for the bottle, then stopped, realizing that both Mithik and Pindrix were staring at him.

"What?" said Pindrix. "What did you say?"

"Nothing. Sorry." Herb abruptly decided that he'd had enough wine, and sat back in his chair. Now why'd you have to go and say that?

"*What* mud monster? Where have you seen it?" Pindrix had risen to his feet, and now glanced toward the door, as if he intended to race right out to the crossroads and circulate a new Rumor. Herb Dierickx of Kemolo has seen a mud monster. Pass it on.

Jesus, thought Herb. "I didn't see any mud monster. Okay? It's just . . . what the Cold Mage told me."

"Cold Mage!" exclaimed Pindrix.

And now Mithik was clucking. "Are you talking about the Epicene?"

Herb nodding, wishing he hadn't said anything.

Marge had always told him, Two drinks, Herb. Any more than two, you start acting stupid.

Mithik laughed, threw a chiding look at Pindrix, then began to collect the dinner bowls. Herb decided to help her, glad to do it, happy to escape the Spellman's stare.

But Pindrix wouldn't drop the subject, wouldn't let it go. He stalked Herb outside, stood over him while he scraped the plates and bowls into a pit then stuck them into a tub of water. Pindrix saying, "What do you know about the Epicene? Why are you here?" He was on the verge of panic, Herb could see it in his eyes. "Is the Epicene alive? The Epicene is alive, isn't it? Isn't it?"

"The Epicene," said Mithik "is a story."

"Then why is he here?" Pointing at Herb. "What is a Kemolon doing in our Moment?"

Mithik folded her arms across her ample bosom, piercing Pindrix with a stony glare (Herb thinking, Now *that's* a glare). "Every time a Kemolon comes to Lostwithal—does it mean we've got monsters running around? Well, does it? Haven't you ever seen a Kemolon before?"

"Well . . . yes," said Pindrix.

Herb thinking, He *has?*

"And so have I," said Mithik.

Herb thinking, *Really?*

"Do you remember the Circus of Kemolo?"

Pindrix muttered, "Yes. All right, all right! But this Herb, a Dierickx said he saw the Epicene!"

Herb saying, "No, that's *not* what I said."

"Well, what *did* you see?"

"Nothing!" Jeez, let's get off this, all right?

Pindrix snorted, and turned his back on both Mithik and Herb.

Back in the hut again, Herb felt stupid for having started such a hoo-ha. He didn't know what he was talking about anyway. Mud monsters. Ridiculous. Godzilla Meets the Mud Monster. Mud monster. *Mud* monster. The more you say it, the more ridiculous it gets. Herb thinking, Mud monster, mud monster. And don't forget your 3-D glasses. . . .

Herb was rubbing his chin, staring at the lamp on the table when Pindrix came back inside, looking abashed. "I'm sorry for my outburst." Then, to Mithik, who was taking down a glass filled with colored stones from a wall shelf: "But I don't know how you can be so sure it's a story."

She frowned. Put the glass on the table, then pulled a tube of thin leather from behind her bed. "You insult me, Pindrix! Do I look like a woman who'd belong to the Cult of the Cradle?"

"You don't have to belong to the cult to allow the possibility of a Fourth Moment."

Herb's ears pricked up: Fourth Moment. Right. He'd

heard that before. From the Walker. From Jack, a Walker, and from Squintik. Who'd also talked about a mud monster.

"Mages of court continue to debate its possibility—that doesn't make *them* cultists."

"Sit down and pick your color," Mithik told him, then smiled at Herb. "Our young Spellman has designs to go to court himself. He's too good for us villagers."

"I never said that!"

Herb clapped his hands together, said, "Now what're these stones all about?" Pointing to Mithik's glass, seeing if he could change the subject again.

Pindrix chuffed, but sat down in his chair and folded his arms petulantly.

The stones, as Mithik shortly pointed out, were could-stones, and the leather, unraveled, was a could-world, and you put them together and you had a game. Herb grinned—a game? really? Hey, neat. He'd always enjoyed board games, Monopoly especially—he and his dad used to play Monopoly a lot.

"I don't think I'm too good for you villagers," said Pindrix, refilling his wine glass. He drained it, filled it again. "And I hope you don't go around *saying* that! If I become a Rumor, *then* where will I be?"

"Certainly not at court," said Mithik.

And Pindrix sulked again.

Could, as Herb eventually gathered, though without much comprehension, was a game of possible fates within the Order of Things. (Oh? Uh-huh. O-kay!) You tossed stones—your "inclinations," Mithik said—across the board, which apparently was a stylized map of Lostwithal. Herb was interested in that, saying, "So where are we on the map?" and hearing Pindrix grunt disparagingly.

Mithik replied, "There are just the main roads, the lake, the Major and Minor Coasts, the Western Hills, and the capital city."

Herb shrugging, saying, "Okay." Then asking, "What are those?" His fingers jabbed at several different-colored diamond-shapes.

"Those," said Mithik, "are could-be's.

Ardor, Illness, Revenge, Travel, Generation, Talent.

Herb nodding, saying, "Why don't we just start the game; I'll pick it up as we go along?"

He never really did, though. He'd toss his stones, in imitation of Mithik and Pindrix, then wait to see what they said before he decided whether to smile or cluck. He simply couldn't figure out who was winning, or even how you might win in the end. When it got to the point of total mystification, he decided to hell with it, and started drinking again, joining Pindrix, who'd been drinking steadily since play commenced.

Suddenly, Mithik laughed at Herb's roll. "Finally," she said, "someone gets a fate."

Herb thinking, Oh really? No one's gotten a fate before now?

You could've fooled him.

He leaned over the leather board, waiting for somebody to tell him what fate he'd actually pulled.

Pindrix, who'd grown surlier than ever, grunted, "Ardor!" Then he laughed in a way that Herb took as mean-spirited. "Better watch out," Pindrix added. "Every time a Kemolon knows ardor, his mother's field burns to ashes."

Herb blinked at that one. Mother's field burns to *ashes?*

"Too-humans squander their ardor. Read the Book of True and Cruel," said the Spellman. "They squander it."

Mithik, with an arched eyebrow: "Unlike Lostwithalians, who horde it till it sours."

"Speak for yourself, woman!"

"Roll," she told the Spellman. And looked at Herb with narrowed eyes and a lissome smile.

For a moment, Herb's stomach folded in upon itself, and his scalp prickled.

They continued to play for another hour, but Herb had lost all interest in the game and merely rolled whenever he was told to. Pindrix, however, played with renewed interest, energy, competitiveness. And it seemed to Herb (though he felt he could easily have been mistaken) that the Spellman kept trying to pitch his stones so they would tumble near, or land directly upon, the blue Ardor diamond.

But none of them even strayed close.

At last, Mithik collected up all the stones (had Herb missed something? had the game ended? who'd won?) and dropped them back into their glass. She rolled up the leather playing board.

Pindrix, who'd been staring at her intently, turned suddenly to Herb, and said, "You will go outside, please. I would speak privately with Mistress Mithik."

Herb was ready to oblige at once, but Mithik put a hand on his shoulder. "Pindrix, I'm afraid, takes the game too seriously. And his life not seriously enough."

"You insult me *again*, woman!"

Herb looked from the Spellman to the charcoal-maker, not having the foggiest idea of what was going on *now*. (Everybody doesn't do the same things that we do, Herbert.) He nodded to them both, then stepped outside.

Man, there were more stars in the sky than he'd ever seen before. He put his head back so far and stared up so long, so raptly, that he got a bad crick, and became slightly dizzy.

Then he heard a loud *whump*.

And when he turned and looked, he saw Pindrix through the window; his left arm was extended, and there was a kind of pink-white cloud enveloping his hand. When the cloud vanished, a bright blue jewel lay in his palm.

The Spellman said something too indistinct for Herb to hear, or even to get the gist of.

All that he heard for certain was the word "ardor."

Then Mithik, whom he couldn't see, laughed.

And the blue jewel in Pindrix's hand turned to a dark-yellow goo that ran off the sides of his palm like egg yolk.

The Spellman exclaimed in outrage and misery.

Mithik stepped into view, looking apologetic.

She lifted a hand and touched the Spellman's cheek, almost tenderly.

Herb started to turn away; jeez, he didn't want to be

a voyeur—talk about being impolite. Before he could, though, he saw the Spellman reach and fondle one of Mithik's breasts, doing it as awkwardly as a fourteen-year-old boy. And with the gooey hand, no less.

She hauled off and cracked him once, hard, across the face.

A moment later, the Spellman came flying out of the cottage, stumbling, and ran past Herb, his eyes bugged in abject humiliation, his right cheek bright red.

Herb thinking, Mom? I think you were wrong.

CHAPTER 2

JERE LEE FINDS
HER COURAGE

I**T TOOK JERE LEE VANCE A**
long time to shake off the dream. She wasn't sure if she'd
woke up groaning, but it wouldn't have surprised her if
she had. A cradle in the oven. Mother of God. A cradle in
her daughter's oven, and that *thing* in it! Sweet mother of
God.

It was nighttime, and Jere Lee was sitting on a
rough-hewn bench in the cavernous hold of a wooden
ship. Some kind of passenger ship or—even a ferry? It
was crowded with travelers. A hundred? Two hundred
people? Hard to tell, too many to count. And it was dim,
almost dark—a few smoky lanterns cast a flickering, anemic light. Very crowded, very dim—very damp. And the
air was foul, close. What am I *doing* here?

And then, with a blast of panic, she sat up, startling a
young woman beside her. She half-stood, straining to peer

through the gloom, swiveling her head from side to side, biting deep into her underlip.

There.

Tingling with relief, she dropped heavily back onto the bench.

He was still standing over there, by a door. *The* door. Just where she'd last seen him, before she'd relaxed and dropped off to sleep.

Master Squintik looked as though he might be sleeping himself. His eyes were closed, his head was tipped back against the bulkhead, his mouth was partly open. To Jere Lee, he certainly didn't look like an important magician at the moment. Dressed in those baggy trousers and that shabby shirt, he looked anything *but* important. Even his exceeding height gave him no distinction down here. Nearly half the other men she'd seen so far were nearly as tall. No, without his cassock, Master Squintik resembled any ordinary almost-old man. His hands, which Jere Lee had seen wield such powerful magic, were veiny and wrinkled, unhealthily white as lard, and as he rested they twitched and clenched almost spastically. Jere Lee was reminded of her grandfather, and didn't wish to be. That *wasn't* the idea. Or the attraction.

"Are you hungry, mistress?" From the young woman, beside her. She was bent over, loosening the neck of her traveling sack, withdrawing a round crusty loaf of bread. She offered it to Jere Lee.

"Thank you, yes. I'd love a piece."

"Take the loaf."

"Oh no. Just a small piece."

But the woman pressed the bread into Jere Lee's hands. "I have no need of it." She was slight, very thin, with short-cropped hair that reminded Jere Lee of Mary Martin's in *Peter Pan*—only Mary Martin's had been dirty-blonde, and this woman's hair was bright orange. And frizzy. And her skin was gray. Racially gray. There were heavy pouches, dark circles, below her eyes, and her lips seemed dry, abnormally shiny. And she was trembling. Poor thing, thought Jere Lee.

"I'm sure you'll have need of it," said Jere Lee,

breaking off a piece of bread, giving her back the rest of the loaf. "I mean, we have quite a trip ahead of us—don't we?" Doing a little detective work, seeing if she could find out where the heck the ship was bound. Not that any port of destination would mean a blessed thing to *her*. Jere Lee repeating, *"Don't* we?"

But the woman only smiled, shrugged vaguely, and turned away. End of conversation.

After she'd finished her little snack, Jere Lee brushed crumbs from her lap, then stood up again to check on Master Squintik.

Still there.

Still oblivious that she'd followed him.

Which had been quite a feat.

Try following an owl through a city sometime. Just try it. Even an owl as big as the one that Squintik had become.

Running blindly, with her face to the sky. It was a miracle she hadn't killed herself. Couple of times she'd nearly collided with some peddler's cart; once she'd even run smack into a wall, bounced, and then kept right on going, loping along for the next several blocks with her nose gushing blood. She'd tried to imagine what she looked like, and the picture she got was almost comic, she'd almost laughed: this lunatic woman running (and occasionally galumphing) after a big white owl. Like the owl on her dad's cigar boxes, only not so fluffy.

If Squintik the owl had gone much farther, she couldn't have kept up. As it was, Jere Lee was in pretty ragged shape, and missing one of her sandals, by the time that he—that it—that he! spread wings and glided down, and down, disappearing behind a long warehouse building on a bustling lakefront street.

It was so much more difficult to negotiate the crowds there—so much tumult, a hurly-burly of maritime activity. She'd gone that far, however, so she'd persisted, pushing, shoving, elbowing, and trying to make her way to the warehouse. She was almost certain that she'd lost him, though—and didn't want to think about what *that* might mean. Could she retrace her route to Dwindling Street?

Unlikely. Jere Lee thinking it'd be some irony—wouldn't it?—if she ended up a street person in Lostwithal, homeless in Beybix?

Some irony, all right. Oh yeah. Great. Tell it to Ripley.

She'd felt the first pricklings of a panic attack, and then her heartbeat accelerated, then her mouth went dry, and then—

She'd spotted him.

No longer an owl: himself.

Though still dressed in baggy trousers and a frayed white blouse.

He was about a hundred yards ahead of her on the cobbled street and was coming directly toward her. She'd stepped behind several huge blocks of salt and let him pass, then followed him again along the chaotic lakefront, reflexively glancing off at the sailing vessels and barges moored at the long quays, but then glancing right back ahead of her, not wanting to lose track of Squintik for more than two or three seconds at a time.

And she was thinking, she couldn't help thinking, of all those boys she'd had crushes on in her late girlhood— how she'd followed them, not just Carl Timm, but other boy's, too, before and after Carl. Oh, she'd been quite an amorous character, she'd had quite a reputation.

She'd followed Squintik into a cavernous building with hundreds of men and women and small children milling around below a high glass roof. The building was open on the lake side and connected to a long wharf from which an ungainly, extraordinarily wide sailing vessel was just then drifting away. With pleasure, Jere Lee watched its bleached sails unfurl, catching the breeze, and sunlight dazzle across its fittings and brassy masts.

Master Squintik had ambled around till he'd found a bench, and sat down.

From twenty yards away, Jere Lee kept her eye on him.

She'd kept her eye on him for three hours. Till another ship appeared at the wharf, for boarding.

She'd kept telling herself to go over to him, present

herself, declare herself. Say to him, What's going on? I
thought we were friends. Why'd you treat me so bad?
What's going on? Can I help you? Let me help.

She knew exactly what she wanted to say to him,
even knew the particular tones of voice she'd use to say it,
but she didn't go near him. Just kept watch.

Wanting to go to Squintik, but staying put.

Because? She was scared.

Scared? Of what, Jere Lee, of what? Of what? she
kept asking herself. Scared of what?

Being rejected. Of being told that she'd misunderstood the . . . situation. Of being told there *was* no situation.

Some people never change, no matter how old they
get. Or which universe they happen to find themselves in.
Do they?

NOW IT WAS THE MIDDLE OF THE
night and she was sitting in a sail-powered ferry boat, and
all around her people were fast asleep, including the
young woman with the orange hair and the gray skin
who'd given her the loaf of bread. Jere Lee was wondering if she should try to fall back to sleep herself. It would
take her mind off her thirst and her full bladder, and
besides it wasn't likely that Squintik was going anywhere.
And even if he did, even if he . . . flew away again, well,
Jere Lee couldn't very well follow him now, could she?
Not out here in the middle of this gigantic lake, she
couldn't.

As she was squirming around, trying to get comfortable, a crew man came in and walked around extinguish-
ing lanterns. All but one. The one hanging by the door.

She watched him leave, and then got hypnotized,
sort of, staring at the quivering flame in the glass chimney,
recalling the long-ago August when she and her husband
and their girls had rented a house on a lake in Vermont.
Primitive place, no plumbing, no electricity. Just lanterns.
She'd read the kids all of the Narnia books that summer,
read them Narnia by lantern-light. And now she fell to

thinking about those books, remembering Aslan the lion, and how sad the story ultimately was, and how Karen had wept when the last novel was finished, and Anne Marie had been so outraged that the children had died. . . .

Suddenly Jere Lee sat up straight.

Master Squintik, his face illumined by lantern-light, opened the door and went out, up the stairs and onto the deck.

He's going to fly away!

And leave me here in this low-rent Narnia.

She was standing before she'd even thought about whether she wanted to stand or not. And then, stepping very carefully, she moved across the passengers' hold, reached the door, paused a moment, then opened it and went up onto the deck.

She could hear the rigging thrum, and several sailors talking in low voices, somewhere. Above her, in the inky darkness, a full moon shone and a crescent one glimmered. She stood very still, hearing the deck creak beneath her, feeling the ship plough sluggishly through the lake.

Then: a beating of wings, and with a pang Jere Lee glanced up, expecting to spot the white owl, but it was just a gull, a filthy thing. And she sighed again with relief, and dropped her eyes, and then saw Squintik.

He was crouched down near the bow, facing away from her.

A mist veiled his back and shoulders.

She approached him slowly, timidly.

You followed him here, so talk to him.

Jere Lee telling herself, Do it.

Find your courage.

But he'll laugh if you tell him what's really on your mind.

Yeah? How do you know?

Or become angry. Again.

But you won't know till you show yourself, will you? So do it. You silly big banana.

Jere Lee talking to herself, coming nearer the mage,

wanting to clear her throat, but thinking, No, that's too obvious.

She halted just a few feet behind him, and slightly to one side. He was hunched down, the mist curling all around him. A skin of ice on his throat.

Jere Lee struggled to swallow.

When he leaned back, a little, she saw it, and her eyes opened wide.

There on the ship's deck was a cathedral-shaped block of ice, the size of a papier-mâché mountain in a model-railroad world. Seated, sleeping, in its hollow—its grotto—was the tiny figure of an old man. His face was deeply lined, the skin so puckered it looked mummified. He was dressed in a mage's black cassock, but the cassock was threadbare. His hands, crossed at the wrists, lay in his lap.

When Squintik spoke suddenly, it caught Jere Lee so by surprise that she yelped in falsetto.

He didn't notice.

"Wake! Hear me now and wake!"

But the old man in the ice cave didn't stir.

Squintik reached a hand toward the ice, and his hand went through it. "Wake! Teacher, awake! Your pupil's pupil is coming to destroy you."

For a moment, it seemed that the ancient man was stirring. His hands moved, slightly. His eyelids fluttered.

But then his head shifted, chin sliding to chest, and the ice block abruptly hazed over, and vanished.

The deck ran with meltwater.

Squintik moaned in frustration and clenched his fists. Then he became aware of Jere Lee, and whirled around.

She stepped backwards, afraid.

Their eyes locked.

Squintik sagged, but then a tired smile crossed his face.

"The kindly woman," he murmured, rising to his feet and taking both of Jere Lee's hands in his. "The kindly woman!"

Jere Lee saying, "So does this mean you're happy to see me?"

CHAPTER 3

REPORTER'S NOTEBOOK (I)

I'M WRITING THIS (PETER wrote) *on the back of one of Gene Boman's Chase bank checks: paper is paper is paper, and I'll take what I can get. There are fifty checks altogether—those, plus the register, should give me plenty of room for notes and impressions, if I write tiny. Which ain't gonna be easy, bouncing up and down in this cramped and crowded John Ford-style stage-coach. Oh: and it's a pretty cool pen. Also GB's. 14-karat gold-plated. Cross. The glitzy kind they advertise in The New Yorker. So I'm all set! And considering that I haven't slept in two days, and that Money's been shanghaied (what the hell's an art-prince?) and that my kidneys are being smashed, I'm feeling pretty good. Things are gonna work out. See what happens when you give me a pen and some paper? My whole outlook changes.*

GENE BOMAN'S NOSE WAS STILL tender, and it was swollen, but he didn't think it was broken. Not that he cared terribly much. If his nose—which he'd always considered an ugly blob anyway—was broken, it was broken. He had more important things to consider. For instance: just what the hell was going *on?*

Before opening his eyes and seeing that big nude painting of Money Campbell on a wall, and then being clocked for his art criticism, the last thing he could remember with any clarity at all was being lost in a castle straight out of Bela Lugosi's *Dracula.* Christ, just thinking about that place again, he got all shaky.

(Peter Musik looking up from his writing, quirking his mouth, and staring with revulsion at Gene Boman seated across from him in this bumpety-bump stagecoach, staring till Boman clasped both hands together in his lap, to stop his trembling.)

Boman thinking, That castle. Then thinking, Richard? What happened to Richard? Where's the Major?

And then it *really* came back to him, all of it, and all in a gush, and he tried to dam it. But then he thought, No, let it come. Time to let it come.

It's time, Eugene, to get your shit together.

And he remembered driving alone to the horse farm, meeting Richard there, Richard babbling about his amazing discovery: *The drug, Eugene, the drug!* Richard had actually ingested one of the Idiot Drugs, and it had deformed his left hand, horribly: claws. Long sharp claws. And with them, his father-in-law had torn a gash in the air, and they'd gone through it, Richard exultantly, Gene reluctantly. Come out in a forest, and then found that castle . . . a small black castle with walls that shimmered, seemed greasy. And Richard had forced him to go inside, prodded him, threatened him, and inside—inside they'd seen that . . . man. Dressed like a priest, whose face was covered with—

(Boman groaning again, involuntarily, and Peter Musik glancing up again, his gaze now stony, now supercilious; and the other man riding with them, the tall, broad-chested wrestler-type in the red tunic and white crossbelt tipping his head quizzically, then saying something to Peter Musik in a sibilant language Gene Boman couldn't understand.)

—covered with wet slugs. And the Slug Man in the black cassock had stared at Richard almost as if he'd recognized him, or *expected* him . . . and as Gene Boman stood there, rooted, in abject terror, his insane father-in-law had walked off with the Slug Man, the two of them disappearing up a staircase. And when Boman had found his voice again, he'd screamed, his scream echoing again and again. He'd tried to follow them, but they went into a room and shut the door, and then Gene had started to run, trying to escape—

Christ, it was the worst experience of his life, being lost in that castle. The worst, and yet . . . He'd almost welcomed it, relished it, it had seemed so *deserved*.

He was being driven insane with terror, and it was exactly what he deserved.

For having said yes, for so long, to Richard Forell; for being blackmailed into giving all those wild-card pharmaceutical drugs to a man who was clearly insane, who intended to use them for his own political and personal agendas.

Boman lost in those corridors, expecting to stay lost forever, expecting to die. Trying to remember childhood prayers, unable to. A rush of words without order, lacking sense. Gene Boman was alone in another world, alone in a nightmare. And then he'd heard, and felt, an explosion.

(Gene Boman looking up now, studying Peter Musik, Peter still bent over, writing, writing on the back of a check.)

An explosion in the castle. Then soldiers. And among the soldiers, a man he recognized. A man he'd tried once to destroy, a man he'd filled with so many Idiot Drugs that his memory had been erased.

Peter Musik. In that castle, he'd seen Peter Musik, coming toward him.

Gene Boman could remember that. Now. But nothing else. Peter Musik in the castle, then—a mural of Money Campbell, in an alley.

And now here he was, riding in some kind of coach, and Peter Musik was seated opposite him.

But, except for punching him, Peter had ignored him, pretty much—had, in fact, treated him as though he were more than just slightly retarded. Or senile. Explanation? Well, Boman wasn't sure, but since he had zero recollection of anything that had happened since he'd glimpsed Peter in that castle, it was entirely possible that he'd . . . wigged out. Gone into shock. And while he was very much aware of his surroundings now, he was thinking that it was probably wise, for the time being, to maintain a certain zombie demeanor. Till he could figure out the situation.

Gene Boman lifted his eyes again. Peter was still writing. The guy in the red tunic was staring out the window. So Boman looked out there, too: what he saw, through a bunch of trees, seemed like the world's largest oil spill. A *lake* of oil.

God, where the hell *am* I?

And why was there a nude mural of Money Campbell painted on a wall in another world?

Jesus, this was insane.

Or maybe just him . . .

                                    . . . *I STILL FEEL*
funny going off without Jack (Peter wrote), *but Ukrops said we couldn't wait around—that weird Finder guy is on the case, and where he goes, we have to go, if we want to find Money. (What is an art-prince?)*

Anyhow, when Zickafooz set out like some kind of bloodhound, Ukrops said we had to get going, too. I picked GB off the ground (that's when I discovered that his checkbook had fallen out of his coat, and confiscated it), and off we went, all of us Merry Spacemen. Zickafooz seemed to know where he was headed, and I got excited, thinking that we'd catch up with Money soon (what is an art-prince?), but I was soon disappointed.

We walked through the city (I wonder, Am I ever going to sleep . . . or eat again?), ended up down at the lake. All these huge barges, wooden ships, long quays. Zickafooz just stood there staring out over the water, then told Ukrops that the woman we wanted had left Beybix by ship. So I figured (who wouldn't?) that we'd try to follow her the same way, but no. Z just told Ukrops to rent a carriage or a coach. I tell U, I think that's crazy, but U just gives me more of that Order of Things crapola.

I'm starting to get the feeling that Lostwithal is kind of a tight-ass place.

So we end up at a stable (it belongs to some relative of Sollox's—what is a sur-brother?), and we hire this coach. Four of those gigundus green horses (the only kind they got here, I think) and we take off (minus the Finder's dog), leaving the city by the same entrance where I arrived with Jack and GB earlier today, taking the same sand road that skirts Black Lake. And that's the situation so far. I'm riding inside with Ukrops and Boman, who's still in diz-city, blank-faced and twitchy. Sollox is driving, and (speaking of twitchy) Zickafooz is riding up top with him. I don't know where we're going, but every so often, we stop, and Z climbs down and walks over to the water and just stares.

Last time he did that, he got all excited when he spotted a ship with square sails way out in the middle of the lake. He ran back to the coach, and we took off again.

The ship, just for the record, kind of looked like one of those 1492-when-Columbus-sailed-the-ocean-blue jobs.

CHAPTER 4

WALKER'S WAIT

RAMPIKE, A RECITER——AND the Prime Minister of Lostwithal——mumbled to himself, slowly rolled several could-stones between his gloved hands, then released them. The tiny yellow stones——bits of gravel——bounced across a leather sheet that was spread open upon his desk. Three corners of the sheet were weighted down with identical blue globes, the fourth with a small glass disk about two inches thick and blemished with spidery cracks.

After the stones came to rest, Rampike studied their configuration, did a few quick sums in his mind, then clenched his teeth——they clicked. He exhaled slowly.

There was a knock at the door.

"Yes?"

A small and wiry man with iron-gray hair and dressed in the dull-green costume of a confidential secretary entered and bowed with flawless precision. "He is here, Prime Minister."

"I'll see him." Rampike, gathering up his stones, jiggling them in his left palm, pulling open a desk drawer and tossing them in. He frowned then, seeing that his secretary had not gone away.

"He is accompanied by the witch Aculita."

"I'll see them both."

"Very good, Prime Minister. Though I should mention . . . she seems distressed."

"Intelligent woman. Show them in, Wid."

"At once," said the secretary, and bowing again, withdrew.

Rampike peeled off his game gloves, folded them together, and tossed them onto his desk. He was rolling up the could-sheet into a tube when the door opened again, and Wid, in stentorian voice, announced, "Jack of Sett, a King's Tramp." Then, scowling, eyes darting sideways, but his voice just as booming: "And Aculita, a Witch of Perfect Order." He moved aside. Lita entered first (which she ought not to have done), followed immediately by Jack, a Walker.

They both arrived themselves at the table which stood to the left of the entrance, dipping fingers into a shallow ceramic bowl then sketching wet loops upon an iron sphere. Finished, they bowed. Rampike nodded. The secretary left.

"He wants to see you," said the Prime Minister (and remembering that he still was holding the could-sheet, tossed it down).

"It would seem, Prime Minister, that Rumors are not what would concern His Majesty at this juncture."

Rampike filled his cheeks, blew out his breath. Then, saying, "I'll take you to him," he crossed the room, pulled the door open, and stepped out.

Jack, squeezing Lita's elbow, then touching her hair.

Lita, pulling her fingers apart, and staring down at them mournfully. Then clenching them, in sudden terror.

She'd told him about her mother's hands.

And he'd spent the afternoon and all of this evening —till the arrival of the Castle Dog—trying to console her.

There hadn't been much he could say, though.

*   *   *

IN THE CASTLE GALLERIES, IT was bedlam—mages of court had gathered, were conferring among themselves, and arguing loudly; their voices rang, ricocheted. As Rampike wove his way through them, head down, jaw set, they plucked at his sleeve, grabbed at his arms, pushed their faces directly into his. "When is the debate to begin?"

"Prime Minister, the debate!"

"The debate!"

"—demand!"

". . . according to the Order of Things!"

"—Agel's summons?"

"Prime *Minister!*"

Rampike shook off the grasping hands, pried away the fingers, and pressed on down the corridor.

Jack and Lita, twenty feet behind him, hurried to keep up.

The Walker kept glancing around, hoping to glimpse Squintik. The Cold Mage was unaccountably absent, but —over there, in that nook: Master Amabeel. Jack moved to speak with him, but he shook his head firmly.

With a frown, Jack continued on, Lita taking several steps to his one, and caught up to Rampike at the end of the long central gallery, where two Red Guardsmen were posted on opposite sides of a doorway that was canted slightly to the left. Rampike, stepping forward, a tired smile playing on his lips: "I trust you can find your way from here."

Jack nodding, then turning to Lita, who looked suddenly ill.

How she hated to make the transformation!

But she could go no farther, as a witch.

Only as the Walker's wasp.

The two Guardsmen, trained not to flinch, flinched when Lita started to flicker. Then her clothes fell in a heap, and a long, thin-waisted wasp, wings quivering, flew up.

The Walker shoved back his left shirtsleeve, exposing

a dark bracelet, and the wasp fitted herself into its single notch.

Fetching Lita's clothes, and with a parting nod to the Prime Minister, Jack passed through the doorway, ascended a flight of stone steps; one torch burned and smoked in a wall fixture.

At the top was a narrow landing, and a door painted green. It had no doorknob. Jack raised both hands and pressed them flat against a panel; he felt a cold jolt as the door opened.

Then he entered Walker's Wait.

It was a large, high-ceilinged room, the floor covered with a woven carpet, its skeins multicolored and meandering. Set around the carpet were a half-dozen highly polished wooden chairs. Standing against a wall, a small table. Upon it, several cruets filled with a dark-brown liquid, and six pewter goblets. Jack strode across the carpet, plucked the stopper from one of the cruets, and filled a goblet. He raised it to his lips, closed his eyes, and drained it.

A shudder passed through him.

And when it had, a roar like an ocean storm sounded in his head, subsided, becoming a sough, then a sibilance, and behind the sibilance: a multitude of voices.

Replacing the stopper in the cruet, he turned and crossed the carpet and sat down in one of the chairs. His eyelids were growing heavy, a small headache had lodged itself between his eyes. He willed away a queasiness at his stomach.

He sat in the room's quietude, hearing Walker's Noise.

Time passed, but he had no way of reckoning how much.

Eventually, he became alert, and fixed his eyes upon a silver door opposite the green one. Hearing a squeak, and a thrum of wheels.

When the door opened, Jack stood, and Sad Agel, in white capelet, black tunic and trousers, but shoeless, was wheeled into the room in a wicker invalid's chair. The king's eyes were all pupil, his hands, crossed at the wrists, lay in his lap.

Behind him, pushing the chair, a young page, a Doveflesh boy.

Page and Walker recognized each other at the same time; the boy's eyes narrowed in hostility, the Walker's remained steady, neutral.

Rolling Sad Agel to a spot in the center of the carpet, the page bowed. Without a side glance, the King of Lostwithal, lifted a hand and touched the boy's cheek, affectionately. The boy shot Jack a malevolent parting glance, then, stepping carefully, he moved backwards (his lips pursing as he counted his steps) to the door. He disappeared into the corridor.

The door shut with a soft click.

Walker's Noise was building in volume, splitting into discreet sonances and clamors—a crowd's roar over there, by the cruet table; a loud whisper, in that corner; a cry of pain, below Jack's chair. Agel's eyes lifted, narrowed, slid sideways, then fixed upon Jack, who recognized the expression. He moved slowly forward, then went around behind the invalid chair, and took hold of the handgrips. Agel nodding to his left, Jack pushing the chair, till the King raised a hand.

Agel cocked his head, attentive. His left arm shot out, fingers spread wide—fingers snapped closed. He held his fist to his ear, listened for a moment, then raised his arm. Jack bent to it, and the King opened his fingers.

A stableman, as he chewed his midday meal, to his wife; the wife at market to a fishmonger; the fishmonger to his son as they scrubbed their stall: *A Finder left Beybix by coach, to seek a too-human from Kemolo*.

Jack's eyes rolled as the mingling voices rose toward the ceiling, and grew faint.

"But the Epicene, my liege. What Rumors—"

Agel cut him off with a curt nod, then pointed, and Jack rolled the chair farther across the carpet. Halting when the king nodded. Agel leaning forward, his shining black eyes fixed on a dark gray whorl in the weave. His left arm dropped, swung lazily, and then his open fingers —snapped shut.

Fist to his ear.

Then he raised it again to the side of Jack's head. Fingers opened.

Girl-child to girl-child to girl-child to a young shepherd, who met a taxman, who told a boatman. Who told his daughter.

The witch-mothers of the Preserve have useless hands of mud.

Jack saying, "It is not Rumor, I have—"

And was stopped once more by His Majesty's sharp look.

Jack continued to wheel Sad Agel from place to place upon the woven carpet, the king catching Walker's Noise like winged insects, sharing Rumors with Jack: of living men and women whose souls had abandoned their bodies; of a small, trembling pythoness whose voice changed timbre with each syllable that she uttered; of a man dragged bleeding from Black Lake, near Soolky.

Agel saying, "Interesting. We find these Rumors interesting."

Jack nodding, agreeing (according to the Order of Things), but thinking, What of the Epicene, what Rumors of the Dark Mage? Saying nothing.

"All these Rumors," said Agel, "we find most interesting. Would you Ramble to seek their provenance?"

"I would Ramble gladly," said Jack. Thinking, But I would rather walk to seek out Rumors of the Epicene, who would destroy us all.

The King's tranquility in the face of Plenary Chaos struck awe into the Walker's hearts. Also (and he reproached himself for so feeling) infinite irritation.

"Be still, Jack."

The King nodded again, and Jack rolled the chair several feet farther, toward the edge of the carpet. Agel sat back and sighed.

"We are aware," he said, "that Perfect Order is in danger of being destroyed." Looked up at Jack, looked away. "We are aware that all human worlds are in jeopardy. We are fully aware. But as the vessel of Perfect Order, we must proceed accordingly. We have consulted with our council, we have engaged eleventh-degree Finders. We are to see our mages of court momentarily."

The King frowned, then adjusted his lap robe.

"And we are greatly pleased with the Walker from Sett. Who must still be fatigued from the ordeal he so eloquently described to me last evening."

"I am not fatigued, Your Majesty. If you would have me seek provenance for you, I am ready to set out, aimless at first. But I would also—" He stopped.

"You would also? Finish."

"My lord, I would also be glad to do whatever I can to seek out the Mage of Four, Mage of Luck."

"But you are not a Finder. A Finder is beneath you. We would insult you were we to ask you to participate in such a direct quest."

"In time of chaos . . ."

The King's face darkened. "Chaos is not upon us yet, Walker."

"My lord," he said by way of apology.

"No, we could not send a Walker in such a pursuit. Even though we mark with pleasure and appreciate your willingness to help Lostwithal in this time of its distress. To send you on such a pursuit would be a violation of Perfect Order. A Walker is moving, but ever passive."

"Yes, my lord."

"The instincts forged in your mother's womb and refined at Walker's Craft are too fine for direct pursuit."

"My lord."

"And as we have both heard here, there are many Rumors your King finds most interesting."

"My lord."

"Any one of them would, we feel, merit a Ramble, and bring honor upon you at Ramble's End."

"My lord." Jack's body was trembling with impatience (which it ought not to have done); he squeezed his elbows to his ribs. His mouth had gone dry long ago. All that my-lording.

The King stared for an uncomfortably long minute

into Jack's face, then cast down his eyes again, to the carpet. A thin voice rose from its tight weave. Agel's arm shot out, a blur, and snatched at Walker's Noise. He stared at his fist, grimly, then lifted it to his ear, cocked his head.

Jack swallowed, his eyes never leaving the King's white fist.

And when it was offered to him, he bent toward it.

The King's hand opened, and the Noise rushed into the Walker's ear, startling him.

Even though a fifth-degree Walker should not have been surprised by anything, he stared at Sad Agel in astonishment.

A Scatterer named Dio telling a gravedigger of his acquaintance about a mage he'd seen on Dwindling Street, a mage upon a rooftop, a mage who'd caused a sleet to fall, then become a great white owl.

"A curious Rumor," said the King.

Jack's heart was racing.

"We are puzzled," said the King with a frown of concentration. "We are curious."

Jack tried hard not to smile.

At the same time, he trembled with anxiety.

Sleet. The Scatterer had said sleet.

Ice.

"We would have this Rumor set to rest, if our Walker is of strong limbs, and willing."

"Your Walker is willing."

"But a Rumor is always dangerous. We would be loath to put so faithful a subject into danger."

"A Walker is not afraid."

"But all humans are afraid."

"All humans, my lord. But a Walker is a ghost of flesh and blood and vitals and bone." Jack stepped back.

"Then I would have you Ramble for us. In which direction will you walk?"

"I shall walk in whichever direction my feet take me, and trust that Accidents will lead me to Rumor's Crux."

All the appropriate folderol finished, the King of Lostwithal slumped in his chair.

Behind him, the silver door opened, and the page reentered. He crossed the room and took up his position behind the invalid chair. Glaring at Jack, who lowered his eyes.

The King glanced over a shoulder, and the boy turned his face. Then, to the Walker: "You are acquainted with this faithful young man?"

"Yes," Jack replied. "Bladen. I say his name twice: Bladen. And would vouch for him."

Suddenly, the boy's face turned red, and he burst out angrily, "I would not have you vouch for me. Deny my name! I demand it."

The King's eyes blazed, and the boy cringed.

"I beg Your Majesty's indulgence! I—I beg Your Majesty's indulgence."

Sad Agel sighed, glanced at Jack. "His sister is known to you as well." A statement, not a question.

And since it was not a question, Jack didn't reply.

But as Bladen, shamefaced, moved to wheel away the King of Lostwithal, Jack said, "Your Majesty?" And when the King had tipped his head: "Thank you."

Alone again in Walker's Wait, Jack closed his eyes, squeezed the bridge of his nose, then sat down in a chair.

Gradually, all Walker's Noise subsided, ended.

And when it was over, he stood and walked to the green door, opened it, went out, and began his Ramble.

CHAPTER 5

DIDGE, A REVENGER

"**I** DON'T BELIEVE IN YOU."

"That's your business. Do or don't, it doesn't matter to me. Your move."

"You speak . . . the liquid dialect."

"Learned it from a previous landlord. Who recently died. Now come on, Didge, it's your move."

"What are those . . . things on your shirt?"

"This is water, what's it look like? And these are palm trees."

"No . . . those."

"These? Are hotels."

"No."

"Well, honey, they sure are. Big hotels in Honolulu."

"What's that word you just said? It's not Losplit. I can't pronounce it."

"Don't let it bother you. Now, are we going to play or aren't we?"

"Who are you? Why are you in my dreams?"

"Are you dreaming? That's funny. Are you *sure* you're dreaming?"

"Who *are* you?"

"Milton Bradley."

"A what? Mil-ton, a what?"

"A what," said Uncle Milty with a soft chuckle. "Yeah, that's about it, honey: a what." He sat back in his chair, clasped his hands behind his head and stretched.

Didge stared at him unblinkingly, then frowned and dropped her eyes to the table. Several blue stones lay upon a could-board.

"Your toss," said Uncle Milty, "your turn."

But instead of tossing, she stood.

Uncle Milty groaned his disappointment and watched her as she roamed around the room, picking up game pieces, examining them, putting them down. "I don't understand."

"It's just a game, we're just playing."

She turned, looked at the little albino. "This room. It's almost like—but not exactly like—a room where I used to spend much time as a girl."

"Well, I do my best. I'm imperfect."

She arched an eyebrow.

"I'm here when you're not. So I wander. I peek through your belongings, what guest wouldn't, alone in a stranger's house? I hope the room pleases you."

She didn't reply.

"Your turn, Didge, your toss."

She was wandering again, stopping finally to regard herself in a small mirror that hung over a sideboard. Didge wearing a heavily mended dark-gray blouse, the cuffs frayed; a rope-belt; stiff and scuffed corduroy trousers. She smiled, then wasn't smiling.

Looked down at her feet: shiny-black walking shoes.

"Did you find these clothes in my memories?"

"Oh, I wouldn't presume to dress you, Didge. You came here dressed that way, don't you remember?"

"I rambled in such clothes." Speaking softly, addressing the mirror, Uncle Milty might've been a million miles away.

"As a Walker," he said, and she turned to him swiftly.

He shrugged. "I snooped. It gets lonely." He pointed to the game board, but she ignored his gesture. "A little girl who wished to run away. *Walked* away instead."

Didge blinked, and glanced toward the albino.

"This Craft," he said, and shook his head in disapproval. "I used to know a fellow—another landlord of mine, as a matter of fact. When he was a boy, his parents sent him off to a military school. It nearly did him in, poor boy. Your Craft, what I've seen of it in your memory, seems the same sort of place. I was *so* glad to get out of there. So glad to get you out of that ditch and take you here. It's so much nicer here, isn't it, Didge? Sit down, Didge. Your toss. Your turn."

She turned back to the mirror.

Uncle Milty sighed, then stood up, lightly scratching at his cheek. He crossed the floor and stooped before a square cabinet. "As you recall and as I saw, your Uncle Jix kept some stronger refreshments in a cabinet just like this one, didn't he? Perhaps we both could stand some refreshment. Before we resume our play, of course." He struggled with the door, and it came open with a pop. He reached in, made a puzzled face; when he pulled his hand out, it was balled into a tight fist, and in the fist, doll-sized, was the squirming figure of the Walking Master.

Uncle Milty whacked him against the side of the cabinet, and he vanished in a puff of smoke. "Well, I think we've seen enough of *him.*" He glanced over his shoulder. "Didge, you're awfully sloppy with your memories, girl, they're everywhere."

Didge had turned from the mirror and was staring at him, openmouthed.

"Now where's that lovely strawberry wine you've always remembered . . . ?" He reached again into the cabinet, but that time, when he withdrew his hand, it was covered with a turbulent swarm of black flying insects. He scattered them with his free hand, and when they had vanished, he regarded his open palm: in which lay a variety of artists' brushes.

Didge groaned.

"Oh," said Uncle Milty. "Yes. Poor Ifnazz."

Didge recoiled at the name.

"Poor Ifnazz," said Uncle Milty. "Poor Didge."

She took a step toward him, reaching for the brushes. But he refused to let her have them, saying, "You don't need to hold onto *these* memories."

"He is dead because of me."

"Love is blind."

She looked at him, bewildered.

He dashed the brushes against the floor, where they broke into vapor, spiraled, vanished. Then he reached back into the cabinet, and withdrew a bottle of strawberry wine.

Didge watched him carry it to the table.

"He was kind to me," she said, to herself, to the mirror. Not to the albino. "Ifnazz was kind to me. I was a novice and he was . . . kind."

"Sit down," said Uncle Milty. He poured two glasses, sniffed one. "Oooo, this really *is* as good as you remember. Didge? Come sit and have a drink with me. And then we'll play."

"He was a prince."

"Yes—yes, I know. All your dirty memories, I've been finding them everywhere. A prince. Very good. Now, shall we play?" He rubbed his hands together in anticipation.

"An art-prince."

"Hmmmm. It's your toss. I tossed Travel, now it's your toss."

"I was his Walker, a prince's Walker. I was so young, just out of the Craft."

"Didge, you're starting to bother me. Let's just play. No offense, but this is starting to sound like Clifford Odets. Come. Sit."

"If I had done him the service he'd requested, instead—"

"Instead of running off to be with your lover. Ifnazz would be alive today. Yes, yes. But what's done is done. And besides, it happens all the time. This universe, that

universe." He shrugged. "Wherever there are humans.
Believe me. I know. Now sit down."

"I heard Walker's Noise, and ignored it." Didge,
speaking to her reflection again.

"Just as you're ignoring me. Now. *Sit.*"

She turned and looked at Uncle Milty, and seemed
suddenly amused. "Who *are* you?"

"Are we back to that again? Oh, please." He reached
out and tapped Didge's chair. "Sit. It's your toss. I tossed
Travel, now let's see about you. Good!" he said when she
came and took her seat.

She picked up her stones from beside her place,
leaned over the board, smiling thinly. "I made you up,
didn't I?"

"Just toss."

She closed her left hand tightly around the stones.
Then mumbling, "Maybe I should . . . shall I?" she
opened her hand, and let the stones tumble.

Eagerly, Uncle Milty watched where they went, tumbling across a black blot, one of them coming to rest upon
a red diamond-shape, another upon a blue scalene triangle.

"Oh . . . my!" Milty grinning, clapping his hands.
"Revenge! Well now, aren't *you* in a spot?" He pointed to
his own yellow stone resting on a green diamond halfway
across the board. "But I've got Travel! Are you willing to
trade? Say, seven turns for my Travel stone?"

"No."

"Oh, where's your strategy, girl? You can't take your
Revenge without traveling to it, and *I've* got the Travel
stone. Take a chance. Use strategy."

"I don't need your stone to travel."

"You do! I know the rules."

She smiled, and rose from the table.

"Your Revenge can't happen without Travel."

"I know."

She crossed the room to the door.

"Didge? Where're you going?"

Smiling mysteriously, she exited, and Uncle Milty

stared glumly at the game board. Then he gripped the edges of the board and flung it away.

DIDGE'S EYES SNAPPED OPEN IN the pitch dark.

One lamp burned weakly by the door.

The woman who'd been sharing the bench with her was gone.

Didge pushing up a sleeve, working a fingertip through a knot in her bracelet, feeling a beetle fidget, then deciding: No.

Not now.

Shoving down her sleeve, Didge remembered. A kindly art-prince named Ifnazz, who'd taken a young first-degree Walker into his employ; his studio on the Bay of Lace, his apprentices strolling the gardens, parties to which she'd been invited. And she remembered the morning when he'd come into her small Walker's Wait, and he'd paced a while, clearly frightened, then stood on the carpet, and Walker's Noise roared around him, and he'd snatched at the air, held a Rumor tightly in his fist, then gave it to Didge, to listen.

A student on the Isle of Mites telling a prostitute, who told a cook, who told a ferryman, who told a gardener, who told his wife as he watched her dress: *An art-prince there is with false heart who would remake the world in his own disorder.*

Didge had heard the Rumor, and was delighted: here, it seemed, was a Ramble more suited to a Walker of much higher degree, and yet she was being asked to seek its provenance. She accepted gladly, and bid Ifnazz farewell, and set off with her legs and feet leading her.

But then—then her Heart of Blood had betrayed her, and taken her to Sett. To *him.* Jack, a Walker.

And when, later, she'd tried to resume the Ramble, her legs faltered, and the Rumor eluded her, and Walker's Noise was gone.

And Ifnazz? Discovered one morning with his teeth

turned blue, and his eyes become roses; and in his chest were two holes, and in the holes, not hearts, but stones.

A Rumor is neither true nor cruel, merely possible, always dangerous.

She'd not found Rumor's Crux, and her patron had died.

So, too, her life as a Walker.

And Jack had denied her name, and then denied it twice.

Ruined, she'd found her way into beetle shops, pressed 'sap to her lips.

Ruined, she'd become a Dispeller.

Ruined, she wished to die. And would. Soon. She'd come to that decision—which was why she'd traveled to Beybix; to see her brother one last time.

Ruined, she would die.

But not before she took her revenge.

A Walker is passive, but Didge was no longer a Walker.

She would ride this ship to the Isle of Mites.

Travel to her Revenge.

According to *her* order of things.

Didge stretched out on the bench, drew up her knees. But did not close her eyes. She had no wish to see that strange little man again.

She had no further need of games.

CHAPTER 6

THE GOLDEN BRIDEGROOM

PINDRIX HAD SLEPT FITFULLY, coming awake with his body slick and his mouth dry, his Heart of Talent sluggish and his Heart of Blood wildly beating. He tossed and turned, stared off into the dark, groaned, made fists and shook them, threw off his cover and ran outside and urinated, slumped against the wall of his rude little cottage, staggered back in, sat in a chair, jumped up, threw himself face-down onto his pallet, then flopped onto his back and rapidly added up a series of numbers, pictured an isosceles triangle and overlaid that with a circle, overlaid that with a lozenge, then blinked and shivered as a perfectly clear, three-dimensional, full-size image of Mistress Mithik shimmered into existence.

Trembling, he stared at her.

And studied her face, and the black braid that hung over the mountain of her left breast, studied the round bulge of her stomach, the fine hair on her arms, the roughness of her hands, the redness of her knuckles, her fingernails.

Pindrix felt dizzy, indescribably confused, and then, with a blast of feeling, was ashamed to be wearing such a shabby white nightshirt. Even though this Mithik was only an illusion, still he felt embarrassed. He leaped up, grabbed his clothes from a peg on the wall, and once again stumbled outside. The sky was lightening, he could hear morning birds, a pertinacious woodpecker.

The Spellman of Soolky dressed hurriedly, brushed his hair with his fingers, and reentered his cottage.

Mistress Mithik seemed to shimmer a bit, her face a blur. Pindrix recollected his final sum, squeezed his nipples, and the image returned to its former clarity. He approached her, stood directly before her, made as if to touch her, then snatched away his hand.

"Mistress," he said in a low quavering voice, "I apologize most sincerely for my . . . presumption. I—I am a foolish, lonely man." He groaned and slapped his hands to his face, shook his head, wheeled around. No, no, *no!* That sounds pathetic: a lonely man! A foolish man! He didn't want her sympathy, he wanted *her.*

With a high-pitched laugh, he flung himself into a chair, the only one in his cottage. Leaned forward, planting elbows on his knees. A lonely man? He, Pindrix of Meeres, a Spellman—lonely? Someone with his talents, his aspirations, his skill, with all of his knowledge? Lonely? No!

(yes)

Lonely and foolish.

Supercilious. And worse of all: a self-deceiver.

All these long months here, wandering around Soolky and its environs with a constant grimace upon his face, hating his life, wholly certain that he was superior to everyone (cartwright, farmer . . . charcoal—maker) and that he was destined by character and native intelligence for higher things, a posting among court mages, a career at Beybix castle, a life of the mind and of Useful Magic, convinced that a terrible error had been made, an injustice done. But: no error, no injustice. His talents matched his assignment, perfectly—or they would, he told himself, if only he'd stop behaving like such an arrogant . . . youth.

He'd been fooling himself, *making* a fool of himself; he'd acted so badly; he'd been so . . . pathetic. Yes. Appallingly pathetic. Thought Pindrix.

The simple truth? I am no scholar, no remarkable talent, merely an ordinary man. Talented, yes—talented, but only moderately so.

An ordinary man who suddenly finds himself—

He raised his eyes slowly to the image of Mistress Mithik.

—in ordinary . . . yearning.

He spread his hands now and said, "I would be grateful . . . I would be happy . . . I would be ecstatic . . ."

He groaned again, jumped to his feet, did subtraction in his mind—and the image vanished.

Would be. Pindrix thinking, I would be a perfect fool —again!—if I sat here pledging love to a shimmer!

With a sharp, almost manic laugh, he slammed out of the cottage, and went running through the sleeping village. A few dogs took idle note of him, and then he was gone.

THE CHARCOAL-MAKER LIVED A half mile outside of the village proper, a distance that Pindrix covered in a scant few minutes. He stood now on the road, sweaty hands flexing and unflexing, trying to summon the final nerve to go and knock upon the door.

So strange: this tiny thatch house, which he'd seen, passed by, visited on dozens of occasions in the last several months, now seemed—enchanted.

Pindrex telling himself, You're stalling. Do it!

With sudden determination and a confident stride, the Spellman of Soolky approached the dark cottage. No doubt Mithik would be startled—but when she understood *why* he was here, why he had come knocking at her door so early in the day, she would be charmed, she would be delighted. She would forgive him for his poor behavior of the night before. When she understood that he now was adding spiritual desire to physical yearning—well, she would be carried away with identical emotion.

Wouldn't she?

He paused, just outside the door.

Wouldn't she?

Living alone, working alone, a widow. Doubtless she would be thrilled to have a young man pledge himself to her as life-mate.

Become her bridegroom.

One of the duties of a village Spellman was to prepare bridegrooms for their wedding ceremonies—mothers took care of brides. Pindrix decided now that he would cast an extraordinary spell upon himself when it came time for his own nuptials. He would have to read carefully in his little red book, but he'd find something truly wonderful, special, different. He would make a bridegroom the likes that Soolky had never seen before. And he'd diligently practice his nuptial magic beforehand, to make sure that it all went perfectly. Smiling, he raised a hand to knock.

Then let it drop.

Thinking, But why wait?

Why not come *now* as a bridegroom? Not only would it make for a moment that Mithik would never forget, it would also spare him the awkwardness of actually pledging his love. Saying it aloud. She would only have to take one look at him to see what his feelings and intentions were.

Good! Good thinking, Pindrix, he told himself.

So, reaching a hand into his bag, feeling around for his spell book, he stepped away from the door.

Since it was still quite dark, he went and stood in the dooryard, under the light of the twin moons; there, he riffled through the book, scowling, shaking his head—no, no . . . no—till finally he paused in his page-turning and gave a single, decisive nod.

It took a full ten minutes to add up all the necessary numbers and visualize all the myriad shapes, but finally the spell began to work, and Pindrix, sporting an almost beatific smile on his long, homely face, stood perfectly still. A tingling that turned almost painful spread through him. For a moment, it seemed as if his face were on fire, and then his legs went numb.

But at last, it was finished.

He didn't know how long he could maintain his spell, so he had to hurry. He raced back to the cottage, grinning in anticipation. And decided not to knock: he would simply . . . appear. Mithik would awake to find him standing at the foot of her bed cloaked in the finest of nuptial illusions—the kind of illusion that only young men of means who lived in the greatest cities of Lostwithal would dare to be married in.

She would look up and behold—the Golden Bridegroom!

Golden, indeed.

His gilded face shone brightly.

So did his hands.

And his threadbare green cassock? Gone. Transformed. Was splendrously yellow.

Anticipating one of the truly great moments of his life, he stepped into the cottage.

And was so utterly appalled by what he saw the following moment that his golden mien flickered and died. He put back his head and wailed.

Mithik and Herb Dierickx were fitted together in the conjugal act.

CHAPTER 7

THE ABOUNDING
WOMAN AND THE
EMPTY MAN

EVEN THE MAGE OF FOUR,
Mage of Luck had no idea how many believers there were
among the humans of Lostwithal. There may've been as
few as a thousand, as many as ten thousand—but no matter how many there truly were who belonged to the Cult
of the Cradle, at dawn they suddenly were all present
among the sand dunes.

Present in the person of a small, hunchbacked old
woman dressed in a brown habit and wearing a heavy veil
that concealed her features. She walked slowly, chopping
a gnarled stick into the sand as she moved. When she saw
the rounded shelter of beach grass and dead wood, she
stopped and genuflected toward its small entrance. Then
she stood again and approached the Dark Mage, who

waited a short distance away on a crest of one of the dunes.

He extended his left hand, and she touched the tips of his second and third fingers, lightly. Then she interlaced her own fingers and moved them as though rocking a cradle. "We are here," she said, and the mage allowed himself the briefest smile.

Ordinarily, she was called Sister Wheel, but this dawn she was called the Abounding Woman.

Because *they* were inside of her. All of them.

All the believers.

As few as a thousand, as many as ten thousand: teeming within Sister Wheel, seeing through her eyes. Eyes that were abnormally bright.

When the Child of Mud comes of age, the Abounding Woman shall be its handmaid.

They were there, all of them, and they said, "We are come, as you called us."

"I expected you earlier," said the mage. He kept looking from the Abounding Woman to the shelter.

"We did not anticipate such a journey. We expected to convene at the Manse Seloc."

The mage's eyes cut suddenly back to the Abounding Woman, and his lips compressed angrily; a glistening slug slipped from his cheek, and fell to the sand. He ground it underfoot. "It could not be helped," he said. "The manse was violated by disbelievers."

"As we understand, great mage." The Abounding Woman made a deferential gesture, hunching her shoulders, then glanced around her.

"And how grows the Epicene?"

"It is nearly grown full."

"You have seen its hands, great mage?"

"Strong. Strong enough to tear through the fabric and into the Fourth Moment of Creation. And in its sleep, it cries."

"To see Bulcease."

"To see Bulcease, and to free the Last Humans from the bondage of time," said the mage, but almost perfunctorily; it was clear that his mind was not now on epigrams

and catechism. He frowned, looked intently at the
Abounding Woman, then his eyes flicked down toward the
water's edge, to the beached flatboat. "Come," he said,
"we need to talk further." He strode along the flank of the
dune, sand crunching underfoot, and then veered off suddenly, heading to the shelter.

The Abounding Woman trembled, pressing her
elbows firmly to her sides, as if trying to keep her body
from exploding outward, and then she followed.

Major Richard Forell flinched alert at the approach
of the Great Mage. He'd been sitting on his heels, rocking
back and forth, hands clasped around his knees; he'd been
trying to think.

(But it was so hard . . .)

When the Abounding Woman saw him, she halted
abruptly and turned to the Mage of Four, Mage of Luck.

"A catechist," he said, indicating the naked man.

"Then why is he not part of . . . us?"

"Upon the back of an empty man," he replied, and
gestured with his hand.

*Upon the back of an empty man, the Epicene is borne
to his Moment.*

The Abounding Woman took a step forward and fell
to her knees. "Then it is to be this day?"

"This day, yes." He reached a hand and pulled the
Abounding Woman to her feet. Then with a cold smile he
stooped, putting his face near to Major Forell's. The Major blinked, tried to return the smile, but—

(it was so hard to think, he *couldn't* think; he *tried* to,
but couldn't . . . his mind was emptying, emptying . . .)

The mage's lips brushed his ear, and when he felt the
mage's warm breath, blowing into him, he shivered—

(numbers whirling through his mind, numbers that
caught fire and burned, flamed out, were gone)

—and turned his head sideways, peering into the
dark opening of the shelter.

For a moment, one thought *did* appear in his mind—
to run, to run now, to escape—but he felt the breath
again, and his stomach was seized by cramps. As the mage

leaned away, Major Forell, empty of thought, fully empty, crawled on his belly over the white sand, and into the shelter.

There was a low rumbling growl, quite inhuman.

Then a high-pitched wail of pain, very human.

THE MAGE OF FOUR, MAGE OF Luck went and stood by the Abounding Woman, and together they turned away from the shelter.

They didn't dare look as the Empty Man staggered out a few moments later, then lurched slowly across the sand and over a dune and down to the flatboat, bearing the monster upon his back—the Epicene Whose Eyes Are Death.

And they spoke no more when, minutes later, they followed, the Great Mage walking with his hands clasped behind him, the Abounding Woman stopping every several feet to pick up gobbets of moist black mud, which she smeared eagerly upon her face.

CHAPTER 8

ADULTERY—A CASE STUDY

IN ALL HIS MARRIED LIFE, Herb Dierickx had never once been unfaithful, not once. Oh, he'd been tempted, and he'd done his share of drooling (and so forth) over girly magazines, but even though he'd had plenty of opportunities to go catting around, he'd just never . . . done it. When he'd been in construction? *Millions* of opportunities. Friday nights after work, at Cavenaugh's Bar? Opportunities galore. But Herb Dierickx hadn't availed himself of any, and after a while, as the years and the anniversaries had piled up, his monogamy had become a badge of honor, sort of. Not that he'd ever let his pals know, that would've been stupid, social suicide, but there was, in his own mind, a large satisfaction in knowing that he'd kept himself . . . well, all right, maybe it sounded too smug and Boy Scout for words, but that he'd kept himself *pure*. In body, if not entirely in mind. And it was the body that counted, right? In the real world? In a marriage? It was the body you worried about, that could cause you grief. Your mind? Was nobody else's business. Not even your wife's. Especially not your wife's.

For almost thirty years he'd kept his marriage vows. Hadn't even gone to a hooker.

And now look. Herb thinking, *Now* look what happens! It's unbelievable! It's crazy.

HERB REPROACHING HIMSELF AS he went running through the woods, his trousers unbuttoned, his shirt tail flapping behind him—thinking, It's the craziest thing that ever happened to me.

THE CRAZIEST.

And it had gone on all night long.

He wasn't excusing himself, but he really hadn't started it, he'd never even considered it—

(well, maybe briefly)

—and, in fact, the whole business (nice euphemism, Herb) had begun perfectly innocently. Really.

What had happened: After Pindrix ran off in such a huff, all red-faced? Herb, feeling embarrassed, had stayed outside, just looking up at the stars, wondering if any of them were stars that he'd seen back home, those summer evenings when he and Marge had parked themselves in the yard, Margie with her Lipton's iced tea, Herb with his bottle of Rolling Rock. Looking up, hoping to catch a glimpse of a comet or a meteor, something out of the ordinary. All those stars. And sometimes Herb would get a funny feeling, that old puny-human feeling that he figured everybody got in the presence of such immensity.

Sitting there in the back yard with Marge, he'd remember his old Baltimore Catechism. First question. Who made us? The answer: God. God made us. And Herb, who hadn't believed in God or any of that supernatural stuff for almost half a century, would get to wondering if maybe he'd been kind of pompous. Who *did* make us? You know?

Lots of stars always did that to Herb, got him wrestling with the cosmic, and they'd done it again to him last night. Of course, the fact that there was a second moon hanging up in the sky added some extra strangeness, yet another dimension of awe.

So he'd stayed there for quite some time, till Mithik wandered out with a cup of tea that she'd fixed him. Hey. Thanks. He wondered if she'd put any more medicine into it, a ground-up root or something, whatever the heck she used. He took the cup, thanked her again, and she went back inside, but then returned immediately with a chair for herself. She sat down and they stayed sitting out there together, both of them looking up at the stars.

Just like he and Marge used to do it.

Both of them looking up, both of them silent.

Till Mithik said, "It is only a story."

Huh? Herb turning to her, tipping his head. What?

"The Epicene," she said. Talking about the mud monster again, that she'd ridiculed earlier when he'd first mentioned it. But that had clearly disturbed Pindrix.

Herb wondered why she was bringing it up again now, though. If she thought it was so dumb.

And then she mentioned that when her mate was alive, he used to read frequently from The Book of True and Cruel.

Herb had turned and given her a funny look; not *her* so much, he was just startled by something. By how peculiar it was to be talking and hearing and understanding another language. What had startled him then was this: in Losplit, "cruel" referred to anything that was not strictly true.

He thought that was odd.

He thought that was interesting.

And he'd suddenly thought, as he stared into Mithik's face, that she had very pretty eyes.

And thinking that, he'd tingled with alarm and something damn close to physical arousal. He'd glanced away, drawing a deep breath.

o   o   o

SEE? HERB SAYING TO HIMSELF
now as he continued to tramp through the dark woods, his lungs on fire, a few of his wounds twinging anew. See? I *tried* to be good. First hint of trouble, I'd turned away. . . .

AND MITHIK HAD GONE ON, SAY-
ing that after her husband had died, she'd burned his book. Which had contained old stories of the Epicene, and of the humans and too-humans of Whole Creation, and of all the Talents, and, naturally, of the Schoolteacher. But she'd had no use for books. Still didn't, she'd told Herb. He'd frowned at that, being a voracious reader himself—not that he was so keen on "serious" literature, but he sure liked to read. He was always reading something. Like, the book he was currently reading—or at least the book he *had* been reading, back in his other life—was a true crime book about Ted Bundy, the serial killer. Herb had always liked reading true crime books, especially those that dealt with psychopaths. He used to tell Marge that they kept him on his toes. It was good to know, he'd say, that there are lots of monsters in the world.

He was absurdly disappointed that Mithik wasn't a reader, but he didn't say as much, of course. No, what he said was, "This Schoolteacher. What's he supposed to be —like God?"

Actually, what he'd said in Losplit was, "What's he supposed to be, the Creator of Three Moments?"

And Mithik had laughed, a little. "No," she'd said, "he's not the creator. He was—a man."

Way she said that, it struck Herb as funny. Funny-peculiar. And familiar. She'd reminded him suddenly of Marge, when Marge'd make some crack about men screwing everything up, rhetorically asking how come men were always in charge—the big screw-ups! The big babies. Same with Mithik. Jeez. Herb thinking, Us men got great reputations, don't we? Every universe we're in, women think we're jerks.

"The Schoolteacher," she'd said. "The Schoolteacher. A man who learned his lessons from Women of Mist, but told the world of men that he'd learned them by himself."

This hadn't been what Herb expected to hear from Mithik—it wasn't so much the content of what she was saying (what content? he didn't know what the hell she was talking about, really), it was just . . . it was just her whole attitude, her tone, that he found startling.

And intriguing.

Mithik smiling then, saying, "I have some Mist in my blood, you know," and Herb nodding, as if he knew what she meant. "So take the words I give you with a skeptical hand."

That had *really* gotten to Herb. Marge used to say, after she'd ranted and raved about something she'd read about in the newspaper, some murder trial or bank scandal or political intrigue, after she'd spent herself venting her anger, damning everybody involved, she'd always laugh, wave a self-deprecating hand and say, "Oh, but what the hell do *I* know?"

Which Herb had always found charming.

Because he knew she didn't mean it, and she knew that he knew it.

So take the words I give you with a skeptical hand.

Mithik had fallen silent after saying that, and just sat there beside him for several minutes more. Then, with a weary sigh, she'd risen, and announced her intention to go to bed. Herb said he guessed he'd turn in, too.

I SHOULD'VE STAYED *OUTSIDE,* Herb was saying to himself now, as he pushed through some undergrowth, switches slapping his face, stinging him. If I'd only slept in the yard, nothing would've happened. I should've stayed outdoors. Slept under the stars. Played the happy camper.

BUT HE HADN'T. HE'D REMAINED in the yard only a few minutes after Mithik had gone in, then followed. She'd blown out the lantern but lit a squat candle, and set out a fresh pitcher of water beside it. She was already in her bed, and Herb felt her eyes on him as he crossed the floor to the pallet she'd prepared for him. He'd already decided that, since there was candlelight, he wouldn't undress. He didn't want to feel self-conscious, though he realized she'd already seen his less-than-gorgeous body totally naked while she'd been nursing him. He said, "Good night"—

(in Losplit, literally: "Hearts beat till morning")

—and then crawled under the light blanket and lay on his back, watching the candle smoke drizzle across the ceiling. He spent a few minutes trying to figure what he should do tomorrow. He didn't have a whole hell of a lot of faith in all this Rumor business—maybe he was being, you know, ethnocentric and stuff, but there you go. He was thinking that maybe he should try to reach the capital city by himself. Walk there. He could ask Mithik to take him to the city; or even Pindrix, if the guy ever got over his pique.

And once Herb arrived there?

Yeah? Once he arrived there . . . ?

Then what?

Herb had scowled in the dark.

In the best of all possible scenarios, Jere Lee and Money and Peter Musik would be there, and Herb could find them, and they'd all tell Squintik, okay, it's time to send us home. And they'd all live happily ever after.

But if none of them had survived the bat attack?

Then?

Well, seeing as how there were no cars here in Lostwithal, he couldn't very well go back to being a chauffeur, could he?

He'd turned over on his side, decided to think things through further in the morning. And falling asleep, he'd dreamed that he was sitting in his living room back home, trying to read his true crime book about Ted Bundy. But he couldn't concentrate because there were howling coyotes outside. Herb putting the book aside, saying to himself, There's no coyotes in the city. What *is* that?

He stood up and went to the window and looked out, and sure enough, there were no coyotes, just the usual parked cars and lawn sprinklers. Then Marge walked into the room, looking very haggard. She dropped into the chair he'd just vacated and puffed. "Herb, would you do me a favor, would you change the baby this time?"

And Herb said, "What? *What* baby?"

Margie said, "I had a baby when you were away, but it's yours, don't worry." Herb was so stunned he could hardly breathe. But still he managed to say, "You mean we have a baby? After all these years?" He was so happy that he started to cry, and she laughed and threw a Pampers at him, being funny. He caught it and dabbed his eyes with it, saying, "What's the baby's name?" and Marge told him, "I thought I'd wait to name it till you got home."

Then he heard it crying again and thought he'd tell Marge that he'd mistaken it for a coyote, but then felt that it might hurt her feelings, so he just gave her a big hug and ran out of the room and started racing upstairs. Then stopped, calling back, "What is it, a boy or a girl?"

For a second, he thought he heard her say it was a boy *and* a girl, but then realized he must've misunderstood and told himself, Oh the hell with it, you'll find out for yourself in a couple of seconds.

He looked into their bedroom, but the baby wasn't there. Then he checked in the second bedroom, which they'd always used as a TV room, kind of a den. But the baby wasn't in there, either. Herb thinking, Where'd she *put* it?

The baby was really howling now, and Herb was starting to sweat. What if he couldn't find it? What if they'd lost it? All those years when they were young trying to have a baby, and nothing doing. At last they get one— and he loses it?

He checked in Margie's little sewing room.

No baby.

He came back out into the hall, panting, and was just about to holler downstairs, ask Margie where the hell she'd put their little baby—when he noticed a door where there'd never been one before. What she'd do, have an addition put on? Jeez, he hadn't been in Lostwithal *that* long, had he?

He braced himself outside for a half-second, trying to regain his composure—after all, this was going to be one hell of a memorable moment in his life—and then he opened the door.

The room was pitch dark, he couldn't see a foot in front of him.

But he heard the baby all right, wailing bloody blue murder.

He fumbled around for a wall switch, couldn't locate one, then reached a hand toward his pocket for his lighter —but even as he was reaching he realized that he wouldn't *have* a lighter, he'd given up smoking. Remember? Yeah, he remembered, except: he found it, his Bic. He rolled the wheel, the flame leapt up, and for a second he was totally flabbergasted.

What the hell was the matter with Marge?

You decorate a little baby's room like *this?*

Mobiles: all right, sure. But *these?* These mobiles were—

Bones dangling on strings. Hundreds of bones dangling from the ceiling.

He brushed past the bones, they clicked and clattered, and searched for his baby. Finally he spotted a wooden cradle on rockers standing against a wall. On tiptoes, he approached, his breathing labored, but with each step that he took, the room seemed to lengthen, and the cradle seemed to be farther and farther away. At last he was running, trying to reach the cradle, and then suddenly: he was there. Beside it.

Brushing sweat from his eyes.

Bending down.

And then screaming at the writhing infant of mud and stones and straw, whose eyes cracked open, opened wide, and were bright yellow.

Herb continued to scream, his screams mingling with the infant's howls, till Mithik had roughly shaken him awake.

He'd been so distraught and so utterly confused that

he'd thought Mithik was Marge—Margie used to shake him like that, then hold him close, that year he kept having all those bad dreams, that year his mother and father and younger sister had all died within months of each other. Margie used to hold him and console him, and brush his damp hair from his forehead, and sometimes she'd make love to him, doing everything, Herb just lying there, Margie saying just to relax, relax, let her be nice to him, he'd sleep better afterwards . . .

Only this wasn't Marge.

And by the time he'd realized that, things were pretty far along, and he just *couldn't* tell her to quit.

Didn't want to.

OKAY. HERB STOPPED, AND leaned against a tree, waiting for his heart to slow down. Okay. The first time you were out of it. You can be excused for the first time. You were still half-asleep. But the second time? The third time?

Herb thinking now, The *third* time?

When was the last time there'd been a third time?

HE COULD'VE STOPPED AFTER the first time.

But he hadn't, and, as the night passed, the dream had receded and kept receding (though he knew that he'd never forget it entirely).

Then came Pindrix.

Barging in, gleaming like some Inca god, and Herb Dierickx got chest pains.

I'm a goner, I'm dead, he'd thought, but then the pains had stopped as abruptly as they'd started, and then Herb was lying on his side, staring at the Spellman's pathetic disintegration.

His bright clothes flickering like theater lights at intermission's end. Then going out, becoming drab green again.

The poor Spellman looked so utterly humiliated that

Herb felt the same kind of pity he'd always felt looking at pictures of starving three-year-olds in a direct mailing from CARE.

Mithik had felt no such pity.

She'd jumped naked from bed and begun to pound and kick Pindrix, screaming at him that she'd said his name and said it twice, that he should die and go to the Void. Herb thinking, Oh Christ, as he'd jumped up and started putting on his clothes.

He felt a monumentally guilty need to explain the whole situation to the Spellman.

But Pindrix, with a final bleat of anguish, had fled the cottage before Herb could even speak a word.

Herb, one leg in his trousers, the other one not, went hobbling outside after him, bouncing across the yard like somebody in a sack race, waving his shirt like a flag, saying, "Wait up!"

How could he have done this to the guy who'd saved his life?

How could he have done this to Marge?

How could he have done this, period?

He ran after Pindrix, and after he'd been running awhile, it had suddenly struck him: Mithik hadn't tried to stop him, or even called after him once to come back.

He'd never understand these people.

Not in a million years, Mom.

THE SKY WAS THE COLOR OF fireplace ashes the morning after. Herb had no idea how long he'd been running, and, further, he had no idea if he'd been running in the right direction or not. Pindrix had cut off the main road, Herb had cut off the main road. After that? It was entirely possible they'd gone in two separate directions.

Who the heck did Herb think he was, Chingachgook?

Was this nuts, or what?

Here he was, wandering around completely lost, and

he'd alienated the only two people he knew in the entire world.

Good going, Herb.

He pressed on, now smelling fresh water (hey, maybe he was Chingachgook, a little), and noticing now that the ground had turned sandy. He walked on, pushing aside brush, wandering through saplings, and then stepped out onto a long, wide beach undulant with dunes.

He pushed a hand through his hair and trekked ahead, the going pretty tough, pretty sloggy, but the sand felt good on his bare feet. He stopped again, to regard his surroundings.

Reminded him of Cape Cod.

When he got home and told Marge? He'd say, It looked like Cape Cod. All those dunes.

And then he thought, Tell Marge?

When am I gonna *see* her to tell her?

He trudged on, shaking his head, and he'd resigned himself to the pathetic truth that he hadn't been trailing Pindrix at all, that he'd just been running through the forest like a nincompoop, a guilt-ridden nincompoop, when—

At the top of a dune, he looked down and spotted the Spellman of Soolky standing in front of a strange-looking dome—an igloo-shaped thing, Herb thought. A dome made of driftwood and beachgrass, with a hole chopped through its top and three perpendicular slits in its side.

Pindrix swayed, then fell forward, flat on his face.

CHAPTER 9

FLESH ON FIRE (III)

Aᔆ ᴀ ʙᴏʏ ʟɪᴠɪɴɢ ᴏɴ Meeres, Pindrix had often visited a peculiar young art-prince who'd maintained a studio in a solitary wold far from the village proper. Pindrix's father was an ink-maker (his yellows and blues were famous throughout all of Lostwithal), and the prince was a good customer, but a customer who shunned all society: he demanded that his colored inks be delivered, and delivered only on the fourth day of each new month (except during the months of Late Blaze, which he spent on the Isle of Mites).

At first, Pindrix had been loathe to make those treks out to the prince's studio. For one thing, the boy had a weak constitution, and the trip, which took almost an hour each way, tired him and always left him footsore and aching, but the real reason he dreaded going was the prince himself.

The prince was as unpleasant and rude in his demeanor as he was eccentric in his attire and grooming habits. He dressed in tight trousers and short, brightly colored jackets and wore high glossy boots. His hair was long, hanging down well past his shoulders, and he sported a thick glossy mustache—no male in Lostwithal maintained any facial hair whatsoever. Thus it was often said around the village that the prince must have once traveled to another Moment, since in several of the poems and stories and parables found in the Book of True and Cruel which dealt with the too-humans of Kemolo and Feerce, it was duly noted (with either amusement or distaste) that it was not uncommon for their men to let hair grow upon their faces.

The art-prince's name was Presquit.

During the first several of his monthly trips to Presquit's studio, Pindrix never went further than the prince's door saddle—thank the 'Teacher. Presquit would promptly answer his timid knock, assume a supercilious pose, make some unkind remark about the boy's posture, or coloration, the set of his jaw, the lack of any character in his eyes, then accept the package of inkpots, dole out the proper coinage, and slam the door. Pindrix would tremble when the ordeal was over.

But around the fourth or fifth visit, Presquit's attitude toward the boy softened, a bit. Instead of blaming Pindrix for his unimposing looks, he would, instead, make some disparaging comment about the boy's parents—it was a pity, he'd say, that they'd foisted their imperfections upon their son. Pindrix was confused by this approach: he felt that he should take umbrage at the denunciation of his mother and father, but since he had no real affection for either of them, he couldn't, not really.

Then, one month, the art-prince had invited Pindrix into his studio, offered him tea. The boy was terrified, but flattered.

The studio was filled with sketches and large drawings and a few oil paintings, all of which were a great shock to young Pindrix. Mostly they were portraits, although the faces and figures in the pictures were distorted, impossible, and the colors demented. Women with fish-eyes, men with tiger-striped faces and mouths like anuses, purple children with two right hands. Pindrix didn't know what to say, so he said nothing. In fact, he tried to keep his eyes lowered, on his teacup, on the floor.

Presquit had studied him with deepening curiosity, and at one point, much to Pindrix's alarm, he'd reached out and gently pressed a finger to his nose, then to his chin. And then, to Pindrix's further alarm, he'd asked him what he thought of the pictures.

Pindrix drew his shoulders up as high as they would go, and lowered his head, cravenly. Finally, he said, "I've never seen anyone who looked like . . . that. Excuse me, sir."

And the art-prince laughed. "I dare say you haven't! Nor have I. It's why I make them."

Pindrix's mouth had dropped open.

"We'd be finished with Perfect Order then, wouldn't we, boy? If everyone were so . . . unique. To the Void with Perfect Order."

Pindrix was astonished, didn't know what to say.

To the Void with Perfect Order?

He put down his cup and said he had to be leaving.

"I've offended you," said Presquit.

"No, sir."

"But I have. Well—good!" And then he'd laughed, and pursed his lips, and regarded Pindrix for a long moment. The boy was afraid he was going to touch him again, but he didn't. He just scrutinized him as if he were imagining him with some extraordinary deformity. Pindrix shivered.

On the way out, he happened to notice a large port-folio of drawings on a table. These drawings were quite different than any of the others, and because they were he let his eyes linger too long upon them. "Have a look," said Presquit, and then swept them all up. Illustrations, he said, based upon the Old Story found in the Book of True and Cruel.

Pindrix looked, and immediately regretted it.

He fled then and ran all the way home, weak consti-tution notwithstanding. He was afraid to tell his father of what had happened because his father had instructed him never to enter the prince's house. But for the next several weeks, the boy dreaded the next trek out to Presquit's house.

As it happened, though, he never had to make it.

One night, the art-prince was seen boarding a ship, and he sailed away, forever.

Pindrix never forgot his visit to Presquit's studio, never forgot the warped portraits that he'd seen, or the illustrations he'd glimpsed on his way out, the ones that had frightened him and entered his dreams, again and again over the years.

A drawing of the Dark Mage fashioning a human form from mud and straw and stone.

A drawing of the mud baby in its cradle.

And a drawing of the Maturate.

Pindrix, the Spellman of Soolky, remembered that last drawing now as he lay terrified on the sandy beach.

The Maturate.

The hive-shaped shelter with three slits in one side to symbolize the three known Moments of Whole Creation, and a round hole at the top to symbolize the Fourth Moment, whence would come the Last Humans, to bring on the End of Everything.

The Maturate.

It stood directly in front of Pindrix on the beach.

Exactly as he had seen it rendered in Presquit's drawing.

The growth-place.

The Maturate.

Pindrix, a Spellman, searched through his memory for an equation of destructive magic, an equation that might destroy this growth-place and the babe of mud he was convinced now slept cradled within it—but though burning numbers flew through his mind, and parallelograms and trapezoids and scalene triangles whirled and collided, he was too blasted with fright to think clearly, and no spell was summoned.

He ground his forehead bitterly into the sand.

And flinched when he heard footsteps behind him.

*　　*　　*

THE EMPTY MAN STOOD IN THE
shallows beside the barge, his face and chest slicked with
ooze, his shoulders and back torn and bloody. He looked
up at the Abounding Woman, who was clutching herself
tight to keep from exploding, then turned to the Mage of
Four, Mage of Luck. The mage had draped a curtain over
the entrance to the small round-topped cabin, and was
now studying the lightening sky. He smiled thinly, then
came across the deck. To the Abounding Woman: "We are
ready." Then he leaned down and blew again, softly, into
an ear of the Empty Man, and the Empty Man twitched,
lifting his clawed left hand.

The Dark Mage touched it, and it burst into flame.

A flame that burned but did not consume.

"When the Maturate is ashes, return to us and the
promise I made you shall be fulfilled."

The Empty Man turned and splashed through the
shallows and walked slowly across the sand, and climbed a
dune, and disappeared down the other side.

HERB HAD SET OFF IMMEDI-
ately toward Pindrix, but he'd not gotten too far along
when his foot struck something cold and hard, something
that gouged his flesh painfully. He stopped, cursing under
his breath, and looked down. It was a pair of pants—what
he'd snagged himself on was the heavy belt buckle.

A pair of pants wasn't all that strange a discovery, but
these were corduroy jeans, and he hadn't seen anything
like *that* in Lostwithal—jeans with an L. L. Bean label on
the back pocket. And there was a shirt, over there. And a
gunbelt and holster. And several feet away, a .45 automatic pistol.

He glanced toward Pindrix again, Pindrix still pros-
trate on the sand in front of that weird little dome, then
plucked up the jeans and dug a wallet from the back
pocket. Flipped it open, and let out a gusty breath.

Driver's license, Visa card, MasterCard, NRA membership card: all issued to Richard D. Forell.

Herb's head went spinning.

Richard D. Forell? *Major* Forell?

Gene Boman's father-in-law?

What in Christ's name was Major Forell's clothing doing here?

Then, looking up, glancing back toward Pindrix, Herb froze.

Seeing the Major himself, naked and covered with mud, staggering toward the little dome. Holding a fiery torch.

PINDRIX SCURRIED TO HIS knees. At first, he'd thought the naked man was slogging toward *him*, but no, he didn't seem to even notice the Spellman. He just walked leadenly, his hand burning, black smoke roiling off it, and when he touched his fire to the Maturate, the dead wood and the grass flared up, instantly.

Pindrix dragged himself to his feet, staring.

He was so focused on the spectacle of the burning Maturate, so enervated with relief—

(The Epicene is being consumed!)

—that he let his attention slip wholly from the figure who'd torched the Maturate.

Who had turned and was now gazing malevolently at the Spellman.

A moment later, Pindrix doubled over in excruciating pain.

He fell forward on his knees, his hands going to his groin.

When he looked up, vision swimming, the naked man kicked him again, this time in the face, and Pindrix, nose spurting blood, shot backwards, crashed down hard.

Pindrix saw the flaming hand plunge toward his eyes, and screamed.

*   *   *

AS SOON AS HERB WAS RUNNING
again, charging fast as he could up the beach between the high dunes, he realized he'd done a very stupid thing. A *very* stupid thing.

Left the goddamn gun lying in the sand, back there. Christ, are you dumb, or what?

He nearly stopped, turned around and sprinted back for it, but it seemed too late for that now.

Major Forell, who'd just kicked poor Pindrix in the nuts . . . now kicked him again, in the face.

And if Herb didn't do something quick, it looked like the son of a bitch was going to keep on kicking the Spellman, to death.

No.

Change that.

He wasn't going to keep kicking him: he was going to stick a torch into his face.

Jesus Christ, what was going *on* here?

Because it wasn't a *torch,* the Major didn't have a torch: his friggen *hand* was on fire!

Herb, who was still at least twenty yards away, felt he had to do something. So he yelled.

Screamed.

The Major's name.

And the Major pulled back his arm, glanced up.

Herb stopped running, kept panting. "Major. It's me, Herb Dierickx. 'Member? Gene Boman's driver? I used to drive your son-in-law's car?" Herb talking, knowing it all sounded stupid as hell out here on a beach on another planet, the guy's hand burning wildly, but, hey, it did the trick.

It stopped the Major.

At the same time, the Major didn't seem to recognize Herb at all. To say the least. He just stared, his jaw hanging open, clots of mud sliding across his chest.

Herb thinking of double features on Saturday afternoons. B-pictures. Zombie movies.

Herb saying, trying to be loosey-goosey, trying to sound like he'd just run into an old acquaintance in the aisle of an appliance store, both of them doing their

Christmas shopping, Hey, longtime no-see—that sort of tone, Herb saying, "Major, what's going *on*?"

. . . As Pindrix, groaning, tried to crawl away.

For a long moment, the Major just stood there, then he tottered, his right hand going to his forehead, like he was trying to remember something, think of something.

But then his hand dropped, and he came at Herb, charging.

What happened to the zombie trudge, huh?

Shit.

Herb thinking, Shit, as he turned and tried to run.

PINDRIX WAS GASPING, TRYING to rise, levering himself up on an elbow, collapsing. Finally, with an heroic effort, he managed to prop himself up, and stay up.

He shook his head to clear the pounding, then saw Herb, a Dierickx stumble over his own two feet and fall, saw the naked man kick him viciously in the ribs, then keep on kicking him.

Pindrix, realizing that he was out of danger now, that he could just get up and flee.

Pindrix, staggering to his feet.

Pindrix, squeezing his eyes shut tight, willing numbers into his mind, adding them, determining sums, sums that lit a slew of rhombuses whirling through his mind's eye.

Thinking, 'Teacher, please let this work.

Wishing he had his little red book.

Sucking up saliva and spitting, hard.

Then: hearing the naked man bellow in pain.

Pindrix smiled.

For the last time in his life.

HERB ON HIS SIDE, KNEES drawn up, spitting blood.

As another kick landed, at his kidneys.

The Major was kicking him with his bare feet.

A bone snapped, but Herb was pretty certain it wasn't one of his.

Jesus God. Herb thinking, I'm sorry, Marge, I really and truly am sorry.

He screamed as fire glanced his shoulder, and his flesh sizzled.

And then: it wasn't him screaming, it was the Major.

The blows stopped. Herb waited for them to start again, but they didn't, and when he ventured to open his eyes, the Major was no longer straddling him, he was stumbling off, his body covered with huge black and red boils.

The Major howling, turning suddenly, aiming his eyes at Pindrix, who stood rooted, arms stuck straight out in front of him, thumbs touching.

Herb tried to call, tell Pindrix to run, but he couldn't catch his breath. Thinking, Run, just run, just get away. Run, you asshole!

But Pindrix didn't; he just stood there, arms stretched, fingers crackling like an electricity exhibit at a science museum. A huge smile on his face.

Herb looked away when the Major snatched Pindrix with his flaming hand. Snatched him by the throat, and the fire enveloped the Spellman's head, flew down his back.

And then Herb was running again, but this time back down the beach. Nothing more he could do for Pindrix, but he wasn't going to let the son of a bitch Major win, oh no, oh no: he was gonna get that gun and he was gonna kill the bastard.

It'd be easy.

He'd read about it hundreds of times in his true crime books.

About how easy it was to squeeze a trigger, when you were angry.

How easy it was to kill.

So many monsters in the world.

He found the pistol right where he'd stupidly left it, grabbed it, and went racing back up the beach.

The dome hut was still burning, and Pindrix was still burning, but Major Forell was gone.

No, not gone.

Staggering away, away from Herb, and away from the corpse he'd made, climbing a dune.

Herb put on a burst of speed. It was gonna be so easy to kill, so easy.

But it wasn't.

"Major!"

The Major kept climbing the dune, he wouldn't look back at Herb.

Herb thinking, Shoot him in the back, go ahead. Shoot the bastard.

But he couldn't. He'd grown up cheering Lash La-Rue and Johnny Mack Brown, Hopalong Cassidy and Roy Rogers and Gene Autry, and he couldn't shoot a man in the back. The American cowboy movie ethic coming into play.

"Major!"

And when Major Forell still didn't halt, didn't turn, Herb's anger went slack. Until he forced himself to look behind him, at Pindrix's charred body. And then he was wheezing up the dune, coughing hectically, spitting blood, flipping the safety off the pistol, clasping both hands around the grip.

There was a barge floating out into the lake, water churning and frothing around it: Herb spotting it, surprised and startled for a moment, thinking, What the hell's making it *go?* Then shaking away the distraction, swiveling his head to find the Major again, spotting him— the Major striding across the beach, his left hand smoking, but no longer burning—and Herb Dierickx extended his arm, pointed the gun, and fired, three times.

One miss, two hits. One to the body, one through the back of his head.

To hell with Lash LaRue and Johnny Mack Brown. To hell with Hoppy and Roy and Gene.

And to hell with Major Richard D. Forell.

Herb began to shake convulsively, and his vision danced with black and red flocking. He dropped to his knees, gulping for breath, then exploded into a coughing jag that went on and on and left him wracked and exhausted. He flung away the pistol and slumped. He felt himself falling . . .

When he opened his eyes again, the sky had turned deep blue, the sun was blazing, the air was thick and moist. Down at the water's edge, the Major's body was covered with gnats and flies.

The barge was gone.

Struggling to his feet, Herb searched around for the pistol, found it, and picked it up, then turned and headed back over the dune. As he crested it, he stopped, abruptly.

Five men stood gathered near the smoking remains of the dome hut, staring down at Pindrix, the Spellman of Soolky.

One of them glanced up, spotted Herb (who lifted his gun, reflexively), and then hollered with near-ecstatic exuberance, "It's Deer-ick, it's Deer-ick!"

Herb tingled, thinking there was only one guy who'd ever mispronounced his name like that.

Jesus Christ, is it possible?

Gene?

Eugene Boman?

That you, boss?

CHAPTER 10

REPORTER'S NOTEBOOK (II)

I *USED TO KNOW AN EDITOR when I worked for the* Enquirer, *a guy named Burns (Peter wrote on the back of a check). A real hardnosed* Front Page *kind of guy; I liked Burnsie a lot. And why I'm thinking of him now is because of something he used to say to us staff writers and reporters. He'd say, "Ain't no such thing as a coincidence. Things happen because." He'd leave it at that: Things happen because. And I always believed it. Things happen because.*

But now I don't know. Maybe in the kind of life I knew before meeting Jack that was true. But now I don't know. I've seen a hell of a lot of coincidences happen in the last couple of days. What Jack calls Accidents. Maybe the patterns of human life aren't

*the same all over? I don't know. Jesus, don't ask me.
As a reporter, I'm with Burnsie. But what would you
call meeting Herb Dierickx this morning? A coincidence, right? You'd call it a coincidence. Pretty far-
friggen-fetched, but there you go: it happened.*

Shit happens.

Why not coincidences?

*It's driving me nuts, though, because I know in
my rational heart that this shouldn't have happened.*

*But I'll try and forget it, leave it to some pointy-
head in a university math department to figure out, if
he/she's so inclined. Leave it go, forget it, and get
back to the facts.*

*And the facts are these: We rode all day in the
coach, stopping every hour, sometimes every half, so
that Zickafooz could jump down and walk to the edge
of the lake, and give it a long hard stare. I kept asking
Ukrops what's he looking for? Is Money out there?
But Ukrops told me, in so many words, to shut up. So
I finally did, and we kept riding.*

*After dark, we stopped for a while, just pulled
off into the trees, and ate a pretty meager supper, just
bread and salted beef, the stuff Sollox had purchased
at one of the market stalls before we left Beybix.
Bread and meat and bitter white wine.*

*GB even got alert enough to eat and drink a
little, but for the most part he still seemed completely
fuzzed out. After supper, Ukrops pulled out his London city map again, poring over it, enjoying a mental
trek. (Note: Ask him about that again, sometime.)*

*Sollox sat with us, but the poor soldier is such a
sad sack/gloomy gus; he just sat there sighing, and he
sighed again, even louder, when it was time to climb
back into the driver's seat, crack the whip and take
off.*

*Zickafooz, the Finder, didn't join us during the
meal break. He just went and stood by the lake again,
staring out over it like Hiawatha or somebody. It's
weird. But, then, what isn't? I'm going to try to remember Dubrovnik: just be here, just be part of*

*things, don't always be asking why. I'm going to try,
but it won't be easy.*

*We continued on through the night, jouncing
along the Sand Road, and finally around dawn I
dozed a little. Thank God, I didn't find myself back
on the Donohue show. Instead, I dreamed I'd found
Money Campbell, turns out she wasn't even lost—
she'd just gone shopping to buy me a present. Woke
before I had a chance to open it, though.*

*Actually, I didn't just wake up; Ukrops shook me
awake. "We'll be stopping for a while. I thought you
might want to stretch your legs." I was kind of irritable that he'd disturbed such a nice dream, but didn't
show it. Just climbed out of the coach, and yeah, it
was good to move around, shake out some of the
aches. It was another bright morning, already hot.*

*I realized after a moment that, for the first time
since we'd left the city, you couldn't actually see
Black Lake: dense forest bordering each side of the
road. As four of the five of us Merry Spacemen emptied our bladders, Zickafooz (who maybe doesn't
have a bladder, who knows?) went traipsing off into
the woods. Ukrops buttoned up (n.b.: no zippers here
—potentially fabulous market some day for the Talon
Company) and then drifted off after him. I collared
GB and followed. Sollox, looking miserable as usual,
came along, too, rather (I suspect) than be left standing there by himself. (He doesn't strike me as a very
courageous soldier.)*

*The woods were only about twenty yards deep,
and they ended at a really beautiful beach; I could
easily imagine some resort company going absolutely
nuts at the sight of it. The sand was white, and sugar-
fine, and the beach seemed to stretch away forever, so
broad and rolling with dunes that we couldn't see the
lake. Which, of course, Zickafooz had set off to find.*

*I decided I'd seen enough of the lake for one day
and just plopped down, took off my sandals, and buried my feet in the sand. Petey the kid again. It felt
really good.*

The good feeling didn't last very long, though.

It was Sollox who first noticed the smoke, coming from the far side of a huge dune about thirty, forty yards to our left. Immediately, Ukrops set off to have a look, Sollox dogging him (reluctantly, you could just tell). I got up, nudged GB, and we headed off after them, me carrying my sandals.

What was smoking was a shell of some kind of beach hut, but what raised the hairs on the back of my neck was the dead body, a dead and burned body lying alongside it in the sand.

Ukrops seemed far more interested in the smoldering hut, though. He walked around it slowly, several times, then said something to Sollox, and I was startled to realize that I couldn't understand him. What's this, another language? I'd thought there was only one. Maybe not, maybe just another dialect, maybe a military language? I don't know. (Check later.) They conferred, and Sollox turned white. Honest to God. White as a sheet. When Ukrops pointed to the burning hut and said whatever he said to Sollox, the poor fat soldier looked like he was going to pass right out.

Naturally, I tried quizzing Ukrops about what was happening, but he suddenly started acting the high-and-mighty Red Guardsman again, no longer the cute Princess Diana fan. He waved me away, and went straight up to the smoking hut. Weird. The dead body didn't seem to interest him at all.

It sure interested me, though.

Gene Boman put a hand to his mouth, like he was going to be sick. Which gave me pause, as they say. If he was so out of it, then how come this was getting through to him? I gave him the old narrow-eyed suspicious-reporter look, and he flinched.

Hmmm.

Eventually, Zickafooz returned from looking at the lake, and got irritated to find us dawdling by this totally unimportant dead body. The guy is a monomaniac: once he's on the case, he's on the case. He *insisted that we leave at once, that we were interfering with his service, but Ukrops wasn't having any of it: he told his brother to go stand over there, right there, and that we'd leave when he decided to go. Then he walked all around the smoldering beach hut again, frowning and rubbing his chin with a hand.*

And then—it made me jump, I'll admit it—Gene Boman let out a war whoop and started to shout and point.

And there was Herb Dierickx standing on top of a goddamn sand dune.

Herb Dierickx, for crying out loud.

Ain't no such thing as a coincidence?

Maybe not, but there he was, there stood Herb Dierickx, and as far as I can tell Lostwithal ain't that small a planet.

Peter paused in his writing, then tapped his pen/Boman's pen reflectively against his lips. He was sitting with his back to a dune, his knees drawn up, a bank check smoothed on a thigh. Several feet away, Ukrops and Sollox continued their scrutiny of the smoldering hut, Ukrops getting down on his knees and poking at embers with a stick that he'd found. Peter was reminded of Master Amabeel, and of how the old mage had crawled around the turret room at Manse Seloc, seeking—what was it? Iteration. Seeking Iteration. The Sherlock Holmes of Beybix, Ukrops had called him. Yeah? So what was the Red Guardsman doing now? Playing Baker Street Irregular?

Beyond the two soldiers, Zickafooz paced angrily, kicking sand, impatient to be off.

Well, that makes two of us, Peter thought.

He frowned, then looked to his left, where Herb Dierickx was sitting on the beach talking with Gene Boman, the pair of them nodding their heads, gesturing emphatically, and every so often glancing up at Peter.

Peter glared back at them, then clicked his pen, and resumed writing.

Big reunion going on. Gene ("Give 'em Blue Mark") Boman reunited with Herbert ("I'll drive you anywhere") Dierickx. The pair of them make me sick. Boman, especially. The son of a bitch has been play-acting ever since we picked him up at Manse Seloc! I give him some credit, though: he never struck me as having the savvy to carry off such a thing. But he fooled me. Know what I feel like doing? Kicking his teeth in. And I'll do it—eventually. I'll have my revenge yet.

But, back to the facts: we found the body of Major Forell on the beach. Herb D. says that he shot him. Well, good for Herb D. Maybe there's some hope for him, after all. But I still don't like him. Anybody associated with Gene Boman—Money excepted—I don't like. Never will.

I wish I could've shot Major Forell.

I feel gypped.

I always feel gypped.

Now, why'd I write that?

And what is this anyhow, a diary? I'm supposed to be taking notes here. Notes. Facts. We found Forell's body up the beach. Herb D. says it was Forell who killed the other guy, some sort of local magician named Pindrick or Pendrik or Pindrix (note: spellings of all names are phonetic/will decide later on official versions). HD also says Forell's hand was on fire—sounds a bit like Frank Luks, no? Except that Luks's entire body was in flames. HD also claims he saw a flat barge that moved without sails, engines, paddles, poles, anything—similar, it sounds, to how the Women of Mist get around the lake. Were they here? Can't tell. HD says he saw no one on the barge. Neither did he see our friend the Mage of 4. So what happened here? Where is the Mage of 4? And what

"Peter?"

It was Herb Dierickx, standing in front of him now, blocking the sun. "Can I have a word with you?" He turned his head to cough, then looked back at Peter, smiling.

Peter folded the check in half, then kept running his thumb and first finger across the crease; at last he lifted his eyes.

"I'm coming to you, like, as an intermediary." Herb nodding back at Gene Boman, who stood ten feet away.

"Is that a fact?"

"Ah jeez."

"Ah jeez *what?*"

"You gonna keep being a hard-ass forever?"

"Screw you."

"Hey, look at me, Peter. You looking? Good. You hate Mr. Boman's guts, and you got every right to. And you don't much care for my guts, and I think you're being a little unfair, but—you can feel whatever you like. That's your business. Thing is. Here we are. That's the thing."

Peter said nothing. He was thinking, though, that Herb Dierickx sounded . . . different, changed somehow, from the last time he'd seen him. Tougher, maybe? Maybe.

"That's the thing," Herb said again. "Here we are. The three of us together—and from what Mr. Boman tells me, we're looking for Money. Trying to put the old gang of four back together again, eh?"

Peter scowled.

"So here's what I'm proposing. For the time being, all grudges are off. Okay? We just get on with whatever we're doing and see if we can come out alive. We make it, we get back home—hey, like I told you the other night, I'll do anything you want to make things up to you. And Mr. Boman will, too."

Peter narrowed his eyes.

"He says you can take your pick: either he'll give you whatever you want, in cash, or else he'll turn himself in to the police, tell everything that happened. Everything about the Idiot Drugs, about the Major, everything. But you gotta take your pick, he says. But he says you don't have to decide now."

Peter couldn't help it, he laughed. "What the hell's

he doing, *negotiating?* Thinks this a friggen boardroom? *I* gotta pick, one or the other? Friggen nerve."

"Well. Maybe so. But I'm just relaying the information."

"Tell him I got a counterproposal. Tell him—how 'bout you tell him this? No money, no cops. All I want, I want to have the pleasure of injecting *him* with Blue Mark. Tell him that'll settle things, far as I'm concerned."

"No, I don't think he'd go for that."

They both turned and looked up the beach: Gene Boman watching them, his face in shadow, impossible to read any expression. Herb waved. Boman waved back. Peter shook his head in amazement.

"Hey, I wanna know something."

Herb saying, "What?"

"He tell you about showing up in that castle, the other night?"

"Oh sure. He came with the Major. And the Major went off with the guy who wanted to kill Jack and Mr. Squintik. Hey, where *is* Jack?"

"Never mind. What I wanna know is: he's been acting like somebody in a trance, two days he's been doing it. Like, his mind was gone. Was that total bullshit? Has he been jerking me around the whole time?"

"Oh no." Herb smiling, saying, "Oh no, up until when you punched him in the nose, he was fourteen years old, watching television shows."

"What?"

"He says he just remembered. He was back home, watching TV." Herb Dierickx leaned in toward Peter, whispered, "Hey, Peter? My advice?" He glanced down at the check that Peter was still rubbing. "Take the money." He started back toward Gene Boman.

"Hey."

Herb turned, an eyebrow going up.

"About that first thing? About all grudges being off, for the time being? I accept."

Herb smiled, and gave Peter a two-fingered salute.

"And—hey!"

Herb cocking his head, saying, "What?"

"How the hell did you ever survive those goddamn bats?"

Immediately, Herb's smile vanished. Then he turned and looked up the beach, where the Spellman's body still lay. Covered now with blankets Soldier Sollox had brought from the coach.

Back on the road again (Peter wrote). *Except we've lost one of our Merry Spacemen. Lost one, gained another. Sollox is gone, Herb Dierickx has joined the club.*

I still haven't figured out why Ukrops told Sollox to stay behind on the road. At first, I thought it had something to do with legal matters—you know, two dead men on the beach, "some explanations are in order"—that kind of thing. But I don't believe Ukrops gives two shits about the dead bodies. (About the dead bodies, no; about that burned hut, yes. He collected some of its charred wood, stuck it in a bag, and then tied the bag to the coach's roof.)

I suspect there's something very "Dubrovnik" about the decision to leave Sollox behind. I tried to get some explanation from Ukrops, but he's turned very moody, very mum. Yesterday, he was carrying on like the search for Money Campbell was a great game; today, he's all-business, all-soldier—and he's treating me like a lowly civilian. Like we're all lowly civilians. He doesn't watch out, I'm gonna cashier him out of the Merry Spacemen.

But about Sollox. As we were coming back from the beach (we left both bodies, by the way, exactly where they were, which disturbed Herb Dierickx greatly: he wanted to bury the magician), Ukrops announced that Sollox would not be continuing on with us. And then he spoke briefly to the soldier in that language or dialect I can't understand. Sollox nodded (and looked greatly relieved), and the last we saw of him, he was standing by the side of the road. Just standing there, waving to us. As we were pulling

*away, Herb Dierickx said, "I hope somebody comes
by soon. So he can start a rumor."*

 *The guy may've changed a little, but not a whole
lot. He's still a flake, in my book.*
 Gene Boman and I are still not speaking.
 Ukrops is our new driver.
 And th-th-that's all for now, folks.

As the coach rolled down the Sand Road, Herb Dierickx suddenly tensed, recognizing some landmarks. Pretty
soon they'd be passing Mithik's place, and he considered
asking Ukrops to stop, just for a minute. But why? For
what? A parting handshake? A last cup of tea? A squeeze?
A kiss?

He closed his eyes, and kept them closed, till they
were well past the charcoal-maker's cottage.

Some things that happened never happened.

That's what Herb decided to decide.

Some things that happened? They never happened.

Life's funny that way.

CHAPTER 11

WALKER ON WATER

THERE WAS A MAN, AND THE man had two small daughters, and on this day, which was a fine, hot, blue-skied day in Late Blaze, the second of the year's four short summers, they all went out from their home and walked down to the lake. Each of the girls carried an oar, and their father carried a hamper of food and a large, illustrated copy of the Book of True and Cruel. The book was one of the father's prized possessions, passed down to him from his sur-father—it was illustrated by the great art-prince Ifnazz.

His wife thought it was foolish to take such a beautiful book out into a boat where it could get wet, become ruined. But he never listened to his wife, about the book. No, it was one of his favorite pastimes to sit reading stories of History and Talent and too-humans to his daughters as they bobbled about aimlessly on the black-water lake.

His wife would finally say to him, as she said to him

just this morning, "Well, all right, if you're so decided, just you be sure you don't read them too much of the Old Story." And he promised, and kept his promise.

It was easy. The girls weren't interested in hearing about the Schoolteacher and his First Pupil, nor did they wish to be disturbed by all the legends of the Epicene, and, naturally, they didn't believe in Last Humans.

The stories they most wanted to hear read to them were the stories of Talent—stories of mages and magic, in particular. But this fine morning, they asked their father to read about Walkers. The Poorest of the Poor, the Richest of the Rich.

And, naturally, their father obliged them—in his youth he'd considered making a tramp's life his thirdwork, but then fell in love with the woman he married. Not that he ever regretted it, of course, but still . . .

Still. . . .

He opened the book and began, "A Walker is a ghost of flesh and blood and vitals and bone. A Walker—"

Just then, his younger daughter, a girl with a head of silky brown curls, suddenly exclaimed and jumped up in the boat, rocking it. She pointed, and then her big sister laughed, and the father just stared, and smiled with rue.

For there was a Walker, walking on water. Walking on water as though it were any road of dirt or sand in Lostwithal. Walking steadily, head down, arms swinging lazily, his hair blowing in the lake breeze, his shabby clothes riffling and snapping, his dark black shoes skimming the lake surface, making tiny splashes. Sun diamonds flashed all around him.

"Oh, and he's got a wasp, Father!" exclaimed the older girl. "See his wasp? His Walker's wasp, Father—see it?"

The father nodded, and kept on staring after the Walker, and his boat rocked gently in the hot, bright, blue-skied day. Then he smiled, telling his daughters to sit down before they both fell out, and resumed: "A Walker is a ghost of flesh and blood and vitals and bone. . . ."

CHAPTER 12

ARRIVAL

DIDGE STOOD IN THE doorway of the game room that looked so much like—but not exactly like—her Uncle Jix's game room, and glared angrily at Uncle Milty, who was arranging glass tiles upon a schema board. Didge slumping against the jamb, shaking her head, saying, "Why are you still here?"

"Why are *you* here? It's all those drugs, you can't keep awake—no matter how hard you try."

Her eyebrows rose, and Uncle Milty chuckled.

"I know all about you—you see, I have access." He nodded toward the dark corridor beyond. "I know it's impolite to snoop, but what else am I supposed to do when I'm down here alone?" He waved a languid hand at the schema board. "Short game?"

"Who *are* you?"

"You used to be quite good at schema."

She turned to leave.

"Didge!"

She turned back, frowning.

"Sit, girl." He stood up from the table and crossed the room, took hold of her hand. She made to snatch it away, but then just slumped, and he guided her by the elbow over to the table. "There," he said, and sat down opposite her. "You really ought to stop with all those bugs. I had another landlord once, did the same thing. Well, not quite. It wasn't beetles, of course, but it was comparable. After a while, he was absolutely *no* fun to play with. His strategy got so sloppy, it was embarrassing. And his conversation! Gibberish." He sighed, then smiled again. "Shall I go first, or shall you?" He propped his elbows on the table and studied the board. "Why don't you go first."

He quirked his mouth and sat back. Studied Didge's face for a minute, then leaned forward. "My most recent landlord—before you? Was under the delusion that I was some kind of . . . advisor. He kept expecting me to tell him what to do all the time, and when I didn't, he just—well, we had our troubles together. The poor fellow. Now, I understood perfectly well why he labored under such a delusion, but still I couldn't help him. I'm not—an advisor."

"What are you, then?"

"It wouldn't make much sense to you—at least, I don't think it would."

"How many hearts do you have?"

He laughed. "My dear, I don't have *any* hearts. I'm just . . . me. But we've gotten off the subject."

Didge exhaled in a burst. Turned in her seat and looked toward the doorway.

"The subject I was moving toward . . . Didge? Are you listening? I was thinking that perhaps, that perhaps in your case, I might. Actually. *Be* your advisor. Seems you could use one. Do you think that might help?"

"I don't need any help."

Uncle Milty reached out and flicked a finger against a schema tile; it tipped over, struck another, and the second one broke, spilling an amber-colored oil on the board. Didge looked, then raised her eyes to Uncle Milty's.

"I don't need any help," she repeated. "I know per-

fectly well what I'm going to do. And how I'm going to do
it."

"Yes. But you see, it's so foolish. To kill a madman—
what will that prove? Will it make you a Walker again?"

"Nothing will."

"Exactly. Exactly! Nothing will. So what's the point?"

"Satisfaction."

"A minor sensation. Believe me, I've felt satisfaction
in a *dozen* landlords—it's minor and it's fleeting. And
death is even a lesser sensation. You won't like it."

"You're not real."

"But I am!"

She looked at him for a long moment, then rose
abruptly. "I have to go, I have to wake."

"Don't do it. Don't do what you're planning. This
art-prince isn't responsible for your misery. *You* are."
They locked eyes, till Uncle Milty glanced back down at
the schema board. "Stay."

For a moment, it seemed as though she might, but
then she wagged her head violently and walked to the
door. There she halted, stood a moment with her back to
the albino. When she turned around, a half-smile flickered. "You're right—you're not an advisor."

Uncle Milty laughed. "I tried."

"Thank you."

"And I know you mean that. I *really* know you mean
that."

Then, as she was leaving, he called after her, "If you
go ahead with your plan, well—I've enjoyed my tenancy.
Brief as it's been."

DIDGE SAT UP WITH A SHARP IN-
take of breath. A crick in her shoulder, her head throb-
bing. Instantly, she was aware of movement all around
her: passengers pressing toward the exit door.

The ship had docked.

Swinging around, Didge put her feet to the floor, and
reached down for her traveling sack. Checked to see that

all the knots were still tight in her wristlet. They were, all eight of them.

Eight beetles.

More than enough 'sap to put an end to everything.

She stood up, wiped a hand across her sticky lips, and joined the crush of passengers streaming onto the deck, toward the gangway, toward the Isle of Mites.

ABOUT A MONTH AGO (WHICH seemed an eternity ago now), during the first week of really cold weather in the city where she was homeless, Jere Lee had gone to the library to get warm for a few hours.

She'd wheeled in her shopping cart, and suffered the disapproving looks of the librarians and the silent readers. As had been her habit nearly all her life in libraries, she first scoured the history stacks. Picked out a book called *Hopes and Ashes*, about the Great Depression, and was on her way to claim a sunny nook for herself when she happened to glance through a plate-glass window into a soundproofed room and spotted a dozen people seated at carels wearing headphones and watching movies on tiny video monitors. Could you do that? Could you get a movie and watch it in the library? She didn't know that. How wonderful! She hadn't seen a movie in months—not since she'd had that operation, lost her job, and found herself without a place to live. Months and months. And she'd always been a great movie buff. About the only thing that she and her husband had had in common by the end of their marriage (after she'd given up the booze, and he hadn't) was a love of movies.

Any kind of movies were okay, but Jere Lee had a special fondness for American movies of the thirties and forties. There were more happy endings.

What's wrong with a happy ending?

She'd gone into the soundproofed room and was shown a small directory by the librarian: all the titles available. What a treasure trove! She could scarcely make up her mind. How about *Bringing Up Baby*? Or *Yankee Doo-*

dle Dandy? How about—oh, how about *The Best Years of Our Lives?* And then she noticed that the library owned a video copy of *Dodsworth*.

Dodsworth!

She hadn't seen *Dodsworth* in ages—it never showed up on TV. And it was one of Jere Lee's all-time favorite movies. Walter Huston and Ruth Chatterton and Paul Lukas and David Niven and Mary Astor. Mary Astor!

She'd gotten the film, and taken her seat at a carel, and spent that afternoon with Sam Dodsworth and his foolish wife on their fateful trip to England. Oh, that wife! Jere Lee thought she was such an idiot, to let herself fall for all those continental gigolos, and lose a good man like Dodsworth. Well, she got what she deserved, Mrs. Dodsworth did. She lost him, and Mary Astor, down-to-earth Mary Astor, ended up with him.

Jere Lee had always thought that Mary Astor was beautiful, and as she watched *Dodsworth* again that day, she thought that Mary never was lovelier than in that scene on the deck of the luxury liner where she first meets Sam. She's sitting under the stars all by herself, and he comes up to see a lighthouse beam, and they start to talk, and you just *know* they're meant for each other. It was a perfect scene, Jere Lee thought. This wonderful man and this beautiful woman alone on the deck of a ship out on the Atlantic Ocean, in the moonlight. Such a quiet scene, no kissing or anything—just two decent people becoming good friends.

Last night, with Squintik, Jere Lee had suddenly remembered that scene from *Dodsworth*.

Two decent people becoming good friends.

Friendship now, the rest of it later. Maybe.

She'd decided she could live with that.

They hadn't gone back down into the hold, they'd just stayed on deck, Jere Lee trying to quiz Squintik, but gently, not wanting to push him—quiz him about just what the heck was going on.

Starting with—that block of ice, that man inside it?

"The Schoolteacher," Squintik had told her.

Jere Lee saying but she'd thought the Schoolteacher had lived . . . thousands of years ago.

Yes, Squintik had told her. And he *still* lived. Squintik telling her that he still lived, and that it was his continued existence that maintained Perfect Order. It was his *faith* in Perfect Order that maintained it.

Jere Lee accepted that. Whenever things got cosmological, she just faded out; it was a failing, she knew, but that's just the way she was. She was a Taurus: down to earth. She liked her reality solid.

"But what were you *doing?*" she'd asked. "You were trying to wake him up?"

"He wasn't actually here—that was merely a vision."

"I understand that," said Jere Lee. "I understand that. But still—you *were* trying to wake him up."

"A dangerous thing—but worth the risk. He dreams of the Three Moments and keeps them Whole. It is a dangerous thing to wake the 'Teacher, but it is better that I wake him than his pupil's pupil."

"You're talking about the Mage of Four?"

Squintik had nodded. "He is coming to wake the 'Teacher, to taunt him."

Jere Lee racking her brains, trying to remember what Jack, a Walker had told them the other day—the Old Story. About the Schoolteacher and his First Pupil. The story vaguely reminiscent of Adam and Eve. The First Pupil convinced there were four Moments, not three, in Whole Creation. The Schoolteacher denying it, forbidding his Pupil to seek proof of that Fourth Moment, the Moment of Bulcease, where the Last Humans were supposed to be.

"To taunt him," Squintik had said. "To taunt him with the reality of the Epicene, to make him watch the monster tear through the veil into the Fourth Moment. To prove to the Schoolteacher that Last Humans exist. And with that proof comes the end of Perfect Order, the end of the Schoolteacher—the End of Everything."

And Jere Lee had nodded, nodded, knowing that she ought to be frightened, knowing that what Squintik was talking about was basically the same as what all the minis-

ters she'd half-listened to during her childhood had
droned on and on about, the end of the world, Armaged-
don, all that fire-next-time sort of thing. But she couldn't
get too excited about it.

Because they were standing talking at the railing of a
wooden ship, under the light of two moons; because she
kept thinking of *Dodsworth;* and because—she realized—
she had utter confidence in this man beside her.

She'd finally asked him, "Why did you . . . chase us
out of your apartment? What did that man Amabeel tell
you?"

"He reminded me that I am not only a Cold Mage. I
had . . . wished to forget."

"What else *are* you?"

Squintik hadn't replied: he'd merely stared off into
space.

"All right," Jere Lee had said, "can you answer this?
Where're we going?"

"The Isle of Mites."

"And what's there?"

He'd turned and looked at her with sorrow. "The
Schoolteacher. And, I fear, the monster."

She'd leaned against him, and they'd fallen silent,
and the ship had ploughed on.

SHE DIDN'T KNOW WHAT SHE'D
expected the Isle of Mites to be like, but it certainly
wasn't *this*.

The first thing she saw of the island was a grassy
hillside strewn with gigantic stone rhombuses and triangles and trapezoids and cylinders and rectangles, and
when she asked Squintik what they were, he answered,
"Grave markers."

Oh. Right. Grave markers.

As the ship rounded a promontory and slipped toward the harbor, she saw a large sprawling village, the
wooden buildings crowded together, canted and dilapi-
dated. Dark, rippling clouds hung over every rooftop, in

every thoroughfare. "What are *those?*" Jere Lee asked, pointing, and Squintik replied, "The mites."

Jere Lee saying, "The mites?"

The mites: as she came down the gangplank, pushed along by the exiting passengers, she had to beat the things away from her face. Little flying bugs. What Jere Lee used to call midges. Those nasty little things that swarmed, got in your nose, in your mouth, into the whorls of your ears. And they were everywhere, you couldn't escape them.

Whatever else these Lostwithalians had, they sure as hell didn't have pesticides. Jere Lee grousing.

As she followed Squintik through the street crowds, she noticed (in between flailing her arms in front of her, trying in vain to keep the bugs from her face) that everybody seemed so . . . haggard, unhappy, slow-moving. It was like a city of manic-depressives and reminded her sharply of the hopeless people she'd lived among in city parks.

They shuffled, their eyes cast down in gloom, or else blazing with anger. So many slumped shoulders, so many clenched fists.

Jere Lee noticed a funeral procession: six men bearing a sheeted corpse upon their shoulders, as a hollow-eyed young boy rang a bell, and a scrawny little blond girl broke twigs in half and tossed them down.

With all the bugs and all these sad-looking people, Jere Lee's own mood plunged. She thought of her daughters, she thought of her marriage, she thought of all those years she'd spent in an alcoholic haze.

Squintik put an arm around her.

"You see why I wished to come alone?"

She smiled weakly. "Aren't you glad you didn't?"

He made no response.

They walked down a winding street, Jere Lee constantly blowing to keep the whirling nuisances away from her mouth, Squintik seemingly unaffected by the mites: his mouth a straight line, his jaw set hard, his eyes unblinking.

Jere Lee saying then as they passed a large ugly

building the color of dark mustard, "Are you sure you got the right island?"

Trying to lighten the mood, but it didn't work.

"He is here."

"You're sure of that?"

He looked at her, but once again didn't respond.

They came out the end of the street, and there the village just ended: before them, dead-looking grass and a hillside that climbed. A dusty road.

Squintik saying as they headed along that road, "At the place where Perfect Order is weakest, he lives."

Jere Lee didn't think that made a whole lot of sense, but, hey, this wasn't *her* world.

Just tag along, see what happened: all she could do.

And maybe in the end, if it wasn't the end of everything, well, maybe she could live happily ever after.

What's wrong with a happy ending?

She slapped at the top of her head, spat, waved a hand back and forth in front of her face—damn bugs!—and kept pace with Master Squintik.

CHAPTER 13

ARTIST'S MODEL

COINCIDENCE? JUST HOURS before Jere Lee Vance and Master Squintik (and Didge, a Dispeller) had sailed into the Isle of Mites, Money Campbell had arrived aboard the *1492*.

Before she was allowed to disembark, however, Mother's Last had gone and fetched a local Spellman. He'd appeared dressed in his drab-green cassock and clutching a red-covered book, taken one glance at Money, down in the hold all trussed up, looking pitiably haggard, totally played out, and he'd wept. Yet another poor wretch! What *was* it about this place that pulled all the flotsam and jetsom of Perfect Order—the lunatics and the suicides and the failed Talents? The Spellman—whose posting to this place was nearing its end, thank the 'Teacher—rebuked himself silently for asking himself, yet again, such a pointless (and impudent) question. Although these sad creatures had fallen out of the Order of Things, they were compelled to come here *according* to the Order

of Things. And a Spellman should not presume to understand that. He'd taken a look at Money and shaken his
head sadly. Turning to Mother's Last: "Mad?" (She
looked too young to be a failed Talent, and since her
hands and feet were bound, she had clearly not traveled
here of her own free will.)

"Oh yes," said Mother's Last. "Very mad." The corners of his yellow lips stretched into a playful smile.

"Well, what service would you have me perform?"

"My master thought . . . something simple. To
make her passage from ship to shelter more . . . conve-
nient. My master said to remind you of a spell in your
budget that is called, he believes, the Obedient Child?"

Money squirmed and struggled and grunted: her
mouth wore a gag. She stared wide-eyed up at the Spellman as he spread his legs, shut his eyes, concentrated,
then gripped his left breast with a hand and squeezed it
till some sort of gluey substance leaked through. Money
thinking, Oh gross. Money thinking, I'm gonna kill somebody for this. Money thinking, God let me out of this, I'll
be good. I promise.

After Mother's Last had given the Spellman several
small coins, he'd gone away. The dwarf had then squatted
down, untied Money's bonds, released her gag.

Money thinking, We're parked—docked, whatever
you call it. We're not out on the water anymore. I'm
gonna make a break.

Thinking, I'm gonna knock this runt into the middle
of next week and make a run for it. Just watch me.

She stood up quietly when Mother's Last told her to.

Money thinking, All I have to do is shove this guy,
run up those steps, jump over the side. Ready?

She obligingly held the fool's hand when he told her
to.

Money thinking, Ready? Go! Ready? *Go!*

She quietly accompanied Mother's Last up the stairs
and over to the gangplank, and down the gangplank and
through the streets of the teeming village, and then to an
old building the mottled color of dijon mustard.

Thinking all the time, Ready? Go! You ready? Go! Ready? Go!

NOW SHE WAS WANDERING IDLY
around a large, multiwindowed artist's studio on the third story of that building. She was alone and kept saying to herself, All you have to do is open that door, go down the stairs, and get away. That's *all* you have to do. Ready? *Do* it!

She looked idly out the window, then turned and made another trip around the room, frowning at all the colored-ink drawings pinned to the gleaming pine walls, the oil paintings propped on easels or standing filed in bins. Most of them were portraits, full-length portraits of some strange-looking people, boy. Freaks, is what Money called them. Freaks. They looked like she *felt*, sometimes.

A sound—a click—behind her, and she whirled. The door had opened, quarter-way, and now a cat scurried in; it was a heavy, short-haired tom, but with markings she'd never seen before on any cat. They seemed very . . . decorative. Starbursts on its muzzle. Parti-colored speckles on its forelegs. The cat leapt up on to a stool and regarded Money with suspicion.

Similarly, Money eyed it right back. Figuring that she'd been here long enough in goofy Lostwithal to know that almost anything was possible. This cat? Could be a person in disguise. She was so busy studying the cat, she didn't hear the man appear, became aware of him only when he laid a hand upon her shoulder.

Money surprised herself by not jumping.

She turned her head slightly, seeing long fingers freckled and smeared with artist's pigment.

Money thinking, Slap it away.

But didn't.

She nodded when Prince Presquit removed his hand to point to a black stool on a raised model's stand. "If you wouldn't mind?"

Money thinking, I sure as hell *do* mind!

She moved across the studio, stepped up onto the stand, sat down on the stool.

Presquit smiled at her for a long minute, then ran both hands through his hair. "Could you just . . . loosen the ties on your blouse, push it down over your shoulders?"

Money thinking, Hell with you! (On the ship, she'd hauled off and kicked this little prick right in the ankle, when they'd first met. Boy, she'd like to do that again. Yeah. Money thinking now, Maybe I will. I *will!*)

She loosened the ties on her blouse, pushed it down over her shoulders.

"Perfect!" he exclaimed, then walked across the studio to a wooden cabinet. Using several keys, which he took from a pocket in his short green jacket, he unlocked it, pulled open the door, and withdrew several jars of thick paint in a variety of colors. He set them down on a table beside an easel. Fetched a blank canvas, set it on the easel ledge. Selected a few brushes. Then stood behind the easel, staring at Money. A moment later, he returned to the cabinet, reached inside again and took out a carton of Vantage cigarettes.

Money's eyes opened so wide they stung.

And it was only then, seeing the cigarette carton, seeing Presquit shake out a pack, unzip the red cellophane, peel open the silver end paper, that she realized that the artist had been speaking to her in English since the moment he'd walked through the door.

English?

Not Losplit, English.

And now he was lighting up a Vantage cigarette. Exhaling. The blue smoke rolled across the room, reached Money's nostrils, and she coughed.

"Now just remain perfectly still," he said. "All right?" And with a smoking cigarette between his lips, he began to paint.

As soon as he did, Money felt an unpleasantly warm sensation on her cheeks. She wanted to reach up and touch it, but didn't. Couldn't. She remained perfectly still.

"Can I talk?" she asked. She'd meant the tone to be surly, but it came out pleasantly, respectful.

"Sure, if you like."

"Why are you doing this to me?"

He smiled. Removed the cigarette from his mouth, tapped ash on the floor, stuck it back between his lips. And saw her looking at it. "Is the smoke bothering you?"

She wanted to say yes; instead: "No."

Then she asked, "How did you get . . . that? Those?" She pointed to the carton of Vantage.

"Please, don't move."

She wanted to tell him, Up yours; instead: "I'm sorry."

And now her forehead was burning, and her lips.

"I stock up," he said.

"What?"

"You asked me how I happen to have cigarettes. Nothing like them here. Smoking is *not* a part of Perfect Order." His tone was light and mocking, smug. Money was reminded, a little bit, of David Letterman. Yeah, even the same toothy smile. "I stock up—every year or so I try to get back, pick up a few things I need."

"Get . . . back?"

"To dear Kemolo!" said Presquit, then his face screwed up in concentration, and he applied himself assiduously to his work.

"You can go back and forth?" Money said.

He didn't reply: he worked.

Her chin burned, her neck felt sore, stinging.

She wanted to scream with pain, with terror; instead, she sat there demurely, hands folded in her lap.

"I can go back and forth, yes," he said after a while.

"How? Are you a mage?"

He laughed. "No, I'm a prince—don't I *look* like a prince?" He stepped away from his easel, and struck a haughty pose.

Money thinking, No, you don't look like a prince.

But she said, "Yes, you look like a prince."

Which caused Presquit to laugh uproariously. "Well,

I'm not—not really!" Then he paused, and said, "Carmel, darling."

"What?"

"California. Carmel, California. Prescott, not Presquit. Harry Prescott." He cocked his head, stretched out his right arm, sighted Money along the tip of his loaded brush. And resumed painting.

The corners of Money's eyes started to burn; then her irises burned, then her pupils.

She wanted to rub at the pain, but didn't. Couldn't. Tears streamed down her cheeks.

"I've been here—forever. Well, not quite. Almost," said Presquit. "How about yourself?"

"Just . . . a few days."

"Is that right! How'd you get through—a Walker? A Finder?"

"A Walker."

"Come as a Witness?"

She nodded.

"Me, too. So *that's* what you were doing at old Agel's castle, the other night. When I saw you. You were in the public gardens? With three other people? I saw you, and that was it—I *knew* I'd found the model I'd been looking for. Funny, though. That I chose a Kemolon. I had no idea. Till I picked you up in the alley. Lifted you up. And I'll be damned, I thought, this girl's got only one heart. Don't move. Stay still."

"My face is . . . stinging. It hurts."

"But you won't touch it, will you?"

"No."

Presquit laughed again. "That's what I love about this place. All these magic spells. Quite wonderful! We put a spell on you, did you know that?"

Money wanted to scream: the pain. But she nodded yes—she knew that.

"And you know what that spell cost me? Take a guess. No? Peanuts. It costs as much to hire a Spellman here as it does to hire some kid to cut the grass. Back home. I'm serious. It's so great. Who *wouldn't* rather live here?"

"My face," Money said. "It *stings.*"

"You can play with the world here, if you learn a few things. Of course, silly old Agel and his deadpan magicians think they've got a hammerlock on magic, they act like the AMA. But they're idiots. You can get what you want, be who you want, if you just know how to do it. You can play with the world here. You can *remake* the world, if you know how to do it." He glanced up at Money. "And I know how to do it."

"My face," Money whimpered.

And Presquit, glancing from his painting to Money, then back to his painting, said, "It's finished."

CHAPTER 14

THIS TIME

THE LAST TIME SHE'D BEEN
on Mites, she'd come as a Walker, catching Walker's
Noise as she moved, seeking Rumor's Crux, passing
through these narrow streets with their whirling insects
and their leaden, lethargic crowds. Didge, a Walker,
dressed in Walker's Rags, not a single coin in her pocket,
gleaming black leather shoes upon her feet. Her Heart of
Talent strong with created instincts.

*An art-prince there is with false heart, who would
remake the world in his own disorder.*

All those many seasons ago, Didge had set out on
Ifnazz's Ramble, trusting her talented heart and following
her feet and speaking not of art-princes, false hearts, and
remade worlds, but trusting that somewhere, somehow
she would, quite by Accident, be led to the Crux. And
she'd come here, to Mites, and camped in a graveyard,
had supper with a man who'd killed himself in the night;
she'd roamed the village, listening to conversations, join-

ing in only when she was asked (a Walker is passive, is . . .), eating whenever she was offered food (not often), and thinking more than she wanted to think of—him.

Whom she'd not seen since they'd entered the Craft.

Of him, whom she'd told, Not now, later. After the Craft. One adventure at a time.

Him.

Who filled her Heart of Blood, and would not be dislodged.

Him.

If only she could see him again, she'd thought—if only we could meet by Accident, as Walkers: I could tell him. He could *know.*

That last time on Mites: feeling her legs being drawn down a certain dark alley, meeting a madwoman who'd pulled a knife and chased her, Didge running into another street, frightened but also tingling with the secret knowledge that this was part of the Ramble, an Accident, perhaps a Perfect Accident. Running, till suddenly: a house, a large dark-yellow house with its door standing open. She'd slipped inside, panting. And the madwoman had gone staggering past.

Didge had smiled in the gloomy hallway, had turned, looked up and then seen him—a man. In shadow at the top of the stairs. Leaning against the balustrade. Arms folded.

He'd invited her up, almost eagerly, and Didge had kept wondering, Am I nearly at Ramble's End, feeling that it might be so. Then becoming almost lightheaded when she'd entered a room that was clearly an artist's studio—all those strange paintings on the wall. Paintings that seemed so . . . distorted.

Disordered.

Was this Rumor's Crux: *this* room?

And the strange bearded man with the long hair and the short jacket and the tight trousers and the high-topped boots? An art-prince? Yes, he'd so introduced himself: Prince Presquit.

But an art-prince with false heart?

What did the Rumor mean: *false* heart?

Walker's Noise buzzed around her head.

He'd invited her to sit, offered her something to eat, to drink, he'd looked at her rags and her shoes, and seemed impressed. He knew of Walkers, expressed familiarity with the Book of True and Cruel—and then he'd offered to paint her picture, but she'd had to decline.

Because you may not paint the image of a ghost: it violates Perfect Order.

And then as she'd stood beside a wall of small-paned windows, Didge had glanced out, and down, and glimpsed a tall shabby man in the street below, a man with straight dark hair, soiled clothing, and dark black boots.

Him!

She'd pressed her fingertips to the glass, seeking a closer look, a confirming look, but the figure had turned a corner by then and was gone, and her Heart of Blood clenched painfully in her chest.

It *was* him, she'd told herself. It *was!*

And she'd stumbled from the room, and Walker's Noise roared in her head, but she no longer listened: Didge running down the staircase, Rumor forgotten, Ramble interrupted, and racing through the streets, stopping people to ask them questions, direct questions, which violated a Walker's created instincts, asking questions, receiving answers. A man with dark hair, in a torn jacket? Yes—headed toward the lakefront. Yes—he'd boarded that ship, that one in the harbor, bound for Sett.

For Sett.

The last time Didge had been on the Isle of Mites: she'd left by the sandbar and walked days to reach the village of Sett.

Where she'd found him.

And slipped into his bed.

And told him what she'd meant to tell him at the gates of the Craft.

And knew that she'd ruined her life: she no longer heard Walker's Noise, and when she tried to walk the following day, she fell, and could only crawl. And he'd looked at her and understood, and he'd denied her name, and denied it twice.

And left her there to crawl on her belly, her legs swollen, no noises in her mind . . .

THIS TIME, THIS TIME ON THE Isle of Mites, Didge knew exactly where she was heading, and had no intention of ever leaving it again.

She walked directly through the heart of the village, ignoring the insects that shimmered in the air, heedless of the groans and cries of the lost souls of Lostwithal.

This time on Mites, no madwoman chased her to the yellow house.

This time she walked there, calmly.

This time on Mites, the door was not open in the yellow house.

She opened it herself, and went inside.

CHAPTER 15

CROSSING BLACK LAKE

THE MERRY SPACEMEN WERE getting on each other's nerves. For one thing, the long, uninterrupted journey in the rattling stagecoach had made everyone irritable, but what actually precipitated a near coming-to-blows among the trio of Kemolons was Peter Musik's incessant writing. He just kept filling the back of check after check with his infinitesimal scribblings, and Gene Boman finally said, "I'd like to know who gave you the right to just . . . steal my checks like that."

Peter, without glancing up: "Stuff it, fat boy."

"Hey," said Herb. "All grudges are on hold, remember?"

"Why doesn't he get his own checks? Why doesn't he get a *pad?*"

"Mr. Boman? Just relax—tune in some old TV shows, why don't you?"

Boman reacted as though he'd been slapped in the

face. "Who do you think you're talking to? I should've known better than to trust an employee with confidential matters."

"I'm not your employee anymore, Mr. Boman."

"I should say you're not. I fired you. I fired you even before I came to this godforsaken place."

Herb saying, "When? *When* did you ever fire me?"

Peter saying, "Shut up, the two of you."

"When?" Herb not letting it go, for some reason: even *he* didn't know why. "When'd you fire me?"

"I told your wife. I told your wife you were fired."

"What?"

"You heard me."

"You told my wife I was fired? You son of a bitch!"

Boman abruptly realized his mistake, and held up a placating hand. "But you can have your job back—as soon as we get home."

"I don't want your dumb job. Keep it. I don't want to be your chauffeur anymore."

"Suit yourself."

Then everybody fell silent for a few minutes.

Till Herb said to Peter, who was still scribbling, "What're you writing? You writing about us? I don't want you saying anything about that woman I told you about. Leave her out of it."

"Whoa," said Gene Boman. "Sounds like Deer-ick has some guilty secrets."

"Just shut up, Boman."

And Peter said, "It's just Boman now? What happened to *Mr.* Boman?"

"Never mind. You just remember what I'm telling you. You can put in the part about Pindrix, but don't—"

"I'll put in any damn thing I feel like putting in. Got it, Herbert?"

Gene Boman, touching Herb's sleeve, a gesture of alliance: "We'll sue."

Herb snatched his arm away, and Peter said, "Sue? Where from, asshole—prison?"

That ripped it. Boman lurched forward, his hands bent like an avenging mummy's, and Peter chopped them away, then tried to slap Boman in the face; he missed, and clipped Herb Dierickx across the bridge of his nose. Herb, startled, pressed his lips together in fury, drew back an arm to pop Peter one, but suddenly—

The coach drew to a halt.

It jounced momentarily as someone up top jumped down to the road, then Ukrops appeared at the window.

"My brother says this is as far as we ride."

"Are we here?" Peter saying, "Has he found her? Where are we?"

"Come see."

Peter was first out of the coach, and he was disappointed to find still more woods, yet another glimpse of the black water. Zickafooz had already started another one of his periodic trips to the lakeshore, but he seemed decidedly more animated this time, more agitated. He twitched and quivered, and then he pointed.

Ukrops and Peter followed, pushing through some heavy foliage, emerging finally onto a narrow and stony beach. Zickafooz still pointing: pointing to a large, hilly island about half a mile out into the lake.

"We're going there," he said, then, leaning toward his brother: "Tides! I know my tides. Tides of the heart, eh?"

But the journey (and the sight of the burned hut, earlier) had taken their toll on Ukrops; he was having none of his brother's antic behavior, and would not indulge him with an encouraging pat. He merely rubbed the back of a hand across his mouth, and nodded sourly.

Peter saying, "We gotta get out to that island? How? Swim?"

"We'll walk," said Ukrops.

"Good trick."

Ukrops was having none of Peter's smart-aleck stuff, either. He frowned, lifted his arm, pointed. "See the lake down there, just down there? Where the water looks almost gray—not black? Sand bar. We can walk from here directly to the island."

"No kidding. What, you've been here before?"

"Isle of Mites."

Peter glanced back at the island. "And that's where Money is? Is he sure?"

They both turned and regarded the Finder, grinning manically, his eyes aimed across the water.

"He won't be sure till he finds her."

"This is so weird."

"Bring the others," said Ukrops.

TEN MINUTES LATER, WITH their pants rolled up (or in Zickafooz's case with his caftan hiked up and cinched around his waist) and carrying their shoes and sandals, the Merry Spacemen waded into Black Lake and started across the sandbar toward the island. The sun was directly overhead. It was murderously hot. Every few feet, Herb Dierickx bent down, cupped some water in a hand, and splashed his face and neck. Gene Boman sat down in the water at one point, and flopped backwards, but then scrambled right up again, and rejoined the others.

When they were about halfway across, Peter glimpsed some movement about fifty yards off to their left; it was hard to tell exactly what it was, with the brilliant sunlight reflecting off the black water—a large bird skimming the surface? A buoy?

Then, under his breath: "I don't believe it."

Believe it: it was Jack, a Walker striding across the lake, moving so as to intersect them just as they made the island.

Peter thinking, Accident, right?

Perfect, right?

Then he raised an arm and swung it semaphorically.

CHAPTER 16

TWENTY QUESTIONS

"**H**OW MUCH FARTHER?"

No reply.

"How do you *know* where the Schoolteacher is?"

No reply.

"Is it because, like Amabeel said, you're more than just a Cold Mage?"

No reply.

"How come you didn't just tell the King about the Mage of Four—I mean, if you figured out what he intended to do?"

No reply.

"Does King Agel know where the Schoolteacher is?"

No reply.

"Does he even know that the Schoolteacher is alive?"

No reply.

"How come you're not wearing your cassock?"

No reply.

"Why didn't you bring Jack, a Walker?"

No reply.

"Why is the Schoolteacher asleep?"

No reply.

"Do you think you can wake him?"

No reply.

"What happens if you can't?"

No reply. (But a frown crossed Master Squintik's face.)

"Is your magic stronger than the Mage of Four's?"

No reply.

"What are you gonna do when you meet him?"

No reply.

"How big is the Epicene?"

No reply.

"Is there a Fourth Moment, really?"

No reply.

"Supposing there is. What happens—what happens if the Epicene tears its way through?"

No reply.

"Who are the Last Humans?"

No reply.

"What's the End of Everything?"

No reply.

Jere Lee expelled a noisy breath and said, "Are you listening to me?"

No reply.

Squintik just kept walking, across the hillside.

Jere Lee stopped, squeezed her eyes shut, flapped her arms, then called out one last question: "What would you say if I told you that I loved you?"

The mage halted. He turned slowly, looked directly at Jere Lee, and smiled. When he lifted his left hand, it iced over; then he gestured with it.

And Jere Lee smelled the sea (the sea?), felt dizzy, sat down on the grass, curled up, and went to sleep.

Master Squintik stared at her for a long minute, then

crouched and lifted her. He carried her to a tree on the breast of the hill and laid her down gently under it. He knelt and kissed her forehead, then rose with a great, trembling sigh, and continued on, alone.

CHAPTER 17

COUNTERFEIT MONEY

EVER SINCE SHE WAS TEN OR eleven years old, people were always comparing Money Campbell to television or movie actresses. At first she was flattered, but then it got to be annoying, even though she realized she was being complimented. But complimented for what? She looked a certain way, she was born with certain genes that gave her certain looks—okay. She enjoyed being attractive, sure, and she used her attractiveness, she'd never deny that. But it sort of made her crazy being complimented for something she had absolutely no control over. It would've been nice, she'd often felt, if she could be complimented for—well, for something else. For *doing* something. For some achievement. But there'd never been any of those, really.

She wasn't talented in any special way. She may've *reminded* people of actress-types, but she couldn't act; she'd tried it once in high school, but kept flubbing her lines, and besides she'd moved awkwardly on stage. And she wasn't especially bright—she'd've flunked out of college her first semester if she hadn't been a good cheat. (Now, there was a skill, kind of. But you didn't go boasting about how cleverly you concealed French verbs and stuff during examinations.)

No, her big claim to fame, all her life, had been her great looks.

Her blond and blue-eyed all-American-actress looks.

She no longer had any such claim to fame.

And the weird thing was—the completely crazy thing was: it didn't bother her.

Perhaps she'd totally wigged out, or perhaps it was that spell the man had put on her in the hold of Presquit's ship, but you know something? She really doubted it.

She would look from Presquit's easel painting to her reflection in a cheval mirror, and think, Why aren't I screaming?

She'd been standing planted between easel and mirror for the past half-hour and still felt no urge to look anywhere else.

She'd touched her face a few times, putting both hands to her furred cheeks, moving them to her gray lips, feeling their new shape, pushing them up under her tapered, yellow eyes, touching the pointy lobes of her ears.

Thinking, Why *aren't* I screaming my head off?

Presquit sat watching her, amused. But anxious. Impatient.

He seemed to be growing very impatient.

"You see now why I like it here so much?" he said. "You can change the world. Back home, you make something, you hang it up, you put it in a museum, or some vault in Japan. You get money, you don't get money. Who cares? The world goes on. People copulate, create, and dress their children. Artists diddle. And their art makes no difference. No difference at all! But here! Look what I can do here! What I've done. I've remade one part of the world today. *You.*"

Money, still looking at herself in the glass: "It's like Halloween."

"It's art!"

"No. No, it's like Halloween," she insisted. "But I don't mind. It'll do." She spun around, cocked her head. "You're wondering why I haven't gone out of my head, aren't you?"

"Of course not. You're beautiful. I've made you beautiful."

"Don't kid yourself. I was beautiful. You've made me up for Halloween."

His face clouded.

"But you're wondering why I'm not half-crazy. Full crazy. Oh come on, Harry, don't kid me. You've been sitting there waiting for me to go all to pieces. Artist. Get off it. You're a sadist." She smiled. "I bet that little midget you got working for you just cried and cried."

They looked at each other again, and Presquit shrugged. "Okay. I admit it. I did expect more of a reaction."

"I bet."

"So?"

"So?"

"So—why *aren't* you . . . reacting?"

Money laughed. "It's driving you crazy, isn't it?"

"No."

"Then I won't say anything else." She glanced at the door (and thought, It was closed a minute ago), then said, "Are we finished? I mean, you've remade a piece of the world. Is the piece of the world free to go now?"

"Go?" Presquit was clearly astonished. "You mean—you'd go away looking like *that*?"

"I thought you said I was beautiful."

"Of course I think you're beautiful, but . . . I expected you'd want to stay."

"Like Mother's Last? Hoping—if I was real good—you'd paint me back the way I was, some day? No, I don't think so. May I leave?"

Suddenly enraged, the painter leapt to his feet, and it seemed to Money that he was actually going to grab her by the throat. She stepped backwards, and assumed what she hoped resembled a karate stance. She didn't know beans about karate, but figured the guy might fall for it. And he did: he stopped, then spread his hands supplicatingly.

"Tell me," he said. Pleaded.

"What?"

"Tell me why . . . you didn't scream."

Money opened her mouth to speak, feeling compelled to answer, feeling compelled to be the Obedient Child, when suddenly Presquit gasped, glanced toward the door, and clapped a hand to his mouth.

A young woman stood there. A grayskinned young woman. And in one hand, which she extended teasingly toward the art-prince, she held a knife with a foot-long blade.

CHAPTER 18

THINGS INVISIBLE TO SEE

SQUINTIK STOOD ON A hilltop, among hundreds of huge, perfectly shaped gravemarkers, and looked down at the great Black Lake. Evening was beginning to fall, and the sky was streaked purple. One of Lostwithal's two moons had just become visible.

The Cold Mage, however, was concerned with those things invisible to see: a flat barge moving slowly into the cove, directly below. Squintik (but no one else, had they been looking) could see that a tall, thin man dressed in black vestments and holding a crozier stood upon it, gazing steadily toward the island. Beside him, a small woman paced anxiously. And Squintik could also see a dark yellow light pulsing through a hole in the top of a dome-shaped cabin in the center of the barge.

As he watched the barge approach shore, then beach

itself, Master Squintik trembled, and crystals of ice formed upon his forehead and across the top of his lip.

The monster had come.

Was here.

And was bringing with it the End of Everything.

Squintik turned away and hurried back through the graveyard, and then up a jagged stony hill. Before he entered the cave, he glanced back once: to see the sky, and the moons, everything in Perfect Order. Perhaps for the last time.

CHAPTER 19

DIDGE, A DISPELLER

MONEY WAS THINKING that maybe she was something of a sadist, herself. Yeah, maybe. 'Cause right now? She was having a real good time —she was having a ball, actually—watching Mr. Harry Prescott of Carmel, California, alias Prince Presquit of Lostwithal (how *had* he managed to pull off such a scam?) squirm around and sweat bullets.

Whoever this gray girl was, with the orange hair? She was okay in Money Campbell's book.

Money watching Didge jab at Presquit's throat with the tip of her knife, Presquit's eyes go wide, go wider; watching him try hard not to swallow, so his adam's apple wouldn't bob and get itself nicked.

Didge had forced Presquit back across the room and into a chair. Presquit turning to putty, to jelly, saying, "What do you want? I don't know you."

Forgetting to switch back to Losplit, which caused Didge a moment's confusion.

Didge thinking, Where have I heard that speech before? *Where?*

Then remembering: Uncle Milty. Every so often he'd slipped into another language, and it was this one, the one that Presquit was babbling in.

But then Presquit was babbling in Losplit. Saying the same thing he'd said in English: "What do you want? I don't know you."

And she said, "Ifnazz," and the painter's attempt at a humoring smile utterly failed.

"You knew him," said Didge.

"Only his work."

"You killed him."

"Is he dead?"

And Didge pushed the knife, a bit: punctured his throat, a little.

"False heart," said Didge.

Presquit shook his head, as best he could under the circumstances.

"False heart and remaker of the world."

"Don't kill me."

"Oh, but I intend to." Didge removed the blade from his throat. His hand went immediately to the puncture; blood ran through his fingers. He watched her move away, and his eyes darted toward the door. She pivoted around, and smiled at him.

He remained seated, perfectly still.

As Didge walked slowly around the room, she reached out with her free hand and tore drawings from the wall, crumpled them and tossed them away, jabbed with her knife hand to slice through canvas after canvas after canvas. When she approached the wet painting of Money, which still stood on the easel, Money exclaimed, "Wait! What's going to happen to *me* if you do that? I mean . . . I'm not up on a lot of magic."

Didge glanced from the painting to Money Campbell.

"Has this false heart remade you?"

"No, I'm just auditioning for 'Cats.'"

Didge frowned, and Money quickly added, "Yeah, I

guess you could say he remade me. So . . . watch what you're cutting to ribbons, okay? Like I say, I don't know the ins and outs of all your magic spells. I don't want to—"

"Spells," said Didge. "The spells of this false heart are—wicked tricks. Tricks a child would play."

"If she had the right paints," said Money.

Presquit had begun to squirm again; he looked as if he might protest this calumny, but then thought the better of it. Wiser to look craven. He slumped in his chair.

Didge stood in thought for a minute, then snorted derisively and reached two fingers down the neck of her blouse and flipped out a small bag that hung on a cord. Roughly, she plucked the bag from its cord, tore it open with her knife, and sprinkled its contents—salt—on the floor around Money's feet.

Money saying, "What're you doing?"

Didge glaring her into silence. Then pricking a thumb with the tip of the knife, squeezing blood, which she smeared over her eyelids, upon her cheek, across her front teeth.

When, behind her, Presquit made to stand up, she said, "Don't." And he sat back down.

Money stood rigid, not even swallowing, watching Didge as she closed her eyes, moved her lips, wondering what was going on.

And as Money wondered, Didge added sums, dismissed them, conjured shapes in her mind, burned them.

Presquit roared in anguish.

Money thinking, What's with him?

Why's he staring at *me?*

Her face, all of a sudden, felt raw. Or like the summer's worst case of stupidity sunburn.

Didge saying, "Remaker of the world!" She spat. "His spells are weaker than mice."

She turned to Presquit and sneered.

Money looked at the so-called art-prince, looked at Didge, then saw herself reflected in the cheval glass.

First reaction? Weirdly enough: disappointment.

Second: a wave of relief.

Seeing the all-American girl looking back at her again.

Hey, you know who you look like? What's her name? Michelle Pfeiffer. No, that's not it. You know who you *really* look like . . . ?

Monica Campbell, from Beimdeck, Ohio.

Money whooping, laughing, forgetting herself and kissing the oranged-haired chick right on her face, planting a big wet kiss and saying, "You're great! *You* did that? That's great!"

Which totally mystified Didge, and caused her to grin.

Didge thinking, Yes, I did that.

Proudly: *I* did.

Then she frowned: Didge, the self-doubter, reasserting her miserable self.

She raised the knife again, studied its edge, then moved her gaze to Presquit: "You left Ifnazz without hearts. I shall leave you the same."

And she would've done it, too (probably/maybe/good chance), if she hadn't, at just that moment, glimpsed something through the studio window: a head of dark straight hair, a shabby shirt.

Him?

It could not be happening again, could not!

Attention distracted, face to the window, she didn't see Presquit lunge from his chair with his arms locked straight out, to push.

She heard Money shout, "No!"

Then she went crashing through the glass.

CHAPTER 20

REUNIONS

AN INFANT? SURE, IF YOU
position yourself correctly, keep your eye on it, and have
some luck. Even a little kid—say, a five- or six-year old.
It's possible; in fact, Peter remembered once writing a
squib about just such a save, some fireman catching a six-
year-old kid in his arms, a girl tossed out of a burning
building.

But it just wasn't possible to catch a full-grown adult.

You'd break your arms, and you'd both go down. Had
to do with velocity, acceleration, that kind of stuff—grav-
ity. Whatever. It just couldn't be done.

Ukrops had done it.

His reflexes? Amazing. Peter couldn't believe the
guy. Crash. Look up. Glass raining down. One second was
all you had: by rights, the woman should've been lying
broken on the ground before anybody even realized she'd
fallen.

In fact, Peter hadn't realized there *was* a woman involved in the rain of glass till he'd felt a thud, and saw her: cradled in Ukrops's arms.

It took a moment longer to realize that he actually *knew* this woman.

Didge. From the Manse Seloc. "Who'd failed through foolishness." According to Jack.

The woman Jack had been so hardcase about, had insulted with bloody spit.

Right here, in Ukrops's arms.

Peter Musik thinking, Hey, Burnsie, I really hate to tell you, pal, but there *are* such things as coincidences.

Happen all the time.

When you hang around tramps like Jack.

Who was standing beside Peter now, just staring at Didge, same as all the other Merry Spacemen.

Didge's eyelids flickered, she groaned, and Ukrops, after kicking aside shards of glass, laid her down on the pavement. Instantly, she sat up, flailing her arms. Ukrops caught her by the wrists. She shook her head violently from side to side—but froze when she saw the Walker approach and then crouch beside her.

"We meet," he said, "by Accident."

She turned her face away, and passed out.

"WELL," SAID UNCLE MILTY, "you've come back!"

Didge stepped into the game room, and as she quietly crossed to the table, she glanced down at herself and realized she was no longer wearing Walker's rags, as she'd worn during every previous visit. No Walker's rags, and no Walker's shoes. Just an ordinary white blouse and coarse gray trousers, a pair of sandals. She sat down, smiled at the albino, then crooked her elbow, planted it upon the table, set her chin in her palm.

Uncle Milty pointed at the schema board, the tiles all set up in straight rows for play. "It's your move, I think. Your move."

"Pass," she said.

٭   ٭   ٭

NOW   THAT   FAKE-PRINCE
Presquit was gone—scrambling down back stairs like his
flat butt was on fire—Money Campbell moistened her
fingertips and then combed them through her hair, trying
to fix herself up a little. Nothing wrong with looking good
as you can.

She walked to the door and pulled it open. Leaned
against the doorjamb, folded her arms, doing Barbara
Stanwyck. It had the desired effect: everybody climbing
up the front stairs stopped dead in their tracks.

Peter exclaiming, "Money!" Then pushing past Zickafooz and trampling up the rest of the way, grabbing her
around the waist and swinging her into the room. Saying,
"Jesus!" Holding her at arm's length, saying, "Jesus—
Money—you okay?" Then pulling her to him, and finally
kissing her like he'd intended to kiss her yesterday morning, like he was Dennis Quaid and she was Ellen Barkin
and this was *The Big Easy*. Yeah!

Zickafooz broke up the embrace—actually yanked
Money out of Peter's embrace, grabbed her by the
wrist—

(Money saying, "Who's *this* guy?")

—and proclaimed, "I declare this woman found. I
declare it twice!"

Then he whirled abruptly and pointed at Gene Boman, who'd just stepped into the room—

(Money saying, "I don't believe it . . . Mr. *Boman?*" and Boman saying, his eyes, as always, going
straight to her breasts, "Monica, great to see you again!")

—Zickafooz saying, "I claim my just and fair
bounty!"

Gene Boman frowned when Zickafooz stepped up to
him, then looked appalled when the Finder shoved back
his sleeve and tried to tear off his Rolex. "Get your filthy
hands off me!"

Zickafooz stiffened, then, to his brother: "I claim my
bounty! Do you want me to get sick? I'll get sick! I'll never
dream!" Then he tried making another grab at the watch,

and Boman shoved him on the chin with the heel of his hand.

Gene saying, "What the hell's going *on* here? What's this sleazebag trying to do to me?"

He still couldn't understand a word of Losplit.

"Give him your watch," said Peter.

"What?"

"Your watch."

"Like hell, I'll give him my watch."

Finally he did—but only after Ukrops had deposited the still-unconscious Didge on the studio's daybed, drawn his fine English sword, and laid the edge against Gene Boman's throat.

Zickafooz clasped the watch greedily in his fist, bowed to his brother, and turned to go.

"Stay!"

It was Jack, a Walker, who punctuated his command by stepping to the door and shutting it.

Zickafooz dropped his eyes to Jack's shoes. Then he looked up, his expression one of utter distaste.

Finders and Walkers: oil and water.

"My service is finished," said the Finder.

"Mine is not."

"That matters nothing to the Finder of Bottles Hill."

They glared at each other for a minute, then Ukrops stepped between them. "Have you need of a Finder?"

Jack could scarcely conceal his disgust. "No. Witnesses."

"You are . . . rambling as the King's Tramp?"

Jack nodding, then looking past Ukrops at all the others, who'd fallen silent and were staring back at him.

"Walk with me," said Jack, then he turned and went out.

No one moved immediately. But, at last, Ukrops followed. Then Peter, exhaling a long breath, and clutching Money Campbell's hand.

Gene Boman scowled, turned to Herb Dierickx and asked, "What's going on? What'd that guy say?"

"He said, 'Walk with me.' "

"Jesus Christ, what the hell is this, a telethon? Where's Jerry Lewis?"

But he went with Herb, reluctantly, throwing Zickafooz a dirty look as he left.

The Finder of Bottles Hill shut the door after them. He opened his fist and regarded his bounty. He held it up to his ear. Then he went and sat on a stool and fitted it on his wrist. And there he sat, staring at the Rolex. Staring at the Rolex. Staring at the Rolex.

Didge remained unconscious.

IN THE STREET, MONEY CAMPbell met Mother's Last, who was returning to the yellow house carrying two sacks filled with provisions. The Fool's eyes widened. "Come, come, you shouldn't be out here—come, he'll be furious. Obedient Child, come along!"

But Money only smiled and gave him a pat on the back. "Listen—listen, would you listen? He's gone. Run away. Out the back door and probably still running. Understand?"

The Fool ducked his eyes, looked devious, winked. Did a somersault, popped back to his feet, spread his hands. "Gone?" And looked suddenly devastated. "Then I'm this way forever? *Forever?*"

He burst into tears, and scuffed off down the street.

"I probably should've told him about the girl with the gray skin," said Money. She waved a hand airily. "Oh, well."

CHAPTER 21

PAPER IN FIRE

IN MOONS' LIGHT THE Abounding Woman struggled and staggered beneath her burden. The Epicene lay heavily upon her, its arms encircling her chest, its forehead resting upon her shoulder, its trunk slopping against her back, its legs dangling, dragging the ground, leaving mud spoor. Even as she climbed the hill behind the Mage of Four, Mage of Luck, the monster continued to grow, increasing in bulk and in weight, and in the ferocity of its growls.

Inside the Abounding Woman, myriad souls clamored for her to turn her head and *look,* to look once, just once, upon the Epicene.

But she would not look; the part of her that was still Sister Wheel, that was still a pythoness, refused to bend to the will of the multitudes.

To look upon the Epicene, Whose Eyes Are Death? What urge was *this?*

If she were to die tonight, she would die look-

ing upon the faces of the Last Humans. Not their li-
berator.

She trudged on, breathing laboriously, stumbling
often, clutching at grass and outcroppings of rock, following the End-of-Everything Man.

Who reached the graveyard and paused, leaning on
his crozier.

He gazed steadily across the field of headstones (of
Perfect Shapes), then made a fist and squeezed it till it
hazed over. He opened his hand, and stared into his palm.

A cave, on a hillside.

He looked up, then raised his eyes still further.

To a cave, on a hillside.

He continued on, the Abounding Woman, with her
heavy burden, stumbling behind him.

JERE LEE WOKE, TOTALLY ALERT.
Sat up, then scowled, trying to remember her dream. She
couldn't, not quite. Almost, but not . . . quite

Which was so strange.

She *always* remembered her dreams.

All her life, she'd wake up from a long sleep, or a
brief nap, and could remember her dreams, clearly, in all
their details.

But this one, this one . . .

She'd been dreaming of Squintik. She recalled a
room, its walls pale gray. And several men, and their
hands were frosted, but their eyes . . .

Something about their eyes. What? Something . . .
odd.

And they seemed to be angry, but Jere Lee couldn't
remember (if she'd even known in the dream) what they
were angry about.

And Master Squintik had torn the sleeve from his
cassock, and the sleeve had burst into bright orange
flames.

There was more. Jere Lee was certain there'd been
more to the dream, but she couldn't . . . remember.

She shook her head, and looked around. Dark.

Sound of crickets, a shrieking bird. She flinched, and pro-
pelled herself to her feet.

Dreaming? Why had she been *dreaming?*

He'd put her to sleep. He'd *made* her sleep, and
gone on alone.

As he'd intended from the start.

She staggered away from the tree, straining to see
through the gloom. Where had he gone to? He'd been
cutting across that field, heading toward that higher
ground, that jutting rock, up there. Last time she'd seen
him.

How long had she been asleep?

Footsteps rustled through high grass behind her.

She spun around. It was too dark to see faces, just
figures, several figures.

One of whom said, "Mistress, we meet by Accident."

SOMEWHERE ON THE CLIMB UP
the last hill, the Epicene had slid off the back of the
Abounding Woman and begun to walk by itself, behind
her.

The souls of the cradle cultists screamed within her
head, urging her to turn around and look, turn and look,
but she steeled herself, sighed with relief that the burden
was off her, and called softly ahead to the Mage of Four,
Mage of Luck, "It is mature!"

Upon hearing this, the Dark Mage, who stood facing
into the mouth of the cave, threw back his head and
ground his teeth. Then stood perfectly still, listening.
Hearing, behind him, the lightened footsteps of the
Abounding Woman, and the heavy trudge of the Epicene.

Ten thousand years of rivalry would end tonight.

The descendant of the First Pupil would take his
revenge.

The Fourth Moment would be cleaved, and the
Schoolteacher proven wrong. And if the cleaving destroyed *all* Moments of Whole Creation, then so be it. So
be it.

His left hand flaring into bright flame, the Mage of

Four, Mage of Luck entered the cave. And descended, moving slowly, trusting his instincts to lead him to the grotto of ice, to the Schoolteacher.

The Abounding Woman stayed several yards behind, the souls within her urging her to turn, to turn, to look upon the monster they'd believed in all their lives, when they'd inhabited the bodies that now lay rotting and bloating with gas in rooms all across Lostwithal.

Turn and look, look! Let us look!

Her body trembling, twitching convulsively, the Abounding Woman refused to look.

Ahead of her, the Great Mage suddenly halted.

"We are close!" he hissed. "Remain here. When you hear me call, follow my voice, and it will lead you to him."

He continued on, heading deeper into the cave, and the Abounding Woman was left alone in utter darkness, with the Epicene.

Turn and look . . .

JERE LEE SAID, "HE MENTIONED a cave, and struck off that way—that way there, but I don't know. I have a feeling it was hours ago."

Jack had nodded, accepting the information which he had not solicited, and Walker's Noise roared in his head. He touched his bracelet, and Lita flew up and embedded her stinger in his scalp, her life in his, and then he walked on.

Jere Lee saying, "Monica, it's so nice to see you again. And Herb!" Wrapping her arms around him, squeezing him tight, saying she'd thought he was dead—was he feeling okay? Then turning to Peter Musik, giving him a big smile, calling him Geebo, by his old street name, and then looking at Gene Boman, and glancing after Ukrops who'd hurried after Jack, and saying well, she guessed there'd be time later for formal introductions.

Trying hard to create an upbeat mood.

Which wasn't all that easy, considering the surroundings and the situation at hand.

Twenty minutes later, when Jack, a Walker stopped

at the entrance to a cave at the top of a hill, and when the giant soldier-boy drew his Conan sword, Gene Boman tried to fizz himself back to age fourteen again, tune into some really good old TV shows, but it was no dice. Didn't work. He was stuck in the now.

Gene Boman saying, "I suppose flashlights haven't been invented here yet. But anybody got a match?"

Nobody did.

But Jack could see just fine in the dark, thanks to Lita's sting: Lita's magic.

He led the way, aimlessly.

THE ABOUNDING WOMAN HUD-dled in the dark, her head twisting to the side, pulling back, twisting half-around on her neck.

Sister Wheel was exhausted.

The souls of the cradle cult were insistent, were angry, were churning and screaming within her.

Look upon it, look upon it! Look!

The Abounding Woman clasped her head in her hands, and rolled forward, writhing.

Behind her, the Epicene breathed thickly, and growled.

Sister Wheel felt her muscles become invaded, overrun.

And she surrendered.

The souls clamored in triumph.

And the Abounding Woman turned.

Two yellow eyes stared back at her.

No form, just eyes. In the darkness: just eyes.

The souls screamed in frustration.

Sister Wheel whistled her own soul into the Void.

And the Abounding Woman shriveled and curled and blackened like paper in fire, and blew away, carried by the tunnel drafts.

CHAPTER 22

GRAYMAN

THE MAGE OF FOUR, MAGE of Luck could feel the cold, could breathe it in now, and it refreshed his lungs. As he approached the ice grotto, his body began to tremble. He knew precisely what he would say to the Schoolteacher: the words had been in the mouths of every pupil since the First.

And now the opportunity, the satisfaction would be his.

The rock walls on either side of him were covered with thick blue ice. Soon. Very soon.

The grotto.

He stepped forward and struck his crozier upon the ground.

And the seated figure, some ten feet away, raised his head, and looked directly into the face of the End-of-Everything Man.

Who was startled. But then smiled. "Squintik," he said. "I often . . . suspected."

"Did you?"

"Yes." He nodded mockingly. "But I am pleased to discover that you are, indeed, a Grayman. Pleased to discover you here."

"I think not."

"Truth. It will give me great joy to show you the Epicene. You and your master both."

"You will not see him. I can assure you."

The Mage of Four, Mage of Luck narrowed his eyes, let go of his crozier, and suddenly his right hand flared into flames. Around him, ice began to melt. "I will see him."

"He is not here."

"He is here."

"I have led you to a false grotto. Of my own making."

"*You* have led *me?*"

Squintik stood. "I will destroy the monster, and I will destroy you. Tonight. Now."

"Squintik . . . Grayman, it has gone too far to be stopped now. The Epicene is fully grown. Is *here*. You would be wise to admit that the First Pupil's Heresy is truth and join us in looking upon the faces of the Last Humans. Or do you still not believe they exist?"

And Squintik said, "We believe. We have always believed. But chose to deny belief, deny certainty, for the survival of all."

"Belief can never be denied."

"Even if acting upon it destroys? Brings upon us Plenary Chaos—the End of Everything?"

"Even so."

The Mage of Four clenched both fiery hands, and the flames leapt from them, met, merged, and flew at Squintik.

Who encased himself in ice.

Wrapping itself around the ice, pythonlike, the fire burned toward the mage protected within. Steam erupted, hissing, and the ice figure—Squintik's Phantom —melted.

Behind the Mage of Four, Master Squintik stepped forth from a glistening cave wall, his fingers extended.

He'd never heard of Lash LaRue, Johnny Mack

Brown, Roy Rogers: from his fingertips, hundreds of tiny, barb-tipped ice slivers flew across the grotto.

The Dark Mage whirled around, met ice with fire, and ice sizzled.

"I will whistle your soul to the Void, Dark Mage," said Squintik. "I can promise you that. But I cannot spare your life."

Widening his eyes in contempt, the Mage of Four, Mage of Luck shook his left hand. The fire there went out. Then he tore one of the gray-black slugs from his face, held it up for Squintik to regard. The slug began to mist, the mist swirled violently, and moments later, a leathery black . . . thing with needle-sharp teeth flew at Squintik, and slashed his throat.

Before it could attack again, its wings thickened with ice, and it plummeted to the cavern floor, and broke there like glass.

Squintik, his wound suddenly frozen, turned again to the Mage of Four and began, softly, to whistle.

"How dare you!" screamed the Dark Mage, and then he glanced up, but too late.

The ice stalactite speared his body—throat, chest, Heart of Talent—and exited through his back; in convulsions, he slid down it, eyes glazed.

The slugs on his face all moved toward his open mouth, and disappeared into it, and wriggled down his throat.

He continued to twitch long after Squintik had ceased his quavering whistle.

CHAPTER 23

EPICENE

BLOWING DOWN THE CAVE
and into their faces: a gust of dry cold air, whirling with
ash flakes. Then: dank, boggy odors, and a heavy dragging
sound. Growing stronger, coming closer . . .

Jack, whispering to Ukrops: "Give me your sword."

"A Walker is passive."

"Your sword!"

"It is the Epicene, isn't it? You walked all of us right
to the Epicene."

"You are a soldier."

"I am. But you brought these others."

Who were huddled behind them, perfectly still,
scarcely breathing.

"I used my judgment. Ramble's End requires Witnesses."

"One would've been sufficient."

"The sword, Ukrops. I can see. You cannot."

Ukrops shaking his head in refusal, then reaching up

and firmly pressing a hand against Jack's chest. "My weapon," he said, "my work."

As Jack moved back slowly along the cave wall, Ukrops moistened his lips, and drew his sword.

THE ICE GROTTO'S ILLUMINATION (which Squintik had created) weakened to a pallid glimmer, then went out, and the Cold Mage stood silently in the darkness, feeling dizzy. He had trouble swallowing (and when he could, he tasted blood). Numbers flared in his mind, but then just dissolved. He slumped against the wall, and listened.

What he heard, moments later, numbed him with terror, and he blindly lurched ahead, reasserting his will, clearing his mind, then filling it afresh with Useful Numbers.

He calculated true sums, superimposed them with Perfect Shapes.

A phosphorescent ball leapt from each of his palms, and his fingers frosted over.

The moving fireballs lit the way, and Squintik followed.

Ahead of him, just a short distance away: it sounded (again) as though heavy canvas were being torn. Slashed.

OF ALL THE MANY LESSONS about violence that Herb Dierickx's true crime books had taught him over the years, the simplest and most consistent lesson was this: a loaded gun in your hand changed you. Absolutely. It empowered you. *Focused* you. One gentle squeeze, and you could protect, you could punish. Do. Undo. Subtract from the world. Maintain your place in it.

Before he'd shot Major Forell on the beach, Herb had never fired a gun. (An ulcer had kept him out of the army, and the Korean War.)

Before this morning, he'd never even *held* one. Not a loaded one.

Before today, he'd always agreed with his wife, that people shouldn't own handguns; no way—you keep handguns away from people, things'd be a lot better all over, all around. There'd be fewer monsters. Less undertakers.

But right now, hunkered down in the pitch-black cave, Herb Dierickx was thoroughly pro-gun.

Well, sure, he was *holding* one—the Major's—in his right hand, and it was loaded, and that changed you. Changed him.

He felt scared, but not helpless.

Something was coming toward them, and he didn't know what it was (mud monster? say it: mud monster, *mud monster*; sounds dumber and dumber, the more you say it, so keep saying it, Herb: mud monster, mud monster . . .), and he didn't know whether or not a bullet would have any effect upon it, nor did he have any idea how many bullets remained in the gun.

But.

But it sure felt good to be holding it.

Felt great to be so empowered, so focused.

Like Lash LaRue and Johnny Mack Brown.

"Hey! That you, Deer-ick? What're you doing?" From Gene Boman, his arm shooting out, grabbing Herb's sleeve.

Herb saying, "Shush!" then moving ahead, in front of Boman, then in front of Jere Lee Vance and Money Campbell.

One gentle squeeze of the trigger, and you could protect.

They were behind him now, under his protection.

He crept ahead, pistol pointing down, finger off the trigger. No accidents. Not while *he* was in charge.

His mouth was dry, his heart was pounding; his face was slick with perspiration.

But it was okay.

He had a loaded gun in his hand.

"Herb?"

"Get behind me, Peter."

"What're you—?"

"Just do it."

In the dark, Herb located Peter's chin, and touched it with the gun barrel.

Peter saying, "Whyn't you give me that—okay?"

Herb saying, "Whyn't you shut up and get behind me? Okay?"

Then saying, "Do it," and creeping farther ahead.

Till he brushed against the Walker's shoulder.

Herb could feel Jack's eyes flick to him, then flick away, and he decided abruptly to stop right there. The hell with going past him—with shielding *him*. He'd led them all into this place, hadn't he? This was his ballgame, wasn't it? Damn straight, to both questions.

So Herb Dierickx wasn't about to offer Jack, a Walker any protection. Be *his* hero. Whatever the hell came at them, they'd face it together.

He wasn't going back, but he wasn't going forward, either.

He was staying right where he was.

Standing here. With his gun in his hand. Not budging.

(Herb suddenly thinking then, Hey, where's the big soldier?)

A moment later: a loud ripping sound, then—

a shimmery glare of white light.

Herb screamed, and screamed again.

Furious for screaming, he squeezed the trigger.

And squeezed the trigger again.

WHEN THE TWO SPINNING FIRE-balls blasted toward him, Ukrops flung himself flat against the wall. The balls halved—two became four. Then four became sixteen, and suddenly the cavern was alive. Shadows flickered and wriggled, collided, joined, splintered, and cold white fire kept bursting, illuminating, with fractured light, slab rock and calcite coral, stalagmites and crystal pools, and an oozing black figure that knelt with its back to Ukrops and flailed savagely with slimy claws. Scoring the air with ragged gashes that crackled, spewed yellow sand, and bulged.

For an instant, the Red Guardsman almost lost his nerve, but then—sword tight in his grip—he hurled himself across the cavern, toward the Epicene.

If he could lop off its head before it could turn its eyes upon him, he might live.

Ukrops thinking, We *all* might live.

First its head, then its hands.

Its head, then its—

A sharp bright pain exploded in Ukrops's left shoulder; then another, in his right thigh.

And the Epicene Whose Eyes Are Death whirled around.

HERB SAYING, "DID I HIT IT, DID I get it?" as light and shadow, shadow and shadow and light flashed and shivered and bounced all around him; Herb suddenly disoriented, overwhelmed by panic. And somebody was tugging at the gun, and he let it go. Then spun away, breathless, and Jere Lee pulled him roughly toward her, and they both crashed down on the dry cavern floor. Jere Lee saying, "It's gonna be all right, gonna be all right, all right, Herb, it's gonna be . . ."

Gene Boman, several feet away, all balled up tight, had his own mantra: "Eight o'clock, 'Flip Wilson.' Nine o'clock, 'Ironside.' Ten o'clock, 'The Dean Martin Show.' Dino. Dino Martin. Dino. Dino Martin . . ."

A howl rose, and kept rising.

"Dino. Dino Martin at ten. Dino . . ."

GUNSHOT, UKROPS WAS TOTTERing, crumpling. Ten fingers opened, hands separated, and his sword fell.

Bright-yellow sand kept spurting from the widening fissures the Epicene had made.

◦   ◦   ◦

MASTER SQUINTIK, HIS MIND
bristling with sums and shapes, flung out his left arm just
as the creature spun toward Ukrops.

Two of the myriad fireballs lighting the cavern suddenly whirled around the Epicene's head, then whirled
around again. On their third orbit, they flared bright as
suns, then slammed into its yellow eyes, and burned them
out.

A howl rose, and kept rising.

A WALKER IS PASSIVE.

Unless provoked.

Jack scrambled through the gushing sand, slipped in
it, dove through it, grabbed the sword (that was already
half-buried in it), stumbled to his feet, regained his balance, and then swung with all his strength.

The Epicene's head was cleaved from its trunk.

It staggered backwards, arms thrashing, claws making further tears in the fabric between Moments. The
Walker stepped after it, striking it again, and again, sever-
ing its hands, then slashing laterally down through its
shoulders. Yanking out the blade, then striking again,
hacking at its legs. It pitched backwards, fell, writhed on
rock, and Jack stood over it for a long moment before
driving the sword deep into its chest, into its heart, which
spewed out stones and pebbles and clotted grass and thick
black gouts of mud.

Sand poured liberally through the tattered fabric,
then slowed to a trickle, then stopped.

CHAPTER 24

LAST HUMANS

DOZENS OF FIREBALLS RE-
joined became two, two became one, hovering high in the
cavern's chimney, burning white.

"So what do you think, Pete, huh? Is it over? We save
the universe, or what?" Money tossed away the gun that
she'd snatched from Herb Dierickx; Peter smiled, and
together they moved slowly across the treacherous hum-
mocks of yellow sand.

Peter wanted to have a good long look at what remained of the Epicene, take a few notes, but Money felt
she could pass on that. She'd seen enough of it, thank you
very much; even in the hectic strobe lighting, she'd seen
quite enough. Its mouth, its claws, its breasts, its penis.

Money thinking, Peter can go check out the local
color, I'll play nurse.

Ukrops was struggling to sit up.

"Don't move, okay?" said Money. Thinking, Oh man,
what a mess. Saying, "You'll be fine." And thinking, I

could strangle that stupid Herb, what the hell did he think he was doing?

The Red Guardsman winced, turning his head slightly to regard his bloody shoulder. Then he looked up at Money and frowned.

"You're not going to believe what happened to you," she said, "so I won't even bother telling you. Oh, all right. I might as well. You were shot. Do you know what a gun is?"

She said "gun" in English.

"Kemolons," said Ukrops.

And Money rolled her eyes (too) and said, "I know, I know. You can't take us anywhere."

On the opposite side of the cavern, the trigger-happy Kemolon was feeling totally disgusted with himself: Herb kept whacking himself in the forehead with the heels of both hands, grinding his teeth, swearing under his breath. "I'm such an idiot, I'm such an asshole-idiot!"

Gene Boman saying, "What, this is news? Wake up and smell the coffee, Deer-ick; you've *always* been an idiot."

"I've heard just about enough out of you. Button it, fat boy."

"You gonna make me, you gonna make me? You and what gun, Rambo?"

"Look, let's just drop this, all right?" Herb shaking his head, watching Jere Lee pick her way across the sand toward Master Squintik. "Let's not—let's just forget it."

"Fine."

"Friends?"

"We never were before, I don't see why we have to start now."

"Fine." Herb watching Jere Lee stop in front of the Cold Mage, and then cock her head, inquisitively; seeing Squintik open his arms. Watching them embrace. "We're alive . . . everything's okay, so let's just . . . forget it."

Gene Boman laughed and suddenly clapped Herb on the shoulder. "Ah, don't blame yourself. You tried. Everybody wants to be Banyon sometimes."

"What? Who?"

"Banyon. You never saw 'Banyon?' Seventy-two, seventy-three season. Fridays? NBC? Robert Foster? Joan Blondell? Richard Jaeckel? Really good series."

Herb saying, "Jesus Christ."

THE WASP LANDED ON JACK'S wrist, flew off, spiraled up, shimmered, became Lita.

Naked, she shivered, leaned against the Walker, and they stood together, not speaking. Just staring intently at the ragged tears in the fabric between Moments. Several had closed, faded, and disappeared.

Finally: "They turned out to be only a story, after all," Jack said. "The Last Humans."

Lita glanced at him, and mutely shook her head.

"Then where *are* they? Why didn't they come through?"

"Perhaps . . ."

More tears sealed themselves, vanished.

Jack saying, "What? Perhaps *what*?"

". . . perhaps they did." Lita glanced down at the yellow sand, toed some, then looked up at Jack again.

She was still looking at him (her life), when the cavern suddenly went dark.

CODA

IN THE MORNING, DIDGE accompanies Zickafooz out of the village and into the hilly countryside. It's fiercely hot, oppressively humid, and the insects are biting, but Didge is happy. For the first time in many seasons, Didge is happy. (And even a Finder's presence can't dampen her spirits.)

She intends to leave the Isle of Mites this afternoon. No plans, no destination: all that will sort itself out, in time. But before she can begin her new life (or resume her old one: she *is* a Dispeller, after all, and a good one, too—look how she handled herself last night, how skillfully she reversed Presquit's magic!), before she can sail away and make herself whole again, Didge has one last thing to do.

Say good-bye to *him.*

Good-bye for good.

She swings her arms as she walks, following Zickafooz off the dusty road and across a green meadow, heading toward cliffs in the distance.

"Is he near?" she asks.

"I will know when I find him," replies the Finder, who has demanded her wristlet as bounty.

Her rag wristlet.

Which she will give to him gladly. Once he finds Jack, a Walker.

Half an hour later, after an arduous climb, they're standing at the entrance to a cave.

"In . . . there?" says Didge, her high spirits slipping, a little.

Zickafooz paces, then sighs, and slaps his hands together petulantly. "Stay here," he says at last, and starts to pick his way back down the cliff.

"Where are you going now?"

"Mistress, can you see in the dark?"

"No."

"Neither can I. Just wait there. I'll be back shortly."

After he's gone, Didge steps into the cave, but then, unaccountably, begins to tremble. She scrambles back into the daylight. Thinking, Is *he* in there? But why? What's—?

But shakes away the anxiety. New Didge, new ways. And sits down with her back to the cliff face, remembering the young man—the boy, really—she'd met one day on the road to Walker's Craft, and how he'd eagerly crept under her blanket that first night, and how silky-smooth his cheeks had felt, and how sweet his breath had been. . . .

And in the heavy heat of the morning, she dozes, and finds herself in a cool unlighted hallway, an open doorway ahead of her, and in the dark of her dream, she smiles, and walks on, and enters the game room, where Uncle Milty is seated at the table, his head bent over the leather could-world. And Didge calls, "I'm back again, and I think I have time for a short game."

When the albino lifts his face, Didge recoils.

His eyes are red-rimmed, and his cheeks are shining with tears.

Didge saying, "Mil-ton? What's happened? Milton?"

He looks at her with such unfathomable sadness that Didge feels an acute pang in her Heart of Blood. "Milton? Why are you—?"

And she bolts awake, Zickafooz bent over her, shaking her by the shoulder. "Come on," he says gruffly. "If you're coming." Clutching the resin torch that he's brought back with him, the Finder turns and heads into the cave. Moments later, as she's climbing to her feet, Didge hears a short scraping sound, a match flares, and the torch bursts into flame.

"I'm coming," says Didge, stumbling after him. "Wait."

And thinks now, Gone.

It's gone.

That feeling? That good feeling?

Gone.

The torch crackles and smokes.

Then: the tunnel widens, opens into a huge vaulted cavern, its floor undulant with bright yellow sand.

Didge suddenly halts, hearing the Finder groan, seeing him clamp his right hand to his mouth.

"What's wrong?" she says. "Where is he?"

Turning slowly, Zickafooz fixes Didge with a panicky stare. Then shakes his head. "The tides," he mutters.

"What?"

"Gone."

"*What?*"

"Gone," bellows Zickafooz, and his voice reverberates: gone, on, on . . .

"So, take me where he's . . ." but she stops, her mouth dry, both hearts thudding in her chest.

"Gone? Gone *where?*"

The Finder jams the torch into the sand, then flings himself down, elbows on his knees, face buried in his hands. "I won't dream, I won't dream, I won't dream . . ."

Didge looks at him for a long minute, then glances all around the cavern, and frowns when she spots—leaning against a knobby growth of calcite—a long sword, its blade encrusted with mud.

Then something that glints catches her eye.

The Walker's notched bracelet, lying shattered in the sand.

ABOUT THE AUTHOR

Tom De Haven has published seven previous novels: *Freaks' Amour* (William Morrow, 1979/Penguin, 1986), *Jersey Luck* (Harper & Row, 1980), *Funny Papers* (Viking, 1985/Penguin, 1986), *U.S.S.A.* (Avon, 1987), *Sunburn Lake* (Viking, 1988/Penguin, 1990), and *Joe Gosh* (Walker & Company, 1988), and *Walker of Worlds* (Foundation, Doubleday, 1990). He has produced the script for a graphic novel based on William Gibson's *Neuromancer*, published by Epic, and has written extensively for newspapers and magazines, including *The Village Voice*, *Goodlife*, *New Jersey Monthly*, and the *Philadelphia Inquirer*. He is a regular contributor to *RAW* and *Entertainment Weekly* and has written episodes for *The Adventures of the Galaxy Rangers*, a syndicated animated television show (1986–87 season). Mr. De Haven is a recipient of two National Endowment for the Arts Creative Writing Fellowships (1979–80; 1986–87) and a New Jersey State Council on the Arts Writing Fellowship (1980–81). From 1987 to 1990 he taught American Studies at Rutgers University and is currently an Associate Professor of Creative Writing and American Studies at Virginia Commonwealth University. He received a B.A. from Rutgers–Newark and an M.F.A. from Bowling Green State University. He lives with his wife Santa and their two daughters, Jessie and Kate, in Virginia.

Here is an excerpt from the triumphant
conclusion to the
Chronicles of the King's Tramp:

THE LAST HUMAN
by Tom De Haven

The Epicene has been destroyed; the King's
Tramp has fulfilled his mission. But all is not well.
Across Lostwithal, visions and portents are seen:
gray-robed men with eyes of flaming green;
golden giants who walk on water; a storm of frogs
and worms. Has the Mage of Four, Mage of Luck
triumphed? Has the Apocalypse arrived?

Watch for THE LAST HUMAN, available in
hardcover and trade paperback in December
1992, wherever Bantam Spectra Books are sold.

"**S**CHOLAR, IT'S ANNGIN. We've summoned the chief physician, he will be here shortly."

Squintik cracked open his eyes, blurrily seeing one of the New Pupils leaning over him. The young man's long, sad, unhealthy-looking face hovered mere inches from his own. Squintik held up a hand, inserting it between them, and the pupil leaned back—the featherbedding lifting when he removed his knee from it and stood up.

"Scholar, I have been requested by your colleagues to offer to you their profound apologies for this violent summons."

"You may tell them I've taken no offense." He moved to sit up higher against the bolster, and winced with a sudden bright pain. He was still bleeding freely from his throat—an injury he'd suffered during his competition with the Mage of Four, Mage of Luck. (In the cave. Only minutes ago. Minutes.) A competition that had ended with the dark mage's death. Fit punishment for the man who'd created the Epicene—the monster of mud and stone and grass that nearly had torn its way into the Fourth Human World. . . . "You may tell my colleagues that now—right now," said Squintik gesturing for the pupil to take his leave.

"Yes, sir." He moved backward toward the chamber door, blindly found the porcelain knob. After performing a curt bow, he was gone, and Squintik let out a long, quavering sigh. He wiped his left hand with the comforter, then curled the fingers and thumb into a cluster. Did various sums in his mind, visualized several Perfect Shapes. And his palm frosted over.

The frost sprinkled away, to reveal a fragile skin of

glassy ice beneath. He lifted his hand to his eyes, and peered into the ice.

. . . SQUINTIK,   YOUTHFUL

again, is seated in a wooden examination chair.

The Schoolteacher—black gleaming hair combed back from a high forehead, deep-set dark eyes, nostrils flared on a strongly arched nose—regards his pupil across a table.

Both of them are dressed in gray school robes.

"Now, this is more comfortable for us both," says the teacher with the trace of a smile. "It's good to see you, Noddy. We've all enjoyed the dreams you sent us, but we'd been hoping to see you again sooner than today. The faculty has missed you."

Squintik nods. Amazingly, he isn't paying much attention to his master. He's looking at his own hands, absorbed with them. They're so—unwrinkled; strong and sinewy. As they were before magic corrupted their bones and triggered arthritis. His hands are beautiful. Smooth white hands that would take delight in touching a woman.

(He thinks of the kindly woman . . . .)

"Noddy!"

Squintik flinches, and turns his attention fully upon the Schoolteacher.

"It was a merry chase the dark mage led you on, wasn't it? And his audacity! To bring the monster here!"

Squintik saying, "He believed that you lived in the cave . . . physically."

"Yes, well there you are, Noddy. The man had no learning at all. A complete imbecile."

"Nonetheless, he made the Epicene live."

The Schoolteacher frowns, saying, "You did well in destroying it."

"It was Agel's Walker did that—as you must know."

The 'teacher stands and moves across the front of the room to a narrow window, cranks it open. Outside it is bright afternoon, Squintik can see new foliage shaking; he draws a deep breath of warm air sweetened by grass and moist earth. Squeezes both hands into fists, and is amazed again by the tightness of his own flesh.

The 'teacher says, "Noddy." And when he has Squintik's attention again: "You did well. It is not your fault."

"My fault? What is not my fault?" Squintik's tone is accusatory, annoyed. Inappropriate.

The 'teacher inclining his head slightly, saying, "One of them came through, Noddy. One of them came through . . . ."

UKROPS HAD SUFFERED TWO wounds (one in the shoulder, the other in his right thigh) and while the physician's aide staunched their bleeding and then blotted them clean, the physician—a fat man who was also very tall, dressed in a dark-gray cassock— muttered underneath his breath the ballad of Reacquired Health. He winced, groaned softly, and his cheeks puffed out, then he bent his mouth to his cupped left hand and dribbled into it a moist green paste. Watching, Lita felt herself go pale (in the Preserve, healing was done differently, far less repulsively) and clung even tighter to the Walker's left arm. Jack looked at her—briefly and without expression—then glanced away, back toward the physician. Who spread the paste in thick layers over the soldier's wounds, red perforations surrounded by dark flesh (they were bullet holes, caused by a Kemolon's panicky tightening of his trigger finger durng the crisis in the hill cave), and then he plucked out the two misshapen nuggets of lead. In fact, he scarcely had to probe for them: they seemed almost to eject themselves. Captain Ukrops never even flinched.

The aide, who was a short, thin boy with sly brown eyes, took possession of the bullets, depositing them both carefully into a small linen bag. After he'd looped the bag on a prong of his belt (he wore flappy gray trousers and a white surplice, both now streaked with blood) he addressed Ukrops, "My master has attended you. Has he attended you well?"

Ukrops nodded.

"Say it, please. According to the Order of Things."

"Your master has attended me well." Ukrops sat up on the table, careful not to look the physician directly in the eye.

"You say it twice?"

"I say it twice."

The assistant walked around the table and presented himself formally to his master. "Your patient," he said, "is satisfied, Lord Pinchbek."

The physician duly struck the assistant a ceremonial slap across the face. Then, with the rigamarole safely out of the way, he cleaned the paste and the blood from his hands, using an edge of the heavy white cloth that covered the surgery table.

"Are *you* Agel's Walker?" he said at last, directing his question to Captain Ukrops.

"No, my lord, I am merely one of his guardsmen."

Jack removed Lita's hand from his arm, and stepped forward, identifying himself as Agel's Walker. Then: "Lord Pinchbek?" he said. "Sir, Rumor had you a Finished Man. Are you *Reedweedt* Pinchbek, healer to the present king's father?"

Pinchbek dropped the cloth—actually thrust it away from himself—and looked peevishly at Jack. "Did Lostwithal truly believe I'd declare myself Finished and take poison on this plum pit of an island?" His stony expression mitigated somewhat. "I suppose they did, yes." A crooked smile, a barked laugh. Then he narrowed his eyes, pinning Jack with a formidable glare. "Obviously, I never did either thing. You've heard of the Gray Man?"

"Are you *Gray*, then, Lord Pinchbek?" This from Ukrops, swinging his legs down off the table and standing up. "Are we in the Undermoment?"

And this from Jack, delivered angrily: "Captain, I am tramping for the King. Accident brought you to me, Captain, you to me. I bid you keep alert, I may present you later as Witness at court if it pleases me. If it pleases *me*, Captain Ukrops."

The Red Guardsman smiled venomously, but fell deferentially silent.

Lord Pinchbek also recognized just authority when he heard it. "Will you tell me, sir, to which of Agel's six tramps am I speaking?"

"Jack of Sett, my lord."

"Sett." Pinchbek screwed up his eyes and regarded the Walker closely. "Jack of Sett. Would you join me, then, Jack of Sett? Since these hands of mine touched blood, I should breathe in some cleansing humors. Would you care to join me?"

"A Walker never declines an invitation to refresh himself." He looked to Ukrops, then turned and looked behind him, at Lita.

She was naked, freshly changed from a wasp, and her skin blue with cold.

"My lord," said Jack, "does your invitation include my companions?"

"I think . . . not." Pinchbek had fitted his hands with gray woolen mittens, and his assistant was holding open the surgery door.

"We'll be fine, Jack," said Ukrops. "Go and enjoy yourself. I'll see that the witch is kept warm."

The Red Guardsmen's implication was astonishingly vulgar! Jack took deep offense, but this was no time to voice it. For now, he merely turned his back on Ukrops, telling Lita, "Make the change."

She quirked her mouth—a gesture of bemusement, even of scorn that Jack recognized only because he'd traveled recently among Kemolons. Among the humans of Lostwithal, it was not a meaningful sign. "I'm afraid I can't do that, my life," she said. And pointed at his left wrist.

Showing him that his bracelet was gone. Somehow lost in the violent transit to the Undermoment.

Lita would not make the change, become his sting, if the wasp had no seemly place to lodge. And the only seemly place—according to the contract Jack had entered into with the Women of Mist—was the notch in his metal bracelet. No bracelet, no wasp.

"So I'll just wait here for you." She lifted one shoulder, let it fall: another Kemolon gesture.

Lita had learned much from the Campbell girl, Jack decided, and thinking now of that too-human, he wondered suddenly where she was. Where they all were. The four Kemolons. He hadn't missed them till this moment. Odd. For a time he'd thought he'd forged bonds with some of them, but obviously he'd been mistaken. They were insignificant. Too-humans.

Lita saying, "Just go breathe a humor, Jack, and see if you can find out what's going on. But Jack? Don't forget. No direct questions."

He smiled, taking pleasure from her legitimate impudence, then turned around and followed Lord Pinchbek through the surgery door. When the assistant made to close it behind them, Jack put out a hand and stopped it. "My companions are high citizens of Perfect Order, close to his majesty."

"What're you telling me for?" said the assistant.

"Edwix!" bellowed the physician. "Bring the Walker's companions some refreshment. And see that the witch is given some clothing. Now, Jack of Sett, if you'll come with me." He struck off at a goodly clip. Jack followed. At the end of the passageway, Pinchbek stopped and opened a door, then ushered Jack into his private quarters.

There were several pillowy gray chairs, a colorless hooked rug on the floor, shelves containing books (whose spines suspired and faintly glowed blue) and other shelves containing bottles of vapors, all hues and densities of ceremonial, convivial, and intoxicant vapors. On a plinx beside the doorway stood a brass arrival globe and a cruit of cloudy water. Jack arrived himself, dipped two fingers and streaking his self-mark on the globe. Pinchbek did not.

He motioned for Jack to be seated, then walked to a set of shelves and reached down a clear flagon that showed wispy yellow vapors stoppered up inside. Pulling the cork, he waved the flagon several times. "I prefer it on the air, if you don't mind." He replaced the cork.

"It is the same," said Jack. "Thank you." Politely, he took a deep breath. It burned sharply and turned him momentarily light-headed.

Lord Pinchbek put the flagon away, then hitching his cassock, dropped into one of the chairs. He looked at the Walker, and the Walker, still distressingly woozy, looked back at him. "We are both men of court, Jack, so I won't go through all the rituals. Let's just both agree that I've done them—and get on to what this is all about."

"Agreed."

Pinchbek smiled, then clenched his teeth, mustering his abdominal and lower back muscles to sit forward. "Jack. The creature freed one of them."

"But we saw—nothing. Nothing come through."

"It is here nonetheless," said Lord Pinchbek. "I regret to say it twice. But I do, I say it twice." He lifted his eyes. "It is . . . here."

THE DWARF HAD A FACE, HERB Dierickx thought, like on one of those dried-apple dolls you see at Christmast time in decorated windows of department stores. A burnt-brown color, and the skin all wrinkled, all pleated. And look, look at how she was dressed: in a fancy gown of dark gray . . . smoke—the smoke drizzling steadily in all directions from dozens of settings in the jeweled necklace that she wore. Two coiling tendrils even sneaked up both sides of her neck, behind the tiny eyes—size of nickels—and then, meeting at the top of her head, knit themselves into a wavering, mirage-like tiara. And get this. Get this. She was seated upon a kind of, well, a kind of throne. Except it was a completely out-of-whack throne, and jerrybuilt from jagged, splintery sticks of lathing. The legs weren't same-sized, and it tilted.

Herb sat ten feet away from her on the cold stone floor, and goggled. He'd done nothing *but* goggle for the past couple of minutes—ever since he'd materialized in this medieval corridor with its block-stone walls hung intermittently on both sides with heavy gray drapery.

He hadn't a clue where he was, or an inkling how he'd gotten there. The last thing that Herb remembered? Before he'd blacked out? Was talking to Gene Boman.

They were in that spooky cave, the whole gang of them—Herb and Boman, and Money Campbell and Peter Musik, and that big soldier called Ukrops, and Jack, a Walker and Lita the pint-sized witch with the epicanthic eyes, and Jere Lee Vance and that bald magician, that guy Squintik—and the mud monster was dead, they'd killed it, chopped it to pieces (well, Jack had), and everybody was feeling good, charged with adrenalin, but suddenly: whoosh! Squintik's big bright ball of magic light went dark. And Herb went tumbling down a well of blackness. For what seemed a long time, but probably wasn't. He'd landed (woken?) with a bruising jolt that rattled his head, clacked his teeth. And when he'd opened his eyes, the cave was gone, and so were his companions. And he was lying on that cold stone floor in that gloomy vaulted corridor—a place straight out of *Hamlet*, or "Prince Valiant."

For a moment, for one very bad moment, Herb Dierickx wondered if he'd lost his mind—if this wasn't just some hallucination. If the whole adventure hadn't been just a long *string* of vivid hallucinations. He was a fifty-six-year-old chauffeur, an ordinary American guy married to an ordinary American woman, they lived in a small mortgaged house and watched too much crappy television. He was a real person, with a Social Security card, prostate worries, chronic pain in his lower back, and real people don't step through a cellophane tear in the world, into some . . . wizardy kingdom. Maybe—Jesus, maybe he was in a *coma*. Maybe he'd had a stroke. Been in a car accident.

Thinking that stuff, Herb Dierickx tingled all over with dread.

But then he told himself no. This is real.

It's real.

Somehow, it's all real, it's happening.

I'm here, she's there. Everything is . . . real.

Although the wrinkled woman in the smoldering dress (Herb thinking, Clothes like that? Could give you cancer) had been talking to him nonstop since his arrival, he couldn't understand her. The sounds she made? Were a cross between a high-speed dentist's drill and a gargle.

It wasn't even a language, as far as Herb was concerned. She used her hands a lot, but the gestures were inscrutable. What do you make of it when somebody lays her index finger alongside a nostril, then stretches her hand across a cheek, touching her thumb to the curve of an earlobe? What do you make of it when she does that three times in a row? Or bites down hard on a pinkytip, then jabs it flat against her forehead?

Herb, trying to be polite, said, "Excuse me?"

The woman lurched from her throne, smoke roiling around her (no longer clothing, merely a chaotic swirl) then realigning (a fancy ball gown again).

Herb scrambled to his feet, just in case he had to run. Run. Good one, Herb. Run *where*? The corridor seemed to stretch endlessly in both directions.

But she didn't seem hostile, she merely . . . studied him as though he were some interesting piece of art in a museum, slowly moving her eyes (as tiny, as bright pink, and as dry as pencil erasers) from his feet (he was wearing sandals; sandals and loose canvas trousers and a soiled white shirt) to his face (he hadn't shaved for days, and his beard was coming in thick, as gray as it was black). She bit down on her small fingertip again, then again jabbed it flat against her forehead.

On impulse, Herb did the same thing. Feeling like a cavalry guy—Joel McCrea, Richard Widmark, somebody like that—trying to communicate with a Apache.

She grinned. Her gums were pebbled with milk teeth.

When Herb started nodding, grinning himself, the woman abruptly scowled.

A moment later, two of the drapes, several yards up the passageway, parted with a loud, carpet-beating thump.

A heavyset man with a round, jowly face and dressed in a million-dollar gray vested suit—the Mafia defendant's suit of choice for corruption trials—stepped briskly through the opening. The knot in his tie was a perfect Windsor, his white shirt virtually glowed. He smiled at the woman in the smoke dress, then shot a thick finger in

Herb's direction. You! Front and center! Herb recognized *that* gesture, all right.

He also recognized the gesturer.

It was Bobby Byrnes, former President of the Amalgamated Rivet-Workers of America.

"Hey Joe!" said Byrnes, gesturing at Herb, "would you please follow me? And get a move on? We got some things to discuss." He snapped his fingers impatiently. "Hey Joe! Whenever you're ready."

"My name's Herb. Are you *really* Bobby Byrnes? Bobby, I was in the union. Sixty-one to seventy-seven. I voted for you, every time. Where are we, Bobby?"

Immediately, Herb wished he hadn't come right out and asked that question.

Because if this *was* Bobby Byrnes, *really* Bobby Byrnes, then Herb was pretty certain where they were.

"Just come on, would you? Herb. Harry. Whatever the hell your name is."

Herb didn't like hearing the h-word, but he forced himself to move toward Bobby Byrnes. He never took his eyes from the woman as he sidled around—then scurried past—her.

"She's human too, believe it or not," said Byrnes. He gripped Herb by an elbow and steered him through the drapery. "And she's okay, once you know her." Then he gave a stag-party snigger. "Put a bag over her head, through—right?"

Male etiquette called for a piggish grunt, and Herb managed that, but meanwhile he was swiveling his eyes all around, checking out the new surroundings. It was another corridor, but significantly wider. The only illumination came from above, where several phosphorescent balls hung suspended and sizzled whitely. In its atmosphere, the place reminded Herb of the pump island at a lonely filling station at two o'clock in the morning.

Bobby Byrnes said, "It's just down the end here."

"What is?"

Herb's voice sounded falsetto—and for a moment Bobby Byrnes chuckled. Then he turned and smiled at Herb. "Lighten up, guy. It's okay."

"We're dead, right?"

There. He'd said it. He'd come out and said it.

"No way!" Byrnes shook his head, and crisscrossed his hands in violent negation. On his fingers he had, altogether, six big diamond rings. "No way. You're alive, buddy, I'm alive, we're all alive."

"All?"

"Your pals. The ones you came with. Only something got screwed up and you got sent to that lovely young lady by mistake. You were supposed to get sent to *me*. Comprenday, amigo?"

No! Yes! Well, yes and no! He was alive, Herb comprendayed that part, all right. But . . . he was supposed to've been *sent* to Bobby Byrnes? To *Bobby Byrnes?* Herb said, "You're telling me nobody kidnapped you and chopped up your body and buried you in a toxic-waste dump?"

"I'd like to see the day!" said Byrnes. *Growled* Byrnes. Then he said, "Right in here. Here we go." He stepped aside, and Herb, with a pang of mistrust, walked through a doorway and into an enormous room that was furnished like an executive suite: cleared teakwood desk, chairs, sofas, a conference pit, a wet bar, a coffee and tea service, a refrigerator, several bronze sculpture pieces on ebony bases and some abstract art. Recessed lighting. No phones, though, or fax, and no computer, no copy machine, no audio or video equipment. And no windows.

The first person Herb saw when he came in was Jere Lee Vance, and she put a happy smile on her pale, lined face and popped out of a leather sofa. "It's Mr. Dierickx! Herb! Hello, hello!" Then he saw the others, taking them all in with peripheral vision: Money Campbell, Peter Musik and Gene Boman. Boman had fixed himself a drink at the bar.

Bobby Byrnes pulled the door shut behind him, and the sound startled everyone to attention.

"Hey, like Charlie Chan says, you're probably all wondering why I brought you here. Well, it's like this, campers: We've got a problem."

He clapped Herb on the shoulder as he passed, heading for his desk.

Jere Lee intercepted him—actually zipped right in front of Byrnes, so that he had to stop. "What about—the rest of us?" she said. "The other four of us. Where's Squintik?"

In a flash, Bobby Byrnes's mild expression turned impatient, and menacing. "All in good time," he said. "You'll find out, you just gimme a chance."

Gene Boman said, "Woman! Why don't you let Mr. Byrnes have his say?" He puffed himself up, the pompous ass. Then saluted Byrnes with his drink. "Bobby, I don't know if you'd remember, but we've met. Eugene Boman —Boman Pharmaceuticals."

"I know who you are, Mr. Boman. Now, if you'd just sit down? All of you?" He waved an arm, then dropped into the highbacked upholstered chair behind his desk.

Money Campbell, giving Herb a cute wink and a sneaky little wave with her fingertips, plopped into a swivel chair and crossed her legs.

Peter Musik remained standing, stone-faced, behind her.

Gene Boman, ice cubes tinkling, fitted himself into a blue sled chair. He got Herb's attention, then pointed to a nearby secretary's chair. The kind with a hard plastic seat, adjustable back, and rollers. Herb ignored the order (heck with that, I'm not his employee anymore, not here I'm not!) and walked over and sat on the glove-leather sofa with Jere Lee Vance.

Jere Lee whispering, "Isn't he the gangster they chopped up and buried in New Jersey?"

Herb whispering back, "That never happened, he says. But yeah, he's the guy you're thinking of. He says he's not dead. He's says we're not, either."

"Well, *that's* nice," said Jere Lee in her normal speaking voice, then she realized that Bobby Byrnes was glaring at her and mumbled an apology.

"Forget it." Byrnes waited a moment and said, "Maybe some of you folks recognize me."

Herb saw Money frown, and turn to ask Peter a question.

"But for those of you who don't, I'm Bobby Byrnes, that's y-r-n-e-s, and I'm not from around these parts, either." Pause. "I come from Detroit. Michigan." He flashed a white smile. (No guy his age—Byrnes had to be close to seventy—had teeth that white. They had to be fake, they had to be false; even so, Herb was a little bit jealous.) "So we're all of us a long way from home," said Byrnes. He leaned back into the chair cushion, Mr. Nonchalant. "All right. Next, let me tell you exactly where you are. You're in Fernando's Hideaway. No, I'm only kidding!" He was also the only one who laughed. "Sorry about that, let's get serious. This place is called—you kids ready?—School. School. Without any 'the'. Just plain School. Now, *technically* we're still in that cave, we're still on the Isle of Mites, we're still in Lostwithal. Only we're not." Byrnes stood up and walked around in front of his desk, then perched on the edge, like a college professor. "Look, we're all from earth. You're from earth, I'm from earth, we don't know from magic, right? Our version of the human race is, what—fairly mechanical. Wouldn't you say that? We're fairly mechanical people? We're rational people. So that's a longwinded way of saying I don't know *where* we are, exactly. Like in the fifth dimension or something. Search me!"

Jere Lee turned to Herb. "I don't know what the hell he's talking about."

"So that's where we are," said Byrnes. "Take it on faith." Bobby Byrnes clapped his hands and rubbed them together like he was trying to work up a lather. "Now. What are *you* doing here? Fair question. But let me tell you first what *I'm* doing here—okay? Indulge me that?" He looked at each person in the room, making soulful eye contact for half a second before flicking to the next. Bobby's eyes were brown and prepossessing—charismatic. "I volunteered to come. I didn't get murdered. You can just forget about that. If *that's* what you heard. Forget about it—no way! I gave *up* my other career—voluntarily. I disappeared *on purpose*. May 12, 1985. Nobody kidnapped me or shot me in the head, nothing like that happened. I simply made a choice to come here. I had the opportunity and I took it. But so what do I do here? What do I do here? Let's see—well, I and a bunch of other people, we kind of exchange information. We bullshit, we play games. It's like a think-tank. You know, like how they got for the Pentagon? We're a bunch of people from three different planets, trying to figure out what's the best way to let everybody else know they're not the only human beings in whole creation. That's what we call everything that exists, we call it whole creation. Am I getting too cosmic for anybody? Just stop me if I am. Please."

He looked around for evidence of bewilderment or complaint.

Money Campbell leaned forward. "No, I think we get you. But is this, like, also a zoo? Because I hope not. All right? Because I want to go home, if that's, like, ever possible."

Bobby Byrnes faced her squarely. "What's your name, miss?"

"That's Money Campbell, Bobby," said Gene Boman. "And that skunk behind her is Peter Musik. That skunk! He's a newspaper reporter, just so you'll know, just in case you're worried about keeping certain things confidential. As I gather you are."

"I didn't ask you, Mr. Boman. Miss Campbell, is it?"

"Monica's fine. I don't like being called Money, though." She turned to Peter. "Well, I don't!"

Peter spread his hands and shrugged.

"Monica," said Bobby Byrnes. "I'd like to send you home right now, I honestly would. But it's like this, sugar, for the moment you'll all—how should I put this? You're all under quarantine."

Bobby Byrnes sucked briefly on his front teeth. Then he pulled on his bottom lip and rolled it between two fingers while he mused. Long, long pause. It was very dramatic. Herb admired the man's showmanship, but he was getting pretty goddamned nervous and wanted Bobby just to—blurt it out. Blurt it out. Oh God. Herb thinking, Oh God, please don't let it be too horrible.

Bobby Byrnes never got a chance to finish speaking his piece, though.

Because suddenly the pores in Jere Lee's face spritzed blood, long fine jets of blood, followed by a raveling out of wire-fine greasy blue filament.

It entangled her head.

Meanwhile, her body had flung itself into spasms. She clutched herself and twisted away, falling to a knee, cramping up, collapsing, huddling into a ball. Then her clothing started to bulge and tear.

There was a crisping sound. Several more.

Herb thinking, Dear sweet Jesus, what's going on now? He fought his cowardly first impulse—to scramble the hell away from Jere Lee—and did the right thing: moved to go down on the floor beside her.

But as he started from the sofa, Bobby Byrnes gripped him by the shoulder, digging in his fingers painfully, and shoved him back. "The woman is gone," he said. "Trust me on this one, Herb. I wouldn't touch her now if I was you."

And when Jere Lee Vance lifted her head, she had another face completely, a face that was elongated and bumpy, and raddled with pulsing blue veins. Her eyes were twice the size they'd been.

Lips slightly parted, she made a quavering sibilance, a whisper that exploded, moments later, into the loudest noise that Herb Dierickx had ever heard.

It was also the last noise that he would ever hear.

From the winner of both the Hugo and Nebula Awards comes a tour de force novel about the ageless issues of evil, suffering and the indomitable will of the human spirit.

DOOMSDAY BOOK

Connie Willis

"No one has reproduced the past that haunts the present any better than Connie Willis."
—*Christian Science Monitor (Lincon's Dreams)*

For Kivrin, preparing for an on-site study of one of the deadliest eras in humanity's history was as simple as receiving inoculations against the diseases of the fourteenth century and inventing an alibi for a woman traveling alone. For her instructors in the twenty-first century, it meant painstaking calculations and careful monitoring of the rendezvous location where Kivrin would be retrieved. But a crisis strangely linking past and future strands Kivrin in the year 1348 as her fellows try desperately to rescue her. In a time of superstition and fear, Kivrin finds she has become an unlikely angel of hope during one of history's darkest hours.

Available now in hardcover and trade paperback wherever Bantam Spectra books are sold.

SPECTRA

AN 417 6/92

Brand new from the author of *The Face of the Waters*, a
story of time travel...and the bewitching power of an
ancient city known as...

Thebes Of The Hundred Gates

Robert Silverberg

At twenty-seven, Edward Davis is a promising rookie in
the Time Service. He has made several jumps in time,
but none as far back as his newest assignment, all the
way back to Eighteenth Dynasty Egypt. It is here in the
teeming streets of the ancient city of Thebes that Davis
must find two members of the Service lost in time. From
the temple districts swarming with worshippers to the
City of the Dead where mummies are embalmed and
tombs prepared, Davis experiences the overwhelming
reality of an ancient world...and the shattering truth
behind the fate of his former comrades.

Multiple Hugo and Nebula award-winner Robert
Silverberg takes his readers on a dazzling tour of ancient
Egypt through a powerful tale of myth, mystery and
adventure.

Now on sale wherever Bantam Spectra
paperbacks are sold.

AN 418 6/92